Any Way Out

Any Way Out

LISA WHITE

CITIOFBOOKS, INC.
3736 Eubank NE Suite A1
Albuquerque, NM 87111-3579
www.citiofbooks.com
Hotline: 1 (877) 389-2759
Fax: 1 (505) 930-7244

Ordering Information:
Quantity Sales. Special discounts are available on quantity purchases by corporations, associations, and others. For details, contact the publisher at the address above.

Printed in the United States of America.

ISBN-13   Paperback   978-1-959682-78-3
                          eBook   978-1-959682-79-0

Library of Congress Control Number: 2023902113

Table of Contents

CHAPTER 1

*T*houghts, those thoughts, they tormented her, yet she couldn't risk telling anyone but she had to make them stop. For now Ashley focused on the clock watching it slowly tick away; any thing to keep her mind busy. How she kept getting in these predicaments she didn't understand. Her friends got away with everything, yet she continually got caught. She knew one thing, detention sucked. Finally the bell rang and Ashley's dark eyes shot to the front of the room.

"Go ahead, you guys." Mr. R. got up and stretched. "Behave yourselves," he added as they started to file into the dark carpeted hallways of their high school with its white walls and blue-gray lockers. Ashley tossed back her long brown wavy hair as she exited the room. She rounded the corner and spotted Kim, one of her best friends.

"Hey, how's it going?" Kim asked, her blue eyes bright and cheerful. "Well, detention's finally over, and I finished all my homework so that's a plus."

"Maybe you should just go to class like the rest of us and do your homework at home." Kim playfully ribbed her with her elbow.

"Yeah, yeah, where's the fun in that?" Ashley smirked

"What are you going to do over the Christmas break?' Kim asked, as they walked towards their lockers.

"Well, I have to figure out a way to ask my mom if I can spend Christmas break with my dad and my grandma, my dad's mom, without her freaking out." Ashley grunted, "It's impossible, I know she'll be mad. I never get to see my grandmother anymore since the divorce. Come on, we have to catch the bus," Ashley added as she closed her locker.

The girls made their way through the crowd of fellow students onto the bus and got a seat together.

"So Ash, tell me again how long your parents have been divorced."

"two years, two long miserable years. Why?"

"Well, don't you do that every other year thing with the holidays?"

"Are you kidding? My family, we don't even do that every other weekend thing.

Kim gently nudged Ashley with her elbow. "Parents can definitely be difficult, so equal it out. Where did you spend the last two Christmases?"

Ashley raised her head. "With my mom and grandparents on her side. In fact we spend the afternoon at my grandparents because my mom always works the 3-11 shift at the old folk's home. Then our grandparents bring us home in the evening and we just hang out by ourselves. I know what you're thinking, just ask since I spent the last two Christmases with you can I spend this one with dad and grandma. Oh, if it were just that easy." Ashley sighed heavily. They spent the remainder of the long ride talking about school and vacation plans.

Ashley and Kim's stop were coming up. They lived just around the corner from one another. It was a country corner, though, the houses were spread much farther apart than say in a more developed area, which meant they had to travel farther to get to each others houses. Although they lived in a little settlement out in the middle of no-where, called North Allentown. They had grown up together, being the only girls in a neighborhood full of boys. They felt a special connection. They spent most weekends at Kim's because church was a must, but Ashley didn't mind. In fact, she rather enjoyed the feeling of community and belonging that the church provided. Kim's parents were very involved in the church and raised Kim to be, so when Ashley spent the weekends at Kim's she also attended church. Kim's family was a very close, loving and open family. They discussed everything calmly and candidly. Deep down Ashley wished to belong to this family instead of her own.

Kim jumped off the last step of the bus and waited (a few feet away) for Ashley, trying to think of some encouraging words for her best friend. Ashley followed a couple of the boys from the area and then caught up to Kim.

"Well, wish me luck; I'm going home to ask." Ashley forced a smile. "Try not to worry; maybe it'll be fine. You never know." Kim added,

"At least we're almost on Christmas break; only two more days." "You're right. My mom's reasonable and she knows I miss grandma. Thanks, Kim. I'll see you tomorrow."

Ashley paced her room for what seemed like an eternity, trying to figure out the best way to ask her mom, Ellen, the big question. Finally deciding to just get it over with, Ashley headed out to the kitchen where Ellen was seated doing her homework. Ellen was currently second in command in the kitchen at a very reputable retirement home a couple towns away, but her true passion was photography, which she hoped to pursue one day.

Ashley marched into the kitchen and nervously stood there. She took in a deep breath. "Mom, you know I love you, right?"

"What did you do?" Ellen interrupted, dropping her pen on her notebook.

"Nothing. Why do you always think the worst?" Ashley held up her hands.

"Because you don't tell me that for no reason. So what is it? what do you want?"

"Well, Grandma Ames called me last week and asked if I would come and spend Christmas with them this year." Ashley's eyes were downcast while she fidgeted with her pant leg.

"With your father, you mean." Ellen's voice started to rise as she glared at Ashley.

"Well… he'll be there too," she meekly answered.

"After all the shit he did to us… waking us up at 2 am, finally home from a drinking binge. Smacking the shit out of us …drunk again… The affairs, coming home with hickeys on his neck. Don't you remember? How can you want to spend even a minute with him, let alone Christmas?" Ellen threw her pen across the room past Ashley and then stormed out in the opposite direction. Ashley stood in silence stunned by her mother's reaction. Ellen reappeared almost instantly. "You want to spend time with him, fine then, go live with him." Ellen marched into Ashley's room and threw her things on her bed, gathering the edges of Ashley's comforter like a sack, dragged it down the hall through the kitchen and out on the back deck. Ashley watched in disbelief. Ellen screamed, "Call him to come get you." she disappeared into her room.

Ashley fought back tears as she dialed the phone, all the while praying her father, Rodger, would answer. Rodger was a tall burly sort of man, with strong facial features; he had jet black curly hair and he usually kept a mustache and goatee, both of which were now starting to turn gray. He was a mechanic, who worked on diesel engines, the big trucks and sometimes drove them on short trips. When Rodger left the family, he (almost) immediately joined up with Ruth who had calmed him down tremendously. She had changed him for the better, and she was also very fond of Ashley. Ruth answered the phone and handed it to Rodger. "What's up, Ash?"

Ashley choked back her tears. "Dad, mom just kicked me out. Can you come get me?"

"What's going on? "Rodger asked

"Well, I asked to spend Christmas with you." Ashley started to cry "OK. I'll be there in a few minutes. Don't cry. It'll be OK."

Ashley hung up the phone. She ran outside crying and continued to cry. After a minute she wiped her eyes and thought that she needed to be strong. If her mother saw how upset she was, she'd win this silent war.

She had forgotten her coat and it was starting to snow, but she thought she would rather freeze than face her mother again. Just then her younger sister, Laura, appeared with Ashley's jacket. Laura was a quiet and reserved girl who had her life planned out since she was about ten. She wanted to work with animals in a zoo or as a vet, and she even volunteered at the SPCA last summer. Besides that she was also all ready to go clean up some Water Fouls and Eagles after an oil spill, In who knows where, but mom wouldn't pay the airfare. You would have thought Laura's best friend died. She has a huge heart, and she and Ashley were close.

"Hey, Ash, here. You're going to freeze. I'm in shock; I can't believe mom threw you out over that." Laura shook her head.

"Thanks for the coat. I didn't want to go back in there. She's a real piece of work." Ashley glared at the snow falling on the ground and kicked the gravel underneath it.

"Yeah, I figured you didn't want to go back in there. Well, make sure you call me and I'll see you at school so…and… well, you know your dad has calmed down since Ruth came into the picture, so it shouldn't be too bad, hopefully." Laura looked at her and half smiled. "Try not to worry, Ash. At least you get to go see your Grandma Ames. At least your dad is taking you there. She'll cheer you up. She always does."

Ashley smiled "You're right. Somehow, all's right with the world when she's there."

Just then Rodger pulled up to the house. Ruth was with him along with her young son, Michael. He was three with blonde locks and sky blue eyes and a handful, but he was crazy about Ashley. She could get him to do just about anything. She had a sweet spot in her heart for him, showing him off to her girlfriends, those blonde locks and sky blue eyes melted their hearts.

As Rodger got out of his beloved truck, a red Chevy, 250, King cab, Ashley started to haul her comforter filled sack off the deck. He immediately went to lend a hand as he greeted his daughter.

"Hey. So it's not going so good over here, huh?" Rodger looked at them. "Ash, we'll talk on the way back. Why don't you just hop in the truck. So how are things with you Laura?" he asked his former step-daughter.

"Pretty good. You know the same old thing. I do not like this too much though."

"Don't worry, everything will work out; it always does." Rodger sighed as he lifted the comforter onto the back of his pick-up.

"We'll take good care of her and I'll see you later." She looked at him. Rodger gave her a hug. (and assured her he would.)

Before heading into the house she popped her head into the truck to say a quick hello to Ruth and Michael and a final goodbye to Ashley.

As they pulled out of the driveway, Ashley vowed to herself not to depend on her mother for anything ever again. It was almost as if a piece of her had died. She hated her life and what it had become. She often wished she had never been born. The fighting between her parents and over them was more than she could stand at times. Her oldest brother, Jeff, never spoke to his father anymore, he was basically crazy. When Ashley was about five, Jeff, Ashley and their mother, Ellen went for a weekend visit, down towards New York city and he sexually abused

Ashley. When they tried to leave he threatened to kill them. The police had to be called so they could leave; it was a huge mess and since then Jeff has never seen or spoken to his father. Jeff was ten years old almost eleven at the time. Unfortunately for Ashley, nothing was ever done about the abuse. Her mother thought that it only happened once, and her being so young it would be forgotten. Many things were like that in their family; if you didn't discuss it maybe it would just go away.

Jeff had gone away, into the Marines as soon as he turned eighteen. This was his second year away, he had found his way. The marines were paying for him to attend college and he hoped to become an officer one day. He was content and happy with the way his life was going, planning on a career in the military, far away from what was left of his home. The reason Rodger was Laura's stepfather also is because he and Ellen were married twice and divorced twice.

Ashley watched the scenery go by as she wondered about her new home. Ruth and Rodger had just bought a house used for a nursing home and moved in a couple days ago. It had not been used as a nursing home for over a decade. Rodger broke the silence. "So Ash, what exactly made your mother toss you to the curb?" He raised his eyebrows

"Well, I told her Grandma Ames called and asked if I would come and spend the holidays with them. Then mom said with your father, I said he'll be there to, and that's all it took. She freaked out and threw her pen across the room and yelled and told me to call you, to live with you. She hates you, and she expects me to hate you too, so here I am." Ashley took in a deep breath.

"Don't worry, honey, she'll come to her senses," commented Ruth, smiling. "I'm glad to have you; you know we love you."

"Hey, think about the bright side of things. You get to eat Grandma Ames' cooking for the holidays," Rodger said. "Not to mention you get a choice between three rooms for your bedroom. We bought that old nursing home on Livingston. Do you know the one I'm talking about?"

"Oh really!! That place is huge, but I heard it's haunted," Ashley remarked.

"Haunted? That means ghosts, right mom?" asked Michael.

"Oh, I was just kidding. There isn't any such thing as ghosts," Ashley quickly stated gritting her teeth.

"Are you sure?" Michael's eyes got wide.

"Of course, I wouldn't kid you about that. Right, dad?"

"Definitely, there isn't any such thing," Rodger added nodding his head.

"Don't worry, honey, there's nothing there that can hurt you," added Ruth, smiling. She had a way about her, giving off a sense of comfort. A vibe she gave off.

"Well, here we are." Rodger pulled into the driveway. The large white house sat on two acres. with six large pine trees spread around the circular driveway and several oak trees were in the back. A small old barn with a hole in the roof leaned against the tallest oak, and a small unkempt garden area was on the other side. The two story white house had a small front porch and a large back deck. "It's in need of a paint job and a couple of windows are broken, but otherwise it's in decent shape," stated Rodger as he got out and started to unload Ashley's belongings.

"Hey, can you give me a hand with this? It's kind of bulky"

"Yeah, no problem," answered Ashley as she checked out her new home.

"I'll go open the door," offered Ruth

"And I'll help too. What can I do? "exclaimed three year old Michael. "Well, grab this side over here. There you go. Hang on. Be careful." The four of them made their way to the house and upstairs, where they plopped down the comforter type sack, and Ashley picked her room. It had light blue paint, a tiled floor, and two windows facing north on the right side and the driveway was on it. Michael's room was across the hall from Ashley's. Both rooms were painted light blue, but he had a dark blue plush carpet, and dad had already put up his car posters on the walls. Just down the hall was a full bathroom with a large old fashion claw foot bathtub, Ash thought nice perfect for a nice soak. She noticed a door in the bathroom, peculiar she thought she opened it and it led up to the attic, she shut it and decided to explore later. Her parent's room was downstairs underneath Michael's. It was large and freshly painted yellow and was the only slightly remodeled room in the place. With a half bathroom across the foyer underneath the stairs, this was the bathroom for the first floor.

"Well, we'll leave you to put your things away." Ruth walked over and hugged Ashley "There's another dresser in the other room if you need it. I'm going to get dinner started. If you need anything, just let us know. Try not to worry; it'll all work out," she added as she left.

Ashley looked around the room and took in a deep breath and thought this is my life now so I may as well make the best of it she started to take care of her belongings. She was about halfway done when she came across a picture of her and her mother. She just sat staring at the picture. She wondered if Ellen had the same painful feeling in her gut as she did.

"Hey, dinner's ready. Come and eat before it gets cold," shouted Ruth.

"I'll be right there," Ashley shouted back, as she put down the picture and started towards the stairs. A feeling as if someone were standing next to her, overcame her. Although it wasn't a harmful feeling, she elected to leave the hall light on while she was up there and would turn it off from downstairs.

As they sat down to dinner, Ashley noticed five empty beer bottles on the counter and wondered if her father had all of them himself or maybe Ruth had helped out. She didn't mention it; she knew it was none of her business. She remembered all the terrible things that came with her dad's drinking, though, and wondered if things would be different now with Ruth.

"Hey, I was thinking since you only have a couple of days of school left before vacation why not just skip them and leave early for Christmas break," Rodger proposed. "Ruthie can call the school and get all your homework and your books and shit. We could pack tomorrow morning and be on the road in the afternoon. This way we could beat all the traffic. What do you all think? "His eyes lit up "I'm already on vacation from work anyway."

"Well, I don't like the idea of Ashley missing school," Ruth commented. "But, they don't do too much the last days anyway. So I think it would be OK."

"Sounds excellent. Let's get out of here." Ashley shook her head. "Me too, me too, let's get out of here," yelled Michael, bouncing up and down in his chair.

"All right then; it's set. We'll leave tomorrow afternoon. You know, Ash, I'm glad you're here with us; it makes us more of a family." Rodger winked at Ashley and smiled. "Ruth, these pork chops are good. Is there any more applesauce?" Rodger put his fork down.

"Yeah, I'll get it for you. I'm glad you like them."

"They are good. Thank you for cooking supper." Ashley smiled "I'll help clean up if you'd like."

"Oh, you know I would. Thanks." Ruth looked at Ashley and smiled back, her eyes filled with warmth as she dished out the applesauce.

That evening after the dishes were done and everyone had turned in for the night, Ashley lay awake staring at the ceiling, wondering and worrying how things were going to go now that she was staying here with her father. She couldn't help but think of her mother. How could she just throw her away like that, knowing how he was? Maybe, though, Laura was right. Ruth had calmed him down, and he would be different, away from her mother. She felt this huge emptiness, dark, empty and alone. Tears ran down her face; she was trying not to make any noise, so as not to disturb Michael. She didn't want anyone to think she was unhappy about being here. The truth was she was unhappy being anywhere. Dark thoughts ruled her mind on an almost constant basis.

shley wiped away the tears and resolved to make it work here, to show her mother. Prove to her that she had made the wrong decision, and that her mother was losing out on her life. She started to cry again, but then the thought came into her head that she would be visiting her grandmother tomorrow, and that could not come soon enough. She imagined Christmas with gram and all the homemade chocolate treats and food, early Christmas morning breakfast, off to church service and then home to open gifts. The thoughts of her grandmother brought a smile to her face even in the darkness of life.

CHAPTER 2

Upon arriving at her grandmother's, Ashley and Michael burst through the door and were immediately hit with the pleasant aromas of apple pies, homemade candies and an elaborate dinner made just for them. Ashley had forgotten how good her grandmother's house smelled.

Her grandparent's house was filled with antiques and decorated with the utmost care. Their motto had always been "If you don't do it right, don't do it at all," but also "to keep on trying until you get it right, and to never give up." Ashley admired her grandparents and their way of life. They lived properly and by the church.

"Hi gram, hi gramps, we finally made it!! "Ashley smiled widely. "Oh, I'm so glad you're here. I've missed you so much. Come here and give me a hug. Oh my, you've gotten so big," Grandma Ames remarked as she hugged her granddaughter. Then she bent down, "Well, hello and you must be Michael. my what a handsome young man you are. You can call me grandma too, OK?"

He smiled ear to ear. "OK. Ashley says you make candy." (as he took off his coat.)

"She does, does she?" She reached up to the counter and grabbed a chocolate Santa. "How's this."

He took it. "Thanks."

She laughed. "Why don't you go get settled and show him around Ash. You guys are sleeping upstairs."

"OK gram. thanks for giving him the candy. It's so nice to see you again; I've missed you so much." Ashley hugged her grandmother again.

"I'm so glad you came too. We'll have lots of time to catch up." She smiled at Ashley squeezing her arm as she went off showing Michael the other rooms.

Rodger and Ruth came in right behind them and greeted everyone with the usual how was the traffic along with the family rivalry of how much time did it take you, how many cops were out and did you get any tickets?

Rodger proudly announced, "No tickets this time, and we made it in less than two hours; not bad huh!!" He gave his parents each a hug and then carried in the luggage.

As they settled in Grandma Ames finished getting dinner ready for them. She always prepared a huge feast to celebrate their visit.

Everything was great for the first two hours, and then at dinner her father dropped a huge bomb on the whole family. Usually Ashley was dismissed with the other children, but not this year. Apparently she had reached some sort of adulthood, or maybe because it affected her so intensely; she wasn't sure. All she did know was that her whole life was going to change.

Rodger stood up and proudly announced, "Ruth is going to have a baby. It's a boy and, in fact, she is five months along." He raised his glass to celebrate, except no one else but Ruth raised theirs. After the shock passed, Ashley partially raised her glass, and the trio drank. Ruth was a beautiful but larger framed woman, so she hid it well. Ashley's jaw just about hit the floor, along with her grandparents'. Her grandfather frowned and sat with his fingers tapping the table. Grandma Ames was normally a refined and distinguished woman, never quick to anger or harsh with words. The kind, sweet and loving grandmother that Ashley had always seen, suddenly stood up and started yelling at Rodger; how could he expecting a son out of wedlock, his first blood son, to bring such shame on the family and how was she supposed to face her friends and family members and what would the pastor say. Ashley sat shocked; she had never seen this side of her grandmother before. She wasn't sure what to do, so she sat quietly, observing.

Ashley wondered if her father expected her to congratulate the two of them and sort of side with them. After all, she thought, I have to go home and live with them. So she gave her father a silent reassuring smile, trying to let him know she was happy for him without letting her grandmother, who she loved deeply, find out. However, deep down she resented him for waiting until this trip to drop the news. She couldn't help but wonder if he actually thought that his parents would be happy about it. They were from an older generation and deeply involved with the church where marriage was a must especially if a baby was expected. Besides, he and Ruth had only been together about nine months and now a baby; they hardly knew one another. Ashley couldn't help but think this is a disaster waiting to happen.

The atmosphere at the house over the next few days was in crisis mode most of the time, and Ashley mainly tried staying out of the way. She covered up her depressed mood so that it didn't register on anyone's radar. Not that they would have noticed anyway; all the attention was given to the pregnancy and marriage situation.

A couple days before Christmas Rodger and Ruth went out very early on a shopping trip for the whole day; they didn't arrive home until very late that night. While they were gone, Ashley spent some much needed time with her grandmother, and Michael mainly hung out with her grandfather. Ashley talked to her grandmother about what had happened with her mother. Her grandmother sat her down and held her hands, "You know your mother. Lord knows she tried with your father, but he was just not happy and he was out of control. Your mother loves you; she just hurts inside. Here your father has moved on and it's a small town you all live in and she is still alone; that probably hurts her. If she had been the one that left or moved on first, it may have been a different story. She may have felt differently; do you understand? So you need to give her a little slack." Then she squeezed Ashley's hands and smiled at her granddaughter.

"That makes a lot of sense, thanks gram." Ash smiled and gave her a kiss on the cheek. They continued to talk throughout the day and by evening Ashley felt much better about the whole situation.

Finally Christmas day arrived. After all the gifts had been opened and shared, Rodger stated there was one more, big gift. It was in a way for Grandma Ames but it was also for Ruth and the baby. Apparently when Rodger and Ruth had gone out on their shopping spree, they had actually gone off and gotten married. It surprised everyone because Rodger had always said he didn't want to ever get married again. But he stated he never loved anyone the way he loved Ruth and the baby to come. It made Grandma Ames extremely happy that they would have the baby in wedlock. So now Ashley not only had a new baby brother on the way but a new stepmother too. She sat stunned; all she could do was smile and say congratulations. Deep down she wanted to run away, but there was no where to run to; she was stuck.

Ellen never bothered to call on Christmas. Ashley told herself that it didn't matter, she didn't matter. Ashley often wished she would get deathly ill, or she would die. Then how would they feel about the way they treated her. But it would be too late, they would be sorry, but she would have the last laugh. She envisioned herself in Jesus' arms, holding her tight, making all the pain disappear.

On the ride home Rodger and Ruth were laughing and joking. As Ashley listened, she realized her father never had that type of relationship with her mother. She basically liked Ruth but was worried how things would be when this new baby showed up.

Monday morning rolled around and Ashley was a bit anxious to get back to school, more or less for her social life. She had served her time in in-school-detention, now it was back to a regular class schedule. That morning as everyone gathered in the auditorium, as usual, to start the day, Ashley ran into Mrs. Burns. She was short with glasses and black curly hair, and she was also one of her favorite teachers. She was the school's tutor although Ashley didn't need her services; she enjoyed spending her free time in her room. Mrs. Burns's husband, Eli, was also a teacher. He was also short with black curly hair, and he had a beard and a mustache that bordered on the wild side. They were like a throwback from the sixties; they always had in-depth conversations on controversial issues. They also never judged anyone for their opinion; they encouraged students to just think for themselves.

"Hey, Mrs. Burns. I have two study halls today. Can I spend them in your room?" Ashley ran her fingers through her hair.

"Yes, stop by and I'll give you a pass."

"Cool, thanks" replied Ashley as she walked away.

"Hey Burn Out," nodded Eddie along with his friends, Troy and Buddy.

"What are you bums up to?" Ashley laughed. "Hey, have you seen Kim?"

"Uh, I think she's already sitting in home row," Troy added as the first morning bell rang.

"Catch you guys later." Ashley nodded; she went and sat in her seat, in order to listen to that morning's announcements. Kim only sat a few seats down from Ashley, so they did the usual trade with Frank. He was a real sweetheart and Kim was kind of sweet on him but was too shy to say so.

"Hey, girly girl, how have you been?" Ashley looked at her in desperation, smiling in a hopeful way.

"Where in the hell have you been?" Kim's eyes were wide. "You just disappeared. Have you even heard of a phone?" Kim held up her hands in frustration.

"I know, I'm sorry. I'll tell you later; it's crazy." Ashley just shook her head and the second bell rang. Everyone had settled into their seats and the announcements started.

After they were over, Ashley and Kim had five minutes to get to their first class. They had already gotten their books, so they headed to the bathroom to hang for a couple of minutes.

"Ash, what happened to you?"

"My mom went totally ballistic when I asked to go to my grandparents. She threw me out, so now I'm staying at my father's. He had no phone because he just moved in; he is getting it hooked up today, thank God. Then we left early to go to my grandparents. My mom never even bothered to call me on Christmas day. Can you believe that shit?" "Wow, I had no idea. I'm sorry, Ash." Kim shook her head as they walked.

"That's not even all of it, it gets better. My dad and Ruth, they're having a baby. She's five months pregnant. They're having a damn baby!! My grandparents were pissed beyond belief, having a baby out of wedlock. So then they went off and got married. I can't freaking believe it." Ashley kept shaking her head.

"Oh my God! You had a hell of a vacation." Kim just looked at Ashley. "I had to just keep saying, 'oh that's great' and smile, and inside I'm freaking out. I mean I like Ruth and all, but a baby, and I gotta live with it. I know my dad. He likes going out, a lot. I hate to say it, but I'll probably become a built in babysitter." Ashley just sighed. "I hate my freaking life."

"Man, that's a lot to deal with." Kim briefly put her hand on Ashley's shoulder as they entered the bathroom.

"Hey, what's going on?" Ashley forced a smile, as she greeted her group of friends.

"Hi, Ash, how's it going?" Karen asked as she took a drag off of her cigarette. "Hey, do we have a lunch date if you know what I mean," Karen added as she raised her eyebrows up and down.

"Why wait till lunch? We have a fourth period study hall together. I'm getting a pass to Mrs. Burns' room; you should too so we can partake beforehand." Ashley smiled and nodded her head.

"Sounds like a plan; see you here before fourth period," Karen replied as she tossed her smoke in the toilet and headed out to class.

Kim looked at Ashley, "I better get going, English with Ms. Sumar. She won't let you in if you're late. Catch you later." Ashley also hurried off to Advanced Geometry, the class she had skipped before vacation. Ashley and the teacher, Mr. B, didn't see eye to eye. He often picked on her in class and she resented him for it. Sometimes she dozed off in class which was probably why she had a hard time with the work. So Ashley went to another math teacher, Mr. Roth for extra help; he was really cool about it.

With her pass in hand Ashley signed out of study hall and bee-lined towards the back hall bathroom. As it cleared Karen showed up with Emily, "OK ladies, let's get down to business and check the hall, Em." Karen directed.

Emily returned. "All clear." Karen took out the joint and lit it; taking a hit she leaned her head back and closed her eyes, as if in heaven. She passed it on to Ashley. When she took her hit it was as if the weight of the world had been lifted. Emily was as cheerful as ever. The trio smoked up, rather quickly, so as not to get caught, being careful to flush the roach. Karen and Emily insisted on having a cigarette before they left. Ashley agreed to be the lookout for them but insisted they hurry because it smelled of pot. While doing so Mr. Shore, the new drug counselor, came strolling along. Ashley gave a quick whistle to alert her friends. He laughed and gave Ashley a business card which said, "Are you Stoned or Stupid?" She looked at it, then at him." I'll see you around; maybe you can drop by my office and we can chat." Mr. Shore gave her a nod and walked away.

As the trio made their way to Mrs. Burn's room, they were laughing and joking.

"Ashley, there's a party at the Bluffs Friday night. Can you go?" Karen asked while they sat at a table in the room.

"Sounds good, but it's awfully cold for the Bluffs," Ashley replied as she sat down and spread out her books on the table, to give the appearance of doing work.

"I'm sure there will be a fire."

"Can you pick me up?" Ashley asked.

"Sure, I'm telling my parents I'm going to the movies at the mall." Karen smiled.

"I'll do the same. Let's tell them we're going to the late show," Ashley laughed.

"Hey, I hate to disrupt your conniving, but I'm getting together a group to take part in a program. It gets you out of school for the day." Mrs. Burns sat down with the girls and folded her arms on the table. She looked inquisitively at each one.

"What kind of program?" Ashley asked sitting up.

"Well, it's a field trip up to talk to some people about their lives and the decisions they have made and how it has affected their lives," Mrs. Burns added.

"It sounds kind of interesting, but why us?" Karen asked.

"It's for troubled youth. Only 20 students will be allowed to participate and you three are on the list."

"There's a list!" Ashley exclaimed.

"Never you mind about the list; this program will be a once in a lifetime opportunity. You will never forget this and it may help shape your future, I promise." Mrs. Burns looked intensely at the girls. "So what do you say, will you go?"

"Yeah, I'll go," Karen said.

"Me too," Ashley replied.

"What about you, Emily? You've been awfully quiet during this conversation." Mrs. Burns looked directly at her.

"Well, if the two of them are going, I guess I could tag along," Emily added a bit apprehensively.

"So where exactly is this place?" Karen asked

"It's at a maximum security prison about an hour from here," Mrs. Burns stated. The girls just looked at one another in disbelief.

"Are you serious?" Ashley's mouth dropped open and her eyes bugged. "With like murderers and rapists and shit. I don't know."

"They aren't allowed to touch you. I'll be there along with Mr. Cromwell. You'll also get a tour of the prison and then just talk to the prisoners. Before we go we're stopping for lunch at McDonalds," Mrs. Burns added. The nearest fast food restaurant was at least 45 minutes away, so that was a huge bargaining chip in Mrs. Burn's corner.

"Sounds a bit dangerous, so I'm in," Karen replied. "Besides we can brag to everyone about it. Come on Ash, Em where's your sense of adventure?" Karen pleaded with them.

"OK if you're going, I will too." Ashley shook her head.

"Well, it makes me a little nervous, but I can't back out if the two of you are going. So count me in too." Emily took in a deep breath and let it out slowly.

"Good. I'll get the permission slips; they have to be back in the next couple of days. We will be going next Friday." Mrs. Burns got up and went over to retrieve the slips.

When Ashley came home from school a few days later, Ruth was sitting at the kitchen table. "Hey, Ash, what's going on with you?" Ruth asked as she stared intensely at her.

"Nothing much; same old thing. Why? Ashley asked somewhat guarded.

"I was doing the laundry and I found these two black pills in your pocket." Ruth put them on the table. "I know what they are," she added.

"Did you tell Dad?" Ashley asked as she took in a deep breath.

"No, I didn't, at least not yet. These things are dangerous. Why are you messing around with this stuff? How often do you take these? Don't lie to me." Ruth looked hard at Ashley.

"Well, I only take them once in a while because I fall asleep in advanced geometry and the teacher picks on me, I swear. It's my first class in the morning. I don't take them very often, honest. Please don't tell Dad, please. I'll do whatever you want me to. I'm trying to clean up my act. Look; look. I've got a permission slip to go to a Scared Straight program."

"What's that?" Ruth asked

"We go talk to prisoners about their lives and choices they made and stuff." Ashley nervously put her hands in her pockets and felt the card Mr. Shore had given her a few days earlier. "And, if you want, I'll even go talk to the drug counselor at school."

Ruth thought for a few moments about what Ashley had said. "What's the counselor's name?"

"Mr. Shore." Ashley readily gave it up.

"I'm going to give him a call. I expect you to start seeing him on a regular basis. If you don't, this won't be our little secret. Deal?" Ruth stood up, grabbed the pills off of the table and tossed them in the garbage. "Ashley you need to stop taking these."

"Ruth, please don't call. I'll do it on my own, I promise." "OK, sooner rather than later." Ruth stood staring at Ashley. "Thank you. Will you sign the Scared Straight permission slip?" "Yes and, for your sake I hope it works; this is serious."

"I know, thank you," Ashley replied, her eyes downcast. "And, for what it's worth, I'm sorry."

That night as Ashley lay in bed she thought about the last few days. Getting high every single day at lunch unless she had a test and, then right afterwards. Just trying to forget about everything. How she needs to be much more careful about leaving things in her pockets. At mom's she did her own laundry. And now Ruth had reason to suspect her of using. So she needed a really good hiding spot. Who knows if Ruth would search her room while she was at school. If Ruth only knew the truth or if anyone knew the truth, she needed to get high. It was the only thing that kept her going. And deep down she really thought about dying, a lot. And now she had to see some head shrink and if he figured it out, they would lock her up for sure. She thought the truth wouldn't set her free, but her father's pistol would. Then she let out a faint chuckle followed by a deep sigh. Tomorrow's another day. God help me because no one else can.

CHAPTER 3

*B*eep, beep, beep. Ashley fumbled with the alarm until she hit the snooze button. Something she did regularly. But it was finally Friday and it had been a long week. Ashley rubbed her face, then stood in front of the mirror thinking about the day ahead. *I can't believe I'm actually going to a maximum security prison.* She took her time getting dressed. As she went downstairs for breakfast, she hoped Ruth would still be asleep. Her father had already left for work and Michael caught the later bus. As she entered the kitchen, much to her dismay, Ruth was sitting at the kitchen table sipping a cup of coffee.

"Good morning, kiddo." Ruth looked up at Ashley.

"Hey," Ashley answered as she looked at the floor on her way to the fridge to grab a Pepsi.

"So today's the big day isn't it? You're going to the prison right?" Ruth took a sip of her coffee.

"Yeah," Ashley started to put her books in her bag.

"Look, Ash, listen to me for a minute. You can be mad at me all you want, but I grounded you this past week because I love and care about you. Maybe your mother had no idea what went on with you or the things you are doing to yourself. But those pills I found I'm sure aren't the only drugs you're doing. I was young once. I'm not so much angry as concerned. Hopefully this trip to the prison will show you what that kind of stuff can lead you to do. You're a smart kid and I want the best for you," Ruth went over and hugged Ashley.

"OK." Ashley shook her head in agreement. "I gotta go." As Ashley went to catch the bus, she wasn't quite sure what to think. Her parents had never really talked to her like that before; they were always too wrapped up in their own lives to care about what went on in hers.

Once at school Ashley attended her first two classes before boarding the bus bound for the prison. Just prior to reaching McDonalds, Mrs. Burns and Mr. Cromwell gave them the speech about staying together and that they only had thirty minutes to eat. Once inside Troy approached Karen and Ashley in a whisper, "Hey, hurry up and eat; we're going to smoke out back before we go in, if you want to join us?"

"You know it." Karen answered for the both of them, nodding her head. After they got their orders, they sat down and ate. Emily joined them, the only other girl on the trip.

"Hey, Em, we're going to smoke. Want to join us?" Karen asked. "I'm not so sure I do. You know how I get paranoid sometimes. I don't want to get paranoid in a freaking prison." Emily raised her eyebrows.

"Yeah, it might not be a good idea for you," Ashley agreed with her. "But it's a great idea for me," she smiled. "In fact, why don't you go over and keep our keepers busy while we're busy," Ashley laughed.

"I can do that," Emily smiled as she crumbled up the wrapper her burger had been in. A few minutes later she got up and headed towards the teachers, tossing her garbage in the trash on the way. While Karen and Ashley slipped out the back door unnoticed.

Troy, Buddy and Ed stood next to the dumpster feeding the remainder of their fries to the birds. "Hey, Burnout, where's Emily?" asked Buddy as he pulled out a fat joint and lit it. He took a larger than life hit, held it, and then coughed it up.

"Believe it or not she's going straight," Ashley answered as Buddy handed it to her, still coughing. "Dude, you sure you're not coughing up a lung?"

"I'm good," Buddy managed to answer.

"Have you seen our jailers?" Troy inquired as he was handed the joint and inhaled.

"Oh, she's keeping them busy for us," Karen added as she was given a turn.

"That's cool. Hey, look over by the back of the bus. Looks like we aren't the only ones smoking up beforehand." Troy smiled. The small group passed it among them.

"What do you think it will be like?" Ashley asked as she took a hit. "Oh, they'll probably lecture us on how Mary-Jane is the gateway drug and we'll all end up on heroine," Buddy stated as he took another hit off the joint.

"Yeah, then they'll tell us how we'll rob people to get money and shit to support our drug problem," Troy added as he took the joint from Buddy.

"Well, I think the tour of the inside will be pretty cool. I'm not too worried. They aren't allowed to touch us," Ashley added "Now, give me that. I need a good buzz to do this." They all laughed as they finished up the joint.

"Thought you weren't worried," Troy teased as he lit a cigarette. Afterwards, as they crept out from behind the restaurant, the bus started up. They climbed on board joining the rest of the group. Ashley found the rest of the group. Ashley found a seat in the middle. Mrs. Burns boarded, did her head count, then sat directly in back of Ashley. As the bus made its way to the prison 15 minutes away, Mrs. Burns started talking to Ashley. Just before they arrived she leaned forward and stated, "What's wrong? You couldn't handle it straight?" Ashley sat bewildered, in shock. Was it that obvious she was stoned? What about the rest of the group? Emily was the only girl who didn't get high. And only a couple of the guys didn't smoke out of a total of 20 students. Man are we busted or what, and then Ashley thought what's done is done.

The state prison loomed tall above them as the students entered its gates. One by one they passed through a metal detector and were patted down. They were also given an orange bracelet, with the instructions that if the bracelet were lost then the students would not be released. The guards meant business; fun and games were over behind these gray walls. They were informed how the outside walls went six stories high and 60 feet underground. They also explained that there had never been a successful escape from this prison. As the group made its way through the yard, made of cement, not one blade of grass was to be seen. Prisoners started to make their way towards them from the far side. They were inside out of harm's way before contact was made. Their guide pointed out the gunmen posted high above, about every 30 feet, ready in an instant to shoot to kill.

Ashley couldn't help but think what a gloomy, dismal, ominously forbidding and threatening place, not someplace she ever wanted to end up in. When they left the yard and entered the cell block, they met inmate Nate. The cell door slammed open and he appeared, "This is it; my home 5 feet by 9 feet. That's with two bunks, a toilet, a sink, and two lockers." Ashley thought that's just too small; my dog has more room.

"Can you imagine living in here for 10, 15, or even 25 years? How about life?" Nate asked. "That's how it is. Then if your bunk mate is crazy, you don't find out until lights out. And your mama ain't gonna save you or the guards," he added. His eyes went all narrow and he tilted his head to the side. "You cute little boys come to prison, you gonna be somebody's bitch." Nate looked hard at a few of the guys. Their eyes got wide for a moment.

"Yeah, that's right. That's how it is in here. Now follow me." Nate led them to a large room. This room was unlike anything in the prison; it was actually cheerful. It had a high ceiling and was made of wood. Half of the room was filled with church pews, the other half had metal folding chairs set up in a large circle. Nate led them to the back of the room next to the pews. "Stand in two lines. Stand up straight. Quit fooling around. This is serious." Nate walked around the group trying to intimidate them. Then he walked over to their instructors and spoke with them for a few moments as other inmates filed in the room. As the group stood in two lines, the inmates gathered together and spoke to Nate.

Another one approached the group, "My name is Ty, but, in here, I'm known only by a number. So, you all like to smoke pot. Yeah, I know. I can smell it on you." Ty made eye contact with several of the students. "You come into my house for help, and you disrespect it." He walked up to another inmate who had wandered over during this and shook his head at him. His eyes got really narrow and his head tilted to one side. "Yo, dog, that's weak." Ty walked around to the back of the group.

"You all don't want to get on Ty's bad side. I'm Frankie." He gave the students the once over and returned to the circle.

"Listen up. I need you all to go over and have a seat in the circle. Do it now and no talking." The other inmates had already taken their seats, leaving it open for two students, then an inmate and so on.

Ashley sat next to a younger man with dark hair, hazel eyes and a mustache. He was also smaller in size compared to most of the other inmates. Ashley felt less intimidated by him. When she sat down, the cold of the metal chair brought her out of the daze that had begun to set in as they stood in line. Ashley watched across the room as one very large inmate came up behind Evan, another stoner; he had taken interest in his watch. Then he just took it. Evan gave it up without a struggle. The inmate put it on and took his seat farther down in the circle, as if nothing happened. Ashley was shocked at first but then she thought he would get it back at the end of the exercise. She was pretty sure they were not allowed to rob them. So she didn't give it a second thought.

Then a very large African American inmate with a shaved head and tattoos started to speak. "My name is Will. I'm here for murder, 25 to life; I've been here for 20 years.

When I was younger I didn't give a damn. I wouldn't listen to my mama or anyone for that matter; I thought I knew best. By the time I was fifteen, I was deep in the gang life; they were my family. For my family I stole, I dealt drugs, and then I murdered. I gave up my whole life, my freedom, for someone wearing another color. It took me over fifteen years in here to realize what a waste it was. Because, when you come to prison, you hang with your gang. They protect you; if you want out they may decide to kill you. Blood in, blood out; I have to be housed in a special unit where, hopefully, they can't get me. I wanted to change, make up for what I did, so I got involved with this program." He sat down.

"As you know I'm Nate, I'm in for life, for armed robbery and murder, and no possibility for parole. I told you about what can happen with a bunk-mate. If you think you're any safer in the yard, you're nuts; that's where most attacks happen. Let me tell you ladies something; if you think it's any different or better for you it isn't. Women's prisons are worse than men's. If you think you can get in good with the guards by being a rat, you're wrong. Other inmates hunt rats and to the guards you're a dime a dozen. Nowhere is safe in here. If you hurt children and we find out, you won't live long. We also hate rapists; they aren't allowed to be part of this group. Even in prison we have a social structure, believe it or not.

A tall white man stood up. "Hey, I'm Thomas; I'm a car thief; 3rd strike for me. I've been in, this time, for 18 years. I've got eight more years before I can get a shot at parole. Let me give you a look at this place, as I see it. This place is a hell hole, you're on your own; you can't trust anyone. Yet you're, never alone, no privacy whatsoever. You can't even take a shit by yourself. I had this female guard watch me take a dump every morning for two years and I couldn't do a thing about it. You don't get to eat what you want. You can only shower twice a week along with ten other men, so you have to watch your back, if you know what I mean. You get strip searched, including body cavities on a regular basis. You don't have control over anything, not even what you wear. That's my life." He took his seat.

Then the prisoner who was sitting next to Ashley stood up; he was tall and lanky. "I'm Jeremy and I'm also a heroine addict. I started out just like all of you, smoking a little bit of pot. I even went to college for a while. Then I started to deal to pay for my ever growing habit. I graduated to doing pain pills, but when I got up to 20-30 pills a day, a so called friend introduced me to heroine. I was hooked, from the very first time. I started out snorting it. It's amazing how when you're young, you tell yourself you'll never do certain things. But then when you're all doped up, wanting to get higher, you do it. So I stuck that needle in my arm. I also shared needles with friends and now I have full blown Aids. I'm going to die in prison, alone in the infirmary. My family won't be here; it's against the rules. If the other inmates want my things, they just take them, I'm too weak to fight them off. And no one protects me, including the guards." Jeremy looked around at the students. "This certainly isn't the life I envisioned for myself when I was a kid." Jeremy sat down. Ashley was moved by what he had said and took it to heart. She started thinking about her life and where it was headed as other prisoners spoke. She thought about going to prison and decided that she needed to make some changes; this was one place she did not want to end up. She decided then and there she would not commit any crimes. Ashley thought, I'll only keep a little amount of weed on me at one time. Then she thought maybe she should just give it up, but it was the only thing that kept her going, kept her from snapping. Her thoughts went back to her parents and the mess of their divorce, all the arguing and fighting. How they were so wrapped up in their lives and their pain that she was just left to her own devices. Left to cope all on her own, and unfortunately, she had stumbled into the world of drugs. How her friends had got her high, trying to help her forget the feelings of loneliness and depression.

All of a sudden Ashley's train of thought was broken by the slamming of one of the chairs down at the other end of the circle. She wasn't sure what had caused it, but Emily had tears running down her checks. One of the inmates had Charlie by the throat. "If I kill you now, it won't matter." He yelled, "I don't care if they put me in solitary, I like it." The other inmates quickly broke it up and calmed him down. By then all of the other prisoners had spoken.

They split up and talked privately, two students and one inmate. Ashley shared about her home situation and that she was unhappy about her parents fighting. After that, Jeremy chose Ashley to do an exercise. She stood in the middle of the circle and four inmates stood around her. She was asked four things her parents asked her to do that she didn't. They were; come home by curfew, don't skip school, don't get into trouble, and do your homework. She was supposed to face each inmate and solve the problem. The inmates each began to say the statements one by one, Ashley looked at them, not sure of what to say, but then they continued, louder and louder faster and faster. Ashley turned, faced each, said nothing and then turned and turned but still said nothing, they were all talking at once, and she was spinning. Finally she just stopped and looked at Jeremy.

Jeremy took her place in the circle and faced each inmate one by one and said, "I will come home by curfew. I won't skip school. I won't get into trouble. I will do my homework." With each statement Jeremy made the inmate stopped speaking. Ashley took in a deep breath and let it out slowly. Jeremy had made it seem so simple, and after that she went over and sat down.

Nate stood. "I hope you all have learned something today about our world and about how things can go so wrong so fast in your lives. All it takes is one bad decision. You're still young and can change the direction of your lives. Most of us wound up here because of some involvement with drugs. They cloud your mind, so remember that, if anything. I hope I never see any of you again. Good luck." After that a few of the inmates went and talked to the teachers for what seemed like forever. A prison guard announced the exercise was over and directed the group towards the exit. As the students left through the yard, the inmates were let out on the other side too soon and the guards started yelling at the students to run, run, so we had to run for our safety.

The bus ride home was quiet; it seemed as if everyone was thinking about what had gone on. As we were nearing home, Mrs. Burns stood at the front of the bus." I just want to let you guys know the inmates told me you were the worst bunch they ever had. I was disappointed in your behavior before we got there, and I'm sure you know what I mean. Whether you couldn't handle it, or what, I don't know. I've decided to let it stay between us, I'm not telling Mr. Mills or anyone else. Mr. Cromwell and I feel that you all still got a lot out of the program and that was the purpose." Mrs. Burns shook her head while she surveyed the group then took her seat. Ashley thought maybe she shouldn't have smoked beforehand but knew there was nothing she could do about it now. She thought that maybe she would apologize to Mrs. Burns on Monday.

When Ashley arrived home, the house was dark and empty. there was a note on the table saying Ruth was at the store; she would be home soon. Ashley was glad to have some time alone in the house or at least in her room uninterrupted. She wanted to hide her drug paraphernalia. Her mind kept going back to the prisoners and she wanted to be sure no one would find anything. She kept thinking I can't believe I'm doing this today of all days. After what I've learned, I should just throw it all away. But I may change my mind and go back to it if life gets out of hand. Where can I put it? Her eyes scanned every corner of her room. Then near her closet the rug was loose. She picked it up and cut out a piece of the padding. She then wrapped up her bowl in a headband and carefully placed it in the small space. She also decided to put the remainder of her weed, which wasn't much, in the space along with a few black beauty speeders she had. Ashley then sat on her bed and examined the area; it was a bit different, kind of lumpy, so she decided to rearrange her room a little to cover the area. But she had to make sure that wasn't the only piece of furniture moved, so it wouldn't arouse suspicion. Her tall dresser just fit into the space on an angle. She moved her bed over closer to the windows and moved her other dressers and made a few more adjustments. She hopped on her bed and examined her handy work, and thought, nicely done.

Later, when Ruth got home, she wanted to ask Ashley how her trip went. Her father was not home yet, and Ruth hoped that maybe Ashley would confide in her. Ruth waited for Ashley to come downstairs. "So how was your trip? Did you get anything out of it?"

Ruth took a seat at the kitchen table.

Ashley joined her at the table "It was definitely an eye opener; they started out just like us. But a few bad decisions and, boom, they wound up in jail. You wouldn't believe how small their cells are and two of them share it. They are constantly attacking each other, and you can't trust anyone. I definitely don't want to end up there; it was scary." Ashley let out a deep sigh.

"So you learned a lot, but did you decide to change the way you live your life?" Ruth asked.

"I'm going to try and straighten up. Believe me, I don't want to ruin my life; jail is not where I want to be in five years." Ashley shook her head.

"Good, I'm glad that you got something out of the experience. I love you too much to see you throw your life away." Ruth raised her eyebrows and gently tapped the table.

That night as Ashley lay in bed she thought about her day and her life. What her future held she had no idea. She had never considered she would end up in jail; jail was scary. She entertained the idea that she would kill herself before going to jail. In all actuality she thought about death and dying a lot these days. The more she thought about it, the less scary it became. As she lay there she slowly realized that even though she thought about dying quite a bit, she still had fun with her friends and still had the ability to laugh and joke and carry on. It didn't make sense in her mind but why question something that brought her some happiness. She felt that reality seemed to be like a candle burning at both ends. She thought, I'm so confused; maybe I better not act on anything permanent until I'm sure. Then she stared out the window at the treetops swaying in the moonlight until she drifted off to sleep.

CHAPTER 4

*T*he bright sun glistened through the window in Ashley's room; spring was finally on its way. She had slept in that Saturday morning. As she lay in bed under her warm comforter, she gazed at the corner of her room where she had hidden her stash over a month and a half ago. She thought of the many times she wanted to break into it, yet resisted. Not that she should be commended though because she still smoked pot with her friends on a few occasions. The awful truth was she wanted to numb herself from reality. At this point, she sat up in bed and snuggled down under her comforter.

She thought about what a failure she was although she had apologized to Mrs. B for her behavior on the trip. But she had basically lied to Ruth's face when she came back from the scared straight program. That had been bothering her for weeks although she wasn't quite sure why. She had lied to her mother a lot and it never bothered her. Having any kind of relationship with her mother felt somehow empty, never filling Ashley up inside. Sort of like a big black hole inside of her, just dark and empty. Ashley tried to justify it by telling herself that her mother had to work full time and went to school part time and then studied constantly. Most of the time, as soon as her mother arrived home, she disappeared into her room to study. She had to have perfect grades which meant there wasn't much time left over for Ashley and Laura.

Ashley thought about Laura and how she felt that she had deserted her and left her all on her own. How lonely she must be feeling, with no one to talk to. They had not been allowed to talk; they had to whisper at night so as not to disturb her mother. Poor Laura. Ashley made a mental note to make sure and call her sister more often. If her mother answered, she would just hang up.

Ashley then realized that it had been months since she had seen or spoken to her mother. She couldn't help but wonder if her mother missed her as much as Ashley missed her mother. Then she thought she really didn't know why she missed her at all, all the yelling. If there was even one dish in the sink or a crumb on the counter, her mother freaked; then no talking at night; and then her mother threw her out. Ashley remembered how she would get nervous as soon as her mother's car pulled into the driveway. Both of her parents made her nervous though. She knew deep down her mother did the best she could. Maybe it was her, maybe she expected too much. Maybe she was just being too hard on her mom. Maybe she just wasn't good enough or wasn't trying hard enough.

Suddenly Ashley's attention was drawn outside to her father as he hopped into his pickup and drove off. She looked at the clock; it read 12:15 pm. Oh shit! She jumped out of bed and threw on some clothes and ran downstairs.

"Good afternoon sleepyhead," Ruth smiled, as she looked up from the table.

"Oh, man, I can't believe I didn't realize the time. I was supposed to call Kim by 11am to go to the mall in the city." Ashley thought no more lying. "Actually I forgot until I saw Dad take off out of the driveway."

"Well, calm down. Call her now. Maybe they're running late. I wish you had asked to go, and then I could have made sure you were up."

"I asked dad three days ago."

"Oh! Well, there you go. He wouldn't remember his head if it wasn't attached."

Ashley ran over to the phone on the kitchen wall and twirled the cord around her fingers as she waited for an answer. She counted twenty rings before giving up. Then she marched over to the table and plopped down next to Ruth.

"I'm sorry, honey." Ruth smiled bleakly. "Well, you can hang out with me. Your dad has to work and Michael is with my folks for the weekend. So I'm free."

"Thanks." Ashley nodded her head. "What are you gonna do?"

"Well, I have a bunch of errands to run and some shopping to do."

"What kind of shopping?" Ashley raised her eyebrows.

"Supplies at K-mart, not the mall, but we could go to the strip mall and look. I'm sure you could use a few things." Ruth looked at Ashley and winked.

"What kinds of things?" Ashley squinted her eyes and tilted her head. "I've been doing your laundry, kiddo, and you're in desperate need of clothes." Ruth took a sip of her juice and patted her large belly.

"Well, I'm on board. Let's go." Ashley grinned from ear to ear. "So when are we heading out?" Ashley asked as she grabbed a Pepsi from the fridge.

"As soon as I finish my list and you're ready."

"I'll be ready in ten minutes; gotta finish grooming." Ashley ran upstairs.

Before long the two of them had zipped through K-mart and finished all the other errands. They were almost to the strip mall and things were going well. Ruth had kept the conversation light and airy but wanted to discuss Ashley's promise to go see the drug counselor at school. They were 45 minutes from home so Ruth decided to wait until they were on their way home to bring it up. When Ruth pulled into the parking lot, Ashley's eyes lit up.

"I still can't believe you're buying me clothes for no reason."

"The reason is because you need them." Ruth exited the car and they went into the store.

"Are you sure you're up to this? I mean you're not too tired are you?" Ash wanted to check on how Ruth was feeling.

"I'm fine. I still have plenty of energy, but thanks." Ruth smiled at her.

"Oh, I also have 20 bucks; Dad gave it to me for the mall. We should use it."

"Well, let's see what they have." The two of them wandered in and out of the aisles. Ashley picked out two pairs of blue Levi's, a pink and white striped button up long sleeve oxford shirt, a bold red and white short sleeve shirt, a solid black shirt and another white button up oxford. They were a smaller size; she had lost a considerable amount of weight over the last couple months.

"Are you sure I can have all these clothes? This is a lot of money." Ashley fidgeted at the register. "Here, take my 20 bucks."

"OK, If it makes you feel better, but don't worry, OK?" Ruth chuckled.

"Thank you so much. I don't want to sound ungrateful, but is dad going to be mad?"

"Honey, it's OK" Ruth smiled as she paid for the merchandise; then they left the store.

"Ruth"

"Yeah"

"Again, I don't want to sound ungrateful, but you got me all these clothes and there's no catch-at all."

"Ash, there's no catch. I didn't plan this out; it was a last minute thing. But I do want to talk to you about a promise you made to me a few months ago. Do you remember?" Ruth smiled warmly at Ashley.

Ashley sat and thought for a few moments. "Yeah, I think so. You tell me, though, so I know for sure."

"Your promise to go see the drug counselor at school," answered Ruth.

"That's what I thought," Ashley sighed

"I think it would do you a world of good to talk to someone about how you feel, about what has happened to you, and about some of the things you do or want to do. Maybe you won't feel so lonely or cry so much."

Ashley shot a look of surprise at Ruth.

"Yes, I hear you cry at night. The heating ducts carry sound incredibly well. Don't worry. Your dad doesn't know." Ruth smiled at Ashley. "I love you so much, and I know you hurt inside, deep inside. You need to get it out."

Ashley started to cry. "It's not that I don't like living with you and dad. It's just that she just threw me away, and she hasn't even called, not even once. It's been months. She didn't even call on Christmas. It's like she forgot all about me, and I don't even exist anymore." Ashley began to sob.

"I know honey, I know"

"Doesn't she love me?"

"Yes, of course she does."

"Then where is she?"

"I don't know. I don't know honey; I'm so sorry." Ruth reached over and stroked Ashley's arm as she drove. They drove on in silence, after a while Ashley sighed deep and stated. "I'll give seeing the drug counselor a try; it can't be all that bad.." Ashley forced a smile at Ruth. Yet she thought at least this one won't be talking to her parents after she sees him, like the counselor did when she overdosed the summer before her freshman year in high school.

"Thank you. I'm proud of you. Talking can be tough, and he won't be telling anyone anything. What's said in there stays in there, unless you want to tell someone."

This will be our little secret. I won't tell your dad unless you want me to."

"No way. He will freak if he even hears drug in the counselors job description." Ashley sighed.

"OK then, what about just telling him you're seeing a counselor?" "Can we just keep it between us for now? Then, later, if we need to, we'll tell him."

"Deal," Ruth smiled.

"Thanks." Ashley sniffled. No one had ever taken the time to talk to Ashley about her life or how she felt. By Ruth doing this, it drew Ashley much closer to her and she began to really respect Ruth and enjoy spending time with her.

"Let's go home and get some dinner and show off all your new clothes." Ruth smiled at Ashley. "You know I love you; you're a good kid."

"Thanks, I love you too; you've been really good to me and I appreciate it. My mom never bought me clothes just because I needed them. I got them at the start of school, Christmas and my birthday, and that's it. So I am so grateful; thank you again." Ashley smiled as she nodded her head.

Ashley went to school with a plan; she was going to try and casually run into the drug counselor. But what she found was that he was quite busy. She also wasn't sure how her friends would react to her seeing him, so she wanted to keep it on the down low. Even though she knew she had to see him, as the days went by, it drifted farther from her mind.

Then one afternoon Ashley and quite a few of her friends were smoking up in the back of the bathroom during their lunch hour, having a grand old time. Ashley was kneeling on the floor, in the back stall, with a sack getting ready to pour out some herb onto a paper.

Suddenly a teacher entered and yelled, "Freeze."

Ashley froze. Karen being a quick thinker yelled, "Put that away." Ashley responded and put it away. A couple of regular smokers got caught because they were in the front of the restroom. As they exited the bathroom, they had to pass between the principal, Mr. Hill, and the vice principal, Mr. Mills. When Ashley passed by them, she saw them looking at each other with a smile on their faces; they rarely busted the girls. As soon as Ashley and Karen cleared the area, they took off and separated. They wanted to ditch their supplies. And, wouldn't you know, Ashley ran smack into Mr. Shore, the drug counselor.

"Whoa, whoa. Where you headed in such a hurry?" He held her arms for a moment.

"It's Ashley right?" He shot her a smile. "You can call me Tim; I've been meaning to catch up with you."

Ashley wasn't sure what to think; she was trembling. "Catch up with me; is my reputation that bad? What exactly have you heard?"

"Well, we could go to my office and discuss exactly how wild you are and maybe talk a bit about what I've heard. How's that sound?" Tim held out his hand in the direction of his office.

Once they sat down in his office, Ashley looked around. His walls were blank, unlike previous counselors she had seen. He was tall and thin and his hair was gray even though, Ashley guessed, he was only in his mid thirties. He also sported a silver gray mustache and goatee, with Beatles type glasses to boot. The way he carried himself and talked was unlike any other adults Ashley was used to, so this helped her to trust him a bit more readily.

"So, Ashley, how's it going on the home front?" Tim leaned back in his chair.

"My parents are divorced, and I live with my dad. My mother threw me out cause I wanted to spend Christmas with my dad and his parents, basically. My stepmother has a four year old son and is going to have another child in March, in just a few weeks." "Are you happy about living with your dad?"

"He's a lot nicer than he used to be when he was with my mom."

"That's not what I asked."

"Ruth, my stepmother is really good to me, better than either of my parents." Ashley looked at the floor, her knee bounced up and down.

"But you're not happy?" Tim studied Ashley. "Do you ever wish your parents were still married to each other?"

"No way; they fought all the time. It was horrible." Ashley shook her head.

"When's the last time you talked to your mom?"

"The night she threw me out, a few days before Christmas vacation. She didn't even call me on Christmas; can you believe that?" Ashley sighed heavily.

"Do you miss her?" Tim scratched his neck.

"Well, a phone call would be nice." Ashley looked at the floor. "What about you calling her?

"No way. She threw me out. When she wants to talk to me, she knows where to find me. I do feel bad that I left my younger sister there, all alone. My mom goes to college part-time, and when she comes home from work she goes to her room to study all night. So my sister, Laura, has no one to talk to. Sometimes I feel like I deserted her."

"How old is Laura?"

"She's 13, almost 14?"

"Does she ever call you?

"No. We see each other on the bus when we ride over to the elementary school to exchange students and pick up the little kids." Ashley bit her lip.

"Well, that's cool. You still get to see each other." Tim smiled. "I'm sure that means a lot to her."

"Yeah, I guess." Ashley forced a smile.

"So let's get down to the nitty gritty. How often are you smoking? I see you wandering around in a haze every so often." Tim smiled again, "Don't worry I'm not going to rat you out to anyone. Whatever you tell me stays with me."

"I don't know, what do you mean, like how many times a week?" Ashley held out her hands.

"OK, let's say a week."

"Maybe four or five times or so, not too much."

"Are you counting the week as in five school days is the week, or the whole week including the weekend?" Tim raised his eyebrows.

"Ah, man, you got me." Ashley smiled.

"That's what I thought. So basically you smoke pretty much every day?"

"Well, I never smoke before a test or important notes. My grades are important to me, I'm in the regents program and plan to stay in it. I only have trouble in advanced geometry, and I get extra help for that on my own."

"So, you're a smart stoner." Tim laughed.

"Ha ha. You think you're pretty funny, huh." Ashley nodded her head up and down.

"I've got my moments." Tim smiled.

"This isn't as bad as I thought it would be." Ashley sighed

"Why? Were you planning on talking to me?" Tim raised an eyebrow.

"Well yeah, kinda. My stepmother found a couple speeders in my laundry and said if I didn't make a point of talking to you, she would tell my dad. So, when you stopped me, I was like OK."

"And here I thought it was my winning personality." Tim smiled. "Whatever the reason, at least, you're here and that's what's important. OK?"

"OK."

"So how is she going to know you're really talking to me and not just giving her a load of bull, anyway?"

"Well, you know it's weird. I can lie to my parents, no problem, but with Ruth it's different. I'm not sure why. She talks to me, really talks to me and takes an interest in what's going on in my life. I don't want to mess that up with a bunch of lies." Ashley bounced her knee up and down.

"I get that. She sounds like she's pretty important to you?"

"It's different, that's for sure." Ashley answered. They continued to talk for quite a while. Then Ashley got a pass for the classes she missed and turned them in. She finished out her day and went home.

Ashley thought about her session with Tim in great detail. She thought about sharing some of it with Ruth but wanted to keep it from her father. Some of the stress she felt seemed to be lifted a little. Yet she still felt suicidal, thinking about it every day, several times during the day. How she could overdose again, like she had the summer before her freshman year, but this time she wouldn't fail. She thought I'm definitely not telling my parents or any counselors that. They will lock me up and throw away the key. She thought I'm so messed up. Here I'm going to kill myself, yet I need to get good grades. I have to accomplish something in life. Ruth was right. I need a counselor.

After dinner that evening, when her father was out of ear shot, Ashley told Ruth that she went and spoke to the counselor. She told her that she liked him and that she would go back; and it wasn't as bad as she thought it would be. When she shared this with Ruth, she was very understanding and sympathetic. Ashley thought long and hard about sharing the rest of her discussion with Ruth. At this point, however, she decided to keep it to herself.

Ashley was helping out around the house much more lately, because of Ruth's advanced pregnancy. The baby was due pretty much any time now so everyone was on high alert. Ashley had never experienced anything like this before, so she was extra sensitive. She kept making Ruth go sit down when she was doing chores. Finally Ruth had had enough of it.

"Ashley, I'm not going to break. Women have been having babies for centuries. In some countries women work, have their babies, then go right back to work within an hour or so. So relax." Ruth got up.

"Yeah, well not in this country. You need your rest. When that baby comes it's going to keep you up all night." Ashley pointed to the chair, as she folded some clothes.

"Honey, I got news for ya; he's going to keep us all up at night." Ruth laughed.

"No, not me. I'm buying a pair of ear plugs, the best they've got." Ashley nodded her head and smiled.

"I just wish this little guy would come out. I'm so tired of being pregnant. Why don't you let me finish folding and you vacuum real quick?"

"All right, I guess that's not too stressful. But if you get tired just sit down and I'll finish." Ashley went to the living room and vacuumed it. When she was finished, she checked on Ruth again.

Ruth lovingly looked at Ashley, "You know if you care for this baby the way you look after me, he's going to have the best big sister in the world."

"What are you talking about?" Ashley squinted her eyebrows.

"You, you have a very caring, nurturing side to you; it's nice. You need to show it more often, instead of that, I don't give a damn side."

"Whatever," Ashley smiled.

The next few days were business as usual, until one afternoon Ashley came home to find a note. It read that her father had taken Ruth to the hospital to have the baby, and Ashley was to look after Michael. Ashley was a little upset that she wouldn't be there for the birth, but someone had to watch Michael. Ashley waited by the phone for updates from her dad, but they never came. The next day she still had not heard from her father so she stayed home from school. She reasoned that she had to get Michael on the late bus, and she stayed up most of the night waiting for a call from her father.

After several hours Ashley was frustrated her father hadn't called, so she decided to break into her stash she had hidden so long ago. She moved her dresser and picked up the rug to find it undisturbed. She plopped down on her bed and filled her bowl; she thought about opening a window but passed on it. She took a hit and another, and another, and so on. She was higher than a kite. She then started to get out her drawing supplies; she had not done any drawing in months. She got it all set up on her bed, and then heard her father's truck pull in the driveway. She started freaking out; she couldn't open the window. He would see her. So she ran to the bathroom, grabbed the air freshener, ran to the bottom of the stairs and sprayed some. Ran back upstairs, saw that he entered the house, and threw open her window, while spraying air freshener all over. She stashed her stuff and put her dresser back, while her father was in the kitchen. She thought maybe she should meet him downstairs so he wouldn't come upstairs. She sprayed the hallway again and the top of the stairway. She bolted downstairs to greet him in the kitchen, far away from the stairs.

"Hi, dad, how's Ruth? Did she have the baby?" Ashley nervously smiled, a bit out of breath.

"She sure did; he's 7 lbs. and doing great and she's doing awesome. He was born this morning at 5:35. I left so Ruth could get some sleep;

she was in labor all night. He is so awesome; I can't wait for you to see him. When Michael gets home, I'll take you guys up to see them. I'm going to hit the sack, I'm bushed, and all I did was coach her. Good night honey, I love you." Rodger put his arm around Ashley's neck and kissed her cheek before wandering into his room.

"I love you too," Ashley answered as her father walked away. She watched him disappear into his room and waited for him to reappear piping mad, but it didn't happen. Ashley stood frozen for about ten minutes, and then she felt the coast was clear for her to return to her room. She thought, talk about a buzz kill. She then went up and fixed her room perfectly. She settled down enough to try to resume drawing a picture of some sort, but mainly practiced trees without leaves.

That evening they all went to the hospital and saw Ruth and the baby; he was introduced as Mr. Jacob Robert Ames. Family had been coming and going all day.

"Hey, honey, how are you feeling?" Rodger asked after they arrived. "Pretty good. Have you seen the baby yet today?" Ruth asked. "Yeah, the kids are up there right now; they'll be here in a minute."

Rodger rubbed her hand.

"Hey, Ruth, Jacob's so cute. How long before you come home?" Ashley asked as she came in from the nursery.

"Actually, we are probably coming home tomorrow afternoon." smiled Ruth.

"That's cool," Ashley replied.

"Yeah, when I went home the house smelled really good, Ash must have been cleaning up a storm." Rodger nodded "She is really helping out."

Ashley just smiled, "No problem really; it's the least I could do." She laughed nervously, hoping Ruth wouldn't notice. Ruth eyed Ashley but was quickly distracted by the nurse who brought in her medication and let them know visiting hours were almost over for the night. Before long Ruth and little Jake were settled in at home and trying to follow some type of schedule. As for sleep, he was waking up about every 3-4 hours to eat which included the middle of the night. Most nights Ashley woke up along with Ruth, so she was sympathetic to her exhaustion. However, Ashley's teachers were not; they did not seem to care if there was a new baby or not. After a few weeks Ashley was exhausted and she had had enough; her patience was wearing thin.

Ashley laid in bed and thought she couldn't handle it anymore. School was becoming a hassle; she just wanted to hide in the bathroom all day. She still talked to Tim but it didn't seem to help much. She thought she was going insane; everything seemed like it was such an effort. I been smoking most every day just to get through, so I don't end it all. She thought tomorrow is Friday; I'm staying home I'm sleeping all day, I just don't care anymore.

CHAPTER 5

Jacob is two months old now and mostly sleeps through the night, much to the relief of the rest of the family. Ashley talked and sang to him constantly; she really enjoyed the time she spent with him. But the minute he would get grouchy, she gave him back to Ruth. Little Michael was having a bit of jealousy as far as the baby went. At other times, though, he was great; it just depended on his mood. Between Rodger, Ruth and Ashley, they tried to spend special time with Michael so he wouldn't feel replaced by the baby. It seemed to be helping him adjust to the new addition to the family. He no longer asked how long Jacob was staying, Ashley informed all of her girlfriends of what is was like to have a new baby in the house. She joked that she was never having one; they were way too much work.

School would be letting out for summer vacation in a couple of months. This meant the weather would be warm which meant parties at the lake. One good thing about being from a small town was there were only a few cops. Two cops would show up at a party of 100-200 kids. They wouldn't even get out of their car, just use their spotlight and leave. They couldn't do a damn thing about it, and the kids knew it. They would just smile and wave at them.

The girls sat in Mrs. Burns room planning their strategy.

"Hey Ash, you're going to the party Friday night right?" Karen asked. "Yeah, what are you going to tell your parents?" Ashley asked. "Probably the mall."

"I think you should say the late show too," Ashley added "Yeah, you're right, I will." Karen nodded her head.

"Is Emily going with us?" Ashley asked "I think so; I'll talk to her later today." "Cool." Ashley rubbed her hands together. "Hey, you know what else I heard?" "What?"

"I heard Thomas has a thing for you, Ash." Karen bobbed her head up and down, smiling.

"Thomas, are you serious? When did you hear that?" Ashley smiled "The other day, and I'm sure it's true because he was there and he started to blush." Karen smiled.

"Really, is he going to be at the party?" Ashley raised her eyebrows. "I'm pretty sure he is"

"Cool. We'll see what happens" Ashley smiled.

The girls continued to talk for the remainder of the hour and then went off to their classes.

Later that day Ashley caught up with Kim and told her about Thomas. Kim was still sweet on Frank, the boy who switched seats with them in the morning. Ashley mentioned the party, but Kim refused to go. She wasn't really into that type of scene. Ashley knew she wouldn't go before she asked. They had a lot of different friends, but they also had a deep connection that would never be broken.

That evening Ashley wanted to wait for just the right time to ask to go out the following day. But her father had been drinking heavily so she thought maybe she should ask Ruth, but she was grouchy and tired from taking care of Jacob. She paced her room for what seemed like an eternity, then finally gained up enough courage and just went for it. When she got downstairs, Ruth was asleep, so she had no alternative but her father.

"Dad, can I go to the mall tomorrow night with my friends? We want to catch a movie or something." Ashley tried to look innocent.

"Go out? Is that all you think about? I would love to be able to just go out." Rodger yelled at her as he swayed back and forth.

"Well, I haven't gone anywhere in a long time. I've been helping out a lot. It's not my baby." Ashley frowned.

"Don't you ever speak to me like that! You're an ungrateful little brat." Rodger gave her the look. The look was terrifying, like he hated her, like he could kill her where she stood; all the kids were beyond scared of this look. It's like the hatred and anger just oozed out of his eyes.

Ruth ran into the room a bit dazed, "What's going on? Why are you yelling?" She looked at both them. Ashley was near tears.

"She wants to go out tomorrow night; she needs to stay here and help out." Rodger glared at Ashley.

"Ruth, I've been helping out a lot and I just wanted to go out for a few hours, that's all. I haven't gone out since Jake was born; it's not fair. We just want to go to the mall and maybe catch a movie. Please, Ruth? I'll do something for you." Ashley tilted her head and tried her best to look pitiful.

"I'll tell you what. Why don't you go out tomorrow and then your dad and I go out Saturday night." Ruth held out her hands.

"Deal." Ashley nodded her head.

"How does that sound Rodger? Ruth looked at him.

"I guess I can live with that," Rodger answered as he staggered away. He wasn't about to apologize to Ashley; he never did. This type of behavior wasn't new to her; it brought back memories of when he lived with her mother. Ashley stormed up to her room, swearing under her breath. She wondered if he was reverting back to his old self. How long now, before this was a regular occurrence. Ashley plopped down on her bed, buried her head in her pillow and started to cry. It wasn't the babysitting; it was him. He was so mean; she hated him when he acted like that. She wished she could just die.

The following day Ashley went directly to Karen's house from school. She had asked Ruth's permission that morning. She wanted to avoid her father at all costs. Karen's house was like a different world; her parents never drank. They treated their kids with decency and respect. Karen was never allowed at Ashley's; it was never spoken, just kind of understood. Karen's parents were very kind to Ashley and she ate it up. She yearned for that type of attention. They were also quite strict which meant that Karen had to lie about where they were going. Ashley always felt guilty about that. She thought if they were my parents I would be good, but Karen didn't give it a second thought.

After dinner the girls took the family station wagon out to pick up Emily and a few other girls, and then headed towards the lake for the party. When they arrived, it was in full swing. They had a huge fire, a keg, and two bucks bought a cup. About 30 cars were already there.

"Hey, Em, Ash, let's try and stick together." Karen pulled over to the side of the dirt road. The three girls spilled out of the front seat, wasting no time going to pay for their cups. The other four girls got out of the back.

"Where's the keg?" Ashley looked around.

"It's in Brian's car," Emily pointed.

"Cool, let's get started," Karen added as they raced over and started to fill their cups.

"Oh, it's good and cold. I love it." Karen raised her cup. "Good stuff makes all your worries disappear." Ashley chugged it down and filled her cup again. "Hey, you want to go over by the fire?" She chugged another and then filled her cup again.

"Yeah, let me finish this first and refill. You better slow down." Karen smiled.

"I will. I just like to get a quick buzz," Ashley replied.

"You two drink up. I'll be the driver tonight; I'll only have a couple," Emily spoke up.

"Thanks, Em, I was just planning on, hell, I didn't have a plan." Karen laughed.

"Well, if I'm not home by 1am my dad will freak," Emily stated. "Yeah, I gotta be home around then too," Ashley added, "but I'm not too worried about it. The hell with them all. I'm here to party," Ash shouted while laughing.

"All right. We'll leave here by midnight. That includes you, party animal. So we will all get home on time. We gotta stop drinking by like 11: 00, so we start to sober up a bit. So, Em, will you be the timekeeper for us?" Karen downed her drink and put her arm around Emily's shoulder.

"No problem. Let's party while we can." Emily took a sip of her drink. "Oh, we gotta tell the other girls that caught a ride with us."

"Yeah, we will; we'll run into them. Do you see Thomas?" Ashley took a drink.

"No, I guess he didn't make it. Maybe he'll show up later and sweep you off your feet." Karen laughed.

The girls continued to drink and party all night. At about 11pm Emily told them the time. Ashley and Karen each chugged one more beer. They were both feeling no pain. They went over to the edge of the lake and splashed water on their faces to help them sober up a bit, not that it really helped. The girls rounded up everyone that caught a ride with them and loaded them in. Emily kept her word and was pretty sober; she could almost walk a straight line. On the way home Ashley rolled down the window and climbed out on the door frame and rode home half in the car and half out. She felt the wind through her hair, against her face, like she was flying, free from life. Her drunken screams cut through the darkness disturbing the cool quiet air of the night.

After dropping the other four girls off, it was Ashley's turn. When they got to Ashley's the house, the lights were still on. She started to laugh, "Think I can pull it off?" she snickered.

"Well, you'll know soon enough," Karen managed to get out before they all laughed.

"Maybe I'll just tip-toe in and they won't even notice." Ashley giggled. "Shh, shh. Guys, this is serious,"

"To hell with them Ash, what are they going to do? They're making you watch that damn baby tomorrow, just to come out tonight. To hell with them. Get some guts about you or however it's supposed to go." Karen was waving her hands around.

"Don't worry, Ash, they're probably asleep and they just left the light on for you." Emily smiled.

"OK. I'm going in. Catch you guys, I mean girls, later." Ashley giggled, as she stumbled out of the car and up the stairs into the house.

Ashley got inside and decided to take off her shoes in order to be quiet; she stretched out her arm for the wall but missed it and fell into a bag of beer bottles. She jumped up brushed herself off and peered around the corner for signs of life. Whoa, that was close she thought. Guess no one is up. Cool. She crept through the kitchen into the living room and there calmly sat Ruth.

"Hi, honey. How was the mall?" She raised her eyebrows. "What movie did you see?"

Ashley glanced at the clock noticing 12:45am "Uh well we uh …" "I can smell what you uh we uh; where were you tonight?" Ruth cleared her throat.

"We were invited to a party, so we decided to go there instead of the mall." Ashley eyed the floor as she tried not to sway back and forth.

"I don't know what to do with you, Ash; you continue to make the wrong decisions. I give you a little freedom and you screw up. Why can't you act responsibly? How can I trust you? Was your driver drunk too?"

"No, she wasn't, and we just wanted to let off a little steam. I don't do this all the time, honest. I'm home most of the time; you know that." Ashley sighed heavily. "Are you going to tell my dad?"

"I haven't decided yet, and you obviously need to stay home if you're going to act like this." Ruth looked hard at Ashley.

"Please, don't tell him. He will just freak out worse than the other day, and I can't deal with him like that. I got a lot on my plate as it is. Please, I'll do whatever you ask."

"I don't like keeping secrets from your father, especially things like this."

"Well, will you at least warn me if you do, so I can prepare for a beating?"

"He won't hit you." Ruth held out her hands.

"You haven't known him as long as I have and he almost hit me the other day. So don't tell me he won't because he has. In fact, he has kicked me down the hall with his pointed cowboy boots on. No matter how drunk I am, I can't get that memory out of my head. There is a lot you don't know about my father, so let's just call it a night. You can punish me any way you want. Hell, shoot me. I just don't care anymore." Ashley just shook her head.

"Ashley!! I'll assume that's the alcohol talking. Just go to bed. You and I will talk tomorrow." Ruth went over and hugged her, "You know I love you."

"I know. I love you too Goodnight." Ashley turned and went upstairs. When Ashley lay in bed, she thought if Ruth told her father, he would beat the snot out of her. Then she thought, I can't believe I actually said it out loud to someone. Just shoot me. How liberating it felt to actually say it; let it out even though she thought it was the alcohol and not her real feelings. She thought, my dad's gun is in the top of the hall closet. I could just get it now and then I wouldn't have to worry if she told him about the party; it would be all over in a matter of minutes. Am I that brave? Do I have that much courage? I could be with God. He would comfort me and love me and protect me, hold me in his arms, fill me up inside. I'm so very empty. My life is so very pointless. No one really wants me anyways. Ashley began to cry. She buried her head in her pillow to stifle the sound. As she cried, she drifted off to sleep.

The following morning came early; Ruth woke Ashley up at 9am immediately after her father left for work.

"Come on kiddo get up. You want to party with the big dogs, you're going to pay the price. Besides your father just left, and you need to get into the shower and wash off the smell of alcohol." Ruth opened the drapes.

"OK, does this mean you're not telling him?' Ashley took in a deep breath and let it out.

"That's what it means. Make sure you do something with that breath; you're getting me drunk." Ruth stood at the foot of Ashley's bed, hands on her hips. "Thanks, Ruth. I'll do better, I promise." Ashley got out of bed.

"Go get your butt in the shower. You have a ton of chores to do before your dad and I go out tonight, Cinderella." Ruth cleared her throat and went downstairs.

Ashley cleaned herself up and reported to Ruth for her long list of chores. She had a full day of scrubbing floors, toilets, tubs, washing windows, doing laundry which included the dreaded mating baskets full of un-mated socks. Ashley did all of these things without a single complaint. Then Ruth took pity on her and allowed her a little cat nap before her father came home and they got ready to go out for the evening.

Rodger whistled as he came through the door. "Hey good looking you ready to go out on the town?" He went over and kissed Ruth.

"You know it baby. I'm almost ready. Why don't you go jump in the shower?" Ruth patted his butt as he left the room.

Ruth went upstairs and woke Ashley, "Hey, kiddo, its 6:30 and we're almost ready to leave. Jake ate about 20 minutes ago and there is frozen pizza and ice cream for you and Michael. Any questions?"

"No, I don't think so. Where are you going?" Ashley got up and brushed her hair.

"I'm not totally sure, to tell you the truth, maybe dinner at The Crows Nest then out for drinks somewhere. We probably won't be too late but then again you never know with your father." Ruth patted Ashley on the head and then went downstairs. Ashley followed a few minutes later; she hadn't spoken to her father since the blow up a few days earlier. She was a bit worried about running into him but figured he would be in a good mood. As she entered the kitchen, Ruth and Rodger were embraced, exchanging kisses.

"Yuck!! Get a room. No don't, that's how Jake got here!" Ashley's face was contorted.

The two of them broke out in laughter. "That's not quite how he got here," Rodger exclaimed smiling.

Michael wandered in from the living room, "How did Jake get here?" "Close enough, now get out of here." Ashley smiled. "Mommy, how did Jake get here?" Michael looked at Ruth.

"He grew in mommy's tummy, honey. Now be a good boy and listen to Ash. We'll be back later." Ruth hugged Michael.

"I wanna go with you," Michael begged

"No, we already talked about this. Listen, there's ice cream for later if you're a good boy, OK?" Ruth gave him another hug goodbye, after that Ruth and Rodger danced out the door.

Ashley watched them leave; she thought they really needed a night out. My dad hasn't been this carefree in a long time. Maybe this was all he needed to get him back on the right track. That night Ashley fed and played with Michael, something she hadn't done in a long while. It actually made her feel good about herself. When she fed Jake, she included Michael allowing him to help, and then she sang to the both of them. After putting Jake down for the night, she let Michael stay up later than usual, more for her company than his enjoyment. At about 9:30 she put him to bed reading him a bunch of bedtime stories, with all the voices. His giggles warmed Ashley's insides. She then went and checked on Jake before turning in herself.

Ashley awoke to Jake's cries. She glanced at the clock 5am. He kept crying and crying. She thought, they are so freaking hung over, they don't even hear him. Ashley went downstairs to her parent's room where Jake slept, and when she went to retrieve him, she looked and they weren't there. She started to panic. What if they got in an accident? What if they got arrested? But then Jake's cries brought her back. Just relax. Just tend to the kids and they will show up; they probably went out to breakfast or something. Ashley fed Jake and then paced the floors, wondering if she should call her grandparents. She opted not to, figuring the police would show up if anything drastic had happened.

When Michael got up, she fed him and had him go upstairs to play with his toys. She let him get his race cars out which were special toys that had to be played with an adult. So he was very happy; she checked on him continually, so as not to break the rule. Ashley fed Jake standing at the window, she kept a vigil at the window looking for their truck. After lunch Michael had questions as to where they were. Ashley answered that they'll be back soon, buddy; don't worry, but that's all she did.

Around two that afternoon Rodger's truck pulled into the driveway, and then the two of them waltzed into the house without a care. They were talking and laughing as if they hadn't a worry in the world. Ashley stood with her hands on her hips glaring at them.

"What's up, kiddo? How did it go? Were the kids good?" Ruth ignored her stance and smiled.

"Yeah, they were great, except I had to keep reassuring Michael you were coming back!" Ashley glared at them. "You should've called. I was worried. You said a night out!" Ashley kept her eyes locked on them. "Oh, please, give me a break! What are you, my mother? For Christ's sakes, grow up. So we stayed out overnight. We're entitled. We work hard, provide roof, food and clothes. Quit complaining. You sound so ungrateful. If I would've known you would whine so much, I would've stayed out longer. Jesus we had a great time and to come home to this." Rodger gave her the look. Ashley cowered immediately, then turned and ran upstairs.

"Rodger! Calm down, you're scaring me and you probably scared her too." Ruth's eyes were wide and her mouth hung open. "Why are you acting like this? I've never seen this side of you. We just had a wonderful time out. She was just worried, OK, just calm down, honey. It's not that big of a deal." Ruth rubbed his arm.

"OK OK you're right. I'm going to go lay down for a while." Rodger shook his head. "You sure tired me out last night, oh man! You were great; I love you baby." He smiled.

"Shh, the kids will hear you." Ruth went over and kissed him, then patted his behind as he left the room. She smiled as she followed him to go check on the children. When she finished, she found herself outside of Ashley's door, wondering what to do. She stood silent for a few moments, then opted to go in.

Ruth cracked open the door, "Hey, mind if I come in?" "It's your house, "Ashley quietly answered.

"Come on now, don't be like that." Ruth sat next to her on the bed. "I'll admit we probably should've called; it never dawned on us that you would be that worried. We just assumed you had it all under control."

"I should've kept my mouth shut; now he's all pissed off at me again. I just can't win." Ashley stared at the floor.

"Don't worry, he's just tired, he'll cool down. Tomorrow this will all be forgotten, I promise you. I'll talk to him if you want me to." Ruth lowered her head so as to make eye contact with Ashley.

"No, you don't need to talk to him; hopefully he'll just let it be." Ashley let out a deep sigh.

"Hey, I appreciate you taking care of the kids while we were gone. Thank you." Ruth smiled and rubbed Ashley's arm.

"You're welcome; they were really good. Michael and I had a lot of fun playing and then I read him some books at bedtime with all the voices. He got a kick out of that." Ashley laughed and then started to relax. "Thanks for coming in and talking to me, and well… you know…saying thank you and all, it means a lot, it really does." Ashley smiled.

Ruth hugged Ashley. "You're very welcome, you're important to me. I know I'm just the step-parent, but I still care about you."

"You treat me better than either of my parents, like how you talk to me. You ask me about my day; they never do that. They are all wrapped up in their own lives; they are too busy to care about my life, and it's sad but true." Ashley shook her head.

"They still love you, Ash. I know your dad does." Ruth took in a deep breath.

"All right enough of this talk. I'm bushed. Do you mind if I take a nap?"

"No, go ahead. You deserve it," Ruth left the room and went downstairs.

Ashley curled up under her comforter and thought about what Ruth said. She always looks at the bright side of life; she sees the best in people. Maybe that is the reason she has so many friends. People are drawn to her. She thought how lucky she was that Ruth had come into her life. She made her life a lot easier as far as her father was concerned. That was for sure. Then she closed her eyes. She felt good for a change; it was a positive change doing something for Ruth, because Ruth went out of her way to do things for her and not many people did that for her.

CHAPTER 6

During finals week Ashley threw herself into her studies. She only had to be at school a few hours each day to take her exams and then back home to hit the books. She looked forward to a carefree summer of fun and friends. That last Friday night was a huge bash at the bluffs that she wanted to attend. Ashley felt she deserved to go after all the hard work she had put into the last semester of her sophomore year.

Her grades had drastically improved since she had started seeing Tim. That was one thing she would miss over the summer. The loneliness had already started to creep in at just the thought of being on her own. Ashley had come to depend on Tim; sometimes she saw him three times a week and now she felt deserted. How was she going to handle all those thoughts, even though she didn't share the deep suicidal ones. Talking was like a pressure valve release, helping her handle thoughts and feelings. She told herself to cheer up; it's only three months. She would just go wild and live carefree.

Friday rolled around and Ashley finished her last exam. She went outside the gym into the hallway and talked with Kim while she waited for Karen to finish up.

"Oh, I'm so glad that's over with," Karen hollered as she ran her fingers through her hair after she exited the gym.

"Well, I guess that's my cue. You know I'll call you over the summer. You better call me too. That's probably the only way I'll be able to come over to your house. See you later Kim." Ashley gave her a hug.

"I'll be talking to you, you know that. Catch you later." Kim smiled at her. "Catch you later Karen." Kim nodded her head.

"See you later Kim," Karen smiled. She looked at Ashley, "Are you ready to get the hell out of this joint."

"Oh don't you know it." Ashley grabbed her by the arm and they marched down the hall and out the door by the gym.

Karen's parents allowed her to take the car to school that day; they only lived a few miles away. The girls were riding along at about 45mph when Ashley looked out the window.

"TRAIN TRAIN!!! "Ashley screamed. There was no time to stop. "TRAIN TRAIN!!" she screamed.

"What?" Karen quizzically looked at Ash, and then "HOLY SHIT." She stomped on the gas. The engine revved and took off. The two of them were in the race of their lives. They flew across the tracks just before the train crossed the road. Then the two girls pulled over and sat there stunned; they looked at each other in disbelief. Suddenly they felt exhilarated, and they started to laugh and laugh; they had danced with death and won.

"Man, can you believe that. They ought to cut down some of those trees or put up some of those railroad crossing guards things so you can see those freaking trains coming. Man, we almost bought the freaking farm. Good thing the old station wagon has some get up and go." Karen shook her head and smiled breathing hard all the while.

"We're lucky as hell. We just fucking made it by like 5 seconds. My heart is pounding out of my chest, I've never felt so alive." Ashley's mouth just hung open for a minute.

They sat on the side of the road for a few more minutes while Karen collected herself, then she took in a deep breath and they got underway.

After a couple of minutes they arrived safe and sound at Karen's house. "Hey, I don't think we should tell my parents about our little race today; they might think we're irresponsible or something. Don't tell my sister Amy either; she could use it against me later. Oh yeah she's driving to the party tonight. She's all fired up since she graduated this year. She wants to party it up tonight, so hopefully Emily will drive us all home, since she's not a big drinker," Karen added as they went in the house.

"Does this mean your parents know we're going to the party tonight?" Ashley asked as they were going in.

"Yeah, can you believe it? They said yes. Because we're going with Amy, they think we'll be supervised. Isn't that funny?" Karen laughed.

"I'm glad my parents said I could come over for the night. They have no idea and what they don't know won't hurt them." Ashley snickered.

The party was in full swing when the girls arrived. Karen and Ashley were on their third drink when Thomas and Gregg showed up. Their knights in shining armor. After a bit of sweet talk and a few more drinks, the girls went off to the beach to make out with them. Ashley, Karen and Emily had a rule between them, to stay within eyesight of each other, so they wouldn't do anything they would regret later. It's hard enough to say no to a guy, but to a guy you like, and still have him be interested. As midnight approached Emily gathered everyone up to leave, drunk as skunks, but right on time. Amy turned the keys over to Emily because she was the only sober one of the group. The four girls arrived at Amy and Karen's house just before one in the morning, beating their curfew, and they quietly made their way upstairs to bed. They were careful to rinse with mouthwash before turning in for the night.

"Hey, get up. It's after 10:30. I'm starving. You guys want something to eat?" Karen rubbed her face.

"Oh, man, I'm beat, and it's already after 10:30 am. Shit, I've gotta be home by noon. But I could eat that's for sure." Ashley got up off the floor and stretched.

Emily sat up and dropped her blanket. "I just want to go back to sleep. I'm glad I only live two houses away. I don't have far to travel before I can hit the sack again, in my own bed. But I'll eat with you all first. I'm hungry too. Think your mom will fix us some eggs?" Emily's eyes got wide.

"Oh, that would be good." Ashley added as she licked her lips. "I'll go ask her," Karen got up and left the room.

Twenty minutes later the girls were enjoying eggs and bacon with toast and orange juice. Ashley thought how lucky Karen was to have such an incredible mother, to just drop whatever she was doing and fix all of them such an elaborate meal. At her house it would have been cereal and then they would have had to clean up the mess.

"So, Ash, tell us. Are you and Thomas an item now or what?" Karen asked in between bites.

"I don't know, maybe. He asked for my phone number, and I gave it to him. How about you and Gregg? The two of you seemed really tight last night." Ashley dipped her toast in her egg yolk.

"Who is Gregg?" Karen's mother asked, her eyebrows raised. "Mom!!"

"What? I have a right to know; you're my daughter." Mrs. D smiled. "Well, he's this really cute guy from school, he's my age, and he's nice and respectable. You would like him mom and that's all, OK" Karen held up her hands.

"OK, OK I was just wondering. I'll leave you girls alone now. Enjoy your breakfast."

"Thank you for fixing this for us. It's really good." Ashley smiled at Karen's mother.

"Yes, thanks" Emily and Karen said in unison.

"You are all very welcome." Mrs. D left the room.

"Your mom is really cool" Ashley stated as she finished up her breakfast.

"You think?" Karen looked at Ashley.

"Are you kidding? My mom would never do this. I hate to change the subject, but I gotta get going pretty soon or my parents will be pissed. I'm surprised they let me spend the night at all. My father thinks I should be at his beck and call or something." Ashley shook her head.

"All right, let's finish up and get going so you don't get the third degree." Karen bit her lip, trying to be sympathetic with Ashley.

Ashley didn't usually share a lot of her home life with her friends except for Kim, but she had started to open up about it this past semester. They were starting to realize what a difficult situation she was in, from tidbits Ashley shared with them.

When Ashley arrived home, her father had left for work. He usually worked a few hours on Saturdays and Ruth was busy with chores.

"Hey, kiddo, did you have fun at Karen's house? I was beginning to wonder when you would show up." Ruth smiled as Ashley sat at the table.

"Yeah, I had a good time. I'm tired though; we stayed up half the night fooling around. If you don't mind, I'd like to take a little nap." Ashley stretched and then yawned.

"Uh, yeah, that would be fine. You do know that we are going out tonight. So you're going to have to watch the kids; your dad said he mentioned it to you."

"No, he didn't, but that's no big deal. Just let me get some shut eye and I'll be fine." Ashley got up and started to go upstairs.

"All right. I'll wake you just before your father gets home." Ruth went back to folding the clothes.

Over the next several weeks Ashley was expected to watch the children from Saturday afternoon until Sunday night without help or complaint. Then towards the end of July Ashley's parents informed her they were going to a country and western music jamboree, out of state. Ashley thought no big deal, until they told her it lasted four days, and they needed a day to get there and one to return. However, they decided Michael would be staying with his grandparents. So Ashley would be alone in the house with the baby for almost a week.

Just before they were ready to leave, Rodger sat down with Ashley at the kitchen table. "I know how you kids think. Parents are away and it's time to throw a huge wild party. That is not happening here. Ruth's parents will be stopping in unannounced, at different times. So don't think for even one second that you're having a party. Got it?" Rodger looked her in the eye.

Ashley looked directly back at him. "I got it. Besides I'll be looking after Jake and there wouldn't be time."

"Good." Rodger got up and started to pack the truck.

Ruth had gone shopping to make sure Ashley had everything she needed for the week. "Ash, I've even gotten extra soda for you. I really appreciate you taking care of Jake for us. I know I can count on you." Ruth gave her a hug.

"Yeah, no problem. How long does it take to get there?" Ashley asked

"About eight hours. We'll call when we get in. That was always a rule when I was young and it's just stuck with me." Ruth smiled at Ashley.

Rodger zipped into the house, "You ready to leave? I want to get on the road and beat the traffic." Rodger sternly looked at Ashley "Remember our little talk."

"I will. Don't worry, we'll be fine." Ashley smiled. She had asked Ruth earlier in the week if her younger sister, Laura, could come over and spend the week with her. Ruth had readily agreed with the idea, thinking that it would keep Ashley company and out of trouble.

Ellen arrived a few hours later with Laura. Ashley thought just keep the past in the past; she's probably just as nervous as I am. It was then she realized she hadn't spoken to her mother in over seven months. Just keep the conversation light and easy she thought. She took in a deep breath and headed outside.

Ellen rushed over and hugged Ashley tightly. "Hey, kiddo, I've missed you so much.

I'm so sorry for how things went. "Ellen then released her daughter. Ashley had hugged her back. "Hi, mom, I missed you too." Ashley was a bit surprised by the amount of emotion her mother had shown her. "Thanks for letting Laura come over; it means a lot to me. So how are things with you?" Ashley smiled at her mother.

"Things are good. You know, basically the same old thing. You look like you've lost weight? So how did you do with school? I know it's been a long time." Ellen smiled and gently squeezed her arm.

"Yeah, I lost about 15 pounds. Stress I guess. As far as school went, I studied hard for finals and scored in the top 15 % so pretty good; not high enough for honor society but I was happy with my performance. Of course, dad didn't comment either way, as usual. I guess I should expect that by now." Ashley raised her eyebrows and bit her lip.

"Well, that's great honey. You should be proud of yourself. I'm proud of you and don't worry about your dad. That stuff doesn't register on his radar. If it was sports then that would be different; he'd rave about it." Ellen smiled. "So what are the two of you going to do?"

"Just hang out really; talk and catch up; nothing too exciting." Ashley shrugged her shoulders. Much to her surprise she started to relax and enjoy their visit. She realized that she actually missed her mother; the sound of her voice, the way she hugged her, how she complimented her.

"Hey, Ash where's the baby?" Laura asked.

Ashley looked up. "Oh, he's inside sleeping. I just laid him down before you got here. I'm sure he's OK."

"So, Ash, I was wondering if you would like to come over and spend a weekend at my house before school starts? I feel bad about how things have been between us." Ellen raised her eyebrows, trying to look hopeful. "We could hang out; I miss you terribly. We could go shopping. I know you need some new things for school."

"Sure mom, I would love to come spend the weekend, and you don't have to buy me a whole bunch of stuff." Ashley smiled.

"Well, I want to get you some things. Maybe not a whole bunch, but some." Ellen hugged her again saying she missed her.

Her mother came over and gave Laura a hug. "Well, I've got to get going. I have to get ready for class tonight. I'm so glad you wanted to spend time with your sister this week. Love you both." Their mother gave them each another hug and then left.

"Well, let's go on in. I'll grab one of your bags; we're going to have fun, trust me." Ashley moved her eyebrows up and down. "Well, today, is only Thursday, and dad won't be back until next Wednesday."

"What do you have in mind?" Laura looked at her sister as they entered the house.

"Well, we are just hanging out until Sunday afternoon, and then I'm going to ask you if I can hire you to keep an eye on Jake. I want to throw a party. You can have a beer or two, but you need to stay pretty sober until Jake goes down for the night, I've got it all planned out; we can put him upstairs and just check on him, often. What do you think?"

"Sounds good to me. I'm not real fond of beer anyway, so I probably won't drink more than a couple." Laura smiled from ear to ear.

"I figured we might be getting bored by then, and also it will give us plenty of time to hang out together before and after. We will have plenty of time to clean up." Ashley let out a sinister laugh.

"Yeah, and nobody thinks there's a party on a Sunday afternoon. You're pretty slick sis, I gotta tell ya." Laura set her bag down on the kitchen table.

"Come on, I'll give you a tour. You can sleep upstairs in Michael's room. It's across the hall from my room. Come on, let's go." Ashley headed upstairs. Laura got settled in and in no time the girls were talking as if they had never been separated. By the following day their conversation had become much deeper.

"Ash, how is it here living with your dad? Is he nicer?" Laura looked at her sister.

"Well, he doesn't hit me but when he's mad he still uses the look. He doesn't ever talk to me; you know really talk to me, like to find out what's going on with me. He still drinks a lot, but he doesn't fight with Ruth when he's drunk; she makes him happy. The main thing I hate is that I'm expected to watch the two kids every weekend. I'm allowed to go out sometimes on Fridays but the majority of the time I'm expected to be here, helping out. Thank God I get along with Ruth; she makes it much easier." Ashley took in a deep breath and let it out slowly.

"Sounds like it's kinda rough. Do you miss me and mom?" Laura shifted in her chair.

"Honestly, before you two visited, I didn't give it too much thought. I wouldn't let myself think about it. Occasionally I would, but I was so hurt, and I figured mom didn't want me because she never called or anything. But now after talking to her, I'll admit it, I miss you both a lot. I also miss my freedom. Here I have quite a few responsibilities; all the time. But Ruth makes it easier. She is so good to me, better than the both of them, and I'm serious." Ashley shook her head up and down. "How is it going with you?"

"It's lonely; she comes home and says "hi," then goes in her room to study, same as when you were there. I don't have anyone to talk to. I want you to move back home." Laura wiped a tear welling up from the corner of her eye. "Please."

Ashley rushed over and hugged her sister. "Oh, Laura Lady, don't cry, I had no idea you were so sad, so lonely. I'm so very sorry. It'll get better I promise." Ashley gently rocked her sister.

"How Ash? How is it going to get better without you moving back home?" Laura sniffled, then looked her sister in the face.

"Well, now that mom and I are talking, I'll come home more," She looked in her sister's weepy eyes. "A lot more, I promise. Especially now, knowing how lonely you are; I've missed you too. You're not the only one who is lonely. Ruth suggested I see a counselor; it has helped. I had this huge, dark, empty hole inside; it's not all gone by any means, but life's a lot easier and I feel better overall. Listen, tomorrow we're going to have a rocking party and you'll feel better, it's going to be awesome." Ashley rubbed her sister's back.

Over the next few days the sister's talked often about their thoughts and feelings and they played some card games, spending important bonding moments in their time together.

The girls had it all planned out. First Jake would be put to bed upstairs and checked on regularly. The party would take place outside. They would only use the bathroom in the basement, using the outside door in the back of the house. Some of the guys were bringing wood. Luckily Rodger had a large fire pit. They had a keg and ice on its way, thanks to Amy. She always came through in a pinch. Laura was in charge of collection two dollars and then giving party goer's their beer cup.

Amy, Karen and Emily showed up at Ashley's house around four in the afternoon. They had the ice and keg in the trunk. The four girls wrestled with the keg to get it down back without shaking it up. The girls started back towards the car when Ruth's parents showed up.

"Oh, shit!" Ashley stopped in her tracks. "Listen, Amy, you and Emily stay here, I don't think they saw you. Karen just say you stopped by and your leaving soon." Ashley started towards the driveway, motioning Karen to come with her.

"Hi, Ash. We just stopped in to see how things are going." Her step-grandparents stood in the driveway and looked around.

"Things are just fine gram. This is my friend Karen. She stopped in to say hi and visit for a little while, that's all." Ashley smiled and nodded her head.

"Do you need anything?"

"No, I'm good. Everything is fine," Ashley answered.

"What are you all doing around back?" gram asked

"Uh, nothing. We were just walking around the lawn. I was showing her the wildflowers." Ashley answered smiling.

"Oh, I would love some fresh cut wildflowers," Gram stated. Ashley looked at Karen and she at Ashley. They were about to be busted.

"We don't have time. The game's on," grandpa insisted, as he looked at gram.

"Well, OK then. We'll let you get back to your visit. If you need anything, just call."

"OK, I will. See you later." Ashley waved goodbye. She was shaking inside but maintained a cool calm exterior. Her grandparents left and after they were gone Ashley just about collapsed. "Man, that was close. Come on. Let's finish setting up." Ashley went to the car to retrieve the ice.

Laura was on the deck holding Jake. She started to laugh. "Ash, you should have seen your face drop when your gram wanted to get those flowers; it was freaking hilarious."

Amy and Emily came out to help finish setting up and they all had a good laugh at their close call, mainly at Ashley's expense. The girls figured that they were home free because the grandparents had checked on them, so they would not be back tonight.

By eight that evening Laura had fed Jake and put him down for the night, so she was basically free to join the party already in full swing. Emily had taken the cup collection job due to the baby. There were about fifty people at the party which was perfect as far as Ash was concerned. The fire was ablaze with wood to spare. They were rocking out to the tunes. Ashley and Karen were pleasantly surprised because Thomas and Gregg showed up. Everyone was drinking and smoking, having a good time. Around one in the morning Laura told Ash she wanted to turn in. Ashley walked her upstairs and saw to it that she and Jake were safely in bed behind a locked door. She told Laura better safe than sorry with drunken guys around and not to open the door for anyone but her.

Ashley returned to the party and continued to drink and hang out with her friends. Many had gone home because of curfews. At some point she joined back up with Thomas and made out with him for a while and then they sat by the fire as it died down. He wanted her to allow him to spend the night, but she wasn't sure it was a good idea. She found Karen and Emily and told them. They all agreed to stick together as the party dwindled. That way the guys couldn't corner them. At around three thirty the last of the party goer's went home, Thomas and Gregg along with them, although they helped the girls clean up a bit before they left. The girls turned in and agreed to clean up the following morning.

The following morning rolled in around noon for everyone except Laura who got up with Jake. Once the rest of the girls regained consciousness and saw the mess left behind they looked at each other in shock.

"How are we going to get this cleaned up in time: the grass is so freakin' matted, cigarette butts are everywhere, there's puke in a few places too, and what about the extra wood and ashes in the pit." Ashley's mouth just hung open.

"You should see the bathroom," Laura added as she nodded her head up and down.

"Don't panic. With all of us, we can do this." Amy held up her hands. "Let's get a game plan. First let's rake up the butts and put them in a bag and spray the puke with the hose. We'll take the extra wood and put it in the trunk along with the keg and put the cups in a bag and put them in the car along with the butts. Then we'll just clean the bathroom. If the grass doesn't pop back up by tomorrow morning, just mow it. Your dad will be proud of you and he'll never know. OK, so let's get busy." Amy stood up and started to delegate the jobs to all of the girls. By late afternoon they had finished and gone home.

The day Ashley's parents were due home, Karen came back to take Laura home and Ashley mowed the grass just to be safe. Rodger and Ruth made it back late that afternoon, tired from their trip. They didn't have much to say and didn't notice anything out of the ordinary. They had a good vacation and so did she; she was home free.

CHAPTER 7

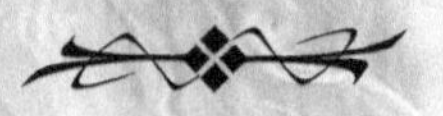

A couple weeks had passed since Ashley's little get together and her parents still had no clue, so Karen called and asked if Ashley could come over to spend the night. Rodger reluctantly agreed. Karen told Ashley to pack a bag for the woods; unbeknownst to her they were kidnapping her for the entire weekend. The girls had planned to attend a music festival, out in the middle of nowhere.

Amy had convinced her parents that she was old enough and responsible enough to take her younger sister, Karen and her friends Ashley and Emily on a safe, quiet and peaceful camping trip. Besides, she told them, her friend Kate was coming along. Mrs. D loved Kate, and Kate could do no wrong in her eyes. After they had a very long what do you do if… talk, Mr. and Mrs. D. allowed the girls to go.

They packed up the old station wagon with all their supplies, Karen even packed extra warm clothes and a sleeping bag for Ashley, knowing she would have no idea of what she was in for. When the four girls arrived to pick up Ashley, Rodger was half drunk out in the yard. As Ashley went to leave he asked, "Hey, when will you be back?" He swayed, fumbling with the grill.

"I'll be back tomorrow around noon." Ashley tried to walk quickly.

"Hey, don't run off. I'm talking to you." He glared at her.

She stopped and turned to look at him, hands on her hips, "What?

"No drinking or anything stupid."

"Dad, I'm spending the night at Mrs. D's. They don't drink, ever! OK. Can I go now?"

Ashley looked at him.

"Yeah, get out of here. Make sure you're home by afternoon. We're going out." He scowled.

"Yeah, what else is new." Ashley walked away.

"Don't get smart or you won't go at all." He kept on scowling at her. Ashley got in the car. "Hurry up. Let's get the hell out of here before he changes his mind."

The other girls didn't say anything, but Ashley could tell by the looks on their faces that they felt badly for her. After a few minutes of silence in the car, Ashley looked around at all the baggage. "What's up with all the stuff?"

"Well," Amy said smiling "we decided to go to a music festival, and you're going too. We didn't want you to miss out on all the fun." Karen and Emily started to chuckle.

"No way. Where is it? Ashley asked, taken aback.

Emily turned and looked at her. "It's in the middle of nowhere." Ashley started to smile. "How long does it last?

"Like two to three days and two nights," Amy answered smiling. "Yeah, your dad will never find you," Karen added. "We all just felt that you needed a vacation, girlfriend, along with us."

Ashley sat silent for a moment. The other girls looked at each other wondering if it was a mistake to kidnap her. Then Ashley started to smile. "You guys are the greatest. Man, this is awesome. Thanks. I hope this pisses him off royally." Then she began to laugh.

They arrived in plenty of time to set up camp; the girls chose a site that was near the stage where the bands played. It was also tucked in underneath huge pine trees and close to the bathrooms; it had a fire pit and plenty of room for two tents. The girls set up their tents and arranged their campsite with camp chairs around the fire, and a lantern near the entrance to the tents; they set up a small grill and table. Mr. D had hooked them up with everything they could possibly need including food and soda. As they were setting up people were walking around smoking pot right out in the open. The girls followed suit and lit up themselves. Amy and Kate told Emily, Sharon and Ashley that they had one main rule to follow and that was to stick together at all times. Amy said she wasn't messing around. We don't know these people; most of them are cool, but it only takes one asshole to mess up your life forever.

The girls were talking to a couple of fellow campers and discovered that cops were turned away at the gate half a mile back because it's private land. Besides, they pointed out, out here there aren't nearly enough cops to storm 300 hippies, even though we're peaceful, at least most of the time.

As night fell on this secret wooded fortress, the bands played a happy hippie tune that an incredible light show played tribute to. The lights bounced off not only the screens but the trees, and poetic dancers waved fluorescent tubes and sticks. The girls wanted to absorb the experience, so they ate mushrooms. This wasn't their first time, but this certainly was an appropriate time. They watched in amazement and wonder, enjoying the festivities, the lights and the colors just danced off the trees and people danced on the waves of the music. They danced until the wee hours of the morning; they laughed and just enjoyed themselves never experiencing such freedom before.

The heat of the day forced Amy out of her tent. She glanced around the campgrounds. It was quiet and peaceful. She decided the smell of food cooking would rouse her sister and their friends. Amy got busy with lighting the grill and getting the food cooking. Then she gently woke the rest of the crew. They stumbled out one by one with the smell of food hanging in the air, it didn't take long for them to wake up.

"That smells good; man wasn't it awesome last night? I had a freaking' blast." Karen rubbed her head as she went and sat in a chair by the fire pit.

"I was trippin' my brains out. That light show was off the top. I'm lovin' it here; I'm so glad you guys kidnapped me." Ashley smiled. "You all are the best, thanks." The other girls all smiled at her, a couple nodding their heads, with gratitude, they knew she needed it with everything going on at her house.

Emily stretched. "Mm, that does smell good. I'm starving. I had a blast last night too, and to think we have another day and night." She went over and got a soda from the cooler.

Amy was busy cooking eggs and bacon on the grill, Kate put the paper plates and forks out on the table. Before too long the girls had enjoyed their breakfast and had cleaned up. They were lounging around at their camp site when a young man came up with a briefcase. When he opened it, it was padded on both sides and was full of glass bowls. He told the girls he had blown them himself. They were all different sizes and colors. He explained to them that the more pot you smoked, the darker they got and the colors would show up brighter. The girls decided that they each needed one of these glass bowls, and immediately started to smoke out of them.

As the sun was starting to set, the bands started to play again. Tonight the girls started a fire and hung out near their site. Every so often a couple of them would walk up to the stage area. The light show captivated their minds and attention, motivating them to dance. In between bands they would check out the vendors and wander back to camp, amazed at what they saw: people dressed in outlandish costumes and hats awesome wild hats. Every type of tie-dye you could imagine, and walking sticks, along with furry boots, tall leather boots, and some even had dark capes. This place was like no other place on God's green earth, and it was peaceful. The girls had plenty to talk about when they got back to their camp site. They continued to smoke and talk as the night went on, finally crashing in the early morning hours.

Ashley woke up and just looked at the ceiling in the tent; she knew she had to go home today. She looked at her watch; it was just after 11am on Sunday and no one else was up yet. She reached over and quietly unzipped the window for a bit of air. She wondered how her dad was going to react. She wondered if he would hit her; then she remembered Ruth was there so he probably wouldn't, but she would probably be grounded until she graduated. She thought to hell with him. I hate living with him: he's so freaking mean I'll just end it; end it all and then I won't have to deal with him ever again.

Just then Karen woke up. "Hey, what are you thinking about? You look so sad."

"My dad and what he's going to do to me for escaping for the weekend." Ashley looked at her.

"Are you scared?" Karen asked

"A little." Ashley rolled over to face her.

"They are just words, Ash. He can only yell so loud and for so long" Karen replied

Ashley sighed deeply and looked at her, then looked down.

"Do you mean he hits you?" Karen's mouth dropped and she sat up.

"He has, but Ruth is there so he might not." Ashley shook her head.

"But please don't tell anyone." Ashley sat up and crossed her legs.

"Do you want me to go in with you?" Karen raised her eyebrows. "It wouldn't happen until everyone left, so it wouldn't help, but thanks." Ashley grimly smiled.

"I'm sorry. Maybe we shouldn't have kidnapped you." Karen unzipped the door of the tent, "It's kinda hot in here."

"No, no I'm glad that you did. It was worth it, believe me," Ashley smiled and squeezed her arm. "That breeze feels good."

About then Emily started to stir. "Hey you two, what time is it?" "It's about 11:30 in the morning," Karen lay back down. "Think we should get up or chill out for a while?" Karen took a deep breath.

"Chill out because I'm not getting any rest when I get home." Ashley chuckled.

Emily stretched under her sleeping bag. "Sounds like a plan to me."

She yawned. All five girls dozed off and on for another couple of hours.

That bit of sleep did them wonders. They decided to get up and moving.

By midafternoon the girls had packed up and were on the road home; they were tired and dirty but in good spirits except for Ashley, but she hid her worries well. As they approached Ashley's house, she began to tremble inside. She was uncertain of what awaited her at home. Well, she was certain her father would flip, but just the level of violence he would unleash upon her, was unclear. When they pulled into the driveway Ashley just sat for a moment. "Wish me luck. I'm going to need it. Thanks again for taking me; see you later."

Just then Rodger came out onto the deck; he glared at the girls in the car. Amy just sat there and looked back. "Man, he's scary. Is she gonna be OK?" Amy asked as they started to slowly back out. Ashley had grabbed her bag and was wandering up to the house. Rodger turned his attention towards her. "Get your ass in this house now! Where in the hell have you been? Who in the hell do you think you are, taking off for the whole weekend?" Rodger yelled at her. By this time Ashley had made it up to the deck. He grabbed her by the back of the neck and thrust her into the house.

The girls had just barely pulled onto the road when they saw Ashley's Father grab her. They were shocked and unsure of what to do. Karen spoke up, saying Ashley would want us to leave it be. She told them the gist of their previous conversation and her wish to leave it be. Her step-mother was there and she would make sure that it didn't get too out of hand.

Rodger seized his daughter by the arm, and then jerked her back and forth demanding answers. "Well, say something. Where were you?" He glared at her. He threw her into the kitchen table releasing his cast-iron grip on her.

"We went camping," Ashley meekly replied as she steadied herself from the throw.

"So when you left, you lied to my face? Knowing you were leaving for the whole weekend, you little S.O.B."

"No, no I didn't. They didn't tell me until we were nearly there," Ashley interrupted. She knew the less she said the better.

"So, why didn't you have them bring you home? You wanted to stay, get one over on the old man, probably laughing all weekend at how pissed off I would be. You think I'm stupid? You little shit, I ought to beat the living hell out of you." He stood glaring at Ashley; she had inched her way to the other side of the table.

Ruth came running in from the other room. "Hey, hey, let's just calm down for a minute, Rodger. You need to relax. Please, just calm down." Ruth was waving her hands.

"Calm down!! Do you realize what she did? She can't get away with that kind of behavior. She's got to learn. I'm no fool." Rodger swayed back and forth waving his hand spilling his beer on the floor.

"I know honey, but I don't think we should beat her. There are other ways, honey, please," Ruth tilted her head to the side.

"You don't know; you've never had to deal with a teenager before. I know what I'm doing. So stay the hell out of it, woman." Rodger started to drink his beer and guzzled it down, wiping his mouth with the back of his hand. He stood glaring at Ashley as his anger brewed.

Ashley knew she was going to have a hard time getting herself out of this one. She stood on the other side of the table trembling, just waiting for him to come after her. Her arm had started to throb from his iron grip.

"Ashley, go get me a beer," Rodger commanded her. She slowly moved from the safety of the other side of the table to the kitchen and retrieved the beer. As she handed it to him, he back handed her across the face with his other hand. As she bent over, he kneed her in the abdomen. She stumbled into the living room with him in hot pursuit; he kicked her in the legs trying to make her fall on the floor. Ruth was in the background yelling at him to stop. Ashley was doing her best to keep her balance. She knew if she fell on the floor she was done for. He then threw his unopened beer, striking the corner of her eye and it immediately started to bleed. He somehow then seemed satisfied and withdrew, shouting, "I'm no fool. Bet you won't try to get one over on me again, you little S.O.B. You're so ungrateful. I should've never taken you in. Your sorry ass isn't worth the effort of trying to raise you right." He went and got another beer, sat at the table and started drinking.

Ashley ran upstairs to the bathroom and started to attend to her bloody eyebrow. Ruth looked at Rodger in disbelief; she had never seen that side of him before. She wanted to scream at him but was afraid he would lash out at her, so she retreated upstairs to help Ashley. When she got up to the bathroom, Ashley was standing in front of the mirror with a washcloth tightly pressed against her eyebrow. "See, he's a different person when he's drunk."

Ruth took in a deep breath. "I don't know what to say. I'm so sorry; let me help you."

"You know the sad thing about it is he probably won't even remember it so he has no idea of how bad it was." Ashley just shook her head and started to cry.

Ruth got some butterfly bandages and put them on her eyebrow, along with a bag of ice to help with the swelling. Ashley's arm was starting to turn black and blue along with her leg and side. The bruises would go away but his words would ring in her ears for eternity and the pain they caused was everlasting.

That night, as Ashley lay in bed, she thought about what happened. She thought, I just can't live like this, so she got up and went to the closet where the pistol was. There were no bullets, she searched and searched, shit she thought, what else could go wrong. She quietly went back to bed and tried to get her breathing under control. Just relax she told herself. Then she thought maybe she should go back to her mother's, escape the madness.

After a couple of days Ashley's bruises were really apparent and she kept her distance from her father. He had not touched a drop of alcohol since that day. He had also been putting in extra hours at work, and, when he was home, he avoided Ashley. One afternoon he approached her with a flower he had picked from the yard. "Hey! Here this is for you. I know things got out of hand the other day. I don't know what came over me. I didn't mean for you to get hurt so badly." He hung his head.

"I know. I shouldn't have stayed out all weekend, but I didn't know before we left. Honest, and I'm sorry for that." Ashley looked at her father.

"I was just so worried about you. I didn't know if you were in an accident or kidnapped and raped, or in a ditch somewhere. Then, when I saw you in the car, laughing and joking, my worry instantly turned into rage. I admit I had had too much to drink. So, I hope you can forgive me?" Rodger looked at Ashley.

"It's over and done with, but I really want you to stop drinking, especially if things are making you upset. If you're in a good mood, then go for it but not when you're mad. Please, will you think about it?" Ashley meekly smiled at her father.

"I'll think about it; it's probably not a bad idea." Rodger hugged Ashley. "I'll talk to you later. Oh, we're going out tomorrow night."

"Yeah, I kinda figured. No big deal." Ashley forced a smile, then turned and went upstairs.

That Saturday night after her parents left, Ashley called her mother; this was the first time she had been alone in the house since her father had gone off on her. She wanted to talk privately to her mother, with no chance of anyone overhearing her conversation. As she dialed the phone number she went over in her head just what she wanted to say. When she got her mother on the phone, they chatted for a few moments. Then she just couldn't hold it in anymore. "Mom, I need to ask you something. Do you think I could move back home with you and Laura?" Ashley was near tears.

Her mother could tell she was upset. "What's going on honey?"

"If you saw me, you would know." Ashley started to cry. "I mean he's fine now, but I don't want to stay here anymore." She sniffled.

Ellen took in a breath. "OK. Yeah you can move back, of course. What does your dad say about it?"

"I didn't mention it to him. I just want to go, and I want you here to tell him. I'm scared to tell him anything at this point." Ashley took in a deep breath.

"When do you want to move? Ellen asked

"Tomorrow morning. I can pack my stuff tonight while they're out and you can come get me in the morning. Please mom. I know it's really short notice, but I don't want to be here any longer than I have to be," Ashley begged

"You sound so desperate. What exactly happened?" Ellen gently demanded.

"Well, I went out for what I thought was just Friday night, but it ended up being the whole weekend, camping without permission. When I got home, dad was drunk and flipped out on me big time. He apologized, but I'm still scared of him, even though he hasn't touched me since." Ashley took in a deep breath and let it out. "Do you think you could bring grandpa, just in case? I mean I don't know how he's going to react."

"So, he hit you?" Ellen asked.

"He did more than just hit me," Ashley told her mother as she was calming down. Now that she knew she could go back to stay at her mother's house, she felt some sense of relief. "So you'll be here by like 9:30 in the morning with grandpa."

"Yeah, I'll call him tonight. We'll be there. I love you," Ellen answered a little unnerved.

"Thanks, mom. I love you too. I'll talk to you tomorrow." Ashley hung up the phone. She leaned up against the wall for a moment and thanked God that her mother was coming in the morning. Then she went upstairs checked on Michael to make sure he was asleep and proceeded to pack all of her belongings. She tried to pack in an organized fashion. She had learned to roll her clothes from her brother and that saved room but it still took a few bags, plus she had all of her little trinkets and art supplies. When all of her things were packed, she put the duffel bags in the closet. She picked up the corner of the rug where she had hidden her stash and packed that carefully, placing back the piece she had cut out of the padding then carefully put the carpet back in place and put her dresser back over it.

That night was a long one for Ashley. She tossed and turned; her mind just kept coming back to what her father's reaction would be to her moving out. For a second she thought maybe he would see it from her point of view. Then reality set in and she knew he would probably be upset, more like mad, pissed off. He would most likely hold a grudge and not speak to her for a long time; he was losing his babysitter, his free babysitter. She knew he held grudges, and even though she was his kid it wouldn't matter. He had that mean streak in him; that's just the way he was, kid or no kid. But Ashley knew she had to get out of there, to save herself, or she wouldn't make it, not there or anywhere.

When Ashley awoke the next morning, it was just after 8:30. She was so relieved her mother would be there soon. She got dressed, packed her pajamas, then jumped back under her covers and snuggled down for the wait. She looked around at her room; its emptiness reminded her that that was just the way she felt deep inside. She thought she couldn't make it work here either. What was wrong with her? Why did she always mess things up? She thought I'm such a failure. Ashley heard Ruth downstairs getting up with Jake, feeding him. The clock read 9:10 am. Only another twenty minutes. Ashley was shaking with anticipation.

Suddenly Michael came bursting in her room "Hey, Ash, will you play with me?"

"Not right now buddy," Ashley answered nervously.

Michael looked around her room "Where is all your stuff? Are you going somewhere?" He asked loudly.

"Just go to your room and play, OK?" Ashley scooted him out and into his room and shut her door.

Ruth had overheard what Michael had said to Ashley and her stomach plummeted. That couldn't be right. Was she all packed up? Ruth put the baby down and rushed upstairs and knocked on Ashley's door. "Hey, Ashley, can I come in?"

"Uh, what for? I'm still in bed." Ashley took in a deep breath; she knew she was busted. A quick glance at the clock; it read 9:20. Oh, Ashley thought, please mom be early.

Ruth opened the door letting herself in. "What's going on Ashley?" "I'm leaving, I'm sorry, Ruth, but I'm terrified of dad. My mother will be here in ten minutes." Ashley looked at the floor, then looked up at Ruth.

"So when were you planning on telling us?" Ruth held out her hands in disbelief.

"When my mom got here. I'm scared he'll freak out and hit me again." Ashley sighed deeply. Looking again at the clock 9: 23. She looked out the window just as her mother pulled in the driveway. "There she is now. I'm leaving."

"Let me at least wake up your father to tell him." Ruth hurried downstairs ahead of Ashley to tell Rodger. He couldn't believe his ears; he jumped up and tried to make sense of it. He rubbed his face looking at Ruth in disbelief.

Ashley ran outside to the safety of her mother and grandfather. "Hey mom thanks for coming; you to grandpa." Ashley sighed deeply.

Ellen looked at Ashley. "What happened to your face?" She cupped her chin in her hand. "He did that to you, didn't he?" Ellen looked at her daughter.

"Yeah, he did," Ashley answered. "Don't say anything. Can we just get my stuff and go?" They went in to retrieve her things.

Rodger stood just outside of his room, his hair a mess. He didn't have anything to say in front of Ellen and her father. They collected most of her things without a word. While Ashley descended the stairs he glared at her. "I can't believe your just leaving without a word,"

She looked at him. "I'm terrified of you. You beat the hell out of me and I'm sorry isn't good enough. Yeah, I was wrong, but when is it going to happen again? I can't deal with it. I'm scared of you. I walk on eggshells around you. I've got to go. I'm sorry dad." She shook her head.

"You know what? You're a little bitch like your mother, so just go. I don't care." It was like he plunged a dagger into her heart. Tears started to well up in her eyes. She ran out of the house and threw her last bag into the back seat of the car, jumped into the front and started to cry. How could she have trusted him, that he cared about her, wanted her, loved her.

CHAPTER 8

*I*t had started to sprinkle when they put Ashley's bags in the car. As soon as they got down the road, the skies opened up and rain poured down.

The windshield wipers were on full blast, the sound drowned out by Ashley crying. Knowing she needed to get it out of her system, Ellen remained silent. Instead of talking she watched her father, Jim, ahead of them in his car; he was headed home. She was grateful that he came with her even though he didn't say a word. Just his presence helped keep the peace. Rodger had always respected him and would never cause a scene or resort to violence in front of him.

Ellen wanted to talk to her daughter about what had just taken place to upset her so much. Yet, she didn't want to push her away; she was just glad to have her back, back in her life. Oh, how she had missed her daughter. She knew she was wrong not to have communicated with her for so very long. And now to look at her, she had grown taller and leaner, her hair was so much longer. She was growing up and she had missed almost a year. She thought never would she make a mistake like that again. Here she was, home finally. She thought she would do a much better job just talking to Ashley, being there for her.

It stopped raining as they entered the outskirts of North Allentown. Her uncle always called it God's country: the sun seemed to shine a little brighter and it seemed to snow a little, well a lot, more often than in the rest of the area; Ashley started to feel better. Just the idea of being back home settled her nerves. Through the sniffles she asked her mother if it was really OK for her to move back in. Did she really want her? The answer was an immediate and emphatic yes; how could she think otherwise. By her behavior this past year she supposed; she knew she had to make it up to her daughter.

"Hey, mom, is Laura home waiting for us? Ashley looked up while taking in a deep breath.

"Yes, she can hardly wait; she's so excited." Ellen pulled in the driveway, smiling at her daughter, feeling complete, with both of her girls at home.

"Thanks, mom. I needed you so bad and you were there for me, thanks…

"Well, that's what moms are for… at least we try; I love you." Ellen reached over and hugged Ashley kissing her forehead as they separated.

The front door flew open and Laura raced out to the car opening the door. "Hey sis." Then she noticed Ashley's eye. "Oh my God, what happened to your face? Are you OK? Where else are you hurt?" Laura didn't waste any time asking the questions her mother was dying to know the answers to.

Ignoring her sister, Ashley got out of the car. "Just help me with my stuff. I'll fill you in on that later." She proceeded to get her things out of the back seat of the car. Both Laura and Ellen helped. It only took a few trips and all of her things were in her old room. Standing in the doorway Laura was smiling. "I'm so happy you're back. Want me to help you settle in?" Her elation at her sister's return was obvious. She didn't want to leave her side afraid she would disappear again.

Sensing her insecurity mixed with excitement at her return, Ashley allowed her to help with the unpacking. Laura was far more organized and wasn't afraid to show it, before long she had taken over. It surprised Ashley, looking at her sister, how much she had grown up in the year she had been away even though she had seen her a few weeks ago. After everything was in its place Ashley supposed it was time to fill them in on exactly what happened at her father's house.

When she went out to the kitchen, Laura on her heels, her mother was already seated at the table. She looked so happy. The light shining in on her face made her seem so young, vibrant, as if she hadn't a care in the world. "So, mom, you want to know what dad did? Well, he hit me in the eye as you can see; it was with a beer can. Then he kicked me in the legs and side." She then proceeded to show her mother the huge bruises on her body and legs.

"Oh my God!! Honey I had no idea it was that bad. I understand why you wanted to get out of there so quickly. I would have been scared too. I'm so sorry he did that to you." She got up and hugged Ashley. Laura looked on in shock. Ellen went over and sat down. "Tell me what was going on?"

"After he hit me, he grounded me from using the phone, so I had to wait until Saturday when they went out, I babysat for them. He made me watch the kids every weekend since the baby was two months old. Lots of times they didn't even come home until Sunday afternoon, and no phone call. I got upset the first time and he flipped out. I thought he was going to hit me but he didn't; I wasn't allowed to complain either. I'll tell you, mom, all I felt like in the end was his little worker, because I had to stay home and help out and I was hardly ever allowed to go out and they went out all the time. He just got mean in the end and I'm not totally sure why. I know I did some stuff wrong, but I don't even think he cares if I live or die." Ashley just shook her head and started to cry.

Ellen got up and hugged her again, then held her at arm's length. "Oh, honey, I'm sure he cares. Unfortunately he's got a problem with drinking, and when he's angry about something and drinks, he loses all control. It's sad but true. That was the main problem we had, and I'm so very sorry you went through that." Ellen shook her head.

Laura remained quiet. Being the baby she had almost always escaped Ashley's father's wrath, and now he had been gone from the house over two years this time. It was hard for her to imagine Rodger inflicting such a beating upon her sister. "What did you do? I mean why did he, well, you know?" Laura asked nervously.

"I stayed out all weekend without permission, but the thing was the girls I went with kind of kidnapped me. I had permission to go Friday night; they didn't tell me we were going camping until we were halfway there. Part of me was glad I was going and part of me knew I was going to get in trouble, but I thought with Ruth there he wouldn't hit me. Guess I was wrong." Ashley just looked at her sister, her eyes filled with tears. She tried to quickly blink them back. It was embarrassing to cry in front of Laura, although she wasn't sure why. This was her blood. She shouldn't feel that way, but she did. Just the thought of being so fragile, so weak; she had always portrayed herself as strong in front of Laura and now she wasn't. Maybe it was a good thing. You can't be on top forever. "Would you mind if I went to lay down for a while? I'm bushed?" Ashley sighed as she asked her mother.

"No, go ahead. You've been through a lot. It's been a stressful day." Ellen smiled at her as she was getting up from the table.

Ashley went to her room and laid down. She looked around and felt this huge sense of relief as if a weight had been lifted off of her shoulders: freedom, freedom to enjoy the weekend, freedom to just be responsible for herself for a change. Not too many sixteen year olds took care of a baby for the weekends for almost five months straight, plus a five year old. Thank God it was over. Never had she appreciated her mother's house so much before. For the first time in months she felt safe and secure; she could even say happy. That was such an elusive emotion, but it was within reach, finally. She wasn't going to screw it up this time. She was going to be a good kid, so her mother would be proud of her, so she would love her. Bouncing between houses sucked. You never felt like you belonged anywhere; home was nowhere. If they got sick of you, they just threw you out, or you left if things got too tough. Nothing was permanent, especially their love.

Later Ashley awoke to the smell of one of her favorite foods Italian sausage with peppers and onions, along with fried potatoes, and she knew there would be a vegetable. She wondered if her mother made it special for her or if she just happened to make it tonight; either way it made her happy. That was one big thing she had missed while she was gone, mom's cooking. She thought her mother was an excellent cook. One good thing she could always say about her mom is that she always cooked a healthy dinner, along with a glass of milk to drink. If you couldn't finish your dinner, you at least had to finish your milk. Some of her friends didn't get a home cooked meal every night; she felt lucky in that respect. Ashley wandered out to the kitchen. "Smells good. I sure missed your cooking. Want me to set the table?" she asked with a smile.

"Sure. Usually your sister does it, but I'm sure she won't mind," Ellen replied as she continued to cook. "Ryan's coming down after dinner. He's going to fix the stereo shelf; it keeps falling. You remember him don't you? He was Brian's friend." She stirred the potatoes. "Why don't you wash up and then call your sister for dinner; it'll be ready in about five minutes."

Ashley did as her mother requested and before long the trio was sitting down to dinner. "It's good mom. Oh how I missed this," Ashley expressed as she ate.

"I agree," Laura chimed in.

"Well, thank you," Ellen answered as she ate enjoying having her two daughters back together again. She had fixed this knowing it was one of Ashley's favorite meals. And now tonight Ryan was coming over. She had always liked him. He was a stand up young man. He took care of his elderly father and worked a full time job since graduating last spring. He and Brian, Ellen's son, had been very close. She knew one reason Ryan didn't go in the military was because of his father. Part of her hoped that maybe Ryan and Ash would get together. He would be a good influence on her, even though there was a bit of an age difference. After they had finished dinner and cleaned up, Ellen went to her room to study for a while. Laura and Ashley sat down to watch some T.V. They only got three stations, so they didn't have much of a selection. That was one of the drawbacks of living out in the middle of nowhere. But if you lived in town, you could get cable. They just made it available in the past couple years. Some people out here got themselves those huge satellite dishes. Ashley and Laura were jealous. How could they not be, with the choice of 300 channels. Although one of Laura's friends had one and he said it's 300 channels of garbage; there's still nothing on. They talked about it and had a hard time believing that you wouldn't be able to find anything on 300 channels.

Suddenly there was a knock at the door. Ryan had arrived. Ashley got the door. "Hi Ryan. How are you?" She smiled at him.

"Good and you…?"

Ellen appeared out of nowhere. "Hey, Ryan, how's your dad?" "He's good." He smiled as he made his way into the house. "So where's your problem shelf?" He asked eyeing the room.

"It's over here." Ellen explained all the problems she had with it and what she wanted. He listened, went back outside, retrieved his tools and got right to work. As he worked, he made small talk with the trio. He couldn't help but notice how much Ashley had grown up over the last year. He briefly thought about their age difference, but it really didn't bother him; something in him wanted to get to know her better although the bruises on her eye made him wonder what type of girl she was. They had informed him she had just moved back that morning, so he couldn't help but wonder if that had something to do with it. As time went by and they talked, he slowed down on the repair job in order to stay and spend more time with Ashley.

Ellen picked up on the maneuver so she excused herself to go to her room and study. She wondered if she should send the two on an errand. The more she thought about it the better it sounded. After a little while she went out into the living room. "Hey, Ryan, would you mind taking Ashley to town to get me some coffee for the morning? I forgot all about picking some up today. I'd really appreciate it."

Ryan looked at Ashley, then at Ellen. "Sure, I could do that. Is that OK with you Ashley?" He looked at her.

"Yeah, that would be fine. What kind do you want me to get?" "Eight o'clock coffee. Thanks, you two," Ellen smiled.

Laura looked at them; she wanted to tag along "Mom, can I go with them?"

"Why don't you let them go by themselves; you can stay here and keep me company,"

"But I want to go with Ashley. She just got here," Laura whined. "I know, but they are older and have more in common; they don't need a shadow and that's that. She will be back shortly, now stop." Ellen stood firm.

Laura sighed deeply and whined "All right,… hurry up though; don't take forever," Laura pouted.

Ashley pursed her lips, "Don't worry Sissy, I'll be quick. Love you lots." She winked at her as they were leaving.

Ryan and Ashley set out for town in his blue four door beast of a car. It would have been classified as a winter rat except for the fact it was summer. It didn't have any dents and the interior was in good shape. It was just big and old, but it was a car.

"So, Ryan, you know I'm a junior this year. I already know you graduated a little over a year ago. Where do you work?"

"At a woodworking place; it's all hand crafted really high end, but they don't pay very well. But I love working with wood, making something beautiful out of a piece of plain wood." Ryan smiled at her. "Sounds rewarding. I mean if you love what you do, it's easier to go to work every day. I remember that grandfather clock you made out of cherry that won best of show in the state fair when you were a senior. It was so beautiful." She nodded her head.

"You remember that?" he cocked his head.

"How could I not!" she smiled. They continued to talk about his work and the art in it, the beauty in it; how she liked to draw and they found out they both loved to work with clay.

Her awe at his work really tickled him and made him feel proud of what he did. A lot of the girls he met only cared about rising up the ladder, or how much you made, not about the art in it or how it made you feel. He found it refreshing to meet someone else who liked to create.

When they got to town, they picked up the coffee. He then invited her to go watch the sunset at the Bluffs before going home and she accepted. He ran back into the store and came out with a brown bag. Ashley looked at him curiously "What's in the bag?"

"For me to know and you to find out." He smiled.

"What's that supposed to mean?" She cocked her head.

"Well, it's a little surprise for when we get to the Bluffs." He winked at her as he drove.

"Surprises already. Are you serious?"

"Well, it's probably more for me than for you. Your mom might get mad at me if I share with you," He raised his eyebrows up and down.

"I know what it is. It's beer, isn't it?" Ashley smiled.

"You will have to wait and see."

The two talked and joked along the way. They reached North Allentown fairly quickly, went past Ryan's house and further down the road past Ashley's house. At the end of the road was a dirt road which led to the Bluffs on one of the great Lakes. Ryan pulled into the parking area, surrounded by huge boulders which gave way to a field full of wildflowers.

The lake was calm and a few boats dotted its surface; the sky was awash in reds and oranges. They had arrived just in time to admire another beautiful sunset on the lake. Ryan got out and went around opening her door; the two sat on one of the boulders to watch. He went back to get the package. "Here we are." He pulled out two Bud lights, smiling.

"Ah, I knew it. A guy after my own heart, thanks." She smiled at him. "Are you sure? What if your mom finds out?" He raised his eyebrow. "That's what breath mints are for, besides I'll only have one. Wait a minute, how do you buy it? You're only 19. Last I knew you had to be 21."

"I got grandfathered in. I just made it too. The law allowed me to buy it because I was already allowed to, so I still can. Pretty cool, huh." He nodded his head.

The two sat and talked watching the sun go down; he had one beer. Ashley only took a few sips of the beer he gave her, explaining it just wasn't going down tonight. Stating she must be full from dinner. She wanted him to think she was cool. But she realized that she didn't want to mess things up at her mother's, especially since she just arrived. She explained her bruises to Ryan and the camping trip. Part of her wanted to say they were totally worth it, but she wasn't sure if they were. It ruined her whole relationship with her father, but what type of relationship was it, really. She was so confused; life was so confusing at times and now here she was sitting on a rock with a boy. To look at him he seemed clean cut and gentle, a quality she was attracted to, her mother approved of him and she liked him at least so far.

After the sun went down Ryan and Ashley decided they had better get her back home so her mother wouldn't worry. It was only a two minute drive which was basically silent. When they got to the driveway, Ashley popped a couple of breath mints. "Well, I had a nice time. Thanks." She smiled at him.

"Ah.. Yeah.. it was fun. We should get together again sometime." He nervously smiled back.

"Yeah, I would like that. I better get going, I'll see you later." She got out of the car, grabbing the coffee. As she was going in, she turned and gave him a little wave, and he waved back. As he left out of the driveway, he thought about what a fun and relaxing evening he had had.

Ashley quietly slipped into the house and put the coffee away and then went straight to the bathroom to brush her teeth. After she finished, she went to her room and Laura came knocking. "Hey, how was your date!!" she giggled, standing in the doorway.

"It wasn't a date."

"I saw you drive by. Where did you go? The Bluffs?" She turned her head.

"Yes, and we watched the sunset." Ashley smiled.

"Oh how romantic; that's what I call a date!! You're not even home a day and you've already got a new boyfriend. So did you kiss?" She raised her eyebrows.

"No!! Of course not!! Nosy." Ashley smiled.

"But you wanted to," Laura teased.

"Oh, and how would you know that?"

"Because that's how it goes on TV." Laura held out her hands. "Laura, TV is fake; nothing on it is real. You're hilarious." Ashley lovingly grasped her hand and squeezed, gave it a little shake and released it. "God girl I love you; you're so funny."

"I'll give you funny." She lightly smacked her sister up side the head. "Listen, funny girl, I'm going to call it a night, so I'll see you in the morning OK? Love you." Ashley turned out the light and climbed into bed.

"Goodnight, I'm so glad that you're home." Laura left her sister's room with a warm feeling in her heart. She felt complete again. Her sister had always been very important to her. She was quite different, yet, ever since she could remember, she always looked out for her. One time in particular she took a beating from her father for her, Laura couldn't remember the reason, but she remembered Ashley lied for her. From then on Laura looked up to her. She knew her sister had her back. She was the one person she could count on no matter what.

Ashley had called her friends and filled them in on the move. Kim was elated about Ashley moving back. They started to rekindle their friendship and since she only lived around the corner, they started hanging out quite often. They also included Laura in most of their activities. Ashley couldn't stand the thought of leaving her at home by herself all the time. The trio started hanging out pretty much every day over the next few weeks before the start of school. Kim was a good influence and her parents were strict.

They spent Sunday mornings in church, and for the first time in a long time Ashley really felt like she needed to be there. They played the music loud and Ashley sang her heart out, she sounded terrible but thankfully no one could hear her. The pastor would call out the words to the songs to the parishioners and they would repeat after him. And sometimes this would go on and on and on, almost hypnotic. Ashley would close her eyes and sway back and forth repeating after the pastor; then he would call on them to pray. She would pray about her relationship with her father, and how it had deteriorated. She would pray for herself asking God for help and strength, and how she did but didn't want to commit suicide. She prayed about the relationship with her mother, mainly not to blow it this time. Many times she was brought to tears during these intense sessions. It didn't matter to her that others saw; she needed to get all of that out of her. It was like a poison, eating away at her soul. She felt that only God could help. Only He could understand the pain and anguish she was going through. He was the only One she could confide in, without fear of something drastic happening. She wasn't sure exactly what would happen if her parents found out her true feelings, the deep dark feelings that she kept to herself.

Although Ashley felt better, much better, living with her mother, the struggle to keep going on still crept in more than she expected. She kept telling herself it would only be a little while before she could see Tim again and that would help. It needed to help, something had to help; she just needed to hang on. In the meantime she reminded herself of the good things that were in her life: she was back at her mother's house, she had freedom, Laura looked up to her, Kim and she were friends and she was attending church plus she met Ryan, and that was going well. Of all the things that were going well, these dark thoughts of suicide still kept creeping in, and she didn't know how to deal with them or how to keep them at bay. She had to hang on to something, anything.

CHAPTER 9

School would be starting soon, so Ellen and the girls were getting ready to go on a shopping spree. Ashley was standing in the hallway when she overheard her mother.

"What the hell do you mean, you're not contributing any money?" she screamed. "Oh, you're a real piece of work… Yeah, well, you also have a daughter over here, or have you forgotten… Screw you," Ellen slammed the receiver down, calling him a few choice words.

Ellen was royally pissed off and complained all day, but she still got her daughters everything they needed. Ashley felt it was her fault because of the fight this last summer. Her mother's constant complaining just drove it in deeper.

Every other day, after work, Ryan had been coming over to Ashley's. Most of the time they would steal away to the Bluffs to watch the sunset. Many times Ryan would bring a joint and they would smoke up and talk. It was easier to get away with than drinking because there was no smell as long as they smoked it outside of the car or as they liked to call it, the beast.

After a few weeks they shared their first kiss. Ashley kept playing it out in her mind, how they were sitting on the largest boulder at the Bluffs, watching the sun as it was about to set. The clouds were strewn across the sky in a brilliant orange red color, and a cool breeze blew off the lake. Ashley had melted in his arms. He was so strong yet gentle, and his lips were so soft; she swore she would remember it for the rest of her life. She kept it to herself that night, but the next day at Kim's she couldn't hold it in any longer.

The trio sat on Kim's front lawn. "Kim, I got my first kiss; it was so romantic." Ashley smiled as she looked up towards the sky, leaning back on her arms. "How come you didn't tell me last night?" Laura interrupted, eyes bugging out.

"Yeah, was he a good kisser?" Kim asked smiling, ignoring Laura. "Absolutely the best; I was in heaven." Ashley sighed lost in romantic bliss.

"So, are you guys a couple? I mean, is it exclusive?" Kim looked at Ashley, picking a blade of grass.

"I guess, I mean I think so. He comes over every other day; he has to take care of his dad on the other days, so I think so." Ashley looked at Kim. "It was so awesome, he is such a good kisser."

"I'm glad you got a good guy, and your mom likes him." Kim nodded her head.

"Well, I'm glad too, Ash, but you should have told me last night, girlfriend." Laura raised her eyebrows and jutted out her head, giving Ash a friendly kick as she sprawled out.

"All right Laura, next time I'll tell you first." Ashley smiled at her. "So today is our last day of freedom," Kim remarked.

"Yeah, I know. Bummer," Laura piped up. Ashley stayed quiet. She wanted school to start.

The following morning went off well. They made it to the bus with plenty of time. This was Ashley's junior year and Laura was in eighth grade. Laura couldn't wait until next year because then they would both be in high school. Ashley sat with Kim on the bus; it took almost an hour for them to get to school. At school Ashley and Kim went to their lockers. They always ended up near each other because their last names were close together. After putting their fresh new notebooks, several different colored folders and some extra pens in their lockers, Kim went to the library to join her group of friends. The library was located in the middle of the school, it was open on both sides, having glass walls on one side, where there was a courtyard, then books on the other end. But Ashley went to the bathroom to catch up with her group.

As Ashley walked in, she greeted everyone. "Hey, how's it going?" she gently shouted, giving a wave to everyone.

A bunch of girls smiled and replied, "Good, and you?"

Karen was in the back. "Hey, Ashley, come on. I'm over here." She waved her hand, then took a drag of her cigarette.

"I figured you'd be here. Where's Emily?" Ashley looked around. "Oh, I'm sure she'll be here soon. So, how's it going at your mom's?" Karen asked

"Good. I have a lot more freedom, that's for sure." Ashley smiled. "I bet you do. That was a fun camping trip, though, wasn't it?" Karen nodded her head.

"We should have done it sooner. Screw the old man." Ashley laughed.

"You're still not talking to him?" Karen asked surprised.

"More like he's not talking to me, so to hell with him." Ashley shook her head as if she didn't care, but deep down it bothered her.

The first bell rang alerting the students to gather in the auditorium. "Come on, gang, let's get going," Karen announced. The bathroom started to empty out at her command. She was definitely a leader to many of the underclassmen. It seemed as if they listened to her rather than the bell or the teachers. She reveled in it, knowing her status, yet she didn't misuse it on the younger students; that was probably why she was so popular.

Throughout the day Ashley saw and talked to most all of the friends she didn't see over the summer. She made it to all of her classes on time and vowed to herself that she would complete all the assignments and study regularly. She always made these promises to herself at the beginning of the year, but, by the end, it was always a different story. This year would be different; she would put in extra effort. Maybe make honor role. It wasn't that hard. She just never put forth the energy to do it; hell, she didn't go to class often enough last year.

That evening Ashley and Ryan watched another sunset while smoking up. She told him all about her first day back. She didn't mention her desire to go see the drug counselor though; she was nervous he would think she was crazy or something.

Over the next few weeks Ashley tried to get in to see Tim, but his door was always closed when she went by. He usually didn't set up appointments, you just stopped in; Tim's unavailability was making Ashley feel like she could explode inside. However, after about three weeks she saw him in the hall and he approached her. "Hey, kiddo, how have you been?" he asked with a grin.

Ashley took in a deep breath. "Uh, OK, I guess. I mean a lot has happened." She looked down.

"Why don't we go sit down and talk?" He motioned toward his office with his head.

"Yeah, OK." Ashley turned and started to walk with Tim towards his office. Once inside, "So what's going on?" He asked looking into her eyes.

"I'm not even sure where to start …."

"The beginning is always the best,"

Ashley then told Tim pretty much the whole story: the babysitting, and how she ended up at her mother's house including the beating and camping trip that brought it about. She also told him about Ryan, how they met and that her mother approves of him, but that they smoke up at the Bluffs at night. She did not tell him she was suicidal, but she did tell him she felt sad about her life right now. Even though she had people in her life, she still felt lonely, and she didn't know how to fix it. He listened to her and was shocked at her father's behavior. He explained that talking helped with the loneliness, that she had been through quite a bit, and that to be sad about it was normal. He also told her that if things got to be too much and she needed to talk and his door was closed, to knock and he would make time for her. Ashley was relieved to hear him say that. In some strange way it made her feel special and she needed that. Over the next few weeks she saw him quite a bit, relieving a lot of her tension. Even though seeing Tim made her feel better, she kept it to herself.

Before long Halloween was upon them and Ashley and Ryan wanted to go to a costume party, but Ellen insisted she take Laura trick or treating. Ashley wasn't happy about that but Laura kept persisting about it. "Please, Ashley, I'll only go for a couple of hours and then you can go to your party. Please, you know mom won't take me." Laura looked at her all wide eyed and innocent.

"Oh, all right, but it's only for a couple of hours." Ashley let out a deep breath, trying to think of a way to ask Ryan to take them in the beast.

"So, I'm going to dress up as Little Boo peep. What are you and Ryan going as?" Laura asked, trying to get on her sister's good side.

"Well, Ryan, is going to be a mummy and I'm going to be a witch, matching my evil personality." Ashley let out an evil laugh.

"Have you been practicing that laugh? It sounds evil," Laura looked at her.

"Yeah, I have. Got to match the costume." Ashley smiled.

"Well, you got it down," Laura shook her head.

Halloween night arrived and Ryan and Ashley took Laura trick or treating. They finished up around eight at night and then dropped her off home and rushed off to the party. She had begged them to tag along but they said no. The people at the party were much older, not to mention the drugs and alcohol that were there. Ashley and Ryan arrived as the party was in full swing. As soon as they arrived, Darth Vader handed them a joint. They started smoking up, passing it on to a zombie. They got themselves some beer from the keg that had been tapped; some people were doing shots, but they declined. Ryan's mummy outfit was a big hit, along with another guy dressed as a girl; the two of them won best costumes. As the night wore on Ashley and Ryan sat down and played cards for small change. As they sat at the table and played, they would pass around joints and drink.

Around midnight Ryan and Ashley got up to leave. When they got outside on the porch, Ashley was so messed up she was standing there then she just passed out, falling down face first onto the deck. Ryan wasn't sure what to do; he figured she was just messed up. He sat down next to her for a few minutes and made sure she was breathing. Then he picked her up and carried her to the car and sat her in the passenger seat. After a few minutes she came around. "Man, you made me nervous." He looked into her eyes.

"What happened?"

"You passed out, and I carried you to the car. Are you OK?" he asked.

"Yeah, I feel weak."

"Let's get you home."

"Thanks for carrying me." She smiled weakly.

"No problem." He smiled back at her.

She laid her head back against the seat and closed her eyes, resting as he drove back to her house. "Do you need me to help you inside?" he asked as they pulled in the driveway.

"No, I can make it, but thanks for your help tonight. I'm sorry for being such a loser." Ashley bit her lip.

"Hey, everyone has a bad night once in a while. I'm just glad you're OK." Ryan leaned over and kissed Ashley. "I'll talk to you tomorrow, OK?"

"Sounds good." Ashley smiled and got out of the car and took in a deep breath, then quietly went into the house. She crept past her mother's room hoping not to wake her. As she flipped on the light in her room, she relaxed, knowing she got away with it. Before turning in for the night, she brushed her teeth and washed up, trying to remove all the smells of the party.

That night, as Ashley lay in bed, she thought about what Ryan had done for her. She was grateful to him for one that he didn't go back inside to the party and tell everyone. It was embarrassing enough that he saw it, let alone everyone else know. Next month, she thought, she would be sixteen and they would have been going out almost five months. She wondered if he was the one, her first. The two of them had brushed on the subject but she had always swayed away from it. She wanted it to be perfect and with someone special, plus they had to use protection; no way did she want some baby. Maybe she could talk to him about it, but what if she chickened out, then what. Would he break up with her? Life could be so confusing not to mention difficult.

Over the next couple of weeks Ashley gave a lot of thought to losing her virginity. She felt as if there was no one she could really trust except Kim, even though she knew Kim was probably saving herself for marriage. After a lot of thought she approached her one day after school, making sure Laura was nowhere in sight. "Kim, I've gotta talk to you about something very important," Ashley looped her arm through Kim's and started walking towards Kim's house.

"OK. What's up?"

Ashley looked around making sure no one could hear. "Well, you know I'm turning sixteen in little over a week and Ryan and I've been a couple for almost five months and, well, I was thinking maybe …" Ash was shaking her head from side to side, gritting her teeth.

Kim stopped in her tracks and looked at her all wide eyed." Are you asking me about the big… you know…? Ash, that's a big question. Are you sure? I mean is he the one?"

"I think so…

"But, do you love him and does he love you?" Kim raised her eyebrows as they resumed their way. "I'm waiting until I get married."

"I know you are, and that's great for you. But, I love him. He is so kind and he has been patient. We didn't even kiss for a few weeks, and my mom approves of him." Ashley clenched her teeth through a smile.

"I don't think she'd approve of sex. Are you really ready? It's not something you can undo, and what if you get pregnant?"

"I already thought about that. We would definitely use protection. I'm not having some baby; they are way too much work, way too much." Ashley shook her head.

"Have you talked to Ryan about it?

"No, not exactly, a little."

"Well, then, good. You can back out. I would. Besides I heard it's painful the first time if you're not old enough. Because you're not big enough, down there." Kim held out her hands as they walked.

"You think so?"

"It's what I heard; anyways what's your rush? It's not like once you do it that's the only time, and he's going to want you to do it with him all the time. Did you think about that?" Kim turned and looked her in the eye.

"You know I didn't think about that but what if I like it too?" Ashley half smiled.

"Well, it's a big decision. I hope whatever you decide it makes you happy, OK?" Kim turned her head and smiled at Ashley.

"Thanks Kim. That's why I love talking to you. You're the best friend I've ever had, love ya, I've gotta get home. I'll talk to you tomorrow."

"All right. See you later." Kim waved and turned to go.

When Ashley arrived home her mother was waiting, "Hey, kiddo, how was your day?"

"It was OK. You know, the same old thing," Ashley sat at the table. "You know your birthday is coming up and I was wondering what you wanted." Ellen smiled at her raising her eyebrows.

"I don't know, maybe some clothes or something." Ashley looked at her.

"Well, it's your sixteenth so I went out and got the book for you to study for your learner's permit"

"No way! Really? You mean to drive?" "Yes, to drive." Ellen handed it to her.

"Wow, that's cool. Thanks mom. When can we go take the test?" Ashley asked all wide eyed.

"As soon as you study the book and feel like you can pass the test… I was hoping maybe on your birthday. I thought we could take the afternoon off and go up and take the test."

"Really, you mean you're going to take me out of school?"

"Well, it's only one time and it's your sixteenth birthday; that's special." She smiled warmly at her daughter.

"Wow, thanks mom." Ashley's face lit up, and she started to read at the table while her mother got dinner ready.

Study, study, study became Ashley's philosophy over the week. She wanted to ace that test. And when her mother picked her up on her birthday, she studied all the way to the motor vehicle department, having her mother quiz her.

"Mom, I'm pretty nervous. I hope I pass." Ash took in a deep breath. "Oh, honey, you have studied so much. Just relax and take your time. You will do fine," Ellen rubbed her arm while pulling into a parking space.

Once inside Ashley took the test, then carefully checked her answers. She went up to get it corrected and came out with a huge smile. "Mom, I only missed one question!! I am officially allowed to drive. Oh, this is the best birthday ever. I love you." Her mom drove out of town then pulled over and they switched drivers. "Are you ready, darlin'?" Ellen smiled at her daughter. She couldn't help but think how fast the years had gone by, and her baby was now driving. She thought soon she would be graduating and going off on her own leading her own life. But, for now, she would just enjoy the moment. Ellen thought she would remember this for the rest of her life that her mother took her to get her permit, not her father. He couldn't steal this from her. The two of them drove home, her mother teaching driving tidbits here and there, enjoying every moment.

That night Ashley hung out at home hoping her father would at least call to wish her a happy birthday. She had it all set up in her mind how he would say hi and apologize for the summer thing, and then she would say don't worry about it; it's done and over with. Even though deep down she didn't forgive him, they were just words. Lying about it just made it easier, easier to get along, something she learned early on in her family. Then he would wish her happy birthday and maybe he even got her a gift. She thought it is my sixteenth. Then everything would start to be all right between them again. After all, this wasn't the first time this sort of thing had happened, maybe not to this extent but still. All he had to do was call, so Ash waited and waited and waited. By eleven she gave up and turned in. She lay down and turned on Ozzy Osbourne; it fit her mood. She couldn't believe she gave up a date with Ryan to wait on a stupid phone call, a call that never came. Tears streamed down her check. Ash couldn't help but wonder if he forgot or was he being intentionally cruel. Either way the pain was the same. Her heart ached and she yearned for someone to hold her tight to make this loneliness disappear. Ashley then thought about Ryan and how he was always there for her and how special she felt around him. Ryan had wanted to take her out tonight, but, no, she wanted to stay home waiting for a call. How stupid could she have been. She should have known he wouldn't call. Now she felt like an idiot, she wasted her birthday, on him. Not anymore. Never again will she wait on her father, expect anything from him, or want anything from him. Ashley thought about how her father might act if she killed herself; would he cry, would he blame himself. These thoughts took up a lot of her time. She wondered if other people felt the same way and just didn't talk about it. She then heard her mother in the kitchen.

Surprisingly enough Ash thought her mother and she had been getting along great over the past four to five months. It was unusual; usually Ashley got into trouble and all hell broke loose. Suddenly there was a crash in the kitchen. Ashley rushed out only to find her mother drunk, passed out on the floor. She shook her mother awake and helped her to bed. Ashley thought, I hope this isn't going to become a regular thing again. She hadn't done this in a long time, since her father had left.

The next day Ellen had no memory of Ashley helping her to bed. If she did, she didn't mention it. Ashley didn't want to shake things up between them so she kept quiet. Ellen was going out on a date and Laura was going over to her friend's house for the night. Ashley had decided she would cook dinner for Ryan, and maybe tonight would be the night.

"So, mom, what should I fix? I don't know how to make a lot of fancy stuff, but I want to make it, I mean I'll probably need you to help but I want to do most of it." Ashley stood in the kitchen with her hands on her hips biting her lip.

"Well, how about spaghetti and meatballs with garlic bread? That's not too hard and it's good. Ellen looked at her daughter with a smirk in her smile.

"What mom? Why are you looking at me like that?" Ashley held out her hands.

"I don't know; you're just growing up so fast. This is your first dinner for a boyfriend. Let's check to make sure we have everything, and then we'll go to town and get dessert and candles. You can't have a romantic dinner without those." Ellen started to gather the ingredients together on the counter. Ashley got the crock pot out and started to cook the sauce, in order for it to simmer all day.

That evening after Ellen and Laura left, Ashley and Ryan sat down to an intimate dinner, candles and all.

"Wow, you really went all out; this is really good too. It's nice to be here with you." Ryan's eyes were soft and he reached out taking Ashley's hand.

"I'm so glad you like it. I got the idea from a movie if you can believe that and I just thought why not." Ashley chuckled. She felt him squeeze her hand and she gently squeezed back. She was getting butterflies in her stomach as they were finishing up dinner. She was thinking about after dessert. Was tonight the night? Could she actually go through with it?

"I also have some cherry pie for dessert." Ashley smiled.

"Hey, why not wait a while for pie, I'm full. You want to go outside and smoke up?" Ryan reached in the pocket of his jacket and pulled out a joint.

"Yeah, I would love to; that's the perfect after dinner dessert." Ashley headed outside onto the back deck. The two took their time smoking the joint, enjoying hitting it. Afterwards Ashley relaxed taking Ryan's hand, leading him into the house and onto the couch. The couple started to kiss. As they made out Ashley got up and led

Ryan to her room and sat on her bed. He looked quizzical at first but then smiled. He started kissing her taking off his shirt, then hers. "Are you sure you want to do this?" he asked in a whisper.

"Yeah, I'm sure." She kissed him running her fingers through his hair." Do you have protection?"

"Yeah, I've got some in the car, I'll be right back." Ryan ran out the door.

He returned and sat on the edge of the bed slowly taking off her pants he ripped his off, laid down next to her, slid his hand up and down her leg removing her panties. Her skin was so soft. He kissed her over and over, and he caressed her with his hands, put on the condom, and then slowly went inside her. A strange sensation rippled across her body, feeling good, a little bit painful at first. Ryan was being gentle with her; she felt his every breath on her neck. She started moving in unison with him; the two of them danced in each other's arms. Afterwards Ryan cuddled up next to her and fell asleep. Ashley just stared at the ceiling; it wasn't anything like she had imagined.

Just then Ashley heard Ellen's car pull into the driveway. "Ryan! Ryan!! Wake up, my mom is home." Ashley started throwing on her clothes.

"Holy shit!" He jumped out of bed and rushed to get dressed. The two of them raced around dressing, and Ashley tried straightening up her bed. "Go out and turn on the T.V. Hurry up, comb your hair, your shirt is buttoned wrong. Oh, shit, she's gonna know…"

"Relax, just blow out the candles and fix your hair. Your clothes look fine." Ryan took the brush and went into the bathroom; he reappeared almost instantly, then shot out to the living room to turn on the TV and sat on the couch trying to catch his breath before Ellen walked in.

"Hey, how's it going? Where's Ashley?" Ellen removed her coat and stood in the kitchen.

"Oh, she just went to the bathroom; she'll be out in a minute. How was your evening?" Ryan asked, silently trying to catch his breath, trying to look as innocent as he could.

"It was good. How was your dinner? I thought you two were going to the movies afterwards." Ellen looked hard at Ryan.

"Well… we uh… finished late …and we uh…"

Ashley rushed out into the living room, "Hey, mom, how was your date?" She stood smiling at her mother, rocking back and forth…

"It actually went pretty well; he was nice. After dinner we went for drinks." Ellen kept eyeing the two of them. "What's going on? You two look like you're up to something."

"Nothing, mom. We were dozing off after diner and you woke us up, that's all, honest." Ashley shrugged her shoulders and held out her hands. "That's it."

"OK. Well it's getting late. I'm going to turn in."

"Goodnight, mom," Ashley answered. When her mother was out of sight she let out a huge sigh of relief. She whispered, "Man, that was close; we were so lucky."

"Tell me about it. Listen I better get going. I'll call you," Then he whispered in her ear, "Tonight was really special." He kissed her and headed out the door.

Ashley stood in silence for a moment, then went to her room. She thought I can't believe we almost got busted. Wait until I tell Kim. She will freak. As she lay in bed she thought about losing her virginity. She knew she loved Ryan and was pretty sure he loved her, at least he said he did. It was a bit more painful than she expected but in a way after a while it felt good too. She hoped it would not be as painful the next time. She thought it probably wouldn't be or why would anyone continue to do it. Overall, though, she was glad she decided to go through with it, with Ryan. She wondered if they would end up getting married. Just then it occurred to her she actually had a positive thought about her future. Something she never thought about. So I guess sex is a good thing. She smiled as she snuggled underneath the sheets and closed her eyes.

CHAPTER 10

Ellen trudged in the house on a Thursday afternoon shouting, "Ashley, Ashley, please come out here!"

She stomped out to the kitchen, "What! I was doing my homework." "Have a seat and lose the attitude. Now that you're sixteen you need to get a job, a real job. Babysitting every once in a while doesn't count," and she tossed the newspaper towards her.

"Where are the jobs?" Ashley shook her hands wrestling with the newspaper.

"In the help wanted section." Ellen snatched it back, spread the section out on the table, and gave Ashley a pen to circle perspective jobs.

Finding only two jobs she qualified for, and one of those was too far away, she called the restaurant for a dish washing job. After the phone call she had an interview; they set it up for the following day.

"Mom, I'm kind of nervous. What do I say? What are they going to want to know?" Ashley started to pace the kitchen floor.

"Relax. First off, you need to get a work permit from school tomorrow. The employer just wants to size you up, see when you can work, stuff like that. It's no big deal, but you want to look neat and capable, it's not a corporate job but it's a job interview, so make sure you sound intelligent, and you'll do fine." Ellen smiled at her daughter.

The next day Ashley got her work permit from the office, and even though it was just a dish washing job she was excited about going to the interview and really hoped she would get the job.

"Come on, Ash, you're going to be late." Ellen was waiting by the door, keys in hand.

"I'm coming, I'm coming. I just had to grab my work permit." Ashley came rushing down the hall past her mother and out the door on her way to the car.

Pulling into the parking lot Ellen remarked, "It's a cozy little place Ash. looks pleasant, now go get-em."

Ashley was immediately met by a huge dog, forcing her to let out a little scream. An older man appeared. "That's just Rosco. He won't hurt you. Go on, Rosco, lay down. It's still early and he has the run of the place. Hi, I'm Don. You must be Ashley Ames right. I've been expecting you."

"Yes, I'm Ashley. This is a nice place." Ashley smiled, as they went inside.

Don explained how things worked and that he was the chef and his wife, Mary, was head waitress and a stickler for details.

"I really want the dish washing job," Ashley remarked after a while. "No one wants to wash dishes; they do it for the money." Don laughed. "Which leads me to my next point. If you get the job, you'll be making minimum wage, OK?" He smiled.

"Yeah, that's fine with me." Ashley shook her head.

Just as they were finishing up, Mary popped in, said hello and talked to Ashley for a few minutes. In the end Ashley felt the interview went well because afterwards they spoke for a few minutes and hired her on the spot. She was to start the following week, one of the other dishwashers would train her.

Ashley got into the car. "I got the job; I'm starting Wednesday. It's OK huh?"

"That's excellent. I'm proud of you. Did they say how much you'd be getting paid?"

"Minimum wage, but it's a start," Ashley sighed.

"It's all part of the master plan," Ellen announced. Ashley just looked at her mother.

That night as she lay in bed listening to Black Sabbath she thought about her new job. What exactly was the point? She had a plan. It was to kill herself after graduating high school. That way she would have accomplished something in her life. Why, when things were going so well, did she still feel so bad? She had all she could do to just hold it together some days. But she was managing to make it to all of her classes even though she was getting high every day, unless she had a test. She smoked so she wouldn't just end it all: it took the edge off, helped her escape, kept her going on. Maybe taking up cigarette smoking would help with the nervousness. But that would probably be expensive and piss her mother off, even though she smoked. What difference does it really make? Time on this earth is limited anyway so I may as well try it. She lay there thinking how she felt more and more scared around groups of people, even her friends, being afraid they didn't really like her deep down. If it was so easy for her to lie, why not everyone else? Man, she thought, I got to stop being so paranoid; it's freaking me out. Then she thought life was like Black Sabbath said, paranoia will destroy you. These thoughts kept popping up in Ashley's mind regardless of where she was or what she was doing. She didn't know what to do, afraid to tell anyone, fearing that they would think she was crazy.

Wednesday rolled around and Ashley reported to work at five sharp. Dan, the other dish washer, was there to explain everything. After an hour he left which was fine with her. It wasn't rocket science or anything. At the end of the night was the only time Ashley got really backed up, because of kitchen clean up. Don had asked her if she wanted him to help, but she declined, wanting to prove she could handle it. Around eleven everything was done and she called her mom to pick her up. Ellen came but wasn't happy about it; she complained the whole way home. Thankfully it was only a five minute drive. Ashley was confused. Her mom told her to get a job but now she doesn't want to pick her up. She thought it was the same thing with making the swim team. She wanted her to go out for sports but didn't want to pick her up so she had to quit, she was good at it too.

After working a couple of weeks, Ellen approached Ashley one afternoon before taking her to work "We need to talk." She frowned.

"What's up?" Ashley sighed heavily thinking what could she possibly want now.

"You need to have Ryan start picking you up at night. I'm too tired in the morning from getting you at 11pm, especially during the week. You need to ask him tonight."

"OK, no problem. I'm pretty sure he'll do it. Is that all you want?" she looked at her mother, thinking she wants me to get a job, but yet she doesn't want to give me a ride. Whatever. . it's one night during the week and weekends.

"No that's it. What, are you mad?" Ellen looked sharply at her. "You have no right to be. I work hard for you and your sister, and it is just too late for me, got it?" She frowned.

"I didn't say anything! "Ashley held out her hands.

"Yeah, well it's that look. I'll slap it off your face!" Ellen glared at her. "Oh, excuse me, for a look! Why are you so mad at me?"

"Since you got this job, you just expect all these rides. You haven't given me any gas money; things are tight as it is." Ellen shook her head.

"Well, I didn't realize that you needed it. I'm sorry. All you had to do was ask."

"I just figured you would offer"

"Mom, I just never thought about it. I'm sorry. Please don't be mad. I'll contribute to the gas to get me to work and I'll ask Ryan to pick me up. I don't want you to be exhausted on account of me, OK?" Ashley raised her eyebrows.

"Thank you. Look I didn't mean to sound so angry; it's not all about you and I took it out on you. I'm sorry for that. Work has been giving me a lot of grief lately. Plus, pretty much every penny is spent before I can make it." Ellen sighed looking defeated, having to ask her daughter for gas money.

Ashley started to smoke cigarettes. She only did it occasionally as sort of a stress reliever type thing. She didn't care what her mother had to say or anyone else. She had the money to buy her own, and Ryan was old enough to get them for her.

As the weeks rolled by, Ashley became much more proficient at her job. Usually Saturday nights they employed two dishwashers, but she worked much harder than her counterpart, so they put her on all by herself. She did pretty well so it was made permanent. Ashley flew around the kitchen, working as hard and as fast as she could.

One slow evening her vice-principal showed up for dinner. Ashley hid in the back as much as possible, but Don went out and told him what a hard worker she was. Usually the only time Ashley saw him was when she screwed up.

"Don what did you tell him? Don't you know you're embarrassing me?" Ashley's eyes were wide open.

"I told him what a hard worker you were. You should be proud of that." Don stood firm. "Can't you take a compliment?"

Ashley shook her head and returned to work without a word, hiding in the kitchen until the vice principal left.

Ryan had become a regular fixture at the bar, waiting for Ashley to finish up at night. "Hey, Ash, want some help?" Ryan smiled.

"Sure, you can take care of the clean stuff for me."

"You want to go out back with me for a minute?" Ryan flashed a joint, raising his eyebrows up and down, "Everyone is gone for the night." "Sounds good to me." They walked out back and lit the joint. "Oh, this is just what I needed," Ashley remarked hitting it again.

"Yeah, it makes the night wrap up easier for us. Did you hear something? Ryan looked around.

"Put it out! Put it out! Here comes Mary. Hurry up," Ashley bee-lined it towards the backdoor of the kitchen.

"What were you doing out there? Isn't that Ryan out back there?" Mary kept looking over Ashley's shoulder.

"We were just having a private conversation. I was taking a break, that's all." Ashley shrugged her shoulders, gently coerced Mary back inside and got back to work. Ryan wandered in a few moments later and started to help out while avoiding Mary as they finished up.

When Ashley arrived home late that night from work, she quietly crept into the house, not wanting to wake up her mother. As she entered the kitchen, she saw her mother passed out at the table with one empty bottle of wine and another half gone. She put her things away and poured herself a large glass adding a few ice cubes. Then after a few gulps she took in a deep breath and nudged her mother to semi-consciousness. "Come on mom, it's time for bed."

"Where did you come from?" Ellen jerked her arm away, slurring her words.

"I'm home from work, mom. Come on, it's late," Ashley tried to rouse her mother.

"You know this isn't what I pictured for my life: no one loves me, your father is already married again with a family and I'm all alone." She started to cry.

"Mom, I love you. You're not alone." Ashley got her up.

"Oh, what do you know? You're young and you have Ryan. I want someone to love me." She stumbled towards her room.

"Mom, Laura and I love you. You're not alone; come on. Just go to sleep." She got her to her bed.

"You will leave me. You'll grow up and go as soon as you can. No one wants to stay with me. I'm going to die all alone. You say you won't leave, but you will, I know." Ellen pulled the covers up around her neck.

"Mom, I won't leave you. You won't die alone. Some man is going to find you and fall in love with you and treat you great; you'll see. So don't worry. Just go to sleep," Ashley left her mother's room after she fell asleep.

After refilling her glass with wine she cleaned up the table, putting the wine bottles on the counter so Ellen would see them in the morning. Ashley knew her mother wouldn't remember how much she drank. She sat at the table and quietly drank the wine while having a cigarette. After finishing her drink, she washed her glass and put it away. She couldn't help but wonder if Laura had seen their mother in that condition. She decided to check on her. Ashley quietly opened her door and whispered "Hey, you awake?"

Laura rolled over. "Yeah, when did you get home?" "Just a little bit a go, you OK?"

"Mom was asleep at the table. I tried to wake her up, but she just moaned and jerked her arm away from me, so I just left her there." Laura sighed. "I know it's from drinking too much."

"Yeah, I just put her to bed. Have you seen her like that before?" Ashley sat down on the edge of the bed.

"She did it a lot when you first left for your dad's, but then it got better. Then when you first came back she stopped I was hoping it was over. Guess not, huh." Laura looked at her sister.

"Well, don't tell anyone and don't worry, OK? Go back to sleep. I'll talk to you tomorrow." Ashley left her sister's room going down the hall to her room.

Turning on Ozzy always seemed to help soothe Ashley's frame of mind. Sometimes she played the same song over and over and over again, just because it fit her mood. She couldn't help but wonder if any of her friends shared the same thoughts as she did. Not only thoughts but situations: did their parents get drunk, pass out and need to be tended to. This type of stuff never happened at Kim's house, but could it happen when no one was there? Like she told Laura don't say anything, secrets in the house, stay in the house. Was everything a front, a lie, a scam, a put on for other people. Because that's what it was at both of her parent's houses. All this thinking was beginning to give her a headache. She thought, well, maybe it was the wine. She turned Ozzy's "Suicide Solution" song on; she had recorded it over and over about 15 times, and she tried to go to sleep.

By the time Ashley came out to the kitchen the following morning, the wine bottles were gone. She didn't know if her mother remembered any of their conversation or not and wasn't sure if she should mention it or just let it go. Deciding it would be best to let the decision fall into her mother's corner, Ashley quietly got herself some breakfast. When she finally ran into her mother, nothing was mentioned about the night before; life went on as usual.

The Christmas holiday was upon them and Ashley was happier this year; she had Ryan plus she had a job. This year it wasn't all about what she would be getting; she was in the giving mood, and she knew her mother would not be springing a new step-father on them or a new sibling. Ashley wondered if she should call her father. After all it had been over six months since the move, and it was the holidays. She decided after much thought to send a Christmas card; she even signed it with love. In the weeks that followed she waited patiently for a response, but none came.

They spent Christmas day at her grandparents as usual and went home in the afternoon so Ellen could pick up the extra shift at the nursing home. Ashley wanted to go out with Ryan but couldn't because she had to stay with Laura, so Ryan came and hung out at the house. Laura had been in her room for a while. Ashley commented, "Let me just check on her real quick," Ashley left Ryan and went to Laura's room; she was sound asleep. Ashley thought, oh yeah! and quietly shut her door. When she reappeared in the living room with a huge smile, Ryan looked at her quizzically. "Guess what? She's asleep." Ashley smiled.

"Want to smoke?" Ryan raised his eyebrows up and down.

"Oh, yeah, you know I do." The two went out on the back deck and lit a joint Ryan had brought just in case they could steal away.

As Ryan lit it, it popped. "Oh a seed." He inhaled again. "Tastes good though."

"Man, this is just what I needed. My dad didn't even call, and I sent them a card weeks ago. My family is messed up." She inhaled and held it, then coughed and coughed.

"Be careful, you'll cough up a lung," as Ryan inhaled and held it. "Yeah, but that's how you get really high." Ashley laughed as she took the joint.

They finished up after a few more minutes, then went in and Ashley rechecked her sister who was still asleep. Ryan wanted to fool around. Since it was Christmas, Ashley consented. They now had a fairly regular sex life. However, Ashley always insisted on using protection, no matter what. By now Ryan knew if he didn't have it, he wasn't getting it.

Ryan had tried to convince Ashley about the no feeling defense. She came back with the getting pregnant, a very painful delivery, with a screaming baby, and no sleeping with a ton of work for the rest of your life defense. Instead of a whole long lecture, where he could lose focus, she had condensed the most important issues into a short list. She told him time and time again a baby doesn't fit in with my plans.

That day Ryan asked, "Ash, what are your plans? Am I in your plans? You never talk about your future or what you want to do."

She took in a deep breath. "I'm not sure what my future holds, but I do want you in it though. Honestly, I feel lost. I want out, any way out of here I can get. Any way out; I don't care what I have to do." Ashley rolled over and looked him in the eye. "Come on. We should get dressed, just in case Laura wakes up."

Ryan dressed and sat on the edge of the bed. "You know I was thinking. My dad is getting sicker and sicker. I don't think he's going to make it too much longer. We could buy the house and move in together, you know after you graduate. I love you more than anything else in this world." Ryan leaned over and kissed her gently on the cheek.

"You really think so?" Ashley answered almost surprised.

"Yeah, why not? We get along great; we hardly ever fight." Ryan took her hand.

"Sounds pretty good," Ashley smiled. For the first time in her life a glimmer of hope sprang up.

"Listen it's almost time for your mom to come home so I'm going to take off. I'll see you later, OK?" Ryan got up and kissed Ashley for a little bit then proceeded to leave.

"Yeah, I'll talk to you tomorrow; you know I love you too." She walked him to the door.

Ashley went back and laid down more confused than anything. She thought about moving in with Ryan; it actually made her smile. Then she thought about how the day went. No call from her father. Why didn't he love her? She just felt this huge hole inside, an ache that wouldn't stop. Maybe she should just try to forget about him; he obviously doesn't care about her. She was damaged goods. Anything connected to her was doomed to fail except for Ryan. He was different and he understood. He was the only thing she really had that was worth anything. She thought everything I touch turns to shit. Maybe in the long run Ryan would be better off without her. He's young and he would get over me in no time at all, but maybe I'll just play it by ear for now.

Ashley heard her mother's car pull in the driveway. She rolled over facing the wall, just in case she came in to check on her. She heard her come into the house, then do some things in the kitchen which, Ashley assumed was to get a glass and a bottle of wine before she disappeared into her room. I bet I could stay out all night and she wouldn't even know the difference as long as I was back before she got up in the morning. Hell, I could sneak in and out of my window. I could stay with Ryan all night; his dad can't get up and down the stairs at his house. No one would be the wiser.

After winter break Ashley went back to school and things were going pretty well for a while. One evening she and Laura got into another argument over whose night it was to do the dishes, and Ellen erupted. "You two are driving me crazy. Here I have given up my entire life for you and all you two can do is argue. I'm sick to death of it. You're so ungrateful for all I do for you. I just can't stand it anymore. Sometimes I just can't stand the thought of coming home to you two. If it isn't one thing, it's another. I hate my life and all the shit I have to put up with and the two of you just add to it. Thanks for nothing." Then she stormed out of the room. They stood looking at each other, unsure of what to do.

Ashley spoke up, "I'll do the dishes." She silently went to the sink. Laura looked at her sister, shocked, then took a deep breath. "I'll help you." They did them in silence, afraid to make a sound.

After they finished, they ended up in Ashley's room. She turned on some Ozzy Osbourne, and Laura sat on the bed. "Ash, do you think mom really hates us?"

"Not deep down, I think she's just unhappy right now." Ashley fumbled with the cassette tape holder.

"But it's our fault, because she had to give up everything." Laura searched her sister's eyes.

"I don't know. I mean we didn't ask to be born; that was her decision. So don't take it to heart OK? We didn't ask to be here. She brought us here, OK? So don't worry." Ashley smiled grimly.

Ashley started to stay at her grandparents one night during the week; they lived in town and got cable. In the mornings they left for work before Ashley had to leave for school, so she started to raid her grandfather's liquor cabinet, mixing it with Pepsi, so she could carry it into school and share it with a couple of her friends. She got away with it for quite a while. No one was the wiser. One spring day she and two friends were sitting in the hallway by the Spanish room. She opened the Pepsi bottle and took a drink.

"Man, this is strong today." She passed it to her friend.

"Thanks for the drink today, Ash. Oh, it is strong." She passed it to Karen.

Karen took a drink and gave it back to Ashley. "Ah, yeah, but it's good." Suddenly Mr. Mills walked by them. He paused momentarily and then entered the Spanish room.

Immediately Ashley exclaimed, "We're busted!"

Almost instantly Mr. Mills reappeared towering over the seated girls. "Hello, young ladies. Could I please see that Pepsi bottle?" He held out his hand and Ashley gave it to him without hesitation and he smelled the contents and frowned. "Please come with me." The trio stood up.

Ashley spoke up, "Mr. Mills, they didn't have any. It was all mine, honest." She tried to look as truthful as possible.

He looked at the other two girls. "Is that the truth?" "Yeah, that's the truth," they replied in unison.

He hesitated for a moment, looking hard at them. "OK, you can go. Come on Ashley." He held his hand out towards the office. One of the other girls touched Ashley's hand as she went with Mr. Mills, as if saying thank you. They walked towards the main office in silence, and upon entering his office Ashley took her usual seat.

"Ashley, what is going on with you? Where are you living now?" He asked.

"With my mom."

"How's it going?"

"It's OK I guess." Ashley's leg bounced up and down.

"You need to stop acting out like this. Don't you think this is a problem? I feel this is just the tip of the ice burg and there is a lot more going on with you. I'm going to stick to you like white on rice. You're going to have to clean up your act. Got it? Now I'm suspending you for three days and to get back in school, we have to meet with your mother." He folded his hands together on top of his desk.

"No, please, Mr. Mills. Please just suspend me for like a week or something. Please don't get her involved. You don't understand. It won't go good for me if you get her involved, please." Ashley wrinkled her brow and tilted her head.

"Ashley, your mother needs to be aware of your behavior. I think you're headed for a disaster. You need some help from somewhere." He leaned back in his chair.

"Oh, and you actually think she's going to help me; that's a laugh." Ashley shook her head, then looked at the floor.

"I'm going to go get the nurse to take you home because you've been drinking. So sit tight I'll be back in a few minutes." He got up and left the office, leaving the Pepsi bottle on the file cabinet. Ashley looked at it and thought well they're taking me home anyway. She got up, went over, and slammed the whole bottle. After waiting a few minutes she got frustrated and left the office. She thought screw them, and she went to the bathroom where she bummed a smoke. After a few puffs she calmed down and just sat on the sink countertop waiting for the nurse to find her. Maybe I shouldn't have downed all that whiskey because it was enough for three people, and it was starting to hit her. In front of the girls in the bathroom Ashley cracked jokes and laughed; she made fun of the teachers and other adults. By the time the nurse caught up to her, she was smashed. The car ride home, however, was a different story. Ashley told her how horrible her home life was and became so upset she cried, telling the nurse about how she missed her father, how he didn't love her, and no one loved her. She was a terrible person, everything she touched turned to shit, and how was she supposed to go on like this. When would it end? The nurse had reservations about leaving her alone but elected to in the end, feeling it was mainly the alcohol talking. Although they were aware that she was tossed back and forth between her parents' homes, there wasn't much they could do.

CHAPTER 11

Ashley stood at the kitchen window watching the school nurse pull out of their long driveway, thinking I can't believe I told her all that personal stuff. Whatever they didn't know about my family they sure know now. She will probably go back and fill the vice-principal in on everything I told her. I'm such a fucking loser. Standing there staring out the window, her thoughts quickly changed as to how she was supposed to tell her mother she was thrown out of school, for drinking no less. It was a Friday so she had the whole weekend to tell her. She thought I'll wait until Sunday night. No sense ruining the whole weekend.

On the countertop was a paring knife. Ashley just stared at it for a while, then calmly took it into her room. First thing, she turned on some Ozzy, hoping it would soothe her, then plopped down on her bed. As she passed the knife from hand to hand, and watched it glimmer in the sunlight, she was deciding whether to use it or not. Eventually she tried to cut the veins in her wrists. Frustrated that they kept rolling out of the way, she stopped. She stared at the scratches left behind. Yet watched the tiny droplets of blood drizzle down the sides of the eight little lines. Strangely, it made her feel a little better. It released some of her tension. It was relaxing in a sense. The knife fell off the bed and clanked on a plate on the floor, bringing her out of the trance like state she was in. She looked at her wrist and thought I must be going crazy. This is crazy. What am I doing to myself? She cleaned up the cuts and thought how am I going to hide this from my mother, and work. Shit, I'm in big trouble. Slitting my wrists is not the way to kill myself; it's just too hard. Those damn veins just kept rolling out of the way.

The clock read 2:00 pm and her mother wouldn't be home for another few hours, but Laura would be home soon. Mentally exhausted and still feeling the effects of the alcohol, Ashley quickly brushed her teeth, climbed in bed and hid herself under the covers hoping to fall asleep before her sister arrived home. The awful truth was that Ashley wanted to go to sleep and never wake up. She knew her mother was going to freak out over her suspension and she couldn't escape to her father's house. There was no easy way to break the news to her, but at least she wouldn't hit her. She was almost certain about that. She couldn't help but wonder what exactly the principal wanted to talk to her mother about. Her parents and the teachers had no idea of what went on with her as far as what she did and what she thought about. If they did, she thought they would lock her up for sure. That's never going to happen, she's not telling them a thing. If they found out about the plan to off myself after graduation, they would try to stop her. What's the point in telling, if you really want to die.

The weekend seemed unusually tedious. Ashley managed to work Saturday night without anyone noticing her wrists. She lucked out and had that Sunday off. Back at home the atmosphere in the house was calm, so that Sunday afternoon Ashley approached her mother. "Mom, I need to talk to you." She fidgeted with her hands

"Sure, honey, what's up?" Ellen sat at the table.

"Well, uh… Friday. I uh.. I got uh…I got suspended." Ashley nervously gritted her teeth and wrinkled her brow.

"You what?" Ellen's eyes got wide. "Why? What the hell did you do now?" Her nostrils flared.

Ashley took in a deep breath. "I got caught drinking." She looked at the floor.

"So for how long?"

"Well, that's the thing. They want you to have a meeting with them in order for me to get back into school." Ashley took in another deep breath, letting it out slowly.

"Why in the hell didn't you tell me Friday so I could've called that evening?" Ellen slammed her hand on the table.

"I don't know. I just figured it would be too late." Ashley shrugged. "Oh, you thought just like you thought it would be a good idea to drink in school. Your thinking is fucked up. Now I have to take time out of work to meet with these people over you and your great thinking. Good job genius. What are people going to think about me? Did you think about that, dumb ass?" Ellen was quiet for a few minutes, pacing the kitchen floor. "Well… I guess.. I'll have to take you to your grandparents tomorrow and see if I can get you in." Ellen put her hand to her head. "Now get the hell out of my sight." Ellen just shook her head.

Monday morning, expecting to set up the meeting, Ellen took Ashley to her grandparents. This way Ashley would be closer to the school, so Ellen wouldn't have to run all the way out to their house to get her. Ellen called Ashley around noon. "Well, they don't have time today, so we have to be there at 11am tomorrow." She hung up without waiting for a response.

After the call Ashley needed to clear her head, so she decided to go out for a walk. As she reached the end of her grandparent's street a car pulled up next to her and parked. Out popped Tim. "Hey, kiddo, how's it going?" He smiled.

"Wow, I can't believe I ran into you," Ashley smiled.

"Yeah, I heard you got into some trouble." Tim leaned against his car.

"What exactly did you hear?"

"You got caught drinking, then polished it off in the old guy's office and gave the nurse an earful on the way home." He wrinkled his brow.

"All that huh? Now I have to have a meeting with my mother no less, to get back in school. She is pissed off beyond belief. She's worried about what people will think of her. Not me. I'm just the problem."

"So what's going on upstairs,?" Tim looked in her eyes.

"I'm worried about what will happen at the meeting, what they will tell her about my behavior? What if I cry or something?"

"What if you do? What's so bad about that?" Tim shrugged his shoulders.

"I can't. That's showing weakness. I can't show that. You don't understand my family." Ashley shook her head from side to side. They continued to talk for an hour or so. Ashley expressed she was feeling a little down. As they were talking, Tim noticed she was wearing wrist bands. "Are those part of the outfit or are they hiding something?" He pointed to her wrists.

She laughed nervously. "They're nothing." She looked at the ground. Tim wasn't sure he believed her, but he let it slide. Making a mental note, to get a good look when she wasn't wearing them. "You know I'm here to help."

"I know. I just need to get my shit together. If my mom throws me out, I don't have anywhere to go." Ashley kicked at the gravel on the side of the street.

"Don't you think if she were going to throw you out, she would have already done it? I mean she is willing to go to this meeting. You can bring up that you're seeing me. That could work for you. It shows that you're trying to help yourself. How's that sound to you?" Tim raised his eyebrow, trying to look hopeful.

"Yeah, that might help. Thanks." She smiled.

"At least I got a smile. Don't worry. It will work out, trust me. They aren't going to kill you or sacrifice you or send you to prison. OK?" Tim cocked his head making eye contact and smiled.

Ashley's first thought was, I wish they would kill me, but she elected to keep it to herself. "Thanks for talking with me. I feel better. Listen, I've got to get going. My mom will be picking me up soon, and if she has to wait, I'll be in even more trouble." Ashley grimly smiled.

"You're welcome. I was glad to do it. You're worth it. I'll see you at school and make sure you stop by and tell me how your meeting went with the old guys. Catch you later." Tim nodded his head as he got in his car. Ashley watched him drive away until he was out of sight. She lit a cigarette and started to walk the short distance to her grandparent's house.

Actually her mother wouldn't be picking her up for about an hour, but she wanted some time, to think about their talk, plus she really wanted a smoke. Tim was cool with some of the older kids smoking, but he didn't allow her to smoke. She thought it was unfair but they were two years older. To look at her, Ashley was often mistaken for 12- 13 years of age, so she kind of understood why Tim didn't allow her to smoke. But she often thought, what a curse to look so young.

On the way back to her grandparent's house, she decided to tell her mother about running into Tim. She thought that her mom would be glad that she talked to someone about the situation she was in. He had given her a different perspective and helped her feel better about it. Overall she figured her mother would be happy that she had met up with him and talked about everything.

As Ashley sat on her grandparent's front porch waiting for her mother, she had another quick smoke. Realizing her mother would be there soon, she threw her smoke away. About a half minute later her car turned up the street. Ashley got an upset stomach at the site of her. She pulled up and Ashley jumped in with a small smile. "Hi mom," testing the atmosphere.

"Hey." She gave her a glance and then looked straight ahead. "Mom, I want you to know that I'm really sorry for what I did. I know it was wrong and I promise it won't ever happen again." Ashley glanced over at her mother, then looked at the floor. Her mother said nothing. "Look, today after you called. I went for a walk and I ran into Tim, my counselor. Well, we talked for like over an hour and it really made me feel better…"

"So you went out socializing while I'm at work, trying to get your ass back in school. Well, it must be nice to be able to just go out and do as you please. What do you think people think about me, huh!!? Do you have any idea!!? I'm working my ass off and you're going off and having a friendly little chat. Well, isn't that just great! I'm so glad that you feel better. People are thinking what a shitty parent I am. That's what they're thinking. I can't change that because of you. You messed everything up. Thanks. But, I'm so happy you feel better. After all, it's all about you, isn't it?" Ellen looked straight ahead.

Ashley's good feeling went straight out the window and, she immediately thought about ending it all. After all, her apology wasn't good enough. Nothing she did was good enough. Upon arriving home she went straight to her room and turned on her most depressing music. Later that night, in secrecy, she cried her eyes out.

As she led the way to the office Tuesday morning, Ashley felt nervous and alone. It was her against them. After the initial greeting they were led into the principal's office. When they sat down, Ellen offered to hold Ashley's hand. She looked at her mother, confused, thinking you hate me. Why lie about it like we're some united front. You wouldn't even talk to me this morning and now you want to hold my hand.

Mr. Mills started off first by explaining how serious underage drinking was, and all of the problems Ashley had. How he thought she had a serious problem. That maybe she should be sent to a treatment center. Out of nowhere, Ellen jumped to her daughter's defense explaining that she was just experimenting, doing the same thing that many teenagers do.

Meanwhile, Ashley had started staring off into the distance, wanting to be anywhere but there. She started to stare at the wall and it mesmerized her. She lost track of what was going on in the office. She lost track of her mother's words. All that she heard was the voice in the back of her mind. Was it her mind? It didn't matter. It was relaxed and soothing asking her to just listen, saying it would all work out. It was her against them. They didn't understand her, they were not there to help her, they were the enemy and not to be trusted.

"Ashley, Ashley. "Startled she looked up, coming out of almost a dream state. She felt insulated against them, and unaware of what exactly they wanted from her.

"Well, what do you think we should do?" Mr. Mills asked folding his hands across his lap, looking directly at her. They were all looking in her direction waiting for a response. She glanced at her mother trying to read if she supported her or not. She heard the voice of her mind again, telling her to tell them, "If you allow me to come back to school, I promise I'll never drink in school again. I will do better overall. I'll make a solid effort to do a better job in all areas. Finals are coming up and I need to be able to take them to pass on to my senior year. Believe it or not, I want to graduate. Plus, I'll keep seeing Tim on a regular basis. I'll do better, I really will." Ashley opened her eyes wide trying to look honest and sincere.

"Why don't you go out and wait in the conference room while we talk to your mother for a few minutes?" Mr. Mills opened the door for Ashley and she left the room. Ashley sat in the conference room, waiting, trying to make sense out of what just happened. She also decided not to tell anyone about the weird mind voice thing. Most likely she thought deep down everyone has a mind voice. Maybe it was just because she smoked up a little before she came this morning. She wasn't sure.

Ellen led the pack walking out to the conference room. They entered and explained to Ashley she would be allowed to return to school, but they would be watching her closely. Any further behavior problems would lead to her direct suspension and she would not be able to return until the following year. This meant she would have to repeat her junior year again, and she would not graduate with her class.

"OK, I'll be on my best behavior. You'll see. I won't screw up anymore, I promise," Ashley let out a huge sigh.

"OK, then. It's 5th hour. Why don't you go on to class?" Mr. Mills shook his head.

Ellen smiled at her daughter. "All right I'll see you at home. Have a good day honey."

Kim and Ashley sat together as usual on the long bus ride home. She filled her in on the meeting, telling her how she zoned out. Telling how her mother was so mean, yet when they went into the meeting, she jumped to Ashley's defense, especially when it came down to sending her away. She asked Kim, "You think that makes her look like an unfit parent, you know, to send me away?"

"I'm not sure. I mean it could go either way." She shrugged. "Yeah, you're right. She would probably look at it like it was a bad thing, like she did something wrong. It's always about how it affects her, how she looks to other people." "Yeah, that sucks."

"But it worked out for me because I definitely don't want to be sent off somewhere." Ashley smiled.

The minute Ashley arrived home she placed a call to Ryan at work begging him to pick her up as soon as he could. She wanted to avoid running into her mother. Forty-five minutes later almost to the minute Ryan was pulling in the driveway. He must have gotten off the phone and immediately jumped in his car to make it there so quickly. Ashley was waiting by the back door having left a note for her mother.

She hopped into the car. "Thanks for coming so soon." She leaned over to kiss him.

"What's going on? What happened today at the meeting?" He asked as he started to back out, heading up to the bluffs.

"They actually told my mother that maybe she should think about sending me away to a place for kids with problems and with drinking. Can you believe that? "She shook her head. "Most of the time I was in there I just zoned out. I didn't want to listen to their bullshit." She got out a cigarette, lit it and then rolled down the window a little to blow the smoke out. "So, anyway you know how mean my mom has been to me. But as we walked in the office she offered her hand to me. I'm like you've got to be kidding me. Oh, it gets better. The principal talks about me going away and she jumps to my defense, I'm confused as to where she stands. Does she hate me or what? I thought I ruined her life, and now she jumped to my defense. I'm not sure how she'll be when she gets home." She shrugged her shoulders looking at Ryan for some advice.

"Well, you can't avoid her forever. It sounds like she's on your side. I think you need to go back home before she has a lot to drink and gets clouded. Your mom does love you, so you need to talk to her. I'll take you back home and we can get back together later. I'll just show up later." Ryan leaned over, and kissed her and, then took her home.

When they pulled in the driveway, Ellen's car was already there. Ashley's stomach immediately twisted into knots. She took a few deep breaths, kissed Ryan goodbye and quietly entered the house, only to hear her mother on the phone yelling, "… They said if you were in her life maybe she wouldn't be acting out like this. She needs her father….

I realize she left, but she is still your daughter. She still needs you. Hell Rodger, she's a kid …. Oh yeah right, like you're so perfect,… Look I thought I would call you and tell you our daughter is acting out and needs help. Obviously you don't give a shit, so goodbye." Ellen slammed down the receiver.

Ashley stood frozen unsure of what to do. Quietly, she crept back outside. With this new information she thought about what she wanted to say to her mother. Ashley slammed the door and walked into the kitchen, and found her mother seated at the table. "Hi, mom. How was your day?… Listen, I wanted to thank you for coming to my defense today in the office; It meant a lot to me. I'm grateful that you're my mom and I love you. Thanks." Ashley smiled at her mother hoping she would be receptive to her comment.

Ellen looked into Ashley's eyes. "You know I love you, right?" Ashley shook her head. " I need you to be straight with me…Do you think you have a drinking problem? I mean in all honesty, do you?"

"No, mom. We were just being stupid. I don't drink very often, in fact hardly ever," Ashley sat down next to her mother putting her hands on the table.

"What about drugs? How often do you use them? They told me they think you use drugs, a lot. Honey, this is important really important. It's not about me or what people think about me. This is your life and your future. They made me see that, and maybe I'm not the best role model for you at times. Maybe all of this with your dad is too much for you to handle and you would benefit going somewhere that could help you deal with all of this. They think you are very depressed. I mean, what do you think about all of this?"

"I don't know. I do feel kind of down at times. But I don't think I need to be sent away." Ashley started to tear up. "Mom, I don't want to go anywhere away from you. That would make me feel worse than I already do."

"So you are depressed." Ellen reached over and held her hands. "Is there something I can do to make you feel better?" She looked into her daughter's eyes.

"You're doing it right now; just being here for me, makes me feel not so alone." Ashley gave a weak smile.

"Oh, honey, I love you so much." Ellen reached over and hugged her tightly.

"I know you do." Ashley hugged her back. "I love you too. Please don't send me away."

Laura was watching unseen from down the hall, tears streaming down her cheeks. She was unsure of whether to go out or to stay back. She had always tried to follow in Ashley's footsteps, although she knew her sister's behavior this time was unacceptable and wrong. Laura was a good kid, headed to college. She had wanted to be a vet since she was about five and wouldn't do anything to ruin her plans. After gathering herself, Laura joined them in the kitchen. "Hey, you two. What's going on?" Laura stood between them, "How'd the meeting go?"

"It went pretty good. I got back in, and I have to be on my best behavior." Ashley shook her head.

"Yeah, but you'll be OK. It shouldn't be that hard. Besides there isn't that much longer you have to go, another month and a half or so. You can do that on your head, right?" Ellen looked at Ashley.

"Yep, no problem. I'm going to study my brains out. Prove to all of them, that they made the right decision. So don't worry, mom, I won't let you down, I promise." Ashley smiled and let out a deep sigh while secretly thinking, yeah, I'm going to get good grades but then after I graduate it will all be over, finally. Just one more year. I will have accomplished something and then I can be done with it all. Man, I sure hope I can wait that long.

Later that evening Ryan showed up as promised. He and Ashley wound up at the Bluffs again. It was their spot; they felt safe there. She filled him in on the phone call she overheard and the talk she had with her mother. Ryan's main comment was, "I told you she loved you even though she has a weird way going about it sometimes." Ashley agreed with Ryan's point of view in the end but still couldn't forget how her mother had treated her earlier in the week. "But I'm going to study hard and pass those exams with flying colors," she told Ryan with determination in her voice.

"Good for you. Then if you decide to go on to college, it will help." He shook his head.

"Yeah." She stared out over the lake. "We probably should get going."

"OK. I'll take you home." Ryan started the car and headed out towards home.

Over the next few weeks Ashley kept her word. She stayed out of trouble and hit the books with a new sense of resolve. Mr. Mills seemed to be sticking to her like white on rice, just as promised. But she wasn't going to give him a hard time. Deep down she knew he only wanted her to succeed. If she needed someone to talk to and Tim wasn't available, she got a pass to Mrs. B's room. That was the one room in school where Ashley really felt like she fit in, like no one judged her. Mrs. B just had this way about her; she made everyone feel important. There were also a few other teachers that were very good to Ashley. Like her art teacher, she continually let Ashley spend extra time in her room. Ashley could also talk to her and she always seemed to cheer her up. Plus Ashley really enjoyed art class, it always seemed to relieve her anxiety, giving her some peace inside. These teachers understood she had a troubled home life and tried to help. Overall, things seemed to be turning around for Ashley. With finals just around the corner, she was in the home stretch for the year. Soon this year with all of its pit falls, would be a distant memory.

CHAPTER 12

*T*here was a knock on her bedroom door, Ashley quickly put out her cigarette. "Uh...Just a second." She fanned the smoke as best she could. "Come on in," as she sat back down to her school books scattered all over her desk.

"Hey, how's it going?" her mother smirked." I see you're studying hard. Look, I know you're smoking. I don't really agree with it but if you're going to do it, you're going to do it, so you don't have to hide it. Anyways, you got a letter in the mail today." She handed it to her.

"Who's it from?" She took it, examining the envelope.

"I don't know. There was no return address on it." Ellen stood in the doorway.

Ashley opened it. "It's from Ruth." She read the letter which basically said Ruth missed her and felt badly how things went between them. She wanted her father and Ashley to make up, that this was not the way things should be between a father and daughter. She missed all of their talks and shopping trips, not to mention how much Michael missed her. Their home was not the same without her, and she was very sorry for taking advantage of her by making her watch the baby all of the time. Would she please give them a call sometime soon? They loved her. Ashley told her mother about what they said. Ellen remarked, "I think you should try and rebuild the relationship if you want to and if you don't want to go over there alone take Laura with you. After all, he was like a father to her for many years too."

After her mother left later in the day, she wasted no time in placing a call to her father's house. He answered, "Yeah."

"Hi, dad, it's me Ash," she offered all hopeful, twirling the phone cord around her finger.

He had been drinking heavily after a miserable day at work. "Well, well, what made you decide to call? What do you want?" He took another swig off his beer.

"I got Ruth's letter today and thought…

"Letter, what letter? Ruth wrote you a letter? What the hell for?" He started screaming, "Ruth, Ruth. Come here. Now."

Ashley couldn't believe her ears; she just hung up the phone and ran to her room to cry in privacy. Crying in the presence of others just proved how weak you were in Ashley's mind, and that wasn't an option. Moments later she heard the phone ringing. She assumed it was probably Ruth to smooth over what just happened, but she wasn't going to fall for it. Laura answered the phone, then knocked on her sister's door. "Ash, Ruth's on the phone for you,"

"Tell her I don't want to talk to her. I got my answer."

Laura returned to the phone and then came back to her sister's door. "She said your dad just had a really bad day at work and he didn't mean what he said. He's so drunk he won't even remember. Honest, he doesn't mean it." Laura waited for a response.

"Just hang up the phone Laura; I don't want to talk to them."

Laura talked to Ruth for a few minutes and then hung up. She stood outside Ashley's door. "Ash, what did he say to you?"

"He asked what the hell did I call for. You know what, I hate him," Laura stood outside her door. "He was drunk, Ash. You know when he's drinking he can be mean and when he's sober he's different."

"I don't care I've given him enough chances. Just go away." Ashley turned up her music drowning out any possibility of conversation, and she just stayed in her room nursing her wounds.

At last finals week had come. Ashley needed to take the regents exams, which were the exams for accelerated courses in high school. She had buckled down the last quarter after goofing off most the year. She was feeling very stressed out, but knowledgeable. She realized this was the last push of the year, so she gave every effort she could muster, studying late into the night before each exam, and studying on her breaks at work. When she had completed the English, math and science regents, she was exhausted. That last Friday afternoon, instead of feeling exhilarated at the successful completion, she felt depleted and depressed.

On the bus ride home Ashley just stared out the window while everyone else laughed and joked with one another, they wrote carefree notes in their yearbooks and shared plans for their summers. Most of the students were going to a farewell party at Chimney Bluffs that night, she had gotten the night off work weeks in advance, knowing she would want to go and let loose.

When she and Laura were dropped off the bus they quietly walked home from the bus stop, Ellen pulled in the driveway shortly afterwards.

"Mom, you're home kinda early," Ashley remarked.

"Well, I had a horrendous day; I just had to get out of that place! Let me tell you those people can drive you crazy at times." She started to look around the house. "You know now that you two are done with school for the year, this house needs a good cleaning, and I mean cleaning. Wash the walls and windows and steam clean the rugs, and a good scrubbing of the floors, plus we should wash the curtains. Besides it will keep you busy while I'm at work; that way we can relax in the place, you know what I mean." She looked at the girls satisfied with herself. Ashley couldn't believe her ears. She hadn't even asked them about how their tests went or even how their last day went and she had already put them to work for the next couple of weeks, and she thought what the hell are we, her slaves?

She cleared her throat and just went for it, "Mom, there's a party at the Bluffs tonight. Can I go with Ryan? I don't want to stay too long or anything, just say goodbye to some of my friends I didn't get a chance to see at school today." Ashley looked wide eyed at her.

"I don't know. There's a lot of drinking at those parties and the trouble you got into. You've just straightened yourself out." Ellen pursed her lips.

"Mom, I need to let off some steam. I'm stressed from all the tests. Please." She held out her hands and took in a huge breath.

"Let me think about it," Ellen sighed heavily, as she turned and walked away.

Ashley looked at Laura. "She better let me go. I freaking did everything I was supposed to do."

"I think you should be able to go. In fact, I think you should take me with you." Laura shook her head up and down smiling from ear to ear, looking satisfied with herself.

"Yeah, like that's going to happen," she laughed.

"Why not? I'll be a freshman next year."

"Right, next year, not this year. You're too young." Ashley pointed at her.

"That's not fair, Ashley."

"Yeah, well life's not fair." Ashley turned and walked to her bedroom. Where she turned on some music and laid down. Her insides felt like they were going to explode. She felt like screaming, standing on the rooftop just screaming to the top of her lungs. No message just a primal scream, to get it all out before it ate her alive.

Minutes later Ellen stood at Ashley's door. "Hey, I thought about you going to the party and I don't think it's a good idea."

"But, why not? I did everything I was supposed to do; that's not fair." Ashley stood up.

"Just listen for a minute. I realize you did everything you were supposed to do and that was great. But now you're on the right path and it took you a while to get on that path. If you go to this party, there are going to be the wrong type of people at the party and you could very easily get sucked back into the wrong lifestyle. You have worked too long and hard to fall back now." Ellen looked her in the eye.

"Mom, everyone's going to be there."

"No, you're not going. That's it." Ellen turned and walked out. Ashley kicked the bed frame quietly muttering to herself, you fucking bitch. Then she went out and called Ryan asking him to come over. The longer she thought about what her mother said, the angrier she got. All she could do was pace back and forth trying to think. Finally she plopped down on the bed, holding her head in her hands. Just then there was a tap on her door, "Who's there?" she snapped.

"It's me, grumpy!" playfully replied Ryan as he opened the door. "Oh, I'm sorry; I didn't think you'd be here so soon. Come on in."

Ashley patted the bed next to where she sat.

"So what's up? You said your mom won't let you go tonight."

"Yeah but listen. I've got a plan. You hang out for like 45minutes and then head home. In like an hour I'll go to bed for the night and sneak out my window. You can pick me up, up the street and we can go to the party for a few hours and then I'll sneak back in, no harm done. She never checks on us….so what do you think?" Ashley sat shaking her head in satisfaction.

"I don't know, Ash; you really think you can get away with it?" Ryan clenched his teeth.

"Are you kidding? Its Friday night. She'll start drinking in a little while and forget all about me. Trust me, I know how she is."

"Well, OK, if you think it'll work."

"Oh, even better! Let's pretend we got in a fight. Yeah that's way better," Ashley chuckled. So they hung out for a while. Just before he was about to leave, they started to put their plan in motion. Ashley started to yell at Ryan and he back at her. They continued their argument all the way to his car. He even slammed the door and peeled out when leaving. Ashley couldn't have been prouder of him and their performance. Once inside, Ellen approached her. "Ash what happened? Why are you guys fighting?" She gently touched her arm.

"He can be such a jerk at times," Ashley sighed heavily shaking her head.

"What did he do?"

"I don't want to talk about it. Men are such pigs, and it's their way or no way. That's all I want to say about it, OK? Please just leave me alone." Ashley plopped down on the sofa to watch a little TV with Laura. Ellen returned to her room to study for her photography course.

Ashley's heart beat faster than the clock. She was deep in thought when her mother came out and opened a bottle of wine. Seizing the opportunity, she announced she had a headache and was going to go to bed. "Oh, let me get you some aspirin," Ellen replied.

"OK. "Ashley stood waiting for her mother. She reappeared with the bottle handing it to her. "Just take two, and then in four hours if you need more, you can take two more." Ellen returned to pouring her wine.

"Thanks, mom. Goodnight, I'll see you in the morning." Ashley walked to her room.

Once in her room she changed her clothes, fixed her bed to look like she was under the blankets, placed the aspirin on her nightstand, turned the radio on low, and grabbed her jacket. As she crept out the window, she sat on the sill with one leg in and one out thinking here goes nothing. Then she jumped, falling to her knees. She thought that's higher than I thought. How am I gonna get back in? Ah, I'll worry about that later. Brushing herself off and looking around, it was starting to get dark so she snuck along the fence line in the yard hoping no one would notice, hit the street and casually walked up to the meeting spot where Ryan was waiting. She hopped in the beast with a smile. "Hey I made it. You were freaking great earlier, and you really sounded like you were pissed off at me. Thanks. I hope you weren't waiting long." She reached over and kissed him.

"No, I went home and ate; checked on my dad," "How's he doing?"

"He's good. He went to bed for the night. I had to change the dressing on his bad foot, but otherwise he's fine." Ryan started the car and they were on their way.

"You're lucky your dad is pretty cool." Ashley lit a smoke. "Hey, what's in the paper bag?"

"Guess?"

"Beer." She opened it. "Oh, a twelve pack, cool." She grabbed a couple, opened them and handed one to Ryan.

"Thanks," Ryan answered.

The party was only about a 15 minute drive by back roads and was in full swing when they arrived. Soon after arriving Ashley met up with her girlfriends and Ryan got together with a group of the guys. They, however, would periodically check on each other. At one point Ashley told Ryan, "Hey, I'm going for a walk on the beach with the girls."

"OK, but don't be gone all night, like usual."

"No, I won't. I'll be back in like half an hour, I promise." She kissed him on the check, as he patted her backside and then she wandered off towards the beach.

"Hey, Ash, I'm glad you made it tonight. This party is rockin'.'" Karen took a drink of beer as they were walking. "Did I mention I had to sneak out? Ryan had to pick me up, up the street." Ashley laughed. Then she took out a smoke and lit it.

"Hey, do you have another one of those? I forgot mine at the car." Karen held out her hand.

"Actually that was my last one, but I have another pack in the car. I'll be right back." When she got up to the car, she grabbed her smokes and while shutting the door, she looked over towards the fire and scanned the crowd. Then she noticed Ryan with one of the cheerleaders hanging all over him. Stunned, she just stared at them. Finally her friends showed up. "Ash, what's going on? What's taking you so long?" Karen and Emily asked.

Ashley pointed in Ryan's direction. "Look, that bitch is hanging all over him, and he's just letting her. What the fuck?" Ashley stood with her mouth hung open. As they stood there, she kissed him on the cheek and he didn't push her away. "What should I do?"

"Oh, no way. What the hell?" Karen commented.

"Well we should watch them for a few minutes to see what exactly is going on. Let's not jump to any conclusions," Emily remarked, trying to be helpful.

"Try to calm down. Then casually walk up to them and ask what's going on, you mother fucker," Karen commented.

Ashley said, "I need a drink" as she walked towards the keg keeping him in her sight. She quickly slammed two beers along with her friends, then snuck up on Ryan and the girl. "Hey what's going on?" Ashley came from behind and stood directly in front of him while this cheerleader had her arm draped over his shoulder.

"Ash, you're back. This isn't what it looks like. She's just really drunk and I'm just helping her stand up, that's all." Ryan held out his hands. Then he let go of the girl passing her off to one of his friends.

"I saw her kissing you and you didn't seem to mind," Ashley pushed his chest.

The cheerleader hanging off another guy spoke up, slurring her words "You don't own him; he can do whatever he wants to."

Ashley marched over and popped her in the face; blood spurted from her nose instantly. She started crying out, "I can't believe you hit me, you barbarian!"

Ashley started yelling, "Barbarian!! Bitch, shut the fuck up or I'll hit you again. You deserved it, messing with my boyfriend."

Ryan pulled Ashley away from the girl as the crowd was gathering. "Calm down Ashley."

Ashley shook her head. "I can't fucking believe you!" and stormed off, Ryan on her heels. "Wait!! Wait! Ashley wait!!" He caught up to her. "I'm sorry, I'm sorry Ashley, please!!" They were away from the crowd, near his car. "Ash, I'm an asshole OK? I'm sorry, I shouldn't have let her hang on me. Please Ash listen? Look it's getting late. At least let me take you home, even if you never speak to me again. Listen to reason, you have to get home before your mom notices you're missing," Ryan pleaded.

"Fine, take me home but no talking to me on the way." Ashley got in the car, slamming the door. They rode home in silence, Ashley opened one of the beers he had bought earlier, and when it was time for her to get out she asked, "Are you going back to the party?"

Ryan looked her in the eye "No, I'll talk to you tomorrow."

Ashley frowned. "Yeah, right!" She snatched the remaining six pack and slammed the door. As she started toward the house she looked back and instead of going straight towards his house, Ryan turned at the corner. She figured he was heading back to the party. As she walked home she started to cry. How could he do that to her, not only cheat but do it in front of all their friends. And now he was headed back to the party without her. After taking a final swig, she threw the empty beer bottle smashing it on the ground.

Sticking close to the fence line Ashley staggered around to the back of the house. She looked around trying to figure out how to get back into her room. She decided to try standing on an old lawn chair; however, it crushed under her weight and caused her to fall down. She sat on the ground, very drunk by now. Then she thought about getting a ladder from the side of the house, it had been stored there since her grandfather repaired the roof this past spring. She grabbed the ladder and pulled, then pulled again and again. With one last big jerk, it freed itself off the brackets which caused her to fall backwards with the ladder on top of her. She shook her head, mumbled "shit" and then managed to get the ladder off of her. While she was trying to get the ladder, she made quite a bit of noise. Finally she dragged it to her window, placed it next to the window, climbed up, but then she couldn't get in because she couldn't cross over from the ladder to the window. So she swore a few more times, basically fell back down the ladder, placed it just up to her window so the top was just below the window opening. Finally she got back in her room safely. She breathed a sigh of relief, and then the light came on. "Hey what's going on?" Ellen stood in the doorway. She was beyond pissed because Ashley was out and obviously drunk, when she had told her she couldn't go out. This was definitely unacceptable behavior.

Ashley sat up on her bed. "Mom I don't want to get into this tonight."

"Well, too bad. I told you earlier you weren't allowed to go out tonight and you snuck out anyways. How in the hell am I supposed to trust you when you blatantly disobey my rules? What am I supposed to do with you? I've had it. That's it. You're grounded for three weeks. You have to stay home and clean this house top to bottom. No friends, no Ryan, no phone, no guests, I mean it… you got it?" Ellen stood glaring at her daughter.

"Yeah, I got it," Ashley moved up and sat on the headboard of her bed thinking about bringing up what happened with Ryan. "Mom.."

"Just go to bed. We'll finish talking about this in the morning." Ellen marched away.

As Ashley watched her mother leave, her heart sank in her chest: loneliness and despair crept in. When she finally glanced over at the clock, it read 11:47. She thought damn, it's still early. No wonder he went back to the party; it must have taken me at least half an hour just to get back in the damn house. She laid down trying to relax, not even bothering to change, but she was restless so she changed the music. The more she tried not to think about everything, the more it raced through her head. How could he do that to her and now she couldn't talk to him. In fact, she couldn't talk to anyone, not even Kim around the corner. Why was it that every relationship she had turned to shit: the one with her dad and now Ryan, plus who knows what her mother was going to do in the long run. What if she threw her out again? Where would she go. Her father hated her. She couldn't talk to Tim. He was off for the whole summer. Hell, she wasn't even allowed to use the phone. She was totally isolated, just her and her thoughts, all alone.

Ashley's heart was aching and her head started pounding. Tears streamed down her cheeks. She looked over and noticed the bottle of aspirin. She remembered her mother's voice saying take two every four hours. She thought about taking them. Not two or four but the whole bottle. That would be it: no more problems, no more heart ache, no more rules to follow, no more anything, just her with God. Surely he would forgive her for killing herself. I want Him to hold me, take away the hurt, the pain, and the loneliness. I'm tired of being so depressed. While the other girls smile and fix their hair in the mirror, I secretly scream I'm going to kill myself. They ask what are your plans for the day. She thought I don't want to wait until I graduate. That's just too long. I just can't hold on any longer. What's the difference between waiting and doing it now? then Ryan's voice, 'Wait, Wait" streamed through her head. Screw you buddy she thought, screw all of you. No one understands, no one listens. They won't even miss me. She started to cry.

She sat and thought and thought about taking all the aspirin. Her insides were aching. Then she realized she needed the beer which was outside. Quietly she snuck outside. Once safely back in her room, she cracked opened the first beer, fumbled with the bottle of aspirin, pouring out five in her hand. She popped them into her mouth, then guzzled the beer all the while staring at herself in the mirror telling herself she was doing the right thing. As she swallowed more and more aspirin the tears streamed down her face. A small part of her felt strangely powerful. After swallowing about 35 aspirin and drinking two beers, she started to gag more and more with each swallow, so she decided to take a break. It had only taken about 10 minutes to take the 35. She examined the bottle and it had about 75 more left. Determined to polish off the bottle of aspirin Ashley took a couple of deep breaths, poured 10 in her hand and swallowed them. Then she gagged and burped almost vomiting but managed to keep them down. She realized she just couldn't swallow any more. She wouldn't be able to keep them down. Then it hit her that she forgot to leave a note in her drunken state. What would she say? She got out a pen and paper and quickly scribbled a brief note,

"Mom, I'm sorry for being such a loser and always getting into trouble. I feel like no one really wants me around because I'm such a screw up. Your life will be better without me in it. And I'll be with God. He will make me feel loved and make the pain go away. My life on earth is just pain, loneliness and depression. I just can't take it anymore. I'm sorry."

Love Ashley

She started to cry. Through her tears she took the aspirin bottle and threw it against the wall spilling the remaining pills all over the floor. She finished her beer. Her plan was to remain in her room just listening to music and go to sleep forever, but she became even more restless and had run out of smokes. Quietly she crept out to the kitchen to grab a pack of her mother's out of the fridge. She discovered her mother's car keys on the counter. She stood frozen for a few moments thinking. Ryan came to her mind. She temporarily forgot about the overdose and thought how could he cheat on her. She decided to go confront him. So she grabbed the smokes, took the keys and quietly left the house. She started the car and left in a rush. She didn't even bother looking back. If she had, she would have seen her mother standing in the kitchen window cursing at her.

Driving down the road smoking a cigarette, she turned up the music and headed towards the party. She started thinking about what had gone on that evening and decided she really didn't want to go back to the party, not with all those people around. Then a sad song came on and she kept seeing large trees along the road go by, telling herself that was a good one. Finally she saw another huge tree in the distance; that's the one she told herself. Don't worry, it will all be done and over with before you know it. She sped up and her heart started racing as fast as the engine. She took a deep breath, braced herself for impact, closed her eyes just before hitting the tree. She screamed, "God please forgive me." Then crashed!!!! .

CHAPTER 13

*B*ack at the house Ellen started screaming, "I'm going to kill her, I can't believe she stole my car, half drunk at that. If she gets one scratch on it she's going to pay for it." With all the noise Laura woke up and wandered out to the kitchen. "What's wrong?"

"I'll tell you what's wrong. Your sister just took off in my car, DRUNK!!" Ellen slammed her hand down on the counter, all the while looking out the window.

"Oh, no," Laura turned to go back down the hall.

"Where are you going? Ellen shouted at her.

"I have to pee," Laura replied, "and don't yell at me. I didn't do anything." Her brow furrowed.

"I'm sorry, you're right. I'm going out of my mind right now." She half smiled at her.

After coming out of the bathroom, she passed by Ashley's room. She had left the light on and her music. Laura noticed the empty aspirin bottle on the floor with some of the pills scattered all over the floor. Confused, she immediately went in her sister's room, picked up the bottle, then she spotted the note on her bed. While reading it, her hands started shaking and she raced out to her mother. "Mom, mom," she screamed, thrusting the evidence into her hands.

Her mother took the bottle and read the note, then dropped them both and ran to the phone. She frantically dialed the police. "Hello, hello."

"Yes, what's the problem?" A female voice asked on the other end. "My daughter, she has taken an overdose of some pills and stole my car. I have no idea where she is. Oh my God, you've got to find her," Ellen desperately pleaded.

"Just try to relax ma'am. We'll send an officer out to your location," the calm voice answered as she took her address.

"But you've got to look for her," Ellen demanded. "What kind of vehicle is it?" The voice asked. "1985 black Thunderbird V-6 and it has a sunroof." "How long has she been gone?"

"About 5-10 minutes. Please hurry. We have to find her," "Try to relax ma'am, we're on our way."

Ashley slowly opened her eyes as if in a dream, but she quickly awoke to reality. She weakly looked around. The steering wheel lodged up into her chest, she couldn't move her legs; they were pinned. Her left arm was pinned tightly against her chest, but her right arm and hand were still free. She felt her face and touched the blood oozing out of all of the areas where pieces of the windshield had embedded itself. Breathing was labored and was becoming extremely painful. She put her head back against the seat and thought, I'm in big trouble. As bad as the car was, strangely enough the radio still worked keeping Ashley company as she lay there dying.

"Honey, did you hear that?" Alice asked her husband of fifty-two years.

Howard replied, "I'm sure it's nothing dear. Go back to bed." "But I'm sure I heard a big noise," she replied.

"You're always hearing things and it's never anything. Go back to sleep."

"I'm positive this time, honest," Alice kept insisting.

"You're not going to quit until I go look, are you?" Howard angrily cleared his throat.

Howard slowly got up, put on his slippers and house coat then shuffled downstairs all the while mumbling to himself. When he got to the front door, he noticed a light in the distance. Then he went out on the porch in the blackness of the night and saw a blinking light and smoke. He immediately knew a car had hit the old oak tree down the street. He screamed up to Alice, "Call the police. There's been an accident!" He started to run up to the car as fast as a 70 year old could run. Alice raced to the phone and completed the call. She started up towards the car herself in just her night clothes.

Ellen lit yet another cigarette while she paced the kitchen floor. She tried to remain calm while she waited for the police to arrive. Laura could hear her mumbling under her breath. She thought maybe she was praying although she had never heard her pray before. She looked at Laura half in a daze "We had better put on some clothes so we look presentable; this could be a long night." Ellen wandered off to her room.

After what seemed like an eternity, a police officer arrived, and took a report. As he was getting in his car to leave, a report came across his radio about a car crash. Ellen overheard and immediately peered into his window, begging him to radio his colleagues to find out if it was her daughter. The officer radioed back to get a description of the vehicle; however, they had not yet reached the scene so none was available. Ellen begged to ride along just in case but the officer denied her request, telling Ellen to wait by the phone. If it was her daughter, they would call.

As soon as Howard got to the car, he saw Ashley, her bloody head resting back against the seat. He thought, oh, no, she's dead. But just then she shifted her torso ever so slightly. He raced over to her, "Hey darlin' helps on the way. Don't worry, you're gonna be OK." He was panting from the short run. After surveying the scene, he felt like he was lying to the young girl, but he wanted to give her hope in her last moments.

Ashley opened her eyes as best she could and gazed up at Howard. "I can't move my legs," she whispered, gasping for air.

Alice rushed up to the car door. "Don't worry sweetie, you'll be just fine. The fire department's coming; they should be here any minute." She looked at her husband with her brow furrowed, just shaking her head from side to side. She too was panting heavily from the run. Howard tried to open the driver's door to no avail, knowing beforehand it wouldn't open, but he wanted to do something, anything, other than stand there helplessly.

The car was a mangled mess. Although there was no immediate danger of fire, the elderly couple stood there unsure of what to do. Alice took Howard's hand in hers and started to pray, "Dear Lord, please spare this child, forgive her of her trespass. Please, Lord, give this child your healing love. Let her have another chance at life. Dear God, please be merciful with her; she is so young, and her life is just beginning. Please, God, heal her, spare her. Thank you. Amen." The couple breathed a sigh of relief knowing they did all that they could.

Breaking through the darkness of the night came the bright lights and roaring sirens of the rescue team. Rescuers jumped off the trucks and immediately started to evaluate Ashley and what would have to be done to get her out and save her life. The captain rushed up to Ashley to assess her condition. He immediately called for a helicopter to airlift her to the city trauma center. Some of the firemen started to rip open the roof of the car trying to get to Ashley. Others surrounded Ashley and started an IV and placed a cervical collar around her neck. One of the team started to talk to her, getting her name and contact information. She struggled to communicate. Removing the car steering wheel from her chest took what seemed like forever, to Ashley. Her breathing was becoming more and more labored and she started to cough. They gently leaned her forward to put a backboard behind her back in case she had broken it. She kept crying out in pain as they freed her from her prison. They had to use the jaws of life again to remove the engine from her legs. Once free, they were able to get her onto the ground to stabilize her while waiting for the helicopter.

The police officer had no more than closed his car door when Ellen turned and raced inside to call her father, Jim, and briefly explain the circumstances. She had overheard the address of the accident and nothing was keeping her from her daughter. Within minutes Jim was on his way to pick Ellen up. While she waited, she paced, chain smoked, and mumbled to herself. Laura watched in disbelief, but finally she gained enough courage to state, "Mom, I want to go with you."

"No, you need to stay here," Ellen shook her head.

"But she's my sister." Laura looked intensely at her mother.

"Laura, it's a car wreck. I don't want that image in your head, OK." Ellen grabbed the back of her neck and tilted her head back, while groaning.

"But mom."

"But nothing. The answer is no. I'll call you if it's her. I uh… Oh, Grandpa's here. I gotta go. Love you." Ellen dashed out to the car, and Laura watched as her grandfather actually peeled out of the driveway. " Dad the address is only a few minutes away. It's just up here over the hill by Howard and Alice's place," Ellen sighed heavily.

"I know where it is. We'll be there in just a few minutes. Try to be positive. Maybe it isn't too bad." Jim clenched the steering wheel with both hands and punched the gas.

The ambulance had arrived ready to transport Ashley to a nearby field in order for the helicopter to land. The paramedics swiftly loaded her in with all of the equipment keeping her in a half-way stable condition. Ashley started coughing and crying out in pain. She had visibly broken her right lower leg, the bone protruding through. Her left arm was also broken and most likely several ribs. The paramedics stabilized her the best they could for her journey. Once loaded in the ambulance they started off for the half mile trip to the field for the waiting helicopter.

The police officer that had been at Ellen's house arrived moments before Ashley left and realized from the description of the car and victim, that this was the young girl he was looking for. He remembered she had taken an overdose and informed the team transporting Ashley. The officer needed to call Ellen. Then he would complete his report of the accident. He approached the elderly couple who were still watching the firemen clean up the wreckage. "Excuse me, but could I possibly use your phone to call her mother?" The officer asked.

"Oh, of course. No problem. Come with me; we live right over here." Howard gestured over towards his house, the only one in the vicinity. As Alice started to follow the both of them towards the house, a car pulled up to the scene and Ellen jumped out of the passenger seat. As soon as she saw the car she started screaming, "Where is she? Where is she? Is she OK?" Ellen frantically started to circle the car. "Where is she?" She grabbed one of the firemen, demanding an answer.

The police officer ran over to her. "Relax ma'am. She has been taken to the hospital."

"Where? How badly is she hurt?" Ellen's eyes were wide and tearful. "She's been airlifted to the city trauma center. She just left, but they're doing everything they can." The officer held her arms trying to keep her calm. By this time, Grandpa Jim had joined them and heard the officer.

"Airlifted! Oh my God, she's been airlifted!?" Ellen sank to her knees, took in a huge breath, then started to cry. Her father went over to her and took her up into his arms.

Jim took his daughter to the car and placed her inside. He returned to talk to the officer, in order to get some details.

Ellen sat there and continued to cry. "Where did I go so wrong? I'm an awful mother. I didn't listen to her enough. My baby wants to die. What am I going to do if she does die? Oh, God, help me." She continued to cry, and her father returned to the car. "OK, honey. I know where we're going. Just try to relax. We'll be there before you know it." He patted her arm and started off towards the hospital.

"Come on, kiddo, stay with me," the medic commanded Ashley, trying to keep her as alert as possible. "What's your name?"

"Ashley," she whispered, forcing out the words.

"How's your breathing?"

"It's hard, and it hurts to breathe in." She looked up at him.

"Can you feel your legs?" He looked into her eyes, softly touching her leg.

"Yeah, but I can't really move them. They hurt so bad, everything hurts." A tear streamed down her cheek.

"I'm sure, but don't worry. We'll be at the hospital in just a few more minutes. It doesn't take long in one of these puppies," the medic replied wanting to reassure her.

A flat bed truck arrived at the scene of the accident to haul the wreckage away, and Ryan was driving by on his way home from the party. He was stopped in order for the crew to hoist the car onto the truck. While he waited, he curiously watched, thinking, wow, somebody must be in bad shape to be in a wreck like that. It made him start thinking about Ashley's and his fight, how wrong he was and how important she was to him. He decided that he wanted to go over to her house and make up with her. He thought maybe he should wait until tomorrow. No, he decided, she was probably up stewing over it anyway. He would go over now. He looked at that car in pieces. What a mess, he thought. Finally the police allowed him to go on his way. He thought, thank God they didn't get him for drunk driving as he slowly pulled off.

When Ryan pulled in the driveway, he noticed all the lights were on. Laura met him at the door. "Oh, it's you. I was hoping it was my mom," Laura sighed heavily and motioned for him to come in. The two of them sat at the kitchen table. "You're not going to believe this."

"Why? What's going on?" Ryan looked puzzled.

"Ashley. She took an overdose, then took mom's car, and I think she crashed it. Anyway my mom left with grandpa a little while ago to go to a crash scene and she isn't back yet, so I'm guessing it was Ash that was in the car that crashed and they're on their way to the hospital." Laura just looked at Ryan.

"Oh, my God. I passed the accident on the way over here." Ryan's eyes got wide.

"Was it bad? You have to tell me." Laura pounded the table.

"Yeah, it was bad. They sawed up the car; it was in pieces. I didn't even recognize it as your mom's car. Oh, my God. What should we do? I don't know where they took her." Ryan took in a deep breath.

"I guess we have to wait for my mom to call us," Laura sighed.

When the helicopter landed, a trauma team was ready and waiting for Ashley as she entered the ER. They immediately did a cervical spine, and chest X-ray, along with blood work and IV's. She was rushed into the CT scan machine for chest and abdominal series, to help diagnose any unseen problems. She had punctured a lung and had to have a chest tube put in. She could only have a local anesthetic because of the overdose and drinking. Luckily she had no internal bleeding, just major bruising. They had to put a tube down her nose into her stomach to give her charcoal because of the overdose. They kept asking Ashley how many pills she took, finally she answered. She kept fading in and out of consciousness, vomiting up the pills and booze she had ingested. She continually cried out in pain, because they couldn't give her much of anything for the pain due to the overdose and drinking. Once she finally became somewhat stabilized they sent her to the x-ray department to x-ray her legs, pelvis, left arm, shoulder, facial bones series, another chest x-ray, abdominal and total spinal series.

While Ashley was in the x-ray department, Ellen and her father arrived. Rushing up to the counter, Ellen asked about Ashley. The intake nurse took their information and had them take a seat. Ellen paced the waiting room for what seemed like an eternity. Finally the doctor appeared and called them. He explained what they had done and that Ashley was stable but was in x-ray right now. They didn't yet know the extent of her injuries, but when she returned they could see her.

Finally Ellen placed a call to Laura. "Hey, kiddo. We're here at the hospital and she's in x-ray right now…"

"How is she?" Laura interrupted.

"Well, she's in rough shape, but she should be OK," Ellen tried to sound optimistic.

"Have you talked to her?"

"No, not yet," Ellen cleared her throat. "I don't even know if she's conscious."

"Ryan showed up. He said they had a huge fight," "Really? is he still there?" Ellen asked.

"Yeah, can he bring me up? Please, I want to see her," Laura begged. "Honey, not tonight. I don't think it's a good idea. Don't worry. You'll see her soon, I promise. Tell Ryan not to show up either. I want to talk to him first. We'll be home in a few hours. All right I've got to go. Love you. Bye honey." Ellen hung up then sighed heavily shaking her head.

Ellen and her father sat waiting. He had called Ellen's mother to let her know what had happened and finally a nurse came out and led them back to Ashley. She lay there unconscious, a tube down her nose from the overdose and on her side going in between two of her ribs was a chest tube it was draining into a bottle on the wall. Clearly her right leg was broken and her left arm, Ellen started to cry. Her father put his arm around her and they stood over her daughter, as if keeping watch, Ellen was bewildered and emotionally exhausted.

Finally the orthopedic doctor, Dr. Connelly, came in to discuss the extent of her injuries: her left arm was fractured, she had also broken her pelvis in two places, and she needed surgery to correct her broken leg. She had several broken ribs and cracked right clavicle. For some reason, wanting to kill herself, she still wore her seat belt which caused the last two injuries and probably helped save her life, the doctor commented. Anyway, she would be scheduled for surgery in the mid-afternoon, not now, due to the overdose and drinking. The tube down her nose was for the overdose and would come out, hopefully, the following day. All of the cuts on her face were from the broken windshield. Luckily, she had not broken any facial bones, but pieces of glass would continue to surface over the next few days and weeks. She had to have the chest tube. She would be moved upstairs on pediatrics within the hour and settled in with her nurse's aide by her side.

"Doctor, do you think she will wake up tonight?" Ellen asked

"Uh, probably not. She had a lot of alcohol in her system, and we pumped her stomach of most of the pills. She probably will sleep it off. Until we take another blood test to make sure she is not under the influence we don't want to give her too much of anything for the pain even though she's in need of it." He shook his head up and down, then turned and left.

Ellen looked at her father. "Well, do you think we should go home and come back in the morning?"

"Yeah, I think that would be OK. She will probably just sleep. You need to get some rest. Tomorrow's going to be a long day." Jim hugged his daughter. Ellen walked over to Ashley and kissed her forehead. She started to tear up again as they left the hospital.

When Ellen arrived home Laura had drifted off to sleep on the couch. She gently placed an afghan over her, and quietly crept into her room and collapsed onto her bed. Just the thought of all that had transpired that night was exhausting. Ellen kept asking herself what signs and symptoms had she missed. How could Ashley have been so depressed and she not even have had a clue. Then she sat straight upright. She had forgotten to call Ashley's father. Oh, God, how had she forgotten to call him? No use calling him at three in the morning; she would call first thing in the morning. She couldn't help but wonder if Ashley called him when she got the letter, and, if she did, how it went. Her mind was spinning. What went on with Ashley and Ryan? Did that push her over the edge. When Ash came home she wanted to talk and she refused to, telling her to wait until morning. Oh, God, if only she had talked to her, maybe she wouldn't have done this. She felt horrible.

Finally, after wrestling with her mind, Ellen fell into a restless sleep, tossing and turning, dreaming and dreaming all night.

In the early hours of the morning Ashley awoke for the first time; she gazed around and realized she was in the hospital, and in fact she had not died. She looked over at the nurse's aide sitting next to her bed; he was reading a book. She just drifted off back to sleep.

Ellen rose early in the morning feeling restless as she fixed her coffee. She was deciding exactly how to tell Rodger that his daughter tried to commit suicide last night. She took in a huge breath and let it out. Fidgeting with the cord, she started to dial the phone. She hung up half way through dialing, hanging her head. Come on Ellen you can do this. You have to do this. So she dialed again. It rang and rang then finally "Hello" in a gravelly voice "Hello, Rodger is that you? This is Ellen," Ellen asked hoping for the strength to do this.

"Yeah, Ellen, why are you calling so freaking early?" Rodger asked all irritated.

"Look, it's about Ashley…"

"What's wrong now! That girls got more problems. Did she do something? Is she in trouble?" Rodger sighed heavily.

"Rodger, she tried to kill herself last night and not a little try but a huge major try," Ellen replied all frustrated.

"What! Last night? Well, how is she? I mean she's OK right. What did she do?" Instantly Rodger's whole demeanor changed.

"She's at the trauma center in the city. First she overdosed and drank, then she stole my car and crashed into a tree. She had to be air lifted last night about midnight. I'm sorry I didn't call. She has several broken bones and needs surgery to correct some of them. I'm headed up to see her in about an hour. My father is loaning us his second car until I can get another one." Ellen breathed a sigh of relief. Talking to him wasn't as bad as she thought it was going to be.

"OK, Ellen, thanks for calling me, I'm sorry for being a jerk at first.

"Rodger swallowed his pride, out of concern for his daughter.

"No problem. Bye." Ellen hung up, thinking, oh, I so wanted to say you were always a jerk and I'm used to it. But after thinking about it, she was glad she held her tongue in the end especially because they would be seeing each other at the hospital, at least she hoped he would show up.

With the call over Ellen went on getting ready and decided to wake Laura. She found her in Ashley's room sitting on her bed. "What are you doing in here, honey?" Ellen asked quizzically.

"How could she do that? Just leave me… forever," Tears streamed down Laura's face.

"Oh, honey, I don't think she thought about anything like that. I think she was just in a lot of pain and she wanted it to stop. I don't think she wants to leave you though. She loves you." Ellen started to cry, along with her daughter. She went over and sat next to her, and she took Laura into her arms and held her tight rocking back and forth, humming ever so softly.

"Mom, why does she want to die?" Laura whispered through her tears.

"I don't know, but we'll get her help, OK" Ellen sniffled.

"I know this is terrible, but a part of me hates her. How could she do this? How could she want to leave me, forever?" Laura breathed heavily still partly crying.

"Honey, you're just really mad at her, and that's OK. She did a really drastic thing to a really temporary problem. She just didn't see any other way out, and she just wanted the pain to stop. You're allowed to be mad. That's OK you're entitled to your feelings. We will work this out as a family, I promise. Things will get better for all of us. Just hang in there. Look, today I want you to go to gram and pop's; it's going to be really hard at the hospital. She has to have surgery so she won't be with it anyway. Plus, I think you need some time to work through your feelings, and gram needs someone to spoil." Ellen held her daughter at arm's length and smiled warmly at her.

"Sounds good to me." Laura took in a deep breath and let it out. "Go get ready. They'll be here soon." Ellen got up along with Laura and they got ready.

"Ruthie. Ruthie you're not going to believe what's happened!!" Rodger went in and shook his wife awake.

"What's wrong?" she sat up straight.

"It's Ashley. She tried to kill herself last night. She's in the hospital." Rodger sat on the edge of the bed.

"Oh, my God, is she OK?" Ruth just looked at Rodger.

"Well, she's in rough shape from what her mother said. I gotta go see her. She's having surgery today to fix some of her broken bones. She actually crashed her mother's car into a tree." He sat shaking his head, "I'm not sure what to do?" He held out his hands.

"I'll tell you. We get dressed and get our butts up to that hospital. Come on, let's get going, I'll get some breakfast ready for us while you get ready. We'll drop the kids at my parents." Ruth jumped out of bed and rushed off to the kitchen. Rodger was lost in thought. Two minutes later Ruth yelled at him to get going and he did, but he was operating on autopilot.

CHAPTER 14

*T*he elevator doors opened onto the pediatric floor, to a calm and inviting atmosphere, however, Ellen didn't feel calm and she certainly didn't want to be there. As she made her way to her daughter's room, she knew her attitude had to be positive, so she took in a deep breath and resolved to be upbeat. Ellen quietly peeked around the corner as she entered the room; she was yet again taken aback by the sight of her daughter with cuts from the windshield all over her head, face and neck. The nasal/gastric tube was still in place which required Ashley's hands to be tied down so she could not pull it out while asleep. She had a chest tube in that drained into a device on the wall next to the bed, along with a catheter which drained her bladder, hanging onto the bed frame. On her left arm was a cast which rested onto a pillow. Her right lower leg had a cast on it, resting gently on the bed, Ellen thought she looked so pitiful laying there all busted up.

Ellen sat quietly next to the nurse's aide. She was about thirty and a tad overweight. Her glasses were red framed and her auburn hair was starting to gray. They exchanged hellos, and the aide went back to her reading.

Soon after Ellen sat down she took Ashley's hand and caressed it, hoping she would sense her presence even if she didn't wake up. Ellen hung her head low. The aide noticed and commented, "We get a lot of teens. It seems like they go crazy with all those hormones." She smiled grimly at Ellen.

"Really? Thanks, I just didn't see it. I had no idea she felt so bad." Ellen breathed a deep sigh. Having that little piece of knowledge would have seemed to make it a bit easier but it didn't. "So someone sits with her night and day?" Ellen asked more to make polite conversation than to search for answers.

"Yeah. She's never left alone even if she's asleep with no chance of waking up. We write down what she's doing every 30 minutes." The aide smiled. "By the way my name's Ann. You'll probably be seeing me quite a bit over the next few weeks."

"Oh I'm,...I'm so sorry. I'm Ellen, Ashley's mother I don't know where my manners are," Ellen shook her head.

"Don't be silly. This is a very traumatic time for you. Manners are the least of your worries; just try to take it one day at a time." Ann gently tapped her leg.

"Thanks. I'll try to take your advice." Ellen smiled as she rubbed her daughter's hand.

Within seconds in walked a team of doctors. Ellen was surprised by the sheer number of them. The head doctor took the chart and started to read, she guessed, what was, a number of different blood chemical levels that Ellen had no idea even existed. The group stood around conversing about what should and shouldn't be done. When they finally stopped talking in medical language, the head doctor introduced himself to Ellen and started to explain, "Your daughter is stable, but she still needs to have surgery to correct her right Tibia, which is the long bone in the lower leg. We are going to put a rod in it to help it heal. After it heals we'll take it out and it will naturally fill back in. Her pelvis is broken in a couple of places but it's non-displaced, so she'll be x-rayed every few weeks. The nurse will be in shortly to remove the N/G tube from her nose. We have her on some meds for pain and with all these broken bones, she'll need to be here for quite some time.

Luckily she had no internal injuries, just a lot of deep bruising. The chest tube is draining nicely and we'll check her lungs progress as it heals. Plus we have a service, which I highly recommend. It is a counselor for her to talk to every couple days while she's here." Dr. Connelly took in a breath and looked at Ellen over the top of his glasses, expecting an answer.

"Sounds good." Ellen nodded her head. "What time is she having surgery?"

"Well, she didn't take as many pills as we suspected, so probably within the next couple of hours." Dr. Connelly closed the chart and placed it back at the end of the bed. "Any more questions for now?"

He looked around at his students then Ellen with no reply he, shook his head and said, " Well if anything should come to mind ask the nurses to get in touch with me, good day to you we will talk later," He and the group left.

"Thank you," Ellen quickly replied, as they headed out the door. Within half an hour a nurse appeared. "Hi, I'm Cori, the R.N. who will be taking care of Ashley during the days." She buzzed around the room, checked on all of Ashley's gadgets and then changed her IV bag. "So are you her mother? She paused making eye contact.

"Yes, I'm Ellen." She bit her lip and shook her head.

Just then Ashley started to stir a bit, and her mother quickly took her hand as she woke up.

"Hey, baby, I'm right here. I love you. You've been through a lot but you're going to be OK." Ellen gazed into her eyes while she stroked her right arm.

"Hey, kiddo, I'm Cori. I'll be your nurse on days. How are you feeling?" She placed herself in Ashley's eye line.

"I'm thirsty, and I hurt all over," Ashley whispered her voice all gravely.

"I'm sure you do. You have been through World War Three kiddo" Cori smiled at her.

"Here, I'll untie you if you promise not to pull out your nasal tube." Cori looked at Ashley.

Ashley nodded her head ever so slightly.

"OK, then. I'll get you some ice chips because you have surgery in about an hour, so you can't have anything in your stomach. Also you need to push the button, right here on this, and that will deliver medicine to help with the pain. Go ahead, you're due." Cori showed Ashley how to operate the IV pain button and the call button. "In fact, why don't we take that blasted tube out of your nose. When I start to pull it out, you need to swallow." Cori gently took off the tape on Ashley's nose and started to pull and pull. "Swallow, hon. Swallow. Good." She continued to pull it out and wound it up as she did. Finally it was out. Ellen couldn't believe how long it was. Ashley took in a huge breath when it was out, and then Cori gave her some ice chips to suck on.

"That tube left a lot of gook in my throat," Ashley commented, forcing the words out.

"That's why I told you to swallow. Here, I'll give you one sip of water, but only one." Cori winked as she fetched the glass.

"Thank you." Ashley took a mouthful "That's much better, thanks." Her voice returning to normal, she smiled, closed her eyes and drifted off to sleep.

Cori looked at Ellen. "The medication makes them sleep; it's pretty strong."

"Thank you," Ellen nodded as Cori left the room.

Before long the surgery techs appeared, they decided to take her in her bed to transport her to surgery. Ellen kept pacing back and forth in Ashley's room, when Ann, the nurse's aide suggested that she go down to the cafeteria to get coffee and something to eat.

"Good idea. Can I get you anything?" Ellen inquired.

"Oh, thanks. I'm good."

Meanwhile Rodger and Ruth had dropped the kids off at her parents and were on their way to the hospital. Rodger was at the wheel, mainly on auto pilot. He was lost in thought. Ruth just didn't know if she should break the silence or leave him alone. For the first time in her marriage, she had no idea how to approach her husband. Hell, she didn't know how to approach Ashley, plus Ellen would be there. They were almost there and suddenly Rodger looked at Ruth bewildered, "I don't know what to say to her."

Ruth took in a deep breath. "Just tell her that you love her." "Then what?" He looked at her.

"I don't know. Tell her everything will be OK, that we'll work everything out, that you're not mad, make some sort of joke, you're good at that. Just be positive." She half smiled at him.

"OK, I can do that." He let out a huge breath as they pulled in the parking lot.

When they walked in, Rodger stopped in the gift shop and browsed around finally deciding on a word search puzzle and a flower arrangement with three white carnations and three red roses, with baby's breath and a couple other flowers in the mix. He came out looking like he was somewhat ready to do this.

"That's nice, honey." Ruth smiled at him.

"I can't go in there empty handed. I love her." Rodger half smiled as they made their way to the elevator.

After arriving on the pediatric floor, they popped into Ashley's room only to find it empty, except for Ann the aide that was assigned to watch over her. "Hi. Is this Ashley Ame's room?" Rodger asked, his brow furrowed.

"Yes it is. May I ask who you are?" Ann smiled. Rodger cleared his throat, "I'm…I'm her father."

"Oh, well she's still down in surgery, although she should be almost done. It's been a couple of hours now. Actually she's probably in recovery by now. Um, .I could call and find out if you want me to? At least I can find out how much longer she'll be down there." Ann got up waiting for a response.

"That would be great, but I don't want to cause a problem." Rodger waved his hand.

"Oh, it's no big deal." Ann got up and went out to the nurse's station. Within five minutes she returned. "Well, Ashley's in recovery. She should be returning within an hour so I'm going to grab a quick cup of coffee and I'll be right back. Do you know where the cafeteria is or do you want to wait here? Whatever you want to do is fine." Ann smiled as she picked up her purse and started to head out.

Rodger looked at Ruth and mouthed cafe'.' "Yeah, we'll go to the cafeteria; it's on the 2nd floor right?" He looked at Ann.

"Sure is. Is there anything else you folks need?" Ann smiled while standing at the door.

"No, we're good." They followed Ann out towards the cafeteria.

After Rodger and Ruth paid for their coffee and donuts they went to sit down when they spotted Ellen sitting by the window alone. "Do you think we should go sit with her?" Ruth asked unsure of what to do. "I'm not really in the mood to deal with her right now. I'm sure she'll blame this whole thing on me." Rodger sighed, then turned and took a seat on the other side of the café. The cafe was quite large but at this time it was virtually empty except for the employees who were cleaning up getting it ready for the noon rush. It wasn't long before Ellen noticed the two of them seated on the other side. She wondered if it was because they didn't want to talk to her, but they would have to sooner or later.

As she sat stirring her coffee, rage stirred in her. It kept brewing with each rotation of her spoon. She started to shake inside. She told herself to calm down but to no avail. She knew this rage was directed at her ex-husband. How could he have been so cruel to their daughter. Ellen wanted to go over and scream at him, questioning him how could he treat her so cruelly, beat her, be so insensitive to her, ignore her pleas for his attention, reject her and swear at her when she wanted to make up. Laura had filled her in on the phone call. Ashley had cried about it for hours, yet felt so ashamed she didn't mention it to her own mother. Ellen sat there starring at the two of them. They glanced back at her every few minutes or so. She felt as if they knew she wanted to scream at them. Finally Ellen couldn't take it anymore and got up with coffee in hand and walked over towards where they were sitting. Each step seemed to take place in slow motion, but her mind was spinning on overdrive.

Ellen glared at Rodger. "So you decided to show up, huh!! All of a sudden you decided to play father? You're a big part of the reason she's here, I hope you realize that!"

"Oh, and you're Mother Theresa, right?" Rodger glared right back at her. "You think you're so perfect. She was staying with you. How in the hell did you let this happen?"

"It's not like I let it happen. I can't watch her 24/7. She stole my car in the middle of the night." Ellen shook her head.

"Yeah, but she was already drunk. You let her go out and drink," he shot back.

"I didn't let shit happen. She snuck out for your information." "What were you drinking? Is that how she snuck out without you noticing?" Rodger sneered.

"Oh, you want to talk about drinking, like when you beat the shit out of her, drunk." Ellen glared at him.

Everyone in the cafe was looking at the trio.

"Hey.. hey you don't need to attack him. He's here now and that's what's important," Ruth stated looking in Ellen's eyes.

"Oh, you think that's going to fix everything?" Ellen frowned at her. "Well, no, but it's a start, and they have to start somewhere," Ruth replied.

"Look, don't start bitching at my wife just because you're mad at me." Rodger scowled.

"Don't tell me what to do, and I'm mad at you because of the way you treat your daughter," Ellen shook her head in disgust.

The trio were so involved with one another they failed to notice a security guard approach them. He was summoned by the staff of the cafe, as the arguing was becoming louder and louder. When the guard arrived on the scene, he just stood next to the trio for a few moments going unnoticed. Finally clearing his voice, "Excuse me folks. This is a hospital. You need to lower your voices and take this quarrel some place else or end it." Almost shocked, looking around, realizing what kind of scene they were causing, Ellen's face turned red, and Ruth felt her ears flush with warmth. They immediately apologized, "Were so sorry… our daughter has suffered an accident. We didn't realize…we were so loud. I'm sorry." Ellen clasped her hands raising them to her face.

"Officer, it won't happen again," Rodger stated. Ruth shook her head in agreement.

The security guard gave them the once over. "So I can leave you folks?" They nodded in agreement. He looked at them and stated, "I understand it can be tough when it comes to your kids. Good luck." He turned and walked away.

"We need to be calm. Blaming each other isn't going to help Ashley. We need to come together and support her, help her get through this. There's no changing the past. It won't help her if we're at each other's throats. We need to come together." Ruth gently grasped her throat and let out a heavy sigh. Ruth had always been the one to stand up for the children. It was as if their parent's hate for one another was stronger than their love for their children. Putting the children first seemed so hard for the two of them.

The trio stood silent for what seemed like forever, just staring at one another. Thinking about what had gone on a few moments ago in public was embarrassing and unacceptable. That type of behavior would have to stop, especially if they wanted Ashley to get better.

"Ruth is right. We need to get along, especially in front of Ash if we expect her to pull through this. I'm sorry." Rodger nodded his head.

"Yeah, I agree, we need to get along," Ellen added. But deep down she still felt this huge amount of anger and resentment towards her ex, but she knew she had to bury it for the time being.

It had been almost an hour since Rodger had arrived, so the trio decided to head upstairs hoping Ashley would be out of the recovery room and back in her room. Plus they wanted to get a report as to how it went and what was next.

When they arrived in her room, she was already there sleeping quietly with Ann sitting next to her. Her right lower leg had a cast on it and was resting on a pillow. Ashley slept for most of the day, only waking up to hit her pain button then nodding off again. Her parents sat with her until it was time to leave for the day.

Throughout the day Ellen had called her parents to update them as to Ashley's condition. When Ellen finally arrived at her parents to pick up Laura, she was exhausted. She only stayed briefly filling them in on what went on, stating she just wanted to go home, get something to eat, and then go to bed. They understood that she needed to get some rest. She filled Laura in on how Ashley was on the way home, and then they no sooner got home and Laura started in.

"Mom, please let me go with you tomorrow. I'll be good, I promise!" Laura begged.

"Honey, not yet. There will be plenty of time for you to go. She's going to be there a long time," Ellen replied.

"But I want to go."

"I know, but she's not even awake yet," Ellen answered.

"Please mom, I'll be good," Laura begged.

"Laura, no. Please stop! I don't need this right now." Ellen's eyes were wide, she gave Laura the look meaning if you don't stop you're going to be in deep shit, as she took in a deep breath.

"OK, OK. You don't need to yell at me."

"I'm sorry. It's just been a very long day, and she'll be in there a very long time. So I'll be making this trip for a very long time and I have to waste all of my vacation time from work to go see your sister." Ellen stood and stared out the kitchen window while she rubbed her forehead.

Laura sat silent knowing she should keep quiet, that her mother needed silence at this time. She had always been better at reading people and knowing what to do than Ashley, it was as if she had an old soul.

The house was strangely quiet without Ashley there. Laura was watching TV when her mother entered the living room. "Hey, have you talked to Ryan since the night of the accident?" Ellen inquired.

"No," Laura shook her head.

"I know you already told me basically what happened between the two of them that night, at least from his perspective, should I call him and let him know how she's doing?" Ellen queried.

"Yeah, I would. He really loves her, mom. That girl was hanging all over him, not the other way around and I think basically it was just a big misunderstanding. I don't think he realized just how important Ash was to him, until he found out it was she who was in the accident. I'm sure he'd be grateful for an update," Laura replied.

"You know, Laura, sometimes you give out the best advice. It's hard to believe you're so young." Ellen smiled at her daughter.

"Yeah, that's what I've been told." She smiled back, and then returned to her television program.

Ellen went over to the phone and dialed Ryan's number, "Hey, Ryan."

"Yeah."

"It's Ellen."

"Oh, how is she? Is she going to be OK?" Ryan asked nervously. "Well, she has several broken bones. She had to have surgery to put a rod in her right tibia, right lower leg broken and her left arm and pelvis are broken, and she has a chest tube. But, thankfully, she didn't have any internal organ injuries. The doctor said just bruising. Her face and neck are full of glass fragments, but they will work themselves out. Today she basically just slept so I didn't really talk to her. Laura told me what happened between you two that night. I hope you don't blame yourself." Ellen paused waiting for a reply.

"Yeah, Laura told me about the suicide attempt, I can't believe she did that, I would have never left her alone if I ever thought she was going to do something like that. Could you tell her I'm asking about her and I would like to come see her, you know, if she wants me to?" Ryan asked.

"Yeah, I can do that," Ellen answered. "OK, then, I'll talk to you in a few days."

"Thanks." Ryan hung up the phone feeling better. Before talking to Ellen, he had blamed Ashley's suicide attempt on himself, but now, as he thought about it, he realized it had to be a culmination of many things in her life that drove her over the edge. He still felt very deeply for her and hoped she would forgive his actions that terrible night. He knew she was going to be in the hospital a long time and after a while, even if she said no, he would just go visit. She would be a captive audience. She would have to listen to him.

Later that night Ellen couldn't sleep so she called her mother, Pat, to talk. She needed someone to talk to. Pat always seemed to have the time, patience and best advice going. She was a really good listener and always put a soft loving touch on her advice. It never seemed preachy or high handed. Even when Ellen was growing up, all of her friends went to her mother for help and advice. They always told her how lucky she was to have such a wonderful mother. While Ellen was on the phone she just completely broke down, wondering where she went wrong, how she could have missed the signs. She just cried and cried. Pat patiently waited while her daughter got those feelings out. Finally, after what seemed like forever, a deep sigh came and then another, cleansing breaths captured and released, starting to ease the pain inside. Pat conveyed to her daughter how she needed to heal herself before she could heal her daughter. How time, patience and a keen ear would be some of the best medicine Ashley could receive. Ellen went on to explain how the doctor recommended a psychologist for Ashley to talk to while she was there. As they talked, they agreed that Ashley definitely needed to talk to someone, a professional, someone she could trust, someone who would hopefully pull these deep hurtful feelings out and help her move on. After all, she was at the beginning of her life. She only had one more year of high school, then maybe, hopefully, college. Ellen paused and reflected for a moment "You know, mom, come to think about it, I never heard Ash talk about her future. It's almost like she has no plan for the future. Do you think she had this in mind for a long time? I mean Laura talks about her future constantly, but Ash never did. In fact, when the subject came up, she would just get a faraway look in her eye. I chalked it up to daydreaming, but now I wonder if she was planning to kill herself all along." Ellen sat wrapping and unwrapping the phone cord around her finger.

"Honey, it's hard to know what was going on in her mind. What matters now is that she gets the help she needs, and that she knows we're here for her," Pat calmly responded. "You could drive yourself crazy trying to figure out all the signs you missed. We need to stick with what is and what has to be done now. Know what I mean?"

"You're right. Thanks." Ellen took in a deep breath as if to clear out the bad atmosphere. As they talked Ellen became more at ease and finally was ready to get a good night's sleep.

The next couple of days were much like the first. Ashley basically slept, only waking long enough to press the button for pain and then falling back asleep again.

By the following weekend Ashley was awake and fairly alert. She seemed in good spirits, although the doctors warned her parents it could be just temporary. Her parents had sat and talked the whole week while she was asleep and decided she needed to talk to someone, so they made arrangements for a therapist to come see her every day. It was to start the following week and they had put off telling her.

Sunday morning, as the trio sat in the cafe', Ellen drew in a deep breath and stated, "Well, I guess there is no time like the present to tell her, so I'm going up." Ellen stood up, grabbed her coffee and looked at Rodger who didn't move so she turned and started walking towards the elevators.

Suddenly Ruth jumped up. "Wait Ellen! Wait!" Ellen turned and stood still, "I'll go with you. You shouldn't have to do this by yourself. You can do the talking, but I'll go with you." Ruth caught up with Ellen.

They looked back at Rodger. He raised his coffee at the two. "Good luck. It's better if you do it. You know it's kind of a woman thing." He went back to reading the paper.

"Whatever." Ellen shook her head and the two left.

When they entered Ashley's room, Laura was sitting next to her sister. This was only the second time she had been there, yet she was fluffing Ashley's pillows and fixing her covers and doing anything she needed. Ellen thought what a cute little nurse maid. Ashley doesn't know how lucky she is; her sister is so sweet and loves her so much.

"Ash, I, well we, need to talk to you about what happened," Ellen cleared her throat as she sat down.

Ashley took in a deep breath and let it out slowly. "What about it? I'll be OK. I feel pretty good."

"Well, we want to make sure. The doctor recommended that while you're here, you talk to someone, and we agree. You need to get these feelings out, deal with them, get over them, and move on. So you can get on with your life and be happy." Ellen raised her eyebrows and shook her head waiting for a response.

"I don't want to talk to some shrink, they'll….

Suddenly Laura jumped up and started screaming "YOU NEED TO TALK TO SOMEONE, YOU CAN'T EVER DO ANYTHING LIKE THIS AGAIN, YOU CAN'T LEAVE ME !!!" Tears started running down her face, and she started to sob. She stood there trembling, almost gasping for breath. She looked into her sister's eyes and managed to squeak out, "Don't you love me?"

Ashley looked down, her face flushed, "Yeah… of course I do." "Then you'll do it," Laura demanded in between breaths.

"Come on, Laura, let's take a walk," Ruth interrupted. "Your mom and Ash need to talk for a few minutes." Ruth wrapped her arm around Laura's shoulders and guided her out of the room.

"Mom, I don't need some shrink." Ashley scowled.

"Listen, you have disrupted everyone's lives; you fucking totaled my car, drunk. You snuck out to a party after I forbid it, took a bunch of pills while drunk and then you tried to kill yourself by driving my car into a fucking tree. Don't you think enough is enough? Not to even mention how upset your sister is. What, you think you can fuck up all over the place and we're just supposed to pick up the pieces and move on. Just forget about what you did like it didn't happen? It doesn't work like that." Ellen paced around the room waving her hands around. There are consequences for your actions and this is it, so suck it up." The rage in Ellen's eyes burst through her formally calm loving façade, giving Ashley a reminder of what her life is really like at home. Even Ashley's aide was taken aback by the sight and tone of the conversation taking place.

"Mom, I feel really bad about wrecking your car, and I'm sorry that I've disrupted everyone's lives, but I don't want to talk to anyone." Ashley frowned.

"Let me tell you something. If you don't talk to this guy and be honest about all your feelings, as soon as they discharge you from this place, which I'm guessing will be at the end of summer. I will put you either into a psyche ward or into a school that will monitor your every move and you will do therapy. Then you won't graduate with your friends and they will all know where you went. I'll make sure of it." Ellen glared at her daughter.

Ashley huffed, "Fine I'll talk to the guy." She glared right back at her mother. The tension in the room was thick.

"Good, thank you, I'll go tell Laura the good news." Ellen strolled out, as if she were discussing lunch plans. Her attitude and mood could change with the wind as long as it blew her way.

Ashley turned and sadly looked at her aide, Carol, who shook her head back at her. "Honey, we'll talk later." They had started to develop a fairly good relationship over the past couple days, Ashley had started to talk to her at night after visiting hours.

"Hey, baby," Rodger called to his daughter as he entered the room, with a big smile. "I brought you some doughnuts, jelly your favorite. Plus they had a couple of books that looked good in the gift shop so I picked them up for you too, along with a puzzle book."

He placed the doughnuts and books on her bed side table and took a seat.

"Thanks, Dad. You didn't have to do that." She smiled.

"So, did your mom talk to you?" He looked sideways at her.

"Oh, you mean about the shrink. It was more like lecture me and make me feel guilty and threaten me if I didn't talk to him. I don't have much of a choice, but, hey, that's my life. So be it." Ashley felt she could express herself safely because the aide was there and her father would not lash out at her. Being sober he was easier to talk to.

"Well, you know your mom. She likes to get her way no matter what." He pursed his lips. Just then Ellen walked in with Laura and Ruth. She overheard what he had said to Ashley. Ellen's blood was soon at a boil. How could he play Mr. Innocent with this. He was in on the decision for her to see a counselor. Why is he making me be the bad guy? That son of a bitch, I hate him more now than ever before. But for now all she could do was keep silent and bide her time. She knew, though, that she would eventually tell her daughter the truth and then she would see her father for the liar that he was. So she stood silent with Laura backing her for sure and with some support from Ruth.

As the day wore on Ellen had another piece of news to tell Ashley. When dinner time came and everyone went to the cafe to eat, she stayed behind. "Listen, kiddo, I have another piece of news to tell you. I need to go back to work tomorrow, but I'll come up afterwards. Your grandparents can take the week off so they can spend the days with you, so you won't be alone." She prepared for the worst.

"That's OK, but they don't have to, I'll be OK. I'm not a baby. I don't need somebody here all the time. Actually it is kind of tiring to tell you the truth," Ashley answered her mother.

"So are you saying you don't want your grandparents to come sit with you?"

"Well, I love them and all, but they don't need to be here all day. They can come after work like you. That would be just fine, unless they really want to. But I'm really tired, and just want to chill for a while. I can watch cable TV or read or sleep." Ashley sort of shrugged her shoulders.

"Well, OK then. I'll plan on coming up tomorrow evening with Laura. It's starting to get late and we've been here all day so is it OK if we get going when Laura comes up from the cafe?" Ellen asked Ash.

"Fine with me"

Just then Ashley's dinner tray arrived. Usually her father brought her something better from downstairs. But he and Ruth had left earlier stating they needed to spend some time with her brothers. So her aide set her dinner all up for her. She carefully examined it, after thanking Carol for setting it up for her: a cheeseburger, French- fries, chocolate cake, milk and an apple. Ashley started to eat the cheeseburger and fries, commenting, "You know this isn't too bad.'" She asked her mom, "Do you think you could get me a couple of Pepsi's?" She smiled. "Then I'll have one for later, and maybe one for tomorrow?"

"Sure, I can do that." Ellen buzzed out of the room. Within fifteen minutes she returned along with Laura holding 4 Pepsi's. Laura immediately spoke up, "I told mom you'll be here all day by yourself, so we better get you a couple more." She smiled.

"Thanks, Laura." Ashley grinned back.

Ellen cleared her throat. "Well, we better get going. We'll see you tomorrow." She kissed Ashley's forehead and waved as they left.

"See you later." Laura waved walking behind her mother.

Ashley let out a sigh as she looked at the clock reading 6:47. She thought now I can just rest. I'm so tired, and I have this jerk coming to talk to me tomorrow.

After Ashley finished her dinner tray and Carol had cleared it away, they sat and watched TV. "Does he tell my parents what I say to him?" Ashley asked.

"Well, he has to give them an overall report but no specifics. What you say stays between the two of you," Carol nodded her head up and down.

"So when he comes, the aide will leave to?" Ashley asked "Yup, she sure will."

"Cool, so I guess it won't be as bad as I thought," Ashley nodded her head.

Later that night, after Ashley was given her night medication and was lying down trying to fall asleep, she kept thinking about all that had happened and what her mother had said earlier about crashing her car and the consequences of her actions. Did her parents come to her bedside out of love or out of obligation? She wondered if deep down her parents were angry with her and when she got home she would get punished. Maybe it would have been best if she just died in the accident. Then they wouldn't have all this mess to deal with. Here she was again the problem child. Was it normal to even feel these things? Tears ran down her cheeks as she silently cried. Luckily it was dark on this side of the room and Carol was engrossed in a book using a small light on the other side of the room. She started getting drowsy and thought she probably should tell the shrink the thoughts she just had, along with the real relationships she shared with her parents. Maybe they do love her and something is just wrong with her, that she just can't feel the love they offer. Maybe she is just not good enough, always in trouble, they just gave up on her, like she doesn't deserve it, that's how she felt deep, deep inside, just not good enough, like a lost cause.

CHAPTER 15

"*R*ise and shine, sunshine," Cori gleefully cheered to Ash as she breezed into her room around 8:30 am, Monday morning. Ashley lazily opened her eyes not yet ready to meet the day.

"Hey, kiddo, the breakfast trays are here, Maria will be in with yours in a few minutes. I just need to give you your medicine and take your vitals. Here take this." Ash held out her hand, popped the pills in her mouth and then took the drink from Cori and swallowed. "You're getting pretty good at taking pills one handed." Cori warmly smiled at her. She was fast becoming one of her favorite patients, always polite and patient, never complaining. She couldn't help but feel sorry for her, wondering what in her life could be so bad that she would resort to such a drastic action. She wondered if she really understood the gravity and permanence of such a decision, not to mention how it would affect those around her.

Although Ashley had only been there just over a week, this was the first day at least one of her parents had not been there. Cori couldn't help but notice the change. "So, kiddo, where is everyone today?" she asked as she sat on the edge of the bed.

"Well, they all needed to get back to work. My mom said my grandparents would take some time off work to come up and sit with me. But I'm not a baby. I don't need constant company. Besides, I have my permanent aides Miss Ann during the day and Miss Carol at night, plus all you nurses and the floor aides. Believe me, I feel guilty enough about all of them missing so much work and having to use their vacation time on me and having to drive all the way up here every day, and also about crashing my mom's car. So now on top of it my mom has to find the time to go out and buy a car and get together a down payment. I know she is really mad about it. I can tell." Ashley let out a sigh and grimly smiled.

"Oh, sweetie, you know what? Having to get a new car is easy. If she had lost a daughter, that could never had been replaced. You are way more important than some car, OK?" Cori rubbed her arm. "Now, I would love to stay, but I've got other patients to take care of. If you need me for anything, just press the button and I'll come in a flash. Oh, I almost forgot, you have an appointment today with Dr. Robert Kelly, at 1:00pm sharp. Don't worry, he's nice." Cori smiled at Ashley as she left. As she turned the corner, she couldn't help but think how Ashley's parents could allow their child to think a car was more important than she was. Maybe the picture her parents painted while she lay unconscious wasn't quite the reality she lived in.

Ashley was ready for the day and just watching TV when a portable x-ray machine and tech showed up around 10:00am. "Hey, are you Ashley Ames? I'm Kathy." She rolled the cumbersome machine next to her bed.

"Yeah, that's me," Ashley answered.

"OK, but I have to check your wrist band to make sure. I'm here to take an x-ray of your pelvis and tibia. Do you know where those bones are located in your cute little body, girly girl?" Kathy smiled at her while taking out the film cassettes and starting to adjust the machine.

"Yeah, I've had them pointed out before, you know, since I broke them." Ashley nodded her head back at the tech.

"Cool, you grab the lift bar above your head so I can slip the film under your butt. Oh it's going to be cold and hard, so you've been warned." Kathy let out a half giggle.

"Oh, you weren't kidding." Ashley's eyes opened wide.

"Well, this one is the worst. Figured we get it out of the way," Kathy spoke with authority.

After about ten more minutes she finished. "So that's it for today, but I'll probably see you again to keep track of how you're healing up. So take care." Kathy smiled as she drove the huge machine out of Ashley's room.

After she left, Ashley turned to her aide, Ann, and asked, "Does the x-ray tech. know that I tried to kill myself because you're here beside me?" earnestly looking into her eyes.

"Maybe, but it's not written in stone or anything." She held out her hands. "Plus, your medical records are confidential so she can't tell anyone that's not related to your care," Ann added hoping this would comfort her. She was hoping to ease her nerves a bit, knowing that she had her first therapy appointment coming up in just a few short hours. She really liked this assignment. Many of the kids who try to kill themselves are very angry and rude or are very depressed and sullen, but Ashley wasn't too bad. She was quiet, but still very respectful. Sometimes Ann wondered if Ashley's parents were abusive to her because she was so well behaved. It was like she could say things here because she was safe, especially to her father, but she wasn't sure. Hopefully, Ann thought, this doctor will really help this child because my instincts tell me she has a lot of secrets.

"So, are you nervous about talking to the doc?" Ann asked raising her eyebrows.

"I don't know. Is he going to want to know everything about me, like today?" Ashley asked wearily.

"Well, he's going to want to get to know you and will want to know why you did what you did, but it doesn't have to be all in one day," Ann tilted her head in response.

"Well, that makes me feel a bit better. I wasn't sure exactly what to do or say. I have never really talked much. I had a counselor at school, so it's probably just like that, right?" Ashley opened her hand.

"Yeah, it will be pretty much like that. You just need to be totally honest. That's the most important thing and remember he's here to help you. He's on your side and he can't help you if you're not honest." Ann shook her head as if making an agreement with her young friend.

"Is he going to tell my parents what I say?" Ashley wearily looked at Ann.

"Well, he will probably let them know how you're feeling, but if you're concerned about that you should ask him what his policy is sooner rather than later, like today, OK?" Ann looked directly into Ashley's eyes, while nodding her head, trying to convey the importance of her statement. Ann wondered why she was so worried about her parents knowing what she talks about. That poor child.

"Yeah, I guess I need to do that then. Thanks." Ashley smiled at her.

"You are very welcome, glad to help." Ann smiled back.

Before she knew it, lunch was done and over. Now Ashley was watching the clock waiting for this so called doctor to arrive. One o'clock came and went with no doctor. If Ashley could have paced, she would have worn out the floor. Finally at 1:30 a smile hit her doorway, followed by an apology. "Hello, I'm Dr. Bob Kelly. Sorry I'm late. In the future, I'll try harder to be on time. You are Ashley Ames, aren't you?" He looked at Ashley, then at Ann.

When Ashley looked at him, he kind of reminded her of Eli, one of her teachers, with his wild black curly hair. Although he was tall and lanky, Eli was sort of short, not too short but short. If he was as nice as Eli, they might just get along. Then she thought he sure was kinda young to be a doctor. Well, at least it wasn't some old man.

Ann stood up. "Yes, this is Ashley She has been waiting patiently, no pun intended. I'll leave the two of you to talk." Ann started to gather her things. Just before she left she asked, "When should I come back?"

"About an hour or so will be just fine. Thanks." He smiled at her as she left, and then closed the door behind her. He pulled Ann's chair beside the bed so they faced one another." So, kiddo, what's the scoop? How did you end up here, all busted up?" He clasped his hands together, placed his elbows on his knees, and leaned forward.

"Don't you already know? Ashley sighed. "OK. What grade are you going to go into?"

"Wait, I have a question." Ashley drew in a deep breath. "Do you tell my parents what I tell you, like our conversations and stuff?" She looked intensely at him, almost scared of his answer.

"Well, no not really. What you tell me pretty much stays between us. I convey how you feel at times, but more importantly I try to have you be honest with them as to how you feel and think about things, OK? Does that answer your question?" Dr. Kelly smiled at Ashley while holding her gaze.

"That makes me feel better about talking to you." Ashley smiled back.

"Good, I'm glad. We try to make this as painless as possible, without involving torture." He winked.

"Yeah, funny! So.. Well.. Uh.. I'll be a senior this year."

"Good, and do you like school? Is it easy or hard?" Dr. Kelly asked. Ashley thought for a moment about being honest with him as her aide had suggested. If he was going to help, she needed to tell the truth so she decided on this topic she would. If her parents found out, her ass would be in big trouble. "I don't mind school. We live out in the middle of no-where, so I mainly go for the social life. Also, it is really easy, but my parents think I struggle so they don't hassle me about my grades. You can't tell them that." Ashley worriedly looked at him.

Dr. Kelly realized she had just revealed a deep secret to him and was happy she trusted him so soon. "Well, as long as you're happy with your grades and you're passing."

"I get mostly B's and some C's." She smiled.

"OK, now can you tell me about mom and dad and if you have any brothers and sisters." Dr. Kelly nodded.

"Well, my parents are divorced about three-four years now. My brother, Jeff ' has been in the marines about four years. He hardly ever comes home. He's stationed in Germany so it's not like it's easy, not that he'd want to. Jeff has a different father but my dad pretty much raised him, not that he was great to him or anything. Then there's my little sister

Laura, she's like an old soul, at least that's what my mother says. She looks up to me a lot of the time, but I just keep screwing up; oh, and we also have different fathers. Now my father just remarried so I have a younger stepbrother who is like six I guess, and they also had a baby who is just over a year. That's it for brothers and sisters, that I know of, although I have overheard my parents talk about my dad's other kids, so I guess there might be some out there I haven't met, but I'm not sure." Ashley sat silent for a moment just thinking. She nervously ruffled the sheet with her fingers wondering why she had told him that.

"So, how are you feeling these days?" Dr. Kelly softly asked. "Are you in any pain?"

"No, it's not really painful, just uncomfortable. They give me medicine for it and not being able to move much is bugging me. I can't go outside or.. well.. anywhere."

"Sort of like you can't get away, or you're trapped?" Dr. Kelly rubbed his chin with his thumb and index finger while he gazed at Ashley, as if he were searching her face for unspoken clues, hints to guide their conversation. "How do you feel about talking with me?"

"I don't know. I'm nervous about when they come tonight. Are they going to ask a million questions about this?" Ashley sighed.

"Do you have a good relationship with your parents?" Dr. Kelly tilted his head.

"No, not really, but my mom is really busy with school plus she works full-time to take care of us." Ashley nodded while raising her eyebrows. "How do you get along with your dad?"

"We either really get along or we don't even speak, but since I've been here he's been really nice, joking around with me and stuff like that.."

"So, if you have a problem can you talk to them?" Dr. Kelly cleared his throat.

"No, definitely not, but sometimes I can talk to Ruth, my stepmother. She notices if something is wrong, you know if I'm upset or not myself. Plus she can keep a secret. Once she could have really screwed me over if she had told my dad, but she handled it just between the two of us. So that made me really trust her and respect her judgment on things."

"So, who do you talk to when things aren't going well?"

"Well, I used to talk to my boyfriend, but I don't know if he's still my boyfriend. My mom says he calls her almost every night to check on me, but he hasn't come up to visit me yet. She also says he still wants to go out with me, but I saw him and some girl hanging all over each other at a party that we went to together." Ashley shook her head and started breathing heavier.

"What did you do when you saw that happen?"

"I went up to them and said what's going on. He gave me some lame excuse about her being drunk. She started to say something so I started beating the shit out of her. Then he actually grabbed me off of her and took Me Home! Me Home! Can you believe that? Then he didn't even go home but turned back towards the party. Jerk!" Ashley felt a tear run down her cheek but quickly wiped it away and looked off out the window, her portal to the outside world. She anxiously thought, think about something else, don't cry. Don't cry. I hate it here. I wish I would've died. This was one of the few times she had thought this since her failed attempt. Damn these thoughts. She was certain they had gone away for good and now they had returned, with a shrink in the room no less. She was instantly worried he would find out and she would get locked up for sure. She definitely could not tell him about these thoughts.

"Sounds like you were very angry. So, then what happened?" Dr. Kelly softly asked as he looked into Ashley's eyes.

Ashley took in a deep breath. She really didn't want to go into details of that night but she kept hearing her mother's voice threatening her if she didn't. She didn't want to spend all summer in some psych. ward with a whole bunch of lunatics. So she relented and briefly explained to him what went on that night. "I was so mad at Ryan, I took a bunch of pills and stole my mom's car, I then crashed into a tree, that's about it," She tried to blame the whole attempt on the activities of that evening.

"So, this boy, Ryan, sounds really important to you." Dr. Kelly stated, trying to get a complete picture of the people in her life. He also realized her attempt was in no way based on one night as she claimed, but he didn't let her know his thoughts.

"He is. We have been going out about 1 ½ years, on and off. He's a couple years older and has already graduated plus he has a good job. He's very talented. My mother really likes him too. We go up to the Bluffs and watch the sunset quite often, especially when we want to be alone." Ashley smiled thinking about those memories. Suddenly she was snapped back to the present.

A cart call was announced to a room just down the hall. Sadly she just looked at the door. Although she had only been there a short time, she knew what a cart call meant. Some little kid was close to death. Something, she thought at times, she wanted, yet everyone else fought so desperately to escape it.

"Does the cart call bother you?" Dr. Kelly inquired, intrigued.

"Well, yeah, it means that some innocent kid is fighting for his life. They didn't put themselves here like I did. I don't understand why God lets stuff like that happen. This whole world is messed up; it sucks. Plus now they have to take care of me instead of other really sick kids. I'm such a loser." Ashley hung her head.

"Your important too and you do need to be here. So don't worry. There is plenty of room for everyone and you're not a loser; you're just a bit confused."

"Yeah, right. That's why I've ruined everyone's summer vacation plans. They had to take vacation time off from work to come see me, so it's a waste of vacation time, all because of me, not to mention crashing my mother's car. She's super pissed." Right after she said it, she knew she had said too much. Ashley remembered her mother's face from the other day seeing the rage in her eyes when the car was mentioned. Ashley felt an enormous amount of guilt for her actions and the damage that had resulted from them.

"I think your mom would be much more upset if she lost a daughter that night than just a car." Dr. Kelly looked at Ashley.

"Yeah, maybe, but she didn't and now she's mad at me, and I'll pay for it for the rest of my life." Ashley sighed.

The doctor made a mental note of this comment. Whether his new patient realized it or not, she had just made a huge statement, giving him a window into her perception of the world she lived in. "So you feel that she doesn't let things go when you make mistakes?" Dr. Kelly asked.

"Mistakes? I crashed her car into a tree, totaling it. That's a lot more than a mistake." Ashley raised her eyebrows, hung her head and dropped open her bottom jaw. It was as if she felt she deserved to be punished.

Dr. Kelly picked up on that feeling. "So, do you feel guilty about crashing her car?"

"Of course I do," Ashley immediately responded.

"Do you feel you should be punished or held responsible in some way?"

"Yeah, I totally screwed up. I messed up my mom's whole summer vacation plans not to mention her savings account."

"How do you know that for sure?" The doctor looked at her. "Because she told me in detail," Ashley sighed deeply. "You see she is one person when everyone is around, then another in private. But isn't most everyone like that?"

"That's an interesting question. Is that how you find people to be?" The doctor asked her.

"Yeah, pretty much in my world. It's all about what everyone is going to think, instead of how do you feel about it or are you OK. Nobody cares how things affect me, just what everyone else in public is going to think about the situation, how my behavior will embarrass my parents. It's like I'm not important or how I feel doesn't matter, but what some stranger down the street thinks and says that matters. To me that feels messed up, but not to my parents. They seem to think it should matter." Ashley shook her head from side to side, with a lost look on her face.

Dr. Kelly sat silent for a minute just taking in what his new young patient had just revealed to him. Their time was nearing the end and he wanted to end on a positive note, so he thought he should speak to her about her willingness to share and be open with him. "Listen, I think you did a really good job today telling me about some of what happened and a couple of the things about your life and the people in your life. You have been through a lot and I think we can start to sort some of this out and get you feeling a lot better about yourself and your situation. It's not going to happen overnight but with a willingness to talk about things we can conquer a bunch of stuff. The process is not always going to be easy or pleasant, but I think you and I together can get a good start on this. Our time is pretty much up for today so do you have any questions for me before I head on out of here?" Dr. Kelly smiled while holding his hands open at his sides.

"What should I say if my parents want to know what we talked about? Because I really don't want to tell them. And are they going to talk to you? And what are you going to tell them?" Ashley's voice was distressed and her face wrinkled with worry.

Dr. Kelly realized her uneasiness and tried to reassure her "You need to tell them that what we talk about is private and I told you to keep it private. As far as for me, I'm not going to tell them anything specific related to what you said. I'll relate just how open and honest you were plus how I feel you are doing emotionally. That's about it, OK? I will not tell them your secrets; they are safe with me, I promise, OK?" He smiled and gave her a quick wink.

Eased by this information Ashley took a huge almost cleansing breath and her face relaxed into a smile. "Thanks. That makes me feel a lot better."

"Yeah, I saw that smile. See, it wasn't too painful was it?" He smiled. "No, it wasn't too bad. I thought it would be a lot worse."

Dr. Kelly got up to leave and went out in the hallway to get Ann so he could leave. Just before he left, he popped his head in and told Ashley he would see her either tomorrow morning or afternoon depending on his schedule, so don't go anywhere. He pointed at her, then chuckled.

"Ha ha, "Ashley replied as he left.

"Well, that sounds like it went well," Ann smiled as she moved and settled into her chair.

"Yeah, he's really nice and I like him." Ashley nodded her head.

The dinner trays were picked up and still no one had arrived to see Ashley. She didn't know what to think. Finally when her mother arrived, she was beyond annoyed, more like totally pissed off. She stormed into the room, not even asking how Ashley was feeling. "Do you know that so-called doctor that we got for you won't tell me a God damn thing about your appointment today, and he actually had the nerve to tell me not to ask you about it. Now we both know that's not what's going to happen here is it? What's so top secret about what you talked about. You need to tell me and you need to tell me now." Ellen slammed her purse down on the side table at Ashley's bedside, placed her hands on her hips and looked Ashley directly in the eye.

Shocked by her behavior, Ashley's night aide, Carol, sat stunned. She didn't know what to do. She didn't know if she had the right to intervene. Should she go get the night nurse to help out, but she couldn't leave her patient. Ashley tried to sit up more in bed to try and handle this onslaught "We….Uh….we just…uh…we just talked about that night and….uh…about Ryan and that I had brothers and sisters and stuff like that. That's all basically." Ashley took it in stride as if it wasn't that big of a deal. The noise had alerted another floor aide to the room along with Ashley's nurse. "What's going on in here? Is everything all right?" The charge nurse asked.

Carol spoke up trying to save Ashley from further badgering, "No everything is not OK, Ellen is demanding to know what happened during Ashley's therapy session today." Carol now on her feet was visibly upset.

"All right let's all just take a breath and calm down, Ms. Ames please don't press your daughter about her session," The charge nurse nodded at her, then stated, "Do we understand one another?"

Ellen looked at the group "Yes, we understand each other. I'm sorry, I just had a bad day, this really isn't me, I don't know what overcame me, I'm so sorry." Ellen pursed her lips while she nodded in agreement. "Well, we all can have bad days. I can understand that, but please just calm down," The charge nurse nodded in agreement and the situation seemed to calm down.

Ashley just settled back down thinking I knew she was going to want to know what I said to that doctor. The only reason she had a bad day was because he wouldn't tell her what went on in our session. She may fool these nurses, but she isn't fooling me. Oh, how I wish it wouldn't have turned out like this. Then I wouldn't have to hear her mouth anymore. I just want to get out of here, any way out, I don't care. She looked at her mother who was searching for something in her purse, "Mom, have you talked to Ryan?" She stopped and glared at Ashley. She clearly had something on her mind.

"Yes, I spoke to him yesterday. He is planning on coming up in the next couple of days or so." Then she sat down very close to Ashley. With Carol seated across the room, Ellen started talking to Ash very quietly. "Listen, I want this conversation to stay just between the two of us, got it?" Ellen looked into Ashley's eyes, then looked over at Carol checking to see if she was following their conversation, but she was reading a book.

"Yeah, sure," Ashley nodded.

"The insurance check came in from the car and after they paid what I owed to the bank, there isn't as much left as I had hoped. So I know you have been saving from your job and I feel like you owe it to me since you're the one who smashed my car. How much do you have?" Ellen asked very quietly.

"Uh.. I have about $ 1,450. You want the whole thing?" Ashley's jaw hung open as she took in a deep breath and let it out.

"Well, don't you feel like you owe it to me? Where's your sense of responsibility? There are consequences to your behavior. You're the reason I have to get a new car. It's your fault and you need to make amends. So I'll tell you what. I'll only take 1,000 and leave you the rest only because I love you and know that you were very upset and made a mistake. So where do you keep it?" Ellen asked all matter of fact as if she was asking to pass the salt.

"I keep it in the top of my closet in the blue shoe box towards the back," Ashley answered as if she were in shock. She couldn't believe her mother was taking her life savings. She was unsure if this was right or wrong, but it didn't feel right. But, it was her fault that her mother had to purchase a new car. She was so confused.

"Well, I probably won't be up tomorrow because I need to go car shopping, and I so appreciate your little contribution. It's starting to get late and I really need to be on my way. I can see that you're OK today, and since you don't want to share about your appointment today, I'll just get going." Ellen got up and kissed Ashley on the forehead and left.

Ashley sat silent just trying to absorb what had just happened. She thought I shouldn't be surprised; that's just how she is. Now I'm not supposed to tell anyone about her taking my money. If it was right of her, why would she care if anyone knew. Not that it would do any good because by tomorrow it would be gone. She thought I hate my life. I'm trapped here unable to do anything. I can't run away. I just have to stay here and take their shit, life sucks. I wish I would have died. She'll leave me $ 450 because she loves me so much, gee, thanks. She loves money more than me. Who's she kidding? Maybe only herself. It's always been about the almighty dollar, with everything not just this. She has always said get all you can get, when you can get it. Go after a rich man so you won't have to work, that's her advice. Oh well, I may as well kiss it all goodbye, because she will probably take the rest and there is nothing I can do about it. So I'll just have to work harder and make it again. To hell with her. I can't depend on her, and I'm not going to end up like her, worshiping money.

CHAPTER 16

*E*arlier that day the nurses had placed a pull up bar on the bar that ran from the bottom of the bed to the top, so Ashley could start to pull herself up off the bed. She would start with this as the beginning of her physical therapy. She was excited to be able to move herself a bit even though it was only a little bit above the bed. Her butt was getting very sore from being on it all the time. They no sooner got the bar on and secured and she was trying it out. Although she wasn't as strong as she thought but she kept on trying. She was not about to give up. She knew the more she exercised the stronger she would get and then the faster she would move on to the next step.

Ashley had been in the hospital about 2 1/2 weeks before Ryan mustered up the courage to visit her. He had felt somewhat responsible for all that had happened that horrible night. The guilt of it all crushed him inside. When he talked to Ellen, she said it wasn't his fault, yet the feeling he got was that she, in part, blamed him, even if she said differently. Ellen had told him to stay away. Ashley needed to heal without distraction, but he just had to go see her. He couldn't wait any longer. So that Thursday morning he put on a smile and brought a bouquet of flowers and popped his head in her room. "Hey there! How's it going?" He walked over to her bedside, tapping his fingers against his jeans with his free hand.

"Ryan, you actually came," Ashley replied with a surprised smile. "And you brought me flowers too! Thanks, that was really nice. You didn't have to do that." She tilted her head.

"Yes, I did. You're still my girl, aren't you?" He opened his eyes wide, as he nervously set down the vase on the window sill. Then he thought shit, I shouldn't have said that right off the bat, but he was dying to know and he just couldn't wait any longer.

"Well, I hope so," Ash stated, as she wrinkled up her brow.

"Well, as far as I'm concerned you are." Ryan bit his lower lip. "So I guess we're still a couple right?" He half smiled, hoping she still wanted him as much as he wanted her.

"I have been trapped here wondering how you have been and hoping you would come up to see me. I thought about calling you, but my mother said I shouldn't, that I should let you sweat it out, but I… I don't know." Ash readily admitted to him." So you want me and not that other girl at the party, right?"

"No, I never wanted that other girl. She was just drunk and hanging on me so she wouldn't fall down, I swear. You're the person I want to be with, honest." Ryan crossed his heart with his index finger.

"I'm glad, that makes me feel a lot better. I've missed you, a lot." Ashley smiled, her eyes bright.

"Well, I have been talking to your mom most every night and she said I needed to wait a bit, until you were feeling better, but I just couldn't wait anymore so here I am." Ryan smiled as he gently caressed her arm. "So, are you in any pain? You really look like you broke a lot of bones." He scanned her up and down.

"Well, they give me medicine for pain so it doesn't really hurt, but, yeah, I really did a number on myself. Plus, they are making me see a counselor. He comes just about every day now, during the week. A few days ago was my first time and when my mother talked to him, she demanded to know what we talked about and he wouldn't tell her. So when she got here she tried to get me to tell her after he told her not to ask me and the nurses came to my rescue. So she got mad and like left 15 minutes later. Can you believe that, but that's her." Ash just shook her head, finally glad to have someone she really trusted to confide in.

"She was probably scared you told him something unflattering about her, you know," Ryan answered, half laughing.

"You mean like how things really are?" They both laughed. The aide overheard the conversation and almost couldn't believe her ears. And thought no wonder she wanted to know what was said in those sessions; this family was very complicated.

"So you mean my mom told you not to come up and see me?" Ash asked a bit confused.

"Yeah, she said you needed your space and time to heal without any drama from me," Ryan confessed.

"Drama? What the hell's that supposed to mean? Ashley asked confused.

"I'm not exactly sure. I guess no problems from me." Ryan shrugged his shoulders.

"Oh, like she doesn't make any drama in her visits." Ashley shook her head and chuckled. "Hey, aren't you supposed to be at work?"

"Yeah, I took the afternoon off so I could visit with you without running into your mom." Ryan nodded his head.

"Smart move," Ashley added.

As the couple sat and chatted catching up on all the latest news, it was as if nothing had happened. Ryan didn't want to push her about the reasons she tried to kill herself and Ashley didn't want to explain the reasons why she wanted to kill herself. At least for the time being the two just sat and enjoyed each other's company. Although it killed Ryan deep down to know that his girlfriend wanted to die, he tried to remain positive, thinking and hoping that it was just an impulsive action. He held onto the idea that therapy while in the hospital would cure her, and when she got home everything would be back to normal or hopefully even better.

They visited all afternoon uninterrupted. As early evening was approaching, their time together was coming to an end. "Well, it's getting late and I don't want to run into your mother, so I better be taking off." Ryan looked sadly into Ashley's eyes.

"Yeah, I know what you mean. I wish you didn't have to go, but for now it's probably for the best. When do you think you can come back?" Ashley took in a deep breath.

"Soon, I promise, but I have your phone number now so I'll call every night after visiting hours are over, I promise." Ryan bent down and kissed her goodbye. He no sooner left her room and not 60 seconds later her mother burst through the door.

"Hi, Ashley. How was your day? Anything exciting happen?" Ellen glanced around the room. "And who brought you those flowers?" Ellen asked curiously with an air of superiority.

"Uh...Oh... Uh... I don't know for sure. I've gotten so many," Ashley answered eyes downcast.

"Funny thing. I thought I saw Ryan on the elevator. He was on the one going down as I got off the one for this floor." Ellen glared at her daughter. "Well, I'm waiting for an explanation." Ellen tapped her fingers on the bedside table, something she did when she was angry.

"What do you want from me? I'm stuck here in this bed. I have no control over who comes and goes." Ashley glared back, giving her mother attitude.

"I made it very clear to him he was to stay away from you. This whole thing happened because of him." Ellen sternly looked at her daughter while she forcefully tapped her foot. "He is not to come up here again. I'm leaving instructions with the nurse's station, that he is to be thrown out should he return." Ellen stiffened and put her hand on her hip as she continued to aggressively tap her foot.

"You can't do that. He's my boyfriend. I love him," Ashley yelled back. "And it isn't the only reason I did it," Ashley screamed. "You and dad are terrible parents,"

Ellen's face went blank. She was taken aback. For the first time since the accident blame from Ashley had been thrown towards her. She stood frozen unable to move, unsure if she should stay or leave. "Oh, give me a break. You don't know what terrible is!" Ellen sternly stated. "You have it so bad; you're ungrateful at best." She glared at Ashley.

"You don't love us. All you care about is how we make you look, how what we do affects you. You continually tell us how selfish we are, how greedy we are. How much you had to give up because of us. How you would be somebody if it weren't for us. You tell us how much money you have to spend on us, like we are such a burden on you. I don't really have a home. When you get sick of me, you just throw me out like trash. I didn't ask to be born and I don't want to be here. There, I said it. Are you happy now, because that's the impression I get from you, every single day of my life! And that's just the tip of the iceberg, so just leave me alone. Ryan is not the problem, you guys are." Ashley sniffled and quieted down, a tear running down her face. She looked downwards away from her mother.

After hearing the rantings of her eldest daughter, Ellen's pride had taken a severe blow. She stood silent for what seemed like forever. Finally she took in a deep cleansing breath and grabbed Ashley's chin tight in order to look her in the eye. "I'm sorry I'm not the perfect parent." Then she leaned in really close so the aide could not hear and whispered, "But if you ever scream out about me like that again I'll kill you myself, you ungrateful brat, and don't even think of repeating this conversation. You have to come home eventually." She then stood up again, straightening her shirt. "I'm sorry for the way things are, but I'm just a single parent and money is tight. I will try harder to get this worked out, but you need to try too." Ellen, out of sight of the aide, glared at her daughter as if she had daggers in her eyes. "Now enough has been said tonight. I'm going home to think about what you said, and you need to think about what I said to you. Goodbye." Ellen squeezed her hand very tightly and then left.

The aide waited several minutes after Ellen left, making sure she was gone for the night, and she went over to Ashley to ask if she was OK. She desperately wanted to know what Ellen had said when she leaned in ever so close, mainly for her own curiosity but also to give young Ashley any support she may need. "Hey, kiddo, are you OK? The aide gently touched Ashley's hand. "You really said a mouthful tonight. In a way it's good to get those feelings out. Of course, I don't recommend that you scream them out, but sometimes you need to in order for that person to actually hear you and hopefully receive the message." The aide just sat next to Ash waiting for some kind of response. Finally, after several minutes, Ashley looked at the aide and said, "It's hopeless. She will never admit fault, especially the way I screamed it out at her. She is so angry now that she won't even think about what I said but the way I said it. Believe me, I know her." Ash just took in a huge breath and let it out. "Hey, could you do me a favor and check at the nurse's station to see if she blocked Ryan from coming to see me. Hopefully she forgot in her rage." Ash looked grimly at the aide.

"Sure honey. Let me get the floor aide to sit with you for a minute and I'll go check."

"Hey, can you tell the nurses I just got in a huge fight with her and she would only ban Ryan just to punish me. Maybe I could override it somehow?" Ashley sadly asked tilting her head.

"I'll see what I can do for you, sweetie," the aide answered feeling sorry for her young patient. She summoned the other aide and left. In about fifteen minutes she returned with somewhat of a smile on her face. "She didn't mention anything to the nurses when she left. Then when I was up there explaining what exactly happened between the two of you, they all felt very bad for you. Then they did receive a phone call from her stating he was not allowed up here." Ashley's face just dropped. "But," the aide went on, "that is not the proper protocol for this type of visitor exclusion and the secretary sort of forgot to mention that to your mother. As long as he comes in the mornings far earlier than she could possibly make it here, you should be OK. How's that sweetie?" The aide just smiled at her young troubled patient.

"Oh, thank you all so very much. If I could get out of this bed, I would give all of you a big huge hug. You have helped me so very much. I just want to cry I'm so happy. Ryan is my only real confidant as far as regular people go. Thank you. Please tell them thank you for me. My life has just been made so much better." Ashley had a few tears in her eyes along with a smile.

"I'll pass the message on." The aide smiled feeling good inside, like she had really helped this child and hoping that things would work out for her. In reality she was sixteen almost seventeen, and she should be in control of her own visitors. She was realizing even more that her parents were not the people they seemed to be.

Later that night just as promised Ryan called. Ashley was quick to fill him in on all that had happened and how her mother actually blamed him. She quickly assured him it had little or really almost nothing to do with him. He was very relieved to hear that statement. It eased his mind tremendously, instantly making him feel even closer to Ashley. Now armed with this knowledge, he felt like he could help her through this ordeal even if it was just sitting and listening to her. He also realized she needed professional help, and nothing could take the place of that. But he was ready to do whatever he needed to do. If he had to come only in the early mornings, then that was what he would do. He would just work late into the evenings. He thought what else do I have to do anyway. Then he would call her after visiting hours were over. Ellen would never find out. They could easily get around her, that witch.

Ashley felt as if she and Ryan were a team of sorts, them against her parents, them against the world. Although her father didn't have anything to do with banning Ryan, she was scared he would go along with what her mother said just to keep the peace and she didn't want to risk it. So she decided that maybe she should ask Ruth what she thought about the whole situation. Then she asked Ryan if he thought that she should ask Ruth about it and explain how her mother totally blamed Ryan and took no responsibility for anything to do with the cause of the accident. "How could she be so blind?" exclaimed Ashley.

"I don't know, babe, some people just can't accept blame or like failure. She doesn't want to be the cause of you wanting to off yourself. I mean that's like so huge, you know," Ryan replied.

"Yeah, I know what you mean, but she's not the only one. My father is right up there too; he's just as bad as she is," Ashley confessed. "I shouldn't have said anything to her. Now I have hurt her feelings really bad and she's never going to forgive me or be the same. I'm such a loser, I wish I could take it back." Ashley sighed.

"But isn't it the truth?" Ryan asked.

"Well, yeah, but I should have been kinder about the way I went about it. She's never going to forgive me or forget about it. I 'm doomed," Ashley sighed heavily.

"Well, at least now it's out in the open, and you all can talk about things and maybe things will get better. You can't change things if you don't know what the problem is. Maybe the doctor you talk to can help you with this. He probably knows exactly how to help with this type of thing," Ryan answered trying to be helpful.

"Yeah, maybe, but she'll probably just throw me out again," Ashley sadly commented.

"Well, you'll be a senior this year. Then you can go off to college if you still want to," Ryan suggested.

"Yeah, I've been thinking about that. One thing about being in here is I have a lot of time to think and I've decided that I want to go to college. I think I want to go into the medical field. I'm not sure which one but something." Ash sounded hopeful about the future for the first time in a long time, and Ryan took note of it.

"You know something? You would never talk about your future before. You would just change the subject. Did you always plan on ..uh .. well .. you know, killing yourself?" Ryan nervously asked.

"Well, kind of, I guess so. I thought about it a lot, that's for sure. I hate to say it, but it's the truth, I hate the way things are with my parents. I feel like they don't give a damn about me and I'm a burden to them. They just get sick of me and pawn me off on the other one for a while; it sucks. It's like I don't belong anywhere or have a real home anywhere." As Ashley talked, she came to a realization of her situation.

"Wow, Ash, that was kind of deep. You need to tell that doctor all of what you just told me. It's important," Ryan assured her. "Please make sure you do, OK?"

"Yeah, I will, I promise. Listen it's getting late and I'm tired, I'll talk to you tomorrow, OK?" Ashley quietly asked.

"No problem. We had a tough talk, so get some rest. I love you I hope you know that," Ryan softly kissed her through the phone.

"I know I love you too. Goodnight." Ashley hung up, then laid back and thought about all she had said to him. She closed her eyes with a tear running down her face.

Unbeknownst to Ashley the aide and nurses had recorded all of the fight between her and her mother and the thing with banning Ryan and how they had kind of gone around it, due to proper protocol and Ashley's age. So when Dr. Kelly came in that early afternoon, he was already aware of the situation and he asked Ashley about it. She was taken aback. "How did you find out about that?" Ashley asked all surprised.

"Well, when you're in these types of places, for your types of problems, people write these types of things down, so we are all on the same page and know what is going on in your world." Dr. Kelly wrinkled up his forehead. "So, will you please tell me your version of what happened?" He half smiled at her.

So Ashley explained the whole thing, "My mother had neglected to tell me she told Ryan to stay away. This left me thinking he didn't want to be with me, and when I would ask my mother about him, she wouldn't really say much of anything. Yet she talked to him most every night. And Ryan had said she made him feel sort of responsible for what happened, not in so many words but in a way. Then yesterday Ryan finally just said to heck with it, I'm going up there. I'll just leave before she gets there. Well she caught him. And then World War

Three. She flipped out on me, like I can control who comes and goes. She said he was the cause of it all and I screamed at her that she and my father were the cause of it. They were terrible parents, which they are. Most of my friend's parents are so much more involved in their lives, like they actually care what happens in their children's lives. My parents are like if you do this, it affects me this way or that way, not is that going to be good for you. My parents are like what are people going to think of me because you did this or that. They constantly tell me how selfish I am or how much money they have to spend on me. One time my father said "You're a little bitch just like your mother." Gee thanks, dad, I love you too. When they get sick of me they just throw me out and the other one takes me until they get tired of me, or until I mess up." Ashley just sighed deeply.

Dr. Kelly just sat for a moment absorbing all of what Ashley had said. After a minute he commented, "Wow, that's a hard situation,"

"Yeah and that's just the tip of the iceberg, believe me." Ashley just shook her head.

"So how do you think we can try and make things better for you?" Dr. Kelly asked.

"I haven't got a clue. One more year and I'm going to go to college. I only have to deal with them until then, then I'm leaving for good," Ashley stated.

"Well, which place is a better fit until then?" Dr. Kelly asked.

"It's hard to say. Now that I screamed that at my mother, she may not let me back and I doubt she will ever forgive me. Then at my father's I risk getting the shit kicked out of me, if I do something wrong and he has had too much to drink. Although Ruth is there and I get along great with her. I know she cares about me, a lot more than both of my parents put together. She actually talks to me and listens to what I have to say. She cares about what goes on in my life. I've never had that before and it feels pretty good." Ash nodded her head.

"It sounds if you stay out of trouble, your father would be the best fit," Dr. Kelly suggested.

"Maybe, but also they make me babysit every single weekend, and I hate that. It's a lot of work and I don't even get an allowance for it, or anything, and if I complain my dad gets very angry, so I'm not real sure about going back there either. It's like I don't belong anywhere," Ashley exclaimed all choked up.

"Well, we don't have to make any decisions for a while. In the meantime, it is a while before you get released. We will have a family meeting with your parents. But for now I just want to talk to you. I need to know all of your concerns and feelings about what's happening in your life and what drove you to try and kill yourself. I want to help you feel better about your situation and your life so you can get past this and move on so you can go to college and have a happy life. So that's my goal with our meetings while, hopefully, you are here healing both inside and out." Dr. Kelly smiled warmly at Ashley.

"If you think you can make things better, then that would be good because I've been feeling bad for a very long time." Ashley looked down.

They talked a while longer about her home life and some of the things that had gone on. Then their time had come to an end. Dr. Kelly agreed with Ash about Ryan being able to come visit, and he left word at the nurse's station that he had overridden Ellen's complaint. Ryan was able to visit without worry of being thrown out. Ashley thanked Dr. Kelly for his help. He said he was glad to do it. He felt that Ellen had done it to punish her daughter for what she had said and the way she said it. He also felt Ryan was good for Ashley. He seemed like someone she could confide in and the more talking she did the better it would be in the long run.

Ashley was grateful to Dr. Kelly for allowing Ryan to come visit, but they kept Ryan's hours in the morning to avoid Ellen, just to keep things quiet and easy. They wanted to keep his visits on the down low, just to avoid any unnecessary problems with Ashley's mother. In the meantime Dr. Kelly wanted Ashley to talk to her stepmother, Ruth, and get her opinion on the whole situation with her mother. Ashley had told the doctor that her mother probably did not tell her father about the fight. In fact, they hardly ever spoke to one another regarding the children or anything for that matter. Most often when they had to talk to each other it ended up in an argument not even over the children but usually how badly they had treated each other.

Later that Friday afternoon Ashley's father and Ruth came in to see her. They hadn't been to see her in a few days and wanted to visit without Ellen intruding upon them. Ruth had mentioned to Rodger that Ash may be more likely to share her feelings if her mother wasn't hovering over them. "Hey, kiddo, how are you feeling today?" Rodger asked as the couple entered the room, bringing a couple of Pepsi's, Ashley's favorite soda.

"I'm OK. Dr. Kelly came and talked to me today. Well, I talked to him mostly. He's really nice and I like him." Ash nodded her head.

"Good. I'm glad. That always helps if you like your therapist." Ruth smiled at Ash as she rubbed her arm. The trio sat and talked about how the family and baby were all doing, and about the gossip going around their small town. Then finally they looked at each other and decided it was time to ask the difficult question on everyone's mind. "So your dad and I were thinking that maybe you might want to share some of what you felt when you crashed the car. You don't have to but we want to know if we need to do something to help you, or do you want to wait and do it with the doctor. We just want to help you in any way that we can." Ruth looked into Ashley's eyes, and Ash started to cry a little. "Oh, honey, it's OK. I didn't mean to upset you. I know this is hard." Ruth tilted her head and stroked Ashley's hair.

"My mother didn't call you and tell you what happened, did she?" Ash looked at both of them, searching their faces for information.

"No why?" they asked in unison.

"Yesterday Ryan came to visit in the morning and tried to leave before she was supposed to get here, but she saw him on the elevator. We got into a huge fight. She told him on the phone not to come visit me. I didn't need any drama. I needed time to heal. Then she told me that this whole thing was his fault and it wasn't. I yelled at her and told her it was because of her and well… you dad. I'm sorry. I hate saying it, but I feel like dying inside. I don't belong anywhere. I don't have a home anywhere. I'm lost and alone, except for Ryan and well, you Ruth. But inside it's empty and a big black hole. I feel like both of my parents, don't love me or want me. I'm sorry dad but that's how I feel and I don't want to hurt your feelings. It makes me feel like a horrible person. I know I hurt my mother's feelings by screaming at her and now she'll never forgive me. So now I'm even more empty and alone. I don't know if there is any hope for the future." Ashley was crying and just looking at the floor.

Ruth and Rodger had discussed his part in her feeling that way, so it came as no big surprise when she stated how she felt. Ruth had very gently gotten Rodger to look at how he had treated Ashley and how things must look from her perspective. He had not been there for several days because he was dealing with his failure as a parent. It hurt him deeply to hear his daughter not only felt alone and depressed but guilty about telling him for fear of hurting his feelings, as if she were more worried about hurting his feelings than being able to express how badly she felt. Rodger knew he had failed his daughter in many ways, but, thankfully, Ruth had helped him deal with that and now he was there to make amends and try to help her heal. "Ash, I'm so sorry. I've failed you as a father in many ways, but I do love you. If you want, you can come back and stay with us if your mom doesn't let you stay with her or if you just want to. I promise it will be different." Rodger sighed trying not to get too choked up. "Listen, I need to get a cup of coffee. You want one Ruth?" He asked

"Yeah, that would be nice." Ruth smiled at Rodger as he left the room. He squeezed one of Ashley's toes.

"So I had a heart to heart with your dad a few days ago, trying to get him to understand things from your perspective. You voicing these feelings today just kind of reinforced how terribly alone you felt. Plus, your dad has quit drinking, since you crashed the car. A few days later he looked at me and said this stuff has interfered with Ashley's and my relationship. It caused me to be cruel to her. I've got to stop." Ruth patted her arm while smiling at her.

"Thank you, Ruth. You are the only real parent I've had. I feel grateful to you for helping my dad see things through my eyes and helping him stop drinking. That's huge." Ashley took in a big cleansing breath.

"Well, you know we love you, and if you did come back to stay with us you wouldn't have to babysit every weekend again. I know that's part of the reason you left and obviously that your dad hurt you, but he promised me that would never happen again." Ruth looked Ash in the eye while nodding her head.

"I'm probably going to be here at least another four weeks and my mother tried to ban Ryan from coming to visit. But Dr. Kelly said I'm old enough to choose my own visitor's list and that she was doing it out of punishment instead of protection. So Dr. Kelly said Ryan could come and visit but to keep it in the morning so as to avoid my mother and any problems it could cause. I don't think it's fair that she can ban Ryan from coming up to visit. He makes me feel good. I have someone that cares about me, he keeps telling me to go on to college after high school, like you said." Ashley looked at Ruth and pursed her lips.

"I think that would be great if you went on to college. Do you realize this is the first time I have ever heard you bring up your future. I think college is awesome. Do you know what you want to study?" Ruth sat holding Ashley's hand.

"I'm not sure but, definitely in the medical field." Ash smiled and nodded her head.

"Well, how about physical therapy?" Ruth offered.

"I don't know. Exercising all the time, I'm not sure I could do that everyday. I don't think that's me."

"Well how about…..? Oh, I know x-ray. You could be an x-ray tech. That's a pretty interesting job and I think it only takes a couple of years training," Ruth suggested eyes wide.

"That might be the one. I think it could be cool. The tech comes in and x-rays me once every couple of weeks and it seems like a pretty cool job. Maybe I'll ask the tech about it," Ashley seemed content with the idea and actually interested in her future, something she hadn't really ever seemed to care about before.

She and Ruth talked a while longer before her father returned. They bounced the idea of college and x-ray technician off of him and he seemed very receptive. Ruth took note of Ashley's interest in her future and thought maybe her talking with Dr. Kelly may actually be starting to be helping. She hoped and prayed it would.

It started to get late and her mother was a no show which did not surprise Ashley in the least, but it angered her father. He didn't let on to Ashley though. Yet Ruth could sense his dismay. The two of them stayed until just before visiting hours were over and had a meaningful and satisfying time actually talking to their daughter. "Well, kiddo, we've got to go. Those kids at home need us to tuck them in," Ruth commented with a half smile.

"Yeah, and I've got to get up early for work," Rodger added as he patted her arm, then leaned over and kissed her forehead. "You know I love you." He looked her in the eye.

"I know. I love you too, and I'm glad you quit drinking. Actually I'm proud of you. And it means a lot to me," Ashley had a tear in her eye and sniffled a bit as they left.

Ashley was left alone with her aide, who was reading, so she sat and thought about the talk they had had that day. She was relieved about telling her father the truth and him not rejecting her. She knew it was all because of Ruth. She had really done a good job allowing him to see life from her perspective. She thought about how it would be now that he had quit drinking. She thought God must have sent Ruth to her because none of this would have happened without her. Then her thoughts went to her mother. She felt so terrible about the way she had told her mother the main reason she tried to kill herself was in large part due to her parent's behavior. And if her mother never forgave Ashley for screaming it for all to hear then she deserved it and would live with it. A tear rolled down her face. She never meant to hurt her mother; she loved her. Ashley prayed: Please, Lord, comfort my mother. Please let her know many of those harsh words were in anger and please forgive me for hurting her feelings. Please, Lord, help my mother forgive me even though I don't deserve it. Ashley was so confused. Sometimes she hated her mother and then others she loved her, but how in the world was she going to fix this? As she lay thinking about this, she drifted off to sleep.

CHAPTER 17

Over the next week or so Ashley had many visitors. Her father and Ruth came about every other day. They had also put the word out that Ashley was up to visitors. So her favorite aunt and uncle came a couple of times which really made Ashley feel good. They had been a big part of her life especially when she was little, taking her to church. This uncle always said North Allentown was God's country and Ash believed him. They would take her camping along with her sister and brother and tons of her other cousins with the help of another aunt and uncle, she had many aunts and uncles, a very large extended family. Year after year they would go down to the lake and camp. They would pack us kids all up with all our supplies half in one boat half in another, they were only like eight- ten foot pond hopper boats. Once the boats were packed they hooked them up to the tractors and we rode in the boats pulled by the tractors from their house up and over the hill, over a rickety bridge, then off the road and all the way down the trail to the lake. The ride took about 45 minutes and we would stay for a couple of weeks. Many of the kid's parents, other cousins, aunts and uncles would come down at night and help cook and everyone would eat a huge dinner cooked over the campfire. Everyone would sit by the huge fire and roast marshmallows. During the day they would water ski or just ride in the boat, swim for hours, not to mention just run wild on the endless rocky beach. This was one of Ashley's most cherished memories; she wouldn't trade that experience for anything.

Also a few of her cousins visited which cheered her up. They spent one whole afternoon cracking jokes and razzing her about all the cute doctors "examining" her. She had a really good time with them and was very glad they came. Her grandparents also visited quite often and brought Laura with them. Laura, at first, was very upset with her sister but as time went on Laura relaxed about the situation and was able to enjoy her visits. Laura had really looked up to her big sister before the crash. She had to really come to terms with what her sister had done, but they shared a deep bond and that won out over the actions Ashley had taken.

Kim and her parents came up to see her which warmed Ashley's heart. They also prayed with her, focusing on giving her comfort and peace of mind. They promised to visit again. They even told her they would call first in order to bring her anything she may want or need. Ashley was so grateful to Kim's parents. She so wished she belonged to their family instead of her own and Kim's parents sort of felt that vibe from her and they responded well to it. They knew her home life was hard at both places, at least from what Kim had told them. She felt as if she didn't belong anywhere, but at their house they wanted her to feel welcome and wanted at all times.

One person, however, did not come up at all, nor did she call. Ashley's mother was missing in action which made Ashley feel terrible about their fight about why she crashed the car. Ashley thought about it constantly no matter what was going on. It was always in the back of her mind. She didn't know how to make it right with her mother. She didn't know what to say when visitors would ask how her mother was. She would just say OK and not mention that she hadn't visited lately. She also had not told anyone about how her mother had taken most all of her money that she had saved. In some ways she felt taken advantage of because whenever she brought up the issue of money and debt of the car wreck, everyone reassured her that her mother had insurance and the car would be replaced at virtually no cost to her. But Ashley felt she owed her something, just not all $1,000 that she took. Knowing her mother had insurance to cover the cost of replacing the car angered Ashley. Here she was trapped in this damn bed while her mother was taking her money for a car she was getting for almost nothing. To add to her anger her grandfather said that the car was in really bad shape and she needed a new one anyway. So the crash happening was the best thing for the car, good riddance to that lemon of a car ", were his words as Ashley recalled. Her grandfather stated the car was some sort of lemon and always needed some sort of repair. The more he went on about the car, the angrier Ashley got. She was on the fence of whether or not to spill the beans about her mother taking the money. Ashley decided she would ask Ryan and Dr. Kelly what they thought about it. Surely they would know what to do.

The following Monday morning Ryan showed up as usual wearing his smile and carrying an ice cold Pepsi. "Hey, how's it going? Did you have a good weekend?" He asked as he opened the soda and gave it to her.

"Hi, yourself. Yes I had a good weekend. Lots of visitors and time flew by." Ash smiled. "But my mother still didn't visit. It's been over a week now, and I only have just over two and a half weeks left until I get released. She's supposed to make a family meeting this week with Dr. Kelly and dad and Ruth. It's supposed to be in two days and I'm nervous she won't show up." Ash took in a deep breath and wrinkled up her forehead.

"Listen, why don't you just call her? What's the worst that can happen?" Ryan held out his hands, palms up.

"Uh, she could hang up on me or tell me she never wants to talk to me again." Ash bit her lip.

"Well, at least you'll know where you stand and you won't be in the dark wondering anymore," Ryan commented.

"Listen, there's something else I need to tell you about. You know all the money I had saved for college?"

"Yeah, what about it?" Ryan answered.

"Well, my mother said I owed most of it to her for wrecking the car. She needed it to help pay for a new car and I was fine with it until grandpa said she needed a new car anyway and her insurance was going to pay for most all of it, except for the deductible. I feel like she just took all of my money just to get back at me for all of this. Is that wrong of me? Am I off base?" Ash asked all confused.

"Well, how much did you have and how much did she take?" Ryan asked his brow all wrinkled.

"Well, I had a total of $ 1,450 and she took $ 1,000" Ash told him. "Really! Why didn't you say something? Have you told anyone else about this?" Ryan started to get loud and his forehead was all wrinkled and his eyes got narrow.

"Well, no. I figured I owed it to her for wrecking the car and she had to spend all that time going out to look for a car, and missing work to come up here to see me. She said she had to use her vacation time to visit me. I'm just a big hassle to her so I figured I owed it to her." Ash breathed deep.

"You're her daughter. You tried to kill yourself. You shouldn't feel like a hassle. That's part of the reason you did what you did. She shouldn't have told you she had to use her vacation time or made you feel guilty. She's supposed to love you." Ryan just shook his head. I'm calling her tonight and having a word with her." Ryan got up and was pacing the room.

"No, please, don't. You'll only make it worse, please," Ashley pleaded. "Well, Ash, you need to defend yourself or have someone do it for you, I don't think you owe her $1,000 dollars for the car especially if her insurance is covering it or most of it. What the hell? She shouldn't do that to you. It's not right. Who else knows about this?" Ryan demanded to know.

"Well, no one. She told me not to bring it up because it wasn't good manners to discuss money with other people," Ash innocently answered Ryan.

"That's bullshit. She didn't want you to tell anyone because she knew it was wrong." Ryan stood there shaking his head back and forth in disbelief. "You said she's supposed to come up for the family meeting in a couple days, right? You need to bring it up then with your dad and Ruth there. Let's see how they feel about it. Also I think you should tell Dr. Kelly about it today when you see him. It's only a couple hours from now. See what he thinks about it." Ryan was breathing heavy and pacing back and forth.

"OK I will, but you need to calm down. It's not the end of the world." Ashley took in a deep breath.

"I'm sorry. I don't want to upset you, but she is taking advantage of you, in my opinion." Ryan nodded. "I just want to protect you, you know." He smiled at her and sat down, trying to calm himself so as not to upset Ashley any more than she already was.

"I know and I appreciate it, but I'm already on the outs with her and I really don't want to make it any worse right now." She smiled back at him.

"OK I can understand that but we need to get this out on the table.

So, you promise to bring it up with the doc right?" Ryan asked.

"Yes, I promise. He'll be here shortly in fact." Ash looked up at the clock.

"Do you want me to stay and help you tell him, or go so you have some time to get your thoughts together or stay a bit longer? Just tell me." Ryan looked her in the eye.

"Maybe go in a little bit so I can just have a bit of time," Ashley responded.

"I just want what's best for you. I just want to help," Ryan confessed, as he forcefully patted his chest over his heart.

"I know. I just need to do this in my own way, or maybe how Dr. Kelly thinks will be the best way," Ashley answered.

Ryan nodded his head. "I understand. Listen, I'm going to get going, so you can rest up a bit before your visit with Dr. Kelly. You've got an important conversation to have. So I'll call tonight to see how things went. Remember, I'm here for you." He leaned over and gently kissed her.

"OK. I'll talk to you later." Ash smiled as he left.

Ashley took in a few deep breaths trying to settle herself down and relax a bit. She had thought about the money situation quite a bit through the last few weeks and had come up with an interesting idea. She felt deep down that her mother took the money to punish her for wrecking the car, a consequence for her actions. It also related to all the time and energy of coming up here to see her and the time off of work and having to spend all of her vacation time. She felt her mother was very resentful of her for what she had done and she wanted to punish her, secretly, without anyone knowing. That's why she told her not to tell anyone. These were the reasons, Ashley felt, why her mother took the money, not to mention all the time and energy that went into finding another car.

Before long Dr. Kelly showed up. At first they chatted about all her new visitors and how enjoyable it was and, about the many different conversations. Then they talked about how her mother still had not shown up or called. Dr. Kelly then stated, "Your mother called me this morning. She wanted to know how you were and she also wondered what she should do with you after all that was said, to move forward. She feels that if she is so terrible why would you even want to be around her. I told her that she is your mother and you love her deeply.

I also told her you feel terrible about what you said and how you said it. I told her we all make mistakes, that there is always room for improvement no matter who we are. We do the best we can even if we are wrong and that it doesn't mean we don't love our kids. She can learn to do better, and so can Ashley; we can fix this. It's not the end of the relationship, but a beginning, a beginning of a new and better way to communicate." Dr. Kelly stopped and looked at Ashley. What do you think about what I said to your mom?"

"Wow, that's great. I feel way better now. How did she feel about what you said?" Ash looked all hopeful.

"Well, I think it gave her some hope about your relationship." Dr. Kelly nodded his head and smiled.

"But what did she say, exactly?" Ashley demanded.

Exactly "She said: did Ashley tell you what she said to me, and I said yes she did, and it must have been very upsetting and even hurtful. Ellen replied with a, well yes it was and it wasn't even true. I told her that perception, even if wrong, is reality for the person. She said she thought long and hard about the conversation and that she feels you don't understand how hard it is to be in her shoes, but she is willing to forgive you. She felt better after I explained about the perception thing she said, but she also explained that you are a very difficult child. I told her that part of it may be the sexual abuse she never got you treatment for. She wants to have a better relationship with you, and I suggested maybe the family meeting this week would be a good start and she agreed."

"Well, that's good. I want to bring up something too. At the start of this whole thing my mother took $ 1,000 dollars of the money I had saved for college, if I went instead of offing myself. Now I only have $ 450 left. She said it was to help pay for the car. At first I was fine with it until my grandfather said that the insurance was going to almost totally cover the purchase of a new car and she needed a new one anyway. So now I feel like she took the money to punish me in some way. She is resentful for having to spend all of her vacation time coming up here all the time. Now this past almost two weeks she hasn't visited. It's almost like it makes her happy that we're fighting because now she has a reason not to have to come up here every night.

Deep down she is glad about it, not that she would ever admit it. It is less she has to do for me and she has more time for herself.

Crazy thoughts but that's her," Ashley burst out.

"OK. One thing at a time. First you really think she took your money knowing she had enough insurance? Maybe she thought she didn't have enough insurance to cover the expenses of a new car, because there can be a lot of hidden expenses, and she didn't find out until later that she had enough and just forgot to tell you. Let's not jump to conclusions. We can ask at the family meeting, but we are not going to jump down her throat, understand ?" Dr. Kelly looked sternly at Ashley. "Yeah, I got it," Ash answered. "Should I bring it up to her before the meeting?"

"If you want to. I think it would be a good idea." Dr. Kelly shook his head.

"I feel badly that you believe she is happy about the fact that she isn't coming up to visit her own child. What makes you believe such a thing?" Dr. Kelly asked.

"Because I know her and it might be hard for you to believe but it's not for me. Trust me, I know her. She has always made comments through the years. At least I don't have to keep doing this or that. It's so annoying and a pain in the ass." Ash was nodding her head. "Well, that's her. She doesn't like having to deal with anything painful or that has her do extra, like go out of her way. If I feel bad she is like let's talk about something else so you don't get upset. I need to get things off my chest, but she just doesn't get it or understand, I guess." Ash took in a deep breath. "Guess that's why I needed a counselor at school and the funny thing is Ruth first insisted on counseling shortly after I came to their house. She could sense I needed someone and then my school principal also insisted and if I didn't go he would hunt me down and escort me to the session himself. My own mother never noticed how depressed I was or that I thought about dying every single day." Ashley took in another breath and then another.

"That's a heavy load to get off your chest. I didn't realize you thought about it that much," Dr. Kelly tilted his head to the side and waited patiently for Ashley to continue.

"No one realized how much I thought about it, although Ruth had an idea. She said she heard me crying at night. She could hear me through the vents." Ashley just stared off into space. "I could tell Ruth cared and that was when, well, she found speed in my pocket, I used to do my own laundry at my mom's. That was when Ruth told me to go see the drug counselor. It was in place of her telling my dad, and she kept her promise not to tell him. Later, I went to a scared straight program and it worked for the most part for a long time until I got too low again. Then nothing worked and suicide was the only answer." Ash confessed it all to him. She didn't want to be alone with all this anymore.

"So, do you trust Ruth?" Dr. Kelly gently asked.

"Yeah, her more than the other two, I'm tired. I'm tired of being tossed back and forth, of feeling like I'm not really wanted. I'm just alone." Ashley started to cry.

Dr. Kelly remained quiet, just listening, letting Ashley sit with her feelings.

"Do you really think this family meeting is going to help? Ashley sniffled.

"Yes, yes I do. I think it is going to change your relationship with all of your parents and for the better. I may as well tell you this now. I'm going to recommend you remain in counseling after you leave the hospital. I don't think in a month and a half we can solve all of the problems you have. You need someone you can trust to help you navigate all you have been through." Dr. Kelly got wide eyed for a second and wrinkled his brow. "Listen, it's about time to end for today. I'll come back tomorrow around the same time and we can chat some more. You did an excellent job today. I'll call your mother today and give her the green light to come visit if you would like me to." He smiled.

"I would. Thanks, that would be great," Ashley brightened right up. "Done deal. OK, I'll see you later." Dr. Kelly gently took hold of her toe and shook it as he left.

Later that day Ashley's orthopedic doctor stopped by on one of his regular visits, "Hey, kiddo, how we doing today?"

"Good. I'm tired of being in bed though." Ash gave him a smile. "I bet you are. Where has your mom been? I want to talk to her about you doing some physical therapy. First I need an x-ray to see how those bones are healing. Has anyone been up to do any exercising in the bed with that bar above your head?" The doctor asked.

"No, but to tell you the truth I've been lifting myself a little because my back and my butt are kind of sore being in the same position all the time. Sorry," Ash said with a half guilty smile.

"No, no, that's good. One thing about you kids, there's no stopping you. You heal up fast and like to get going." He patted her leg.

"Well, when your mom gets here, have her get in touch with me, through the nurse's station, OK?" He smiled as he was leaving.

"OK "Ash answered.

Not an hour later and the x-ray tech rolled in with her machine ready to take the films. "Hey, kiddo, I'm going to take some films. Let me check your name tag. You're Ashley, right?" The tech looked at her.

"Yes, that's me," Ashley answered.

"OK. Let's get this done." The tech. started to have Ashley lift herself to get the film cassette under her. As they went on, Ashley started to talk to her.

"So, do you like your job? I was thinking this might be something I could go into as a career, or at least to start my life in the medical field. Is it interesting?" Ashley asked as they did the x-rays.

"Yeah, I like my job. It's somewhat different every day. You get to help people and I enjoy it. It took just over two years of training and you can basically go anywhere and get a job," the tech answered, as they proceeded with the x-rays. The tech sort of explained what she was doing and why to Ashley so she could understand, and the more she explained the more Ashley liked the idea of getting into the field. Ashley was grateful for the mini lesson and asked to see the x-rays when they were developed.

"Well, I can ask the radiologist. He is the x-ray doctor. If it's OK with him, then I don't see why not." The tech smiled feeling good her patient was interested in her future. She was aware of the reason she was there. She actually took care of her the night she came in. She was sure Ashley didn't remember her and hopefully not that horrible night.

Ashley was thankful to the tech and read her name tag. "Kathy, thanks for taking good care of me. I appreciate it." Ash smiled at her nodding her head.

"No problem. Besides it's my job, but I love it. You take care and behave yourself. Don't be too hard on your nurses," Kathy said, as one of Ashley's nurses came in and was washing her hands.

"This one, she's not too bad!" Anna smiled as she winked at Ashley. Then she finished up and as she left she told Ashley, "As of right now there are a lot of job openings for x-ray techs, so it's a good field. Good luck." Then she packed up her machine and went on her way.

Ashley felt good about the little talk she had with the tech. She was interested in the x-ray field and the tech made it seem like it was something she could actually get training for and then get a job in the field. For the first time she felt like maybe she could have some sort of future instead of throwing in the towel. She took in a deep cleansing breath and actually felt good deep down. This was really the first time she had a direction for her future that didn't have a dismal outcome for her and her family. Having had such a heavy talk with Dr. Kelly left Ashley drained so she just lay back and drifted off to sleep.

Later on that afternoon Ashley awoke to the sound of Kathy, the x-ray tech., returning with her x-rays, in order to show her the films. She actually brought two sets one taken straight on and another taken sideways in order to show the breaks in detail. Kathy held them up in the window and pointed out the breaks and how they were healing up.

Ashley was amazed and extremely grateful. "Thank you so much for taking the time to come back here and show me all the x-rays and explain it all to me. It's very interesting, I'll never forget this. You made my day, thanks." Ashley smiled ear to ear.

Kathy smiled. "No problem, you're a good kid. Listen, I'll see you later. I've got to get back before they miss me." She winked at Ashley as she left.

Ashley then looked at the clock. Almost 3pm. She wondered if Dr. Kelly had called her mother yet. If he had, she would probably arrive around 5pm. Even though things were rough between them, she still missed her mother and longed to see her. As she lay there and thought about things between the two of them, she thought most likely she actually did owe her mother at least the $500 dollar deductible for the wrecked car. But then she also thought if she just let her keep the other $500 dollars, then maybe her mother would like her more and wouldn't be as angry with her. She rubbed her hand back through her hair regretting telling Ryan about the money situation. She knew he would not let it go as she was thinking about doing. She still had time to talk to Dr. Kelly about allowing her mother to keep it, no questions asked. What to do? What to do? How was she going to get out of this predicament without someone getting pissed off. She knew Ryan would be a challenge. Trying to keep him quiet would be hard at first but as time went by it would be easier. Besides, she thought trying to get the money back from her mother would be virtually impossible without a big fight. Privately Ellen would hold it against her for the rest of her life. Ashley knew deep down that she was never going to see that money again, so she may as well get used to it. She resolved herself to the idea of it and decided she was just going to have to get another job and save, save, save. Then when she goes off to college, she will just get another part-time job to help with expenses. As she lay there thinking about how she could afford college, it dawned on her that she could apply for financial aid. Yes, they had to give it to her. Her parents were not wealthy and were not going to pay for college. Hell they weren't even going to help. They told her she was going to flunk out of college her first year. Only Ruth believed she would be successful. Thank God for Ruth, Ashley thought. She was truly a God send, and Ashley was grateful she was in her life. If it hadn't been for her, she wouldn't have even gone to the counselor in school. At times Ashley felt Ruth cared more about her than both of her other two parents and that hurt her, but that's how it felt.

Ashley sat up in bed pulling herself up with the pull bar. She told her aide "Man my butt is getting sore from laying in one position all the time." She turned and chuckled a little bit.

"Yeah, it can get that way. Try turning… here let me help you." She got up and helped Ashley turn onto her side a little. "How's that?" she asked.

"Well, it's better, but not great," Ash commented.

"You fractured your pelvis, kiddo, so you can't exactly move all over the place, understand ?"

"Yeah, I know. Thanks for trying to help me." Ashley smiled at her. A few minutes later she was back to agonizing over thoughts about her relationship with her mother. She wondered why it was so hard for them. Her friend Kim and her mother had a great relationship. She was envious of them and wished she could have that with her parents. At times like this, when she felt so helpless and empty, she wished she had just died in that crash. It would be so much easier. Ashley thought, all of this, everything combined, is just too much, it's just too hard. I can't do it, I can't make it right. I can't fix it. Ashley looked at her aide and asked, "Can I get an Ativan, like now?"

"Yeah, no problem," she rang for the nurse.

Cori came in the room immediately with the medication. "What's up honey? You feeling anxious?" She gave Ashley the pill with water, "You having a hard day? Just try to lay back and relax. Let the medicine work, Ann will be here with you. I'll come back in a little while to check on you." Cori patted her foot and left the room. Soon after Ashley started to feel drowsy and then drifted off to sleep from the effects of the medication.

CHAPTER 18

*T*he sun was high in the sky and Ellen was feeling a sense of accomplishment. After days and countless hours of searching for just the right one, it was finally over. Excitement and satisfaction overtook her as she beeped the horn and raced out of the parking lot in her late model red Volkswagon bug, a car she had always had her eye on and finally it was hers. She flew home to scoop up Laura, Ellen beeped the horn all the way up the driveway. Laura ran out of the house and her eyes got big. "Oh my gosh, mom. I love the car. It's the coolest." Her smile stretched from ear to ear.

"So, I take it you approve?" Ellen got halfway out and stood behind the door.

"Definitely, are we going up to see Ash in it?" Laura raised her eyebrows.

"As soon as we are ready." Ellen cocked her head.

"I'm ready!" Laura smiled.

"Then, let's go," Ellen jerked her head towards the road. Laura immediately raced over and jumped in. "Hold on one minute. We've got to lock up and get a few things for Ashley first." She laughed as she went into the house for a few minutes. After what seemed like forever, Ellen returned to the car with two six packs of Pepsi and a couple of books, one being a new journal. Ellen was hoping to make a small peace offering to smooth things over between them. When she got into the car, Laura had already checked most everything out and she was impressed.

"Mom, this is a really nice car. In a way I'm glad the other car got wrecked. I'm not happy that Ashley did what she did, but I really like this car. It is so much nicer than the old one." Laura's smile was wide. "I can't wait to tell Ashley about it. It's too bad she can't leave her room to see it, but she'll see it soon enough, right?" Laura looked over at her mother.

"Yeah, she'll see it soon, that's for sure. I hope she likes it." Ellen half smiled, feeling a bit uneasy.

"How can she not like it. It's wonderful." Laura gazed at it all over again taking it in as if it were the air she breathed, full of life and bright like the summer sun.

Ellen looked at her daughter, full of life and joy. She sat there ready to go, her eyes bright and cheerful, as if she could take on the world. Ellen had thought long and hard about her life and the girls over the past week or so. They were so different, Laura never gave her a problem. Could it be that she just wasn't a teenager yet? She wasn't sure. She was such a joy to be around especially compared to her sister, Ashley, who was always in some kind of trouble or something. Being bounced between her and her father's house, sometimes it felt like she was a stranger. She never shared her feelings or plans about her future, unlike Laura who was an open book sharing everything.

Ellen just couldn't get over the thought that it had been partly her fault that Ashley had tried to kill herself. When Ashley hurled those words towards her they dug in deep like a dagger down into her soul. It was going to take a long time to heal those wounds. Deep down Ellen didn't really feel responsible for Ashley's decision to take her life. But she wondered how had she missed the signs of her deep depression. Hell she didn't even realize she was depressed at all. Maybe blue on occasion but aren't all teenagers moody at times. When she thought about the situation she thought maybe she was not as involved in her life as she should have been. But then Ashley wasn't open like Laura. She was very private and hard to talk to, especially about her feelings. Maybe she should have tried harder to interject herself into her life. She had thought about all of this and decided to just take it day by day and try to build a new relationship with her daughter, one that was built on honesty and trust. Ellen was really hoping that Ashley would get better by talking to Dr. Kelly maybe the family meeting coming up would help. This being the first time they saw each other since the big blow out, Ellen wanted Laura there to hopefully ease the tension between the two of them. She was really very nervous about coming to see Ashley, but she knew she had to visit her at some point especially before the family meeting.

"Mom, do you think Ash is better? I mean like in the head? Laura asked all worried.

"Yes, yes I do. I think her talking to the doctor has helped a lot." She smiled as she briefly looked her in the eye. "But I also think she will have to continue talking to someone after she leaves the hospital," Ellen added as she shook her head.

"Will she be home in time to go back to school? It's her senior year and that's your best year, or at least they all say it is." Laura asked.

"I'm almost positive she will be home in time, but we will just have to wait and see what the doctors say." Ellen pursed her lips with a sort of smile.

"Well, I sure hope so, cause I sure miss her being around the house." Laura took in a deep breath and let it out.

"I hope so too. It's not the same her being here instead of home but she needs to get better first, even if that means going to another place after this place, but that's between you and me. I doubt she will have to, but we need to do what the doctor says is best for Ash, OK?" Ellen tilted her head down and sternly looked at Laura. "Remember not a word about that to Ash, OK?" she reiterated.

"OK, I got it," Laura answered with a bit of an attitude. She knew not to disobey her mother, even if she felt she needed to side with her sister. Mentioning that to her sister would be disastrous and Laura knew she would be in big trouble if she did.

They were pulling into the parking lot just as it started to rain. They quickly parked and ran inside, experiencing a mid-summer thunderstorm. Shaking off the rain as they made their way up to Ashley's room, Laura was the first to pop her head in the door. "Hey there, sissy. How are you?" She ran over shaking her wet hair onto Ashley's face.

"Well, I can tell it's raining out," Ashley laughed. "It's good to see you. How's it going?"

Laura gave her big sister a hug and said, "I'm good, but it's kind of boring not having you around the house." She put her hand on her hip.

"Hi, mom. What's up with you?" Ashley nervously asked.

Her mother walked up and gave her a hug. "Things are good. I've missed you. How are you is the question?" She half smiled, her face not showing any real emotion.

"Well, Dr. Cohen wants to talk to you. He comes most everyday but yesterday he said he wanted to talk to you. He said just have the nurses call him. They want me to start physical therapy sometime in the next couple of days.

"OK, I'll go tell the nurses in a minute. Well I see you no longer have the nurse by your side, so you must be doing better." She nodded her head in approval

"Yeah, she left a couple days ago. It feels good to know that they feel I'm progressing as much as I am." Ashley smiled.

Laura, on the other hand, could hardly contain herself, "Ash, you should see the car mom got. It's a little red bug. It's so cool. Definitely our style; you'll love it," Laura was flying around the room.

"Really?" Ashley replied. She couldn't help but wonder how much her mother paid for it or how much of a down payment she put down. Had she spent the entire thousand she had taken from her. Ashley wavered constantly, sometimes she felt responsible and owed the money towards the car, then other times she thought that her mother needed a new car anyway and had insurance to cover the cost. Ashley also felt that her mother's actions or lack of interest in her life, helped drive Ashley to crash the car. Everything was just so confusing. She just felt it was so hard and she was never going to get it all straightened out. But she put on a good face and smiled at the two of them. As the conversation continued, there were several uncomfortable long silences. The trio talked about gossip running through the neighborhood and other trivial matters, always avoiding the really important conversation they needed to have. As the evening went on they felt the tension. Shortly before they were going to leave, Laura remembered the supplies they had in the car. She wanted to have a few minutes alone with her sister, so she hoped her mother would go.

"Oh, mom, we forgot the stuff in the car." Laura looked at her mother, it was getting dark so Laura hoped her mother would retrieve the items. Ellen felt awkward in the room and this was a good excuse to change things up plus she had to check in with the nurses so she offered to go "I'll go get the stuff. You two can visit for a bit." She cleared her throat looking at Laura as she left, as if giving a message to Laura to remain silent about their conversation earlier. She was no sooner out the door when Laura ran to check, making sure she was really gone. Then she started shaking her head. "Sissy, you have to get almost all better before you leave here, or else, I mean like really better. I promised mom I wouldn't tell you but I can't hold this in, not against you. The more I think about it the worse it makes me feel. It is like they are betraying you, conning you into telling them your secrets and then saying you're too sick to come back home. Oops, I wasn't supposed to say that part." Laura was all wide eyed and shaking. She rarely went against orders from her mother. Yet she had an alliance with her sister. They were close, really close especially deep, deep down when it really counted.

"Why what is she planning on doing?" Ash looked into her sister's eyes." Is she planning on leaving me in here or sending me away somewhere or locking me up in a crazy place?" Ash's eyes were wide with her mouth half open.

Laura just nodded her head up and down. "But listen. You can't let on that you know something because then I'll get in big trouble. Just get all better. If you get all better, you can come home. She says it's for your own good. Whatever you need mom and the doctors are going to do. So just get all better in their eyes. We have convinced people of things plenty of times so just do it all over again. This doctor that sees you, he was the one that told them about another hospital at the beginning of him seeing you. But the decision is theirs, I know that for sure because he said you know her the best. I'll keep my ears open as to how he thinks you are doing and let you know what he tells them." Laura ran to check the door. "Please, Ash, don't say anything to mom or your dad cause I'll get it really bad. Plus they will know you know and they may question your honesty and all that. Just get all better in their eyes, or like almost all better." Laura kept nodding her head. "Now when mom gets back here, tell her we talked about you and Ryan or the car so she won't get suspicious, cause I'll get it bad, OK?" She looked at her sister.

Ashley took in a few deep breaths trying to calm herself before her mother returned. "Yeah, sissy, that sounds like a good plan. We can do this. Thanks for the heads up. I will get totally better I promise. You're a good sister. I owe you big time. Don't worry I can pull this off, besides I really am much much better so everything will be OK." Ash kept nodding, then put her hand out to grasp hold of her sister's hand. "So you like the new car huh?" Just then her mother entered the room. "Surprise! I got you some Pepsi and some books along with a journal. I thought you may need something to keep you busy and it's a kind of a peace offering." Ellen smiled at her daughter as she set the materials down and gave her arm a heartfelt squeeze.

"Thanks mom. That was very nice of you. I appreciate it." Ash smiled while underneath she was seething. She wanted to yell and scream asking how could you even think about sending me away but she couldn't betray her sister, one of the few true people she had in her life. So she put on a false face and acted like all was well and good. "So when did you get the car? It sounds cool. Laura was raving about it while you were out getting my gifts. Red sounds real sporty. I can't wait to see it. Pretty soon I'll be out of here, only a few more weeks. I'm feeling better and now I'm starting P.T. I think things are going good, mom," Ash smiled big while nodding.

Ellen had been a bit nervous about their meeting but Ashley seemed really receptive to her visit, although Ellen still harbored resentment towards her for how she had blamed her for her suicide attempt. She knew that Ashley was still a bit confused with all that she had been through. But she did seem much better than before. Ellen thought it was amazing how far she had come in the week she had not seen her. After speaking with Dr. Cohen about Ashley starting physical therapy, Ellen and Laura left for the night.

Ryan showed up the following Tuesday morning with a smile as usual. Ash was waiting anxiously to tell him what her sister had revealed to her. After she explained everything that had happened during their visit, he sat there stoned faced. After it soaked in, he asked, "So like where are they going to lock you away? I mean is it … it's not written in stone, right?"

"Well, no, only if… Oh how do I say it? If I need it, I guess, that's what they said. It just sounds like punishment to me. They just don't want to deal with me for another year until I graduate. I feel like they want to get out of the deal as soon as possible. You know they want to be done raising me they are just tired of me and want to be done You know she was up here yesterday acting all nice because she was probably thinking she doesn't have to deal with me on a day to day basis. She is most likely counting the days. My father is probably in on it too." Ashley shook her head in disgust.

"So, what are we going to do?" Ryan held out his hands.

"Well, I've been thinking about this all night and first off I'm going to show this doctor how much better I am. Then I'm going to have a secret conversation with my mother. It is going to be about how no one will ever find out about the money I gave or should I say that she took for the car, if and only if I am allowed to come home after this hospitalization. Otherwise, everyone in our small town will find out about how the money switched hands. So what do you think about my plan?" Ashley raised her eyebrows up and down with an evil smile. "Well, you know she did tell me it was bad manners to discuss money with anyone other than who you are doing business with, so I would hate to develop a bad case of bad manners." Ashley laughed.

Ryan took in a deep breath and then stated, "Why don't you get emancipated and come live with me. I know my house is old and needs a lot of work but I could support you and you have your job, that would help. I know you have mentioned college, but you could still go if you stayed with me. I know I love you and I'm of age. You're seventeen. You should be able to go where you want. Then you can tell your parents to go to hell." He softly looked in her eyes.

"Oh, Ryan, you are so awesome. That sounds so totally perfect. Do you really think that they would let me move in with you?" Ash let out a sigh of relief.

"Why not? It's not like they are fighting over who gets you." He held out his hands.

"But what if I have to come back up here once a week for therapy? I mean how would that be?" Ash looked concerned.

"Well, I'm coming up here five times a week right now so once a week is no big deal," He grinned at her and gave her a kiss. "We could do this. I'm pretty sure your parents wouldn't care as long as they don't have to do much of anything, or anything at all."

"Well, the only problem is how they would look in other peoples eyes. That's their only problem, or our only problem. Wait a minute.

If we just tell the doctor I'm going to live with my mom and then when I get home I move in with you and I convince them to just let me see the counselors at school, maybe it could work." Ash sighed again trying to think of a plan that would work. She was getting lost in the moment. The longer she thought about it the more she realized her mother would never go along with such a deceitful plan or idea. Deep down Ashley knew this. "We can't do that. Scratch that idea. I just don't know if they will let me move in with you because of all that has happened and that I'm still in high school. It's like they don't really want me, but they don't want people to think they don't want me." Ashley sighed heavily. "I'm doomed."

"Well, if you're not allowed to move in, you can just spend all of your free time at my house. How's that sound?" Ryan squeezed her hand.

"Yeah, that's probably how it's going to have to be. I'm sorry. I would have loved to move in with you." Ash pursed her lips as a tear rolled down her cheek. Ryan got up and wiped it away. "Don't cry. You'll make me start to cry. I love you so much. We will be together soon enough." He caressed her cheek.

Ash sniffled briefly, then took in a cleansing breath. "I know I need to get the hell out of here first and foremost." She glanced up at the clock. "Holy shit, it's almost time for Dr. Kelly to come." She looked at Ryan.

"Well then, I better get going. Stay strong and remember our plans," He gave her a kiss and headed out.

Ash sat there for a moment and thought, plans what exactly were our plans. Oh yeah, just to be really better right, yeah that's about it. She wondered if she should discuss the money thing with him. If he is going back and telling her parents things, then how can she trust him. However, she did recall how he said he only told them how she was doing emotionally and not particulars of their conversations. So she needed to decide to either trust him with this or not. Oh how difficult this was. But if she did mention it to him and he told her mother, then it would definitely prove to her his trustworthiness in the future. So she decided to just go for it and tell him and maybe get his opinion on it.

Soon enough Dr. Kelly arrived with his soft demeanor and smile the same as every time, just welcoming her to entrust him with her secrets, right from the start. She wasn't sure how he emitted such a warm and caring vibe, but he did and she soaked it up. It felt good just being in the room with him, like it was starting to fill some huge hole inside of her. Yet, she thought, she had better not share that because she didn't want him to think she was needy or weak or sick. She needed to put on a strong solid face like at school with her friends how they all acted, happy and cheerful that would work, she thought.

As Dr. Kelly sat down, he smiled at Ashley and asked, "So, kiddo, how are you doing? I heard you had a visit with your mother. How did it go?" He tilted his head and gently rubbed his hands together.

Ashley let out a big sigh. "Well, it went pretty good. She brought me up some Pepsi and a couple books and a journal. I guess she wanted to maybe bring some type of peace offering, I'm not sure. She also brought my sister along so we really didn't discuss anything serious, or anything about our argument. It was kind of awkward throughout the visit, with a lot of tense quiet moments but my sister helped a lot because she broke it up quite a bit. So we really didn't solve anything. We just danced around the elephant in the room. She also bought a new car to replace the one I crashed. Laura said it is awesome compared to the old car, like a hundred times better and it is cool. I guess it runs way better too. You see our old car my grandpa said was a lemon that didn't run very well and he said we needed a new one anyway so I shouldn't worry about wrecking the car." Ashley suddenly stopped and took in a deep breath, wondering if she should continue.

Dr. Kelly commented, "Yes, so how does that make you feel?"

"Well it's kind of … kind of complicated I guess," she looked down and away.

He softly asked, "Maybe you could tell me and we could sort your feelings out. Then you could have a better understanding of the way you feel and maybe how things are." He leaned in towards her.

Ashley sighed heavily, then again, and she decided to just go for it, and tell him what happened, so she started. "Well, when I was first in here like after the first week, my mother was very upset about the car. You know that I had crashed it. She was really angry at me because she had to go out and search for another car, you know, all the time and energy it takes to find a car. She felt that since I crashed her car I should come up with some money to help replace the car. Now I have had a job and have been saving, just in case I go to college, and she knew this. I had 1,450 dollars saved. So she demanded that I give her 1,000 dollars towards her new car. She also said I am not allowed to tell anyone because it is very bad manners to discuss money with people you are not doing business with. It was just between her and me and I was not allowed to tell anyone. The longer I thought about it, the more I kind of thought, it was a lot of money to have to give to her for a car that was no good anyway. And her not wanting me to talk to anyone else about it makes me think that she is taking advantage of me. She also got money from the insurance company and my grandpa said it was enough to cover the cost of a similar vehicle." Ashley just looked at Dr. Kelly, unsure of what he was going to say.

"Wow, that's a lot to keep inside all this time. Did you tell anyone else?" He asked.

"Yeah, I told Ryan and he was very angry about it, but I told him not to say anything to her about it," Ashley admitted to Dr. Kelly.

"How did his reaction make you feel? He asked.

"Well, that he thought she was taking advantage of me, and that he wanted to take care of me. You know, make everything all better, fix the problem," Ashley answered.

"Sounds like he cares about you," he commented.

"Oh, I know he loves me. We are going to be together forever, I just know it." She smiled. Ash thought for a moment about how Ryan had suggested her moving in with him but decided not to mention this to the doctor. "Plus Ryan is already mad at my mom because she told him he is not allowed to come up and visit me. That's why he comes in the morning, just to avoid her. Then he works late to make up the time. He thinks she was wrong to take the money, especially because it was for college." Ashley raised her eyebrows and pursed her lips.

"What do you think?" He asked

"Oh, I am so confused over this whole thing. Sometimes I think I owe her some money, just not all of what she took, maybe half of what she took. Then at other times I feel like she got a bunch of insurance money, and her old car was a junk heap. She needed a different car anyway, so I shouldn't have to give her anything. My grandpa said she got a large check from the insurance company and he told me not to worry my mom would be just fine. She made out great, and he said except for me crashing the car and feeling so bad it was the best thing that could have happened, because mom made out just fine. So if she made out so well, why did she need my money too?" Ashley shook her head. "I didn't tell Ryan the part that grandpa told me because he would have flipped out on my mom. It makes me feel like she wants to punish me for this whole thing and that's how she is doing it, with the money. She knows the money means something to me, whereas nothing else really does. I mean what can she really do to me. Plus she resents having to come up here every night after work. She was probably in her glory when we were fighting because she didn't have to come up at night. She could just go home and relax." she sighed deeply.

"It must feel pretty bad to think your mother doesn't want to come up and visit you, that you're a burden," Dr. Kelly replied softly.

"Not really. I'm used to it. Neither one of my parents ever want to go out of their way for us. We all have learned from a very early age not to ask for anything that would make them commit to anything. We can't go out for sports because we would need a ride, I was expected to get a job, but Ryan has to pick me up because it's too late for them; shit like that. So the money is just her way of privately screwing it to me." Ashley just shook her head.

"Why don't you bring this up with your mother, instead of just stewing about it. Maybe you could renegotiate the amount of money that you say she took from you, and arrive at an amount you both could be happy with?" He suggested.

"Well I kind of want to ask my grandpa if he thinks I should have to give her any money at all. I mean if it is such an OK thing then why I am not allowed to talk to anyone else about it. That docsn't make sense to me." She frowned.

"I think getting it out in the open is a very good idea. Would you like to bring it up in the family meeting next week?" Dr. Kelly rubbed his hands together.

"Yes, definitely. Now who exactly is going to be there?"

"Well, both your mom and dad, and Ruth. It depends if you would like your grandparents there, and I think your sister should be there for just part of it. What do you think?" He adjusted his seating position.

"Yeah, that sounds pretty good. Maybe Laura and my grandparents could just be in the same part though. Would that be OK?" Ash looked him in the eye, something she didn't do very often and he took note of it.

"That would be just fine. It's your meeting. You are the one that's our main focus." He smiled at her.

"Dr. Kelly? I'm nervous about this meeting, I'm afraid that my parents are going to…well kind of… kind of gang up on me, yell at me. I know I've done a lot of bad things in the past, but now I'm… well .. I'm better. I'm actually thinking about my future. I want to go to college and be an x-ray tech. I never used to think about my future before just dying, but that's not the case anymore. I just feel so different now and I want to thank you for helping me feel better. All my friends, their parents are so much better than mine. I'm not stupid, besides my friends tell me they feel sorry for me. No one ever comes over to my house. I always go to my friends' houses and I see how their parents are compared to mine. But it will be OK I only have another year and then I'm off to college to start my life the way I want to live and it will be fun. I mean I know it is going to be a lot of studying and stuff, but my friend's sister says that college is also lots of fun, so" and she left it at that waiting for the good doctor to put in his words of wisdom.

"Well, we need to get you out of the hospital and into an acceptable living situation first and foremost, not to mention a whole year of high school. I think you need to slow down a bit and take it one day at a time for now. But I'm liking your enthusiasm. It's nice to see you're feeling better, even with all that you're going through." He smiled and nodded his head.

"So I hear you're starting physical therapy tomorrow. How does that feel?" Dr. Kelly asked.

"I can't wait, I'm excited just to get going again. Over three weeks of just healing my pelvis bones is boring beyond belief. I'll be happy to get out of this room for a while." Ash smiled wide. They continued to talk for a little bit, until their time was up.

"Well, kiddo, I've got to go, so I'll see you tomorrow probably after you have your first physical therapy session, so you can tell me all about it," Dr. Kelly got up and waved as he left.

Ashley sat alone just thinking, thinking about how she was going to talk to her mother about the money. Part of her wanted to just forget about it, just bury it. Then another part wanted justice, at least part of the money back. She decided that she could live with her mother taking half of what she had taken. This amount was much easier to swallow than 1,000, and it's not like she was saving for some material thing, it was for college, her future and her mother knew this. None of this seemed fair but life wasn't fair. She might as well get used to it. Something made her think of her father. She wondered what he would think of all of this. She doubted he would come to her defense. Most likely he would make his usual statement, "I'm not getting involved, it's between you and your mother." His indifference towards their struggles never ceased to amaze her. He never wanted to get involved in any disputes they had and especially with their mother. It was as if she had some sort of spell over him. He rarely if ever crossed her. He used avoidance as his tool to get on in life, even at the expense of his children. Thankfully Ruth was not a confrontational person as was Ellen. Ruth believed in calmly and quietly talking things through.

Ashley just sat thinking, what am I going to do? Where am I going to live? I don't really think either of my parents want me, especially to live in their house. Heck, I'm not even sure they even love me. Why would they with all the trouble I got into. And they wonder why I've been suicidal.

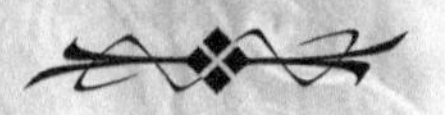

CHAPTER 19

*I*t was late afternoon when Ashley returned from physical therapy. She was exhausted and, even though they had worked her hard, she loved every minute of it. Just being somewhat active again made her happy, not to mention she got to leave her room for a while. Once back in bed she dozed off to sleep for a few hours until her dinner tray arrived. Her meal was a Cheeseburger and French fries which were a bit soggy but not too bad and she got a soda that was usually a little watered down by the ice but drinkable, along with her favorite sugar cookies for dessert. And boy was she hungry, she gobbled down her whole dinner then rang for her nurse, to ask for more.

"Hey, sweetie, what can I do for you?" Amie asked, another nurse who sometimes took care of Ashley. She had long brown hair and was short on everything but humor.

"I ate my meal but I'm still really hungry. Could you order me more? I had physical therapy today for the first time and I guess I used all my energy up," Ash smiled.

"They gave you a good work out huh? Sure I'll get you something more. You want another cheeseburger and fries?" Amie checked a few things while she was there.

"That would be great. Thanks. Oh, don't forget the sugar cookies." Ashley raised her eyebrows.

"No problem." Amie walked out and gave Ash a quick wink.

Ashley settled in to watch some TV while she waited for her tray. As she was flicking trough the channels, her mother popped in, alone. Ashley was nervous that she was alone, but she knew they needed to talk about the money situation and she was sure that was why she was here. "Hi, mom," Ashley nervously stated.

"Hi, Ash. I can't stay real long but apparently we really need to talk. Dr Kelly called. He said you're doing very well but you want to talk to me about a sensitive subject. He didn't say what, but that maybe we should talk about it before the family meeting." Ellen looked her daughter straight in the eye. This look made Ashley feel quite nervous about things, the look had always had that effect. "Just what did you tell the good doctor about us that we need to talk before the meeting? That you want to bring up at the meeting? Ellen stood firm looking at her daughter as if she was not to be crossed.

"Well… I.. uh. . mentioned how grandpa said the wrecked car was basically a lemon and you needed a new one anyway…"

Meanwhile Ashley's second tray arrived and Amie grabbed it to deliver it but as she got to the door she overheard the conversation and didn't want to interrupt, she stood for a few moments trying not to listen but that proved impossible.

"And grandpa said you got an insurance payment too, and you told me not to tell anyone that you took all the money I had saved for college…"

"Stop, I did not take all the money, although maybe I should have. Do you have any idea of how expensive it is to come up here all the time, and then on top of it buy you soda, books and magazines, or whatever else you might think you need. Then, of course, there is your sister, the good one, who never does anything wrong. She sees you get all this stuff so I have to buy her things to make up for your bad choices." Ellen stared down her daughter who was starting to get very anxious.

"Well, I am sorry I am such a burden to you. I realize that I smashed your car, but grandpa told me it was on its last legs. This way you got an insurance check for it, which was way higher than what they would have given you for a trade-in. He told me that too. Maybe I do owe you some money but not a thousand dollars. That was almost all the money I had. I can't believe this all boils down to money. It's like that's all you think about. So, if I'm too expensive, then don't bother coming anymore because I really don't need you." Ashley's anxiety slowed as anger overtook her.

Just then Amie saw her cue to enter the room. "Hey, Ash, here's your second tray. Oh, hey, your mom's here. Where do you want me to set it down?" Amie set it up on the bedside table, then made herself busy in the room checking this and that, stalling for time and, hoping things between the two would calm down.

Ellen was furious with Ashley for even voicing the situation to her doctor, let alone bringing it up now within earshot of others. "Are you almost finished?" Ellen snapped at the nurse.

Amie took offense mainly at Ellen's tone. She may talk to her daughter like that but who does she think she is talking to. "I still have to take her vital signs." She really didn't but she wanted to stay in the room for as long as possible. Boy, did she want to give Ellen a piece of her mind. Who says things like that to their child. It only took a few minutes to take Ashley's vital signs. "Well, kiddo, you're still with us. If you need me just ring your buzzer." She put it right next to Ashley and glared at Ellen as she left.

After she was out of earshot, Ellen looked Ashley in the eye. "Now see what you've done. You turned the nurse against me because of this. Thanks a lot." Ellen breathed heavily while shaking her head. "Oh, yeah, it's all my fault," Ashley sarcastically replied.

"You better check that attitude right now little girl. I can make your life miserable or wonderful at any time, so watch what you say. I am not fooling around. You need to accept the fact that you willingly donated every dollar to me and bury this money thing or else. That's that, done and over. Got it?" Ellen glared straight into Ashley's eyes as if she were burying her words deep down into her soul.

Ashley didn't know what to say so she just agreed. "Got it," she answered beaten down.

"Well, now that we have reached an understanding I've got to go, I'll be up soon enough." Ellen patted her leg, then left.

Ashley sat there stunned. She felt totally beaten down, destroyed, pulverized. She decided she definitely did not want to return to her mother's house when she got out of the hospital. How could she trust her mother? Now she felt as if her mother only came up for show, so she would look like the caring mother to others. That is what she cared about what other people thought of her. If she could get out of coming to see Ashley, she would, no doubt in Ashley's mind. The doctor said she wasn't thinking in her right frame of mind at the time of the crash, yet her mother acts as if she were making a rational decision. What happened to love and understanding? Her mother didn't have any of either for her anyway. She was hurt by what her mother said and felt very alone. She was questioning herself again: am I really such a burden? Then she thought, I'll just do better in life, make better decisions. I'll do better in school and she'll see, she's wrong.

Now she thought she had to convince her father and Ruth to take her in, yeah convince because no one really wanted her. She can't really blame them. She did get into trouble sometimes. She had two younger brothers at her father's house, and she enjoyed spending time with them. Hopefully, they would realize that she would be a big help with the children. The more she thought about it, the better it sounded. She and her father got along most of the time. It was just when they didn't, they really didn't. Ruth, well, she was awesome. Ashley enjoyed spending time with her. She hoped they would take her in because, in a way, they were her last chance.

Ashley knew if she brought the money up again, her mother would make her life a living hell so she may as well kiss that money good bye. She would get even though. Maybe not now, but in the future, somehow she would get even. After she gave it some thought, she recognized how sad it was to want or need to get even with her own mother. Why, God, why did You put me in this family? I just want a family that wants me, maybe even loves me; a tear rolled down her cheek.

Later that evening she called her father's house and talked to Ruth. They talked about the children and this and that. Then she asked Ruth when they were coming to the hospital. Ruth told her they were coming up to visit her on the weekend. She explained that it was hard to get a sitter for the kids, but her parents were kind enough to watch them this weekend. Ashley was anxious about asking but decided to just do it over the phone, "Ruth, I've been thinking. Do you think when I get out of the hospital that maybe I could come live with you and dad and the kids. You know, kind of get a fresh start. I promise to be good, I won't disappoint you, I promise." Ashley sighed heavily. "If you think dad will say no, then don't mention it to him. Just keep it between us."

"Oh, Ash, I'm sure it would be fine with your father. I know it's OK with me. I would love to have you. Are you sure you don't want to stay with your mother?" Ruth inquired.

"No, definitely not. I don't want to stay with her at all." Ash breathed a sigh of relief.

"I'll mention it to your father when he gets home. I'll tell him the good news," Ruth answered, "I'll talk to you later. Love you, bye."

"Thanks, Ruth. I love you too, bye." Ash hung up the phone, happy as she could be. She so hoped that her father would agree to letting her come live there. Ruth sounded hopeful so she was pretty sure. If this worked, it would be the first step in alienating her mother from her life.

Ruth finished up the dishes and then went in the living room and sat down next to Rodger. "Honey, we need to talk about something." Ruth rubbed her hands together.

"Is everything OK? Rodger inquired.

"Oh, yeah. I spoke with Ashley today and she wanted to know if she could move back in with us and the kids. She promised to be really well behaved." Ruth chuckled.

"Really? What's Ellen got to say about it?" Rodger asked.

"I don't know. In fact, I'm not even sure she knows Ash has asked us, but she sounded so sincere and a bit desperate actually," Ruth explained. "I don't know, Ruth. She was such a handful last time and when all that happened." He tilted his head, frowning, while looking her in the eye.

"I know, but she promised to behave and she needs us. Obviously she isn't getting along with her mother if she has asked to move in with us. Remember she is great with helping out with the kids. Rodger, she is your daughter and she needs you, us. We need to be there for her, especially after what she has been through. Obviously Ellen has checked out on her. How did she get in such a mess on her watch? She needs to know that we care about her, love her, want her and she can get a fresh start here." Ruth gave him her please look.

"Oh, honey, I can't win against that look on your face. Oh, all right. But if it goes all wrong, you and you alone are cleaning up the mess." Rodger sighed.

"Thank you. Don't worry. It will be just perfect, well maybe not perfect, but great. Thanks, honey." Ruth smiled

Rodger laughed shaking his head side to side. Ruth was so excited by his answer, she called Ashley with the good news. They also agreed not to tell Ellen about the move until the family meeting which was only about a week away, and then the following week Ashley would come home. After the phone call, Ashley felt a huge sense of relief. She knew she wouldn't be sent away if she said the wrong thing especially about her mother. She knew it would be better at her father's this time because she had goals and it was her senior year of school. She needed to buckle down and focus on getting all of the classes she needed and good grades to get into college. There was no room for messing around this year. It was going to be all business.

Ashley then called her sister Laura who just happened to answer the phone. "Hey, girly girl, it's me. Listen I need you to do something for me, OK? Go into my room and in my closet on the top shelf under my art books there is four hundred fifty dollars. Take it and give it to Ryan tomorrow morning. I already told him to come by and get it from you,

Can you do that for me?" Ashley asked.

"Sure, sissy, no problem," Laura answered.

"Don't tell mom. I can't explain now. If she hears us…" "Oh, she's not home. She's out on a date,"

"If she asks what happened to it, you tell her Ryan came and got some things out of my room at my request, OK?"

"Sure. But why do you think she will take your money?

"Oh, if you only knew."

"What's that supposed to mean?" Laura questioned her sister.

"I'm not allowed to say, but at one time there was another thousand dollars to go along with that four-fifty, but I'm not allowed to say a word. It's only because I trust you, so mums the word, got it?"

"Wow, I got it. Mums the word," Laura answered, shocked. Laura immediately went and got the money just as Ashley told her and gave it to Ryan the following morning. Ryan went directly to the bank and deposited it into an account he set up for Ashley and himself, since she was a minor. Then he set off for the hospital, bank book in hand to show Ashley. When he arrived she was down in physical therapy so he waited in her room for what seemed like forever. It was getting close to the time that he needed to leave when she returned to her room. "Hey, how long have you been here?" Ashley asked surprised to see him.

"Oh, not too long" he lied smiling. "Look what I've got!" He shook the bank book in his hand.

"You put it in the bank. That's so cool." She smiled.

"Now she can't touch it. It's safe and sound." Ryan grinned.

"Thank you so much. You're the greatest boyfriend ever." Ashley breathed a sigh of relief.

"Just looking out for my girl." He winked. "Got to save for college." He gave her a kiss.

"I love you so much; you're the best," she kissed him back. "Hey, I've got to go to work. You spent all our time in physical therapy, but that's OK because it means you're getting stronger, I hate to leave, but I have to." They kissed again and again and again. "So I'll call you later. Love you. See you later."

"I'll talk to you later. Be safe. Love you too." Ashley waved.

Ashley thought about Ryan and a smile came to her face. She thought how handsome he was and so smart to put the money in the bank. Now her mother could never get her hands on it, and that brought a bigger smile to her face.

Ellen had been stewing about her conversation with Ashley for a few days when her new insurance bill arrived in the mail; it went up significantly. As far as she was concerned it was totally unreasonable. How in the world, she thought, could it possibly go up that much. She ranted and raved about it, to an empty house. Then she thought, I know exactly where I'll get the extra money. Unfortunately, Laura came home to find her mother tearing apart Ashley's closet. She suspected she was looking for the money that she secretly removed so she quietly went to her room. Ellen noticed her walk by and immediately swung around. All disheveled she demanded to know what had happened to the money. "Where is it Laura? Where is the money? You and I are the only ones who live here, so if anything has been moved, it has to be either you or me. So where is it?" Ellen stood with her hands on her hip's eyes glaring at Laura.

"Uh.. Well.. uh Ryan came the other day and went in Ashley's room to get some things for her. He could have taken it, I guess," Laura answered just as Ashley had told her. Yet she was scared, scared her mother was going to explode on her.

"Why didn't you tell me he was here? When he came?" Ellen furiously demanded.

"You weren't here. I didn't think it was a big deal. What are you looking for that is so important?" Laura added. She quickly thought this was a good reply to make her mother stop and come to her senses.

Ellen took in a deep breath and just looked at Laura, disgusted. She marched to the phone and punched in the numbers to Ryan's phone ready to unleash her fury. When he answered, she didn't even give him a hello. "What do you think you are doing coming into my house and removing property. I ought to call the police on you. That is called robbery," Ellen screeched.

Ryan gave it right back. "Oh yeah? What you did is robbery, taking her college money, you. You…" He wanted to call her a bitch but he knew it would ruin any future with her, so just in case he needed to deal with her, he held back. "In fact, why don't you call the police. I would like to hear what they have to say about it." Ryan's nose was flaring. He was shaking, but he knew he had to stand up to her and for him it was better over the phone.

"You need to stay away from my house. You are no longer welcome here." Ellen backed down because she didn't really want to call the police. Being a small town, word would get out and she didn't want that. She just slammed down the receiver and yelled out. She was now boiling, seething with anger, feeling she was outsmarted by some kids. Then she thought, she will get what's coming to her one way or another, both her and Ryan.

Ryan no sooner got off the phone with Ellen and he placed a call to Ashley, telling her what took place just so she was informed. "Hey I'm still shaking from it, I never had to stand up to your mother before, but it was kind of scary." Ryan readily admitted.

"Tell me about it I've had to do it for years, by myself. Lots of times I would do most anything to avoid it." Ashley nervously laughed. "But not anymore, I'm moving in my Dad's and Ruth's house, goodbye Ellen, she doesn't even know it yet. We are going to tell her at the family meeting it's in three whole days, I can't wait." Ashley breathed a sigh of relief.

"Well it's farther away for me but I don't mind. I'm sure I'll get along with your Dad and Ruth just fine," Ryan answered. They said their goodbyes with peace and a touch of happiness, each realizing Ashley was going to be safe at her father's house.

Ashley thought this whole situation with the money had just gotten out of control, she decided that she would not bring it up at the meeting unless her mother put up a fuss about her moving in with her father. She just wanted it to be over and done with, she thought I can always make more money, but I only have one mother. And she hates me right about now, all I wanted was for her to love me. Well if she doesn't want to come up she doesn't have to, then a tear rolled down her cheek. What is wrong with me, it is like trouble just follows me, I just have to do better, I have to. She rolled over and quietly cried herself to sleep.

Before she knew it the day for the family meeting had arrived, Ashley was now able to leave her room in a wheelchair a couple times a day, she had healed faster than expected. The doctors chalked this up to her being so young and healthy before her injuries. So as time came for the meeting she sat in her room waiting for everyone to arrive. She had asked her father and Ruth to come a bit early so she didn't have to be alone with her mother, and they agreed, unfortunately her mother came even earlier. "Hey Ash how are you doing today?" Ellen asked.

"Oh hi mom, I'm OK, how are you?" Ash asked surprised. "I'm OK I just wanted some private time with you. I hope we can put all that ugliness behind us and start over? OK?" Ellen looked sternly at her, but not the mean look.

"Yeah sure, we can do that," Ash answered in compliance.

"Great, OK" Ellen nodded her head in satisfaction, letting out a sigh of relief. I'm going to grab a coffee I'll be right back.

A few minutes after she left Rodger and Ruth strolled in "Hey babe" her father greeted her with a kiss on the forehead. "Hi honey" Ruth smiled at her.

"She is here, she went for a coffee, she said she wants to put all the ugliness behind us," Ashley was breathing heavy.

"Well that's OK, just relax, we're here now, you're OK, she can't hurt you," Ruth immediately answered.

"Yeah don't worry, just relax," Rodger gently motioned his hands up and down to settle her down.

Then in walked her grandparents and Laura, "Hey sissy I'm here for you,," she smiled

"Hi honey, "Her grandparents said almost in unison

"Hey thanks for coming" Ash smiled at them. I guess we're pretty much ready, mom went to get a coffee she'll be right back. Now we just wait for Dr. Kelly he should be along in a few minutes he's hardly ever late.

Everyone was gathered in Ashley's room when Dr. Kelly arrived, he lead them to a conference room and had just Ash and her parents and Ruth go in. At first they discussed her medical issues how she was doing in PT and what her needs will be when she goes home. Then her relationship with Ryan came up for discussion, not only how important she felt he was but also how much older he was. Such as what his expectations are in a relationship verses hers, like sexual, Ellen jumped on this and suggested maybe they should see less of each other. She was still very angry with him for that little stunt they had pulled. Ashley became very upset and jumped to his defense. She told them he had never ever forced her to have relations with him. Which he hadn't, she had always wanted to, but she didn't offer that piece of information, as far as she was concerned it was none of their business. Dr. Kelly also suggested Ashley is hungry for male attention and that's why she was so involved with Ryan. Rodger then informed the Dr. that he would do his best to spend more time with his daughter. Ellen jumped in and sarcastically said "yeah right like when".

He came back with a resounding "a lot more time, since she will be living with me."

Ellen was shocked, she sternly objected, how could they do this behind her back, "that's not going to happen" She snapped.

Rodger just shook his head and said "Yes yes it is, look at what happened on your watch, it's definitely going to happen," he shook his head.

r. Kelly spoke up "Listen we all need to calm down the both of you need to be on the same page when it comes to Ashley, she needs stability," He looked at both of them.

Ashley sat back listening, amazed that her parents were actually fighting over who was getting her, she had always felt they fought over who had to take her. Why would they even want her in the first place, should she say that to them, let them know how she has always felt, she really needed to talk to the doc privately, she wondered if she could ask him for a private moment, so she just took a deep breath and went for it. "Dr. Kelly I was wondering if I could just talk to you for one minute by ourselves, please?" Ashley's forehead was all wrinkled up with worry.

He thought for just a moment "Yeah we can take a five minute break," Dr. Kelly excused her parents and sat next to Ashley "What's up kiddo, things getting to hard for you?" He gently asked.

"Well you see how they are fighting about who gets me, I've always felt they fight over who has to take me, like they don't really want me. I know I get into a lot of trouble so I can understand why, but now I'm confused because deep down I feel like they don't even love me, so why would they want me. Should I tell them that or will they get mad because I shouldn't feel that way." Ashley asked in desperation.

"I see, that is quite the predicament. It must feel terrible to think your own parents don't love you." Dr. Kelly turned his head to the side and gently looked at her. "I think they need to know how you feel, I doubt you will get into trouble and I'll be right here to support you, OK?" Dr. Kelly nodded.

"Well I finally said it to someone so I guess there's no turning back now," Ashley agreed.

With everyone back in the room Dr. Kelly made an announcement, "Ashley has something very important to tell you, it is very sensitive and hard to say so I need you to pay attention and think before you respond, remember it is how she feels," Dr. Kelly nodded at Ashley.

"Well I don't exactly know how to say it so I'll just say it, my whole life it's always seemed like you two fight over who had to take me, not who gets me, like you don't want me. I can understand the fact I get into trouble, I'm sorry for that, but I feel like you don't really love me, there I said it," Ashley let out a deep breath. Glad in a way she let it out but nervous that she did, now they would be able to get at her, hurt her with their words.

Ruth was the first "Oh Honey," she started to cry, "Oh I'm so sorry, if I ever did anything to make you feel like that, I love you so very much. I realize I'm only your stepmother but I love you as if you were one of my own, I will do everything in my power so you never feel like that again, I'm so very sorry," Ruth swallowed hard with tears in her eyes.

Rodger and Ellen spoke at about the same time, each telling Ashley they did in fact love her and were sorry she felt that way. It was as if the whole tone of the meeting took on a different vibe, more sensitive and caring, not the anger and fighting from before. So Dr. Kelly directed the meeting back towards the living situation, and asked Ashley "So Ashley you want to go live with your father and Ruth correct?"

"Yes, I think I need a fresh start and I only have one year before I go to college, plus I plan to go back to my job, and that way I can save up some money for college." She looked at her mother as she said the last part.

Dr. Kelly asked "Have you decided what you want to study?"

"I want to be an x-ray tech, I talked to them when they came in and did mine and it sounds like it would be a good job for me," Ashley answered "But I'll have to buckle down in school and make up some courses, which will also keep me out of trouble" she nodded.

"Cool, sounds as if you're making goals which is good." Dr. Kelly smiled.

They talked about rules and guidelines she needed to follow while in her father's house and how she would need further treatment, it was then determined she should continue therapy. If she couldn't get it set up through the school or somewhere near their house she could return to see Dr. Kelly after she left the hospital. They then had her sister and grandparents come in and they all talked about how the suicide attempt had affected them, especially the fear and thought of losing Ashley. They all, but especially Laura, expressed the huge fear that if things went badly she could do it again. They also discussed how important each one of them was to each other and how important it was to keep the lines of communication open. Then they ended the meeting with a group hug, most everyone was happy with the outcome and glad the meeting took place.

Ashley was happy and since she was already out of her room she took a quick trip outside to see her parents off, this was her first time outside since being admitted to the hospital. She took in a deep breath and looked at the sky, the sun was setting on the horizon, it was beautiful. She saw them off then went up to her room and collapsed on her bed totally wiped out. She thought about today and the meeting couldn't have gone any better and moving in with her dad and Ruth, she thought life's getting better.

CHAPTER 20

$\mathcal{T}$he last week in the hospital dragged by, each day slower and slower, one bright spot was seeing Dr. Kelly every day, he was so easy to talk to and Ashley had become quite fond of him. Not to mention she actually trusted him to an extent, something she had never really done with an adult. Ashley felt a little sad that she was not going to be seeing him very much after she left the hospital, but her joy about leaving overshadowed it. Finally her day came, after she said thank you to all of the staff she was wheeled out to her father and Ruth who were happily waiting. "Come on Ash, let's go home," her dad smiled as he carefully shuffled her into the car.

"Well how's it feel to be out of that place?" Ruth cheerfully asked as they pulled away.

"Great, I can't wait to get home, see the boys and get on with my life" Ashley smiled wide, feeling a sense of freedom almost a liberation from captivation.

Once home they helped her into the house, she hadn't walked all that much in the hospital. She was supposed to go to physical therapy at the local medical center starting the very next day. In just a few weeks school was supposed to start, no one knew if she would be strong enough to start, except Ashley. She was determined to go back with everyone else, home school was not an option in her mind. As they made it up the stairs she went to her room and laid down exhausted from the trip and short walk. Ruth had gone to her mother's house and gathered her things with Laura's help and set them up for her, Ashley looked surprised. "Ruth you did this for me?" Ash asked astonished.

"Well yes, with Laura's help, I thought you would want your things, that it would make you more comfortable," Ruth smiled at her and caressed her arm.

"Thank you, that was so nice, I really appreciate it" Ashley answered in awe someone would go to such lengths for her.

"Well we love you and want you to be comfortable, I'm so glad you're here, really I am," Ruth started to get chocked up, so she turned and left not wanting Ashley to see it. Ruth felt terrible that Ashley thought that her parents didn't really love or want her. She thought how awful it must have been for her, how lonely she must have felt, she just shook her head in disgust. She wanted to make it up to her, although she realized she could not parent her out of guilt. This was a slippery slope she must navigate with caution, patience and stability.

Rodger had gone and picked up the boys from Ruth's parents, Michael and Jacob burst through the door, ready to play with their sister. After some more explaining they quieted down and agreed to be easy with her and allow her to rest. However as soon as their parents were out of sight, up the stairs they crept, "Hey Ashley" Michael whispered desperate to hear her voice.

"Hey you monkey's," they quietly heard back.

"Boys, boys where are you," Ruth called from downstairs.

"You better go before you get in trouble, I'll read you a story later, OK," Ash winked at them from her bed.

"Promise, "Michael answered. Ash gave them a nod and they scampered off back downstairs to play.

After a short nap Ashley got up and went downstairs, she sat at the kitchen table, the hub of the house, and asked Ruth if there was anything she could do to help with dinner. Ruth got her some potato's and a peeler "There you go, are you sure you're up to it?" Ruth asked.

"Believe me this is great compared to just sitting around all the time, it's nice to feel useful," Ashley answered as she started to peel away. "Besides I could do this in my sleep, from doing it so much at work,"

Later that night after the boys took their bath they settled down for bed and as promised Ashley went in and read them not only one story but three and she was glad to do it. Even being so much older she enjoyed spending time with her younger brothers. She felt special when they would run up to her and hug her leg or pound on the window when she got off the bus glad to see her, they made her feel loved. An emotion she was so desperate to feel she enjoyed those little boys so very much and loved them back just as much.

The following day was Ashley's first appointment at P.T. so Ruth made the appointment time to coincide with Michael's afternoon baseball practice and it worked out perfectly, they were even finished at about the same time. While they were busy with that Ruth actually had time to run a few errands, with just Jacob, so she was happy. When they arrived home Ashley was tired but she asked Ruth "Do you think your parents would let me borrow their exercise bike? I need to get into shape if I'm going to start school in a couple weeks, can you please ask them for me?" Ashley asked.

"Well I don't see why not they don't ever really use it, I'll give them a call," no sooner did she quit talking and she was on the phone asking.

Not an hour later and her father showed up with the exercise bike "Anything we can do to help" her father, Bart, remarked. They were good people always ready to help in any way they could. "So you going to ride this old thing are you?" Bart winked at Ashley.

"That's the plan, thanks for letting me borrow it, I really need it," Ashley patted the seat. They had placed it in the living room so she could ride it in front of the T.V.

"Well somebody might as well get some use out of it, at our house all it did was collect clothes. Well alright I've got to go, see you later," Bart left with a wave, he was never one to stick around long. He hopped back in his pick-up truck and on down the road he went. He was not out of sight when Ashley jumped on that bike and started to ride at first it was on an easier level, she pedaled and pedaled, working up a sweat. She kept pushing herself but finally she could go no farther, the bike read almost 2 miles, she was not satisfied but stopped and after she rested went and showered. Later that evening she got back on the bike and started to ride again. And that's how it went for the next week Ash would get up in the morning and try to ride for about 45 minutes, get ready go to P.T. come home ride for a while then again after dinner. By weeks end she was riding at least a few miles each time she hoped on the bike, Ruth and her father were impressed to say the least. Her determination was fueled by her intense desire to start school with everyone else.

One morning after her routine she sat at the table with Ruth "Do you think I'll be strong enough to start school next week? I mean it's

6 days away, we go to the doctors in three days. What do you think he will say?" Ashley wrinkled her forehead, looking all worried.

"I'm not sure what he'll say, but I think you're strong enough, even if maybe you get tired and have to go to the nurse's and lay down for a while, but that would be OK," Ruth nodded her head very optimistically. "Have you given any thought to what the other kids might say? You know about all that has happened," Ruth raised her eyebrows and wrung her hands a bit.

"No not really, I mean what can they say that can hurt worse than what my mother said," Ash just shook her head and looked at the floor.

"Well sometimes other kids can be very cruel," Ruth hated saying that, but she knew she needed to at least to warn her.

"Yeah I know, but if it's that bad I'll just beat the shit out of them," Ash commented, Ruth looked shocked her jaw almost hit the floor. "I'm just kidding, besides I'm not strong enough, so I'll have my friends kick the shit out of them," Ruth's eyes got big, "I'm kidding, I'm kidding, relax," Ashley chuckled.

"You are going to give me a heart attack" Ruth shook her head while smiling.

"Yeah I had you going there didn't I, sucker!! Don't worry I'll be good, besides I need to concentrate on my studies to get into college." Ashley smiled. But deep down she was worried about what was going to happen at school, although she tried not to dwell upon it. As long as her friends still accepted her then she really wasn't too worried about what the other kids would say.

Since school was starting soon Ruth and Rodger decided to get Ashley all the things she would need to start along with the rest of the kids including new clothes. Ashley was pleasantly surprised by her shopping trip with Ruth, she enjoyed spending one on one time with her, not to mention getting new clothes.

Ryan had been coming over to see Ashley quite often since she had been home, he fit in well at her fathers the two got along very well. Rodger actually trusted Ryan he even allowed him to take her up to see Dr. Kelly twice since she had been home. He wanted to stay in contact to make sure the transition went well. As far as she was concerned it was going great, she was determined to make it work this time. Ashley felt she had grown up a lot since the last time she lived with her father and would not act out as she had before, so there was no reason for anyone to worry. Her last session with the Doc went well and she was actually kind of sad that she had to say goodbye to him. But he told her if she needed him she could call and they could talk over the phone. Over the summer she had grown to be quite fond of him and knew she would miss talking to him. She was going to switch over to the school psychologist once school started. Dr. Kelly also told her to give the new counselor a chance to get to know her before judging him. She had given him her word that she would and that she would be honest with him even if it was hard. Ashley wasn't too sure about that part of their deal, she wasn't one to be to forth coming, especially about deep secrets. She didn't trust very many people hell she didn't really trust anyone with her deep secrets. No one not even Ryan did she trust with her personal secrets. Although she had been thinking about how Dr. Kelly said it's lonely to not let any one in, so maybe she should let Ryan in, he is worthy. She thought he is a really good guy, most of the time. He has been coming over a lot and just hanging out, because her parents won't allow her to go out. But he doesn't seem to care, he acts as if he is having a good time just hanging out with Ashley and her parents and he even plays with her and her little brothers, Ashley realized that he's actually having fun.

So Ashley got the OK from the doctor to start school with the rest of the kids, she was beyond elated. After she and Ruth arrived home her first phone call went to Ryan "Hey guess what? The doc said I could go back to school Tuesday along with everyone else, isn't that awesome."

"Oh that's great, I'm so happy for you" Ryan answered.

"Well I told him Ruth's idea that if I get too tired I could always go to the nurses office and lay down for a bit then go back to class, but that I doubt that I would need to do that since I've been riding the bike so much and far several times a day every day, and I don't want to miss any more school than possible. I said my education is important and I need to get good grades this year because I goofed off the last few years. And I discovered I want to go to college for x-ray, that I never had a goal before but now I do, so I want to pursue it. So I told him all of that and he agreed it was important and I was strong enough." Ashley breathed a sigh of relief. Ryan heard it over the phone.

"Well I am so happy for you, I know you have worked so hard for this and it has paid off big time. I just want to jump through this phone and give you a big hug. Look I would love to stay and chat but I've got to get back to work so maybe I'll talk to you after work, OK?" Ryan asked.

"Yeah that would be great, so I'll talk to you later." Ash hung up the phone.

Finally Tuesday had come and Ashley was nervously on her way to school, Ruth had agreed to drop her off, because Jacobs daycare was just up the road. Ruth had also just returned to work herself as a nurse's aide. They pulled into the parking lot and Ashley got out without hesitation "See you tonight Ruth thanks for the ride" Ash waved goodbye.

"Have a good day" Ruth smiled as she drove off.

Ashley went in and waved to some fellow classmates, many other kids just looked her way. She was nervous that they all knew what happened over the summer. Then Mr. Mills caught sight of her and immediately came over. "Hello Ashley, how are you feeling?"

"I'm OK" She nodded trying to get away.

"Well if you need anything I'm here to help" Mr. Mills offered. "Thanks, but I'm OK, really I am" Ashley answered as she gently walked away trying not to be rude. She thought this may be harder than I realized, I hope the teachers just leave me alone. After a short walk she entered the main hangout bathroom and pretty much everyone stopped talking and looked at her, so she just looked back and said "Hey how's it going?" … silence… then Karen spoke up "Hey Ash, come over here" as she waved her arm and then everyone sort of started talking again, yet also paid attention to her.

"Hey Ash don't let anyone get to you, how you feeling anyway, you seem OK to me, glad to see you" Karen smiled and patted her on the back.

"Thanks Karen I'm doing pretty damn good" as most of the room listened "I'll tell you though, it was a fucking ruff summer that's for sure" Ash chuckled while she shook her head.

"Well you look good, don't let any of those ass holes get to you, your OK in our book right girls?" she spoke up to the whole room. And all in unison "Right" came back from the usual gang.

"Thanks" Ash shouted back, feeling good. She knew where she belonged, the group she hung with were an OK group as far as she was concerned, and at that moment she really needed them and they were there. This made her feel a much needed acceptance which made coming back to school so much easier, because she knew there would be some who would give her grief about what had happened.

During lunch Ashley bumped into her sister Laura she was a freshman this year. "Hey girly girl" Ash put her arm around her.

"Hey sissy how's your day going?" Laura asked surprised to see her. "Good my crowd has been very excepting, Thank God because I was worried about it to tell you the truth. What about you, how's your day going?" Ash asked looking in her eyes.

"Well it's OK, a couple of older girls kind of pushed me around a bit" Laura confessed as she looked down, and gently kicked at the floor.

"What girls?" Ash demanded wrinkling her brow.

"Well I don't know, just older with blond hair pulled back" Laura replied.

"You come with me" Ashley gently took her by the arm and lead her into the bathroom.

"Hey" she sort of shouted, "Hey guys this is my little sister, Laura, she is a freshman this year and someone is giving her crap, if you see anyone giving her a problem do me a favor and slap them, thanks" Ashley shouted over the chatter.

"No problem….OK....Glad to….sure…..sounds good" were several of the responses of the girls in the bathroom.

"Thank you, all of you" Ashley answered. The two then left the bathroom arm in arm and went and had lunch together. Laura was grateful to her sister for helping her out, not to mention having lunch with her, being a senior having lunch with a lowly freshman. Ashley mentioned how they should meet for lunch everyday, so they could spend time together. Laura thought it was a great idea and readily agreed to it, she told Ashley it was very lonely at the house without her so this way they could talk everyday, Ashley really missed her little sister so this was perfect for now, the two girls were happy to be in the same school it helped them remain close.

Later in the day with two hours left until she caught the bus home she had a class College Comp. It was supposed to help teach you how to write an essay to get into a College. The teacher was explaining how the assignments were going to be given when a girl, as Ash would say a goody- goody, spoke up, "Mrs. Williams you better be careful with these assignments some of us may not be able to handle them because they can't deal with life itself. We wouldn't want them to hurt themselves." And she looked directly at Ashley, as did the whole class.

Mrs. Williams spoke up "Tiffany that was uncalled for, now stop it" Mrs. Williams tilted her head and looked at Ashley with the I'm sorry expression. But Ashley had started a comeback, "It's sorry ass people like yourself that cause people like myself to do the things we do so go to hell, I'll kick your ass" Ashley was standing pointing her finger at Tiffany. Who was a bit wide-eyed, "Mrs. Williams you're not going to let her get away with that are you?" Tiffany protested. On the inside Mrs. Williams was cheering Ashley on but on the outside she could not allow that kind of behavior "Ashley you can't talk like that or threaten her I have no choice but to send you to the office for the remainder of the hour. She then wrote a note and sent Ashley on her way.

Down at the office Mr. Mills read the note and had Ashley join him in his office. "Well I wanted to talk to you privately anyway. I was worried about you, I heard what happened."

Ashley exhaled "Yeah you and the rest of the world" she shook her head.

"Well how do you feel now? Who are you living with?" Mr. Mills asked.

"I'm OK really I talked to a doctor every day in the hospital and I'm supposed to talk to someone here and I'm living with my dad again along with my step-mother, Ruth she's great." Ash smiled.

"So what happened in class? Your already in trouble" He commented. "Tiffany came out with some of us can't handle assignments or life, I said shut up or I will shut you up, basically" Ashley waved her hands. "It's tough enough coming back to school I don't need to take crap from her"

"Watch the language"

"Sorry but she is so…ugh…just so…difficult" Ashley teared up a little.

"Well I can understand your dilemma, I will speak to her privately" Mr. Mills answered.

"I really don't want you to it'll only make things worse" Ashley replied.

"Well I don't condone her behavior either, she should have been sent down here along with you and I'll convey that to her." Mr. Mills commented. "Now it's almost time for your last class so why don't you go make a guidance appointment and then go to class and I'll catch up to you later, oh and I'm glad you're OK" He motioned her towards the door.

"Thanks, see you later" Ash left and went to the guidance, she quickly made an appointment then off to the bathroom to hang before her last class for the day. She had quit smoking in the hospital and wasn't sure she wanted to start again. After all she wasn't working to pay for them and Ryan didn't smoke so maybe she should just stay stopped, at least for now. Yet she enjoyed hanging out with this crowd this was where she felt she belonged, besides this was where they got high and discussed who had what, maybe not today, but she knew it would happen soon enough. So she chatted with a few of the girls and now after hanging out that morning and part of lunch they treated her like nothing ever happened and she was glad. She told a couple of the girls what had happened with Tiffany and they were not too happy about it, swearing and vowing to give it back to her. Ashley told the girls how she said she was going to kick her ass but in reality she was still too weak, they offered to help make her life a bit more difficult, nothing too serious but difficult. Ashley chuckled and said do what you got to do, thanking them for their help. She couldn't help but think what good friends she had as she left for last class. That was one thing about small schools everyone pretty much knew everyone else and their business.

Before she knew it her day was over and she was getting off the bus, glancing up at the house there was her little brother pounding on the window as she made her way up the driveway. She did it, made it through the day without going to the nurse's office to rest.

She made it with out to much grief and not too many people asked her if she needed their help, so it was a success. Her little brother came up to her and hugged her leg to say hello, she played with him for a few minutes then went to talk to Ruth.

After telling Ruth about her day including about being sent down to the office and how Mr. Mills said Tiffany should have also been down there. She explained that this was not how she envisioned it to have been, she wanted to just focus on her studies, why did they have to say shit to her.

Ruth sighed heavy and said "You know some people have boring or uneventful lives so they need to stir up trouble with others. It's a lot harder to walk away and take the high road than to stay and fight even though it would feel really good to kick the heck out of her" she stood shaking her head.

"Yeah I suppose, but Mr. Mills said he would talk to her, Ruth you know he's only going to make it worse. She's going to be like oh you got him to fight your battles now and I told him that. Oh I don't condone either behavior, well that's not how it's going to come across" Ash just sighed.

"I'm sorry honey," Ruth tilted her head.

"Yeah well I would just appreciate it if you wouldn't tell my dad I already got sent down to the office" Ash asked.

"OK just this once" Ruth shook her finger at Ash.

"Thanks, I just don't want him to regret taking me in because I'm not going to be in trouble all the time, that's just not what I'm about anymore. I really want to just go, get good grades, graduate and get into college. I want you both to be proud of me for a change." Ashley confessed.

"Ash you have come so far, we are already proud of you" Ruth softly clapped her hands, now let's get supper ready.

Over the next few days school became a real battle, Ashley was continually battered with verbal assaults from this one particular group of girls. They found it quite amusing to loudly berate her about the cause of the accident, claiming Ryan truly wanted the cheerleader, Vanessa, that night. That he actually made plans to see Vanessa on the side just before she went in the hospital. He only stayed with her because he was afraid she would actually kill herself if he broke up with her and he didn't want her blood on his hands.

The first time Ashley heard this she couldn't believe her ears then she almost went up and punched the girl, Mary, in the face but she immediately ran up to a teacher and found refuge in class. So Ashley looked at Mary and mouthed I'll be waiting for you later. Mary's eyes got wide and before she could say anything to the teacher Ashley disappeared. Ash went straight to the bathroom she was so upset she wasn't sure what to do. Nervously pacing back and forth Ash just kept repeating don't let them get to you, over and over again. The bathroom had cleared out by the time she had calmed down and classes had begun, Ash knew she was late and needed a pass to get in, so she went to the guidance office, hoping she could get a pass. Once there she noticed Mr. Shore's office door was open so she thought maybe he would give her a pass he was nice like that. "Hey, I know you're probably busy but do you think you could give me a pass?….. Please" Ashley's brow all wrinkled.

"Well well,well… No, hi how are you, how did your summer go, just can I get a pass, huh. Why don't you come in for a minute and explain why you need a pass. You look kind of…..well out of sorts, what's going on?" Mr. Shore raised his eyebrows while he motioned her to sit.

Ashley took a deep breath and sat while he shut the door behind her. "I'm sure you heard all about my summer just like the whole freaking school" Ashley looked at the floor, her knee shook up and down.

"Well I may have heard a bit, but I would rather hear what happened from you" Mr. Shore rubbed his hands together.

So Ashley proceeded to tell him all about the night of the accident and then her stay in the hospital and most of what her parents said and did throughout the summer along with her relationship with Ryan. She also informed him how Laura was a freshman this year and how she didn't want her to know about her drug use and reputation, how she didn't want her following in her footsteps. She explained that she was a good kid and already had a plan for her life so she didn't want anything derailing that. That seemed to impress Mr. Shore he had never really seen that side of Ashley before but he liked it.

Finally Ashley confessed about all of the taunting and teasing from the group of girls and how she wanted to beat the living hell out of them yet her hands were tied because she was still too weak to do it. And how she was toying with the idea of having her friends do it for a bag of weed because they were making her life unbearable.

Mr. Shore suggested "Listen there has to be a better way, maybe Mr. Mills can speak to the girls and explain that they need to cut the shit or get the shit kicked out of them" He chuckled.

Ashley laughed along with him, "Yeah like he would say that" "But that's the gist of it right?" Mr. Shore asked with all sincerity. "You know it"

"I'll talk to him, see what we can do to fix this without anyone getting the shit kicked out of themselves, OK? He nodded. "So it's almost time to go for the weekend, let me write you a pass for class then just go home and try to relax and hopefully Monday I'll get Mr. Mills to talk to the girls and things will get better." Mr. Shore looked sympathetically into her eyes.

"OK I'll give it a chance, but if things don't change quickly I'm going to get someone to teach them a lesson in manners, you don't mess with a crazy person" Ash smiled.

"You're not crazy"

"How do you know, you have no idea of what goes on inside my head" Ash sighed heavily.

"Well then I guess we have a lot to talk about?" He raised his eyebrows.

"Too scary"

"Well we'll just take it one step at a time." He tilted his head and pursed his lips.

"See you later" Ashley got up and went on her way.

Being a Friday night Ryan was coming over and Ashley had a lot she wanted to talk to him about. Had he really had feelings for Vanessa? Did he really go back to the party to see her? Did he go see her while she was in the hospital? All of these questions echoed in her mind. The more she thought about it the more upset she became, by the time she arrived home she was visibly upset so Ruth asked her what was going on.

"I can tell something is wrong? Did you have more problems with those girls? Did you get into trouble again? Ruth looked into her eyes.

Ashley started to tear up "Those girls, well one of them told me that Ryan went back to the party that night to be with a girl, Vanessa, then she said that he is seeing her on the side that he has the whole time I was in the hospital and is only with me because he's afraid I'll kill myself and doesn't want my blood on his hands." she was crying at this point.

Ruth could not believe her ears "No I don't believe that for one minute, and neither should you" Ruth came over and started to stroke her hair. "Those girls just get some sick satisfaction out of tormenting you, you need to stop listening to them because they are full of shit" Ruth shook her head in disgust. "This group gets their power every time you react to their stupid ranting, Ryan loves you, he is not seeing anyone else, that's just plain crazy." Ruth sighed deeply "Listen you've had a long week and you're tired, Ryan isn't coming over for at least 3-4 hours why don't you go up and take a nap. Things won't seem so bad when you've had some rest, because deep down you know he loves you and this is just a bunch of girls trying to get under your skin" Ruth Patted her back.

"Yeah maybe you're right" Ash gathered her things and headed upstairs. She flopped down on her bed all these thoughts going through her head, she wasn't sure what to think. What exactly happened when she was in the hospital she didn't know. But as for what was going on now she believed he was being true to her, at least she hoped. He didn't seem like he was just fulfilling an obligation as far as being with her so she wouldn't kill herself. At one point she thought maybe it would have been better if I had died at least I wouldn't have to put up with all of this bull shit. Tears ran down her cheeks as she drifted off to sleep.

CHAPTER 21

Ryan walked up to the Ashley's parents' house, knocked as he let himself in with a "Hello anyone here?" as he strolled into the kitchen. Ruth met him with a "Hi, Ryan. How was your day? Oh, listen, I just want to give you a heads up. That group of girls is still tormenting her and now it's about you and her, so be warned she's very upset." Ruth shook her head in disgust.

"They don't know anything about me so how can they say anything?" Ryan waved his hands, his palms started to sweat thinking about what they could have said about him.

"Well, they are letting her have it …. And she is letting it get to her, so I had her go lay down for a while, hopefully to help her relax. Things always look better when you're well rested. Anyway, why don't you go up and roust her out?"

"You mean you're letting me go in her room all by myself?"

"Make sure you leave the door open all the way. I will be checking in on you." Ruth lowered her head and pointed her finger at him.

"Yes mam" Ryan shook his head as he headed for the stairs.

He was trying to be quiet but the creaking of the old staircase gave him away and it awoke Ashley, Ryan peeked his head in the door only to see her just waking up.

"Hey, there's my girl. You're so pretty when you first wake up." Ryan smiled at her.

"Thanks." Ash sat there, now even more confused. She thought how could he cheat when he talks to me like that, or maybe he talks like that to cover it up. No, don't think like that. Oh, I hate my mind.

"So I heard you had another bad day at school,"

"Those girls, they just can't seem to leave me alone." Ashley sighed while shaking her head.

"What exactly are they saying about me or us? I mean they know nothing about me so how can they say anything?" Ryan shook his head.

So Ashley filled him in on all that was said and how upset it had made her. She was so confused. Part of her wanted to ask, yet she wanted to believe he would never cheat on her. But for her own piece of mind she needed to hear him say it. "So did you?" She implored him.

"Did I what?" He answered.

"Did you go back to the party to see her? Ashley looked into his eyes. He looked at the floor. "What does that matter. We are here now together. To hell with the past." Ryan retorted.

"So that means yes right, you did, I need to know the truth so I can fight these girls off. I need to know all of the grueling details as painful as they may be for me to hear. I can forgive you, but only if you are being true to me now. If you really want to be with me, that's great. But if you're only with me because you're afraid I'll kill myself, then we need to part ways now." Ashley looked him directly in the eyes as tears started to roll down her cheeks.

"Ash, I want to be with you. I do, I really do. Don't let those girls get between us," Ryan pleaded with her.

"Well, then, tell me the truth." She sniffed as she sat upright in bed ready to hear all he had to say. She took in a deep breath and let it out, then looked him straight in the eye.

"OK…The night of the party I did go back to see Vanessa and I kissed her, but that's all, I swear. Then I felt bad about it and left. I ended up at your mom's house with Laura. Then when you were in the hospital, she called me a few times. It was when you first went in and your mom told me you didn't want anything to do with me; you hated me. I was thinking we were pretty much over. But that's why they know so much about you because all I did was talk about you and what was going on with you." Ryan was continuing to look at the floor, too worried and ashamed to look at Ashley.

"So that's it. You just talked. Did you kiss her or did you sleep with her?" Ashley demanded to know.

"Oh, Ash, I love you not her," Ryan stated.

"That's not what I asked." Ash glared at him.

"She is nothing to me. I'm here with you. That's what's important," Ryan pleaded.

"Ryan, tell me the truth now. All of it," Ashley demanded.

"OK, OK I did sleep with her but only one time. It was only a rebound thing, honest. But let me tell you it was nasty. I mean nasty. She is like a wet sock she has been with so many guys. Afterwards, I just got up and left, I was so disgusted. Seriously, she has nothing on you. I know I'm the only guy you've had. So I started asking other guys if they have had Vanessa and like after fourteen guys I stopped asking. They all say she's a slut so you can use that against her. She has given practically the whole soccer team blow jobs, some on the same night." Ryan was hoping to divert her attention away from his actions and on to Vanessa's.

"Did you use a condom?"

"Of course, I'm not taking a chance of having a baby with that slut or getting some disease," Ryan immediately responded.

"Part of me hates you right now. In fact, you need to leave." She frowned getting angrier by the minute.

"But…but you said you.. you could forgive me," Ryan weakly appealed, trying to hang on to their relationship.

Ashley stood up and got in his face. "But that was before you said you slept with her and I never said how long it would take. Now get out of my room before I punch you in the face." She turned around and faced the window. After a few moments Ryan quietly left her room. As he was leaving he said, "I love you Ashley Ames. That will never change. Please give me another chance." He descended the stairs defeated and in tears. He never thought she would find out about Vanessa because she had told him she wouldn't say a word to anyone about their hook up. Rotten bitch, he thought. He wanted to get even with that whore. Mess up his relationship, over a nasty hole. Shit, he thought, now what was he going to do. The love of his life may not take him back. Man, I can't believe I did that. What was I thinking? My life is over. He passed through the kitchen and Ruth saw him, tears running down his cheeks. "What happened?" she asked.

"Ashley broke up with me because I'm an asshole that made a huge mistake and I can't take it back." Ryan kept walking, looking at the floor trying to hide his tears.

Ruth was on his heels. "What? Wait. What are you talking about?" Ryan kept walking.

"Hey, wait. Come back here and talk to me," Ruth insisted. Ryan stopped briefly, turned around and said, "Ashley broke up with me because I'm a loser. I'll let her tell you why because it's even unbelievable that I even did it but I did, so I've got to go." He turned and departed, now a stream of tears running down his cheeks.

Ruth stood bewildered for a moment as she watched him drive off, then turned and ran upstairs to Ashley's room. Winded from the climb she asked, "What happened between the two of you?"

Crying in front of the window Ashley turned around exclaiming, "He cheated on me when I was in the hospital with that slut, Vanessa, so they are telling the truth. Now how am I supposed to fight them off when they are telling the truth?" she cried out.

"Oh, honey, I'm so sorry." Ruth went over and hugged her tight.

"I just don't know what to do. At first, before he told me, I said I could forgive him but that was when I thought he just made out with her or something, not slept with her." Ashley sniffled. "I just can't believe this is happening, I mean what else can go wrong." She stood embraced in Ruth's arms, crying, just wanting this to go away.

Later that night, as Ashley lay in bed, she thought about her relationship with Ryan and how much she loved him. He had really hurt her, yet she knew she couldn't just let him off the hook. He had to know his actions were serious and there were repercussions. He had to earn her trust back and make this up to her somehow, but how? She didn't even know how. Never had she imagined he would cheat on her. The saying, once a cheater always a cheater, yeah that kept ringing in her ear. Her mind kept going and going. Somehow things would work out, they just had to. Finally she drifted off to sleep with all this going around in her head.

After a couple of days Ruth and Ashley sat down Sunday night to talk this over, before she returned to school. "So, when exactly did he do this and for how long did it go on?" Ruth gently inquired.

Taking a deep breath to calm herself Ashley began to explain what Ryan had said. Ruth listened carefully and then sat calmly and began to tell Ashley what she thought. "From what you told me I think he thought that you didn't want to see him anymore. Your mother told him you hated him, you had just tried to kill yourself and he may have thought in part it was because of him. He, it sounds, was with this girl because he was trying to get over you and apparently all he did was talk about you or how would she know all this stuff about you. It sounds like, to me, that even though he was with her, he was still crazy about you. And it was just a rebound thing because from the information he was getting, you hated him and never wanted to see him again. Think about it for a minute. How would you feel if you were in his shoes and he just tried to kill himself and you were told he never wanted to see you again? For guys it is different than girls. They get over things by moving on where we sit and cry to our girlfriends and eat ice cream and watch sad movies, but guys they need to get on with it. Move on, that's how they deal with things. So it wasn't that he wanted to hurt you. He just wanted to heal his own heart because it was broken. Does that make any sense to you?" Ruth reached over and patted her arm.

"Well, when you put it like that, I guess it makes sense, but it still hurts that he did it and now she knows all this shit about me. What am I supposed to do? How am I supposed to fight them off?" Ashley sighed heavily.

"He says he only slept with her once, right. So you can remind her she was only a one night stand and wasn't good enough for a return visit and he went back to you, the love of his life. I mean I hate the thought of you fighting with this type of ammunition, but I also hate the way they are treating you. It's not exactly very mature to be caught up in this type of rivalry. You know what I mean, and you should tell her that. She should be ashamed of that type of behavior. I wonder what her parents would say if they knew what was going on," Ruth added while shaking her head back and forth in disgust. "In fact maybe we should just call her parents and explain the situation and all that has transpired. See what they have to say about it because this has got to stop." Ruth shook her head.

Ashley spoke up quickly "Wait. Then I'll be known for that too. Please let me try to handle this on my own. But I do like what you said about him only being with her the one time because he thought I hated him and she was just a rebound thing. That all he did was talk about me and her bringing all this up and her keeping this going is so immature and she doesn't have anything better to spend her time doing. Hopefully that will put an end to it and she will stop because I'm tired of fighting with her and reliving this shit everyday." Ashley weakly smiled at Ruth. "I just want to get good grades and go on to college and start my life over somewhere where no one knows me." Ashley sighed, putting her head in her hands.

"Sounds like a plan." Ruth smiled at her.

Later that evening she called Ryan and they talked about things, making up. He swore to her that he would never be unfaithful again and she was the love of his life. He also told her again that Vanessa was nasty and he regretted sleeping with her. He was so very sorry that it had gone down that way. If only her mother had never told him she hated him and never wanted to see him again. That had crushed him inside. Part of him wanted to die when he heard that. She was the most important person in his life and Ashley told him he was also the most important person in her life even though it didn't always seem so. They talked for a while and when they finished, she actually felt really strong in their relationship.

She placed another call that night. It was to Kim. She felt unsure about this whole situation. After explaining everything in detail, she asked Kim what she thought she should do. Kim suggested that she pray for guidance and pray for Vanessa, not only to stop tormenting her but pray for her soul. She said to let God deal with her and not to take harsh actions against her. Ashley answered with, "I figured you would say something like that."

"Then why did you call?" Kim asked.

"Because I guess I just needed to hear it from you," Ashley responded. "But I'm not sure I can do it, but I will pray for all of them."

"I'll pray too," Kim answered. "And I'll talk to you tomorrow at school. You know I'll always be on your side.

"Yeah, I'll catch you later, thanks" Ashley hung up

As Ashley lay down to go to sleep she thought about all that had gone on and she decided she was going to stick up for herself. She was still riding the exercise bike everyday and she was getting stronger and stronger. If it came to blows, she felt she was prepared, yet she hoped it wouldn't. They were cheerleaders so they probably wouldn't want to fight and she didn't want to fight other than with her words. So she tried to come up with several different scenarios that could come up and have come backs to them, in order to verbally annihilate them and embarrass them in front of their classmates. But before she gave up for the night she did put in a rather lengthy prayer for the girls and for herself, praying mainly for strength and all of this nonsense to just end. By the end of her prayer, after she had asked God for guidance, she really wasn't out for revenge against these girls and didn't really want to embarrass Vanessa in front of everyone. Her desire to really hurt this girl had diminished, although she couldn't forget what she had done. A sense of letting go had emerged. She lay in bed and thought some more. She decided if they come after her then she'll go after them, but only if they do it first.

When she arrived at school the next day, she headed straight for the bathroom to gather with her friends. They never hassled her for any of the problems she faced during the summer. In fact they helped support her. She actually asked Karen and Emily along with Amy, this was Amy P, an underclassman they were friends with, not the Amy who graduated last year. Amy P. was also in their circle of friends to help just kind of watch her back a little. They all said, no problem, they would. One thing about a small school is that most everyone knows everyone else's business so this was no real secret. And other smokers also volunteered to step up and help out, without being asked to. Ashley thought, oh man, I don't want some kind of war happening here.

Now all of these cheerleaders would walk down the hall and their books would continually get slapped out of their hands onto the floor. "Oh, were those your books, so sorry!" and they would laugh as they left the scene. Not to mention all the times they got slammed into their lockers by Ashley's crowd. The girls would laugh and talk about it in the bathroom in between classes. It made Ashley feel as if she wasn't alone against these girls. So she didn't know what to do but part of her was glad her friends stepped up to these girls.

At least she wasn't alone with this anymore. She also decided to still stand up to them if they came after her again, but her friends hardly ever left her side, so she was almost neveralone and that's usually when they struck. Finally a few days later Ashley went up to Vanessa and said, "Look I've had enough of all this shit. If you leave me alone,

I'll make the other girls leave you alone. No more slamming you into lockers or slamming your books to the floor Just shut your mouths and all of this will end" Ashley looked her in the eye.

"Swear." Vanessa just stared at her.

"No, I came here to blow shit up your ass. You idiot." Ashley just shook her head.

"I'll talk to the other girls. I'm sure they'll agree." Vanessa turned back to her locker.

"Oh, and Ryan, he said you're like a wet sock, all used up. Bye," Ash turned to leave.

"Whatever, you bitch."

"Slut, blowing the whole soccer team." Ash took off down the hall.

Vanessa just stood there in the midst of everyone staring at her. She shouted, "She's lying you idiots. Leave me alone. Mind your business," slamming her locker and marching off, head held high.

So Ashley announced to her friends, "I want to thank all of you for standing up for me and helping me out but you don't have to anymore. We've called a truce, but I owe it all to you so thank you again. But they have agreed to stop bothering me, so all of you don't need to stick up for me anymore. You are the best group of friends ever." Ashley smiled and gave a high five to all her friends. She thought thank God this is over and done with.

A couple weeks later classes were in normal progression and Ashley was in college comp class. They were instructed to write an essay and Ashley wrote hers in 20 minutes. When she turned it in the following day, she received an A for her grade. When she showed it to Mrs. B she insisted she take the SUPA English course from the University. She would have to make up a couple of essays but she was up for the challenge so she decided to take the course. It was grueling. Every other week she had to turn in a 500 word essay, then two weeks later a 1,000 word essay, both had to be typed. This was grueling for her not only making up the back work and doing the current work, but she had also returned to her job washing dishes at the restaurant two nights a week and all weekend. Ashley had also met with her adviser and signed up for all the courses she needed to take to get into college. These were courses she blew off in her underclass years because she was too busy partying not to mention she had planned on killing herself after graduating. Plus she was supposed to see a counselor at least once if not twice a week. Sometimes she would get frustrated waiting for him in the guidance office and take off and then the vice-principal would hunt her down and haul her back there for her session, which pissed her off. After lunch instead of the usual getting high in the bathroom she elected to go down the hall and sit at the end of a connecting dead end hall and read a book. It was next to the boys' bathroom, so she also watched for the guys who were in there smoking. Mr. Mills would wander down and check the boys' bathroom. Before he got too close she always said hello, a bit loud, to warn the guys. Then he would clear the halls of all the other students yet he would allow her to remain there to read her book, although sometimes he wanted to just chat with her, more like 20 questions. "Who are you living with now? How's that going? How are classes going? How are you doing?" After answering his questions and he felt satisfied he would say, "If you need anything, anything at all, I'm here for you, OK?".

"Thanks Mr. Mills but I'm OK, really I am. Everything is going fine. Nothing is wrong, but thanks." Ashley looked up at him towering over her and she then tried to get back to her book. Then Tim Shore showed up on the scene, "Hey, what's going on? You and Mr. Mills having a pow wow?" He smirked.

Mr. Mills chuckled and said "Well, we were just chatting, but I'll let you take over. See you later." He wandered off down the hall.

"Well, you and the V.P. are getting to be regular pals. He is always chatting with you. So, anyway, are you free? You feel like talking to me?" He motioned to his office.

"Yeah, I guess. I don't have class until next period." Ashley stood up and walked with Tim to his office.

Once in there, they bullshit for a few minutes then started getting into more important things. "I'm so tired of everyone asking if I'm OK and they are there if I need them. I just want to be left alone." Ashley shook her head.

"Well, when you try to knock yourself off, it scares people and they care about you. They want you to know they are around if you need them. They just want to help. For some strange reason they like you and care about you even though you can be a tough nut to crack. You don't let people in, so no one knows what is going on in that head of yours, and that my friend is scary." Tim sighed and lightly clapped his hands.

"You want to know what's going on in my head? I feel overwhelmed at times. I'm taking all these extra classes plus college English and making up back work for it. Then I have to stay after school to type the papers because I haven't saved up enough to buy a typewriter yet. Then on top of it, I work three to four nights a week, then I have to find time for my boyfriend and I have to watch my little brothers when I 'm not working. I don't have an extra minute to do anything but sleep. I am so tired I fall asleep in my first period math class and the teacher picks on me about it, embarrassing me in front of the whole class. I hate that dude." Ashley rubbed her face with both hands and sighed.

"So you have a lot going on." He held out his hands. Ashley thought, oh shit I told him too much. Now he's going to think I can't handle things and I'm going to throw in the towel. "Well, I may have a lot on my plate, but I feel up to the challenge. It's good that I'm so busy. It keeps me focused." She thought that should satisfy him.

"Listen, you know that what ever you say in here stays between us. I don't go out and announce it to any of the staff. I don't tell anyone," Tim told Ashley trying to persuade her to tell him the truth about how she was feeling.

Ashley thought about what he said for a minute, but she still decided to play it safe and keep her suicidal thoughts to herself. It wasn't like she thought about it all the time like she used to. In fact she thought more about going to college than suicide so she thought she could handle those suicidal thoughts on her own. Besides, she knew if she told him she thought about offing herself sometimes, he would be obligated to inform the proper authorities. "I just have a lot going on right now. Pretty soon it will be Thanksgiving break and I'll be able to rest some so I'll be fine. I just need to hang in there. In the hospital a nurse told me a saying: This too shall pass. Plus I haven't been smoking any pot in school so I don't have that as an outlet. Actually I haven't really been smoking much at all" Ashley just looked at Tim.

"Yeah, well, that's good. Do you feel like the fog is lifting at all?" Tim raised his eyebrows.

"I don't know." She shook her head.

"So in a couple weeks it will be Thanksgiving. Will you visit your mother at all?" Tim asked

"I don't know. I mean I live with my dad so I doubt it. Usually when I live with one, I don't talk with the other. She hates me right now anyway, so I doubt it." Ashley looked at the floor.

"Well, what if you called her? What if you made contact with her?"

"I'm not sure if she would want to talk to me plus I don't want to piss my dad off," Ash responded.

"You really think it would piss him off if you called your mother on Thanksgiving? Maybe you could do it when he's not around. At least you would know if she was receptive to you or not. You might be missing out on a good relationship. Who knows, maybe she thinks you don't want to talk to her." Tim suggested as he sat there twirling his pen on his desk.

"Yeah maybe…you think she misses me?" Ashley asked staring off into space.

"I can't speak for her, but I would miss you if you were my kid. Believe me, you're not as bad as you think you are." Tim looked her in the eye.

"Is that some sort of compliment?" she huffed.

"Yes, and you need to learn how to accept one." Tim smiled with a quick wink.

They talked a while longer about this and that, nothing too heavy but shit that bothered her. Then he gave her a pass for the class she was late for and she settled in and tried to pay attention to the teacher, but all she could think about was the idea of calling her mother. She missed her but she was so scared to call for fear of rejection. Yet, maybe Tim was right. Maybe she was waiting for her to make the first move.

Ashley stayed after school and went into Mrs. B's room to talk to her. She was someone Ashley confided in at times. In fact, she was in high demand. There were almost always other students in her room wanting to talk with her. She would talk privately with you and keep it private, but many times the discussions would turn into some type of group session where everyone got to put in their opinions and be heard. She and her husband always tried to encourage students to think about things from all different directions. They taught kids to think for themselves and question authority, not to blindly follow. Ashley looked up to them and enjoyed spending time with them.

"Mrs. B, do you have a minute?" Ashley stood in front of her desk. She looked up from a stack of papers, red pen in hand, "Hello Ashley, what do you need?" taking off her glasses with her other hand.

"Well, I was wondering if I could talk to you for a couple minutes?" She sighed.

"Sure what's going on?"

"Uh…well…Tim suggested earlier today that I should maybe call my mother, but the thing is I'm kind of afraid she won't want to talk to me and that if I call her and my dad finds out he will be mad at me and then he might throw me out. That's all" Ashley wrinkled her brow.

"That's all. Oh, kiddo, that's a whole lot. You are afraid of rejection from not one but both of your parents. That is a huge deal. You must be freaking out inside. I know if it was me I would be. So what are your options? Can you maybe call when your father is not around or do you want to just leave things the way they are. I don't know your father, but it's hard for me to believe he would throw you out just because you spoke with your mother. But I just don't know what you should do,. I'm so sorry I can't be better help to you. Go with your gut with what it says deep down. That's usually the right choice. "Mrs. B tilted her head and pursed her lips.

"Thanks, believe it or not, that helps." Ashley smiled then waved goodbye.

"Good luck." Mrs. B waved back.

Late that night as Ashley lay awake trying to fall asleep, the thought of making contact with her mother kept going through her head. She couldn't help but worry about how the conversation would go. What was she going to say besides hey, how's it going? She thought she could always tell her about taking the college English course and how she was saving for a typewriter. That was a safe topic. Her mind went from this to how her parents got along.

She just couldn't understand why she had to shield her parents from each other.

Weren't they the adults? Her friends had divorced parents and they encouraged their kids to see the other parent. Why, then, did she have to do it in secret; it just wasn't fair. Sometimes she thought it would have been better if she would have died. Tears rolled down her checks; she began to pray. "Dear Lord, thank you for all you do for me. You are wonderful. Please help give me strength to deal with my parents and school so that I can make it to go on to college and just start my life over. Help me get through this and give me the strength I need to go on and not try to kill myself again. Also, please help my parents get along and not get mad at me for talking to the other one. love you God. Thank you." Ashley felt better after her prayer and rolled onto her side and just looked out the window and watched the trees blow in the wind as she drifted off to sleep.

CHAPTER 22

It was a Tuesday afternoon and Thanksgiving break had finally arrived and no one was happier than Ashley, she had decided to take some time off of work so she could finally spend some much needed time with Ryan and maybe her parents plus grandma Ames was coming, along with grandpa of course, her sidekick. Ash always looked forward to grandma Ames coming, she felt very close to her even though they didn't get to see one another often.

Although she had not yet contacted her mother she planned on calling her from Ryan's place, just to keep it private. Ryan had also decided to take a couple days off for the holiday so he was on his way to pick her up and they were going back to his place to make the all important call to Ellen. When he arrived Ashley was busy pacing the floor which alerted Ruth that something was about to happen.

"So what exactly are the two of you going to do today?" Ruth suspiciously eyed the both of them.

"Nothing really… why? Ashley cleared her throat.

"Don't even try to get out of here without telling me what's going on, I can tell when you're up to something? So let's have it what are you up to?" Ruth demanded as she tapped her foot.

Ryan looked at Ashley and she at him then Ash spoke up "OK I'm going to make some phone calls that's all like my grandparents and stuff " Ashley shrugged her shoulders hoping that explanation would be enough to satisfy Ruth's curiosity.

"So if that's all why can't you make them here?" Ruth inquired.
"Well I could but I was just going to do it from Ryan's that's all."

Shrugging her shoulders, trying to down play it as much as she could. "So really you also want to call your mother right." Ruth bluntly stated.

"Well I was thinking about it, but if you don't want me to I won't" Ashley added starting to feel a bit guilty about it.

"I think you should call her, I mean it's been a long time and she is your mother and it's a holiday and you two need to mend fences. Although I don't think we need to mention it to your father right now, but I think it's a good idea" Ruth nodded her head and smiled, glad to have gotten to the truth.

"Wow really, thanks Ruth you're the best" Ash went over and hugged her, relieved that she was OK with her talking to her mother. It was as if someone took a huge weight off of her shoulders, to know she didn't have to hide this from Ruth.

"Well thank you," she chuckled "I didn't expect that."

"You know sometimes you seem like the best parent I have" Ashley lovingly admitted, with a huge smile, totally relieved she didn't have to lie.

"Oh well I try to do what's best for you, what I would want for my child and in a way you're my child too" Ruth held her at arms length and smiled. "So go make your calls and good luck," she smiled as she let her go.

Once the two of them were on their way and arrived at Ryan's it was late afternoon almost quitting time for Ellen, so Ash decided to call immediately. She nervously dialed the number and it rang and rang then finally a "Hello"

"Yes hello may I speak to Ellen Ames?" Ashley nervously announced

A few minutes later "Yeah this is Ellen Ames" "Uh… Hi.. Mom ..it,,.. it's me, Ashley" Silence…

Then after a few moments "Ashley…. Uh.. Hi, how are you?…

I'm…. I'm so glad you called, I've… I've.. missed you."

"I…I'm good, I've missed you too," Ashley answered a bit relieved.

"So what's going on? How's school?"

"Things are good, I'm actually taking a college English course from the university and I've returned to work. In fact, I'm saving for a typewriter for the course because I have to type all my papers." Ashley replied with a large sigh, trying to keep a light conversation going.

"Oh really, well.. you know we sell typewriters in our employee store for a reduced price, I could get one for you, you know, as long as you pay for it" Ellen offered.

"Uh.. yeah that would be great, I have like $200 saved do you know how much they are?" Ashley asked a bit excited.

"Well actually I think they are around that but I'll have to check to be sure" Ellen answered happy to be able to help. "Listen do you think maybe you could come over sometime during your break to visit?" Ellen eagerly asked.

"Can I bring Ryan mainly because he could bring me and it would be easier that way?"

"Yeah sure no problem, he's always welcome" Ellen assured her. "Uh…well then I'll call you tomorrow and you can tell me how much the typewriter is and when we can get together and all that" Ashley breathed a sigh of relief.

"Bye, I love you" Ellen squeezed in.

"Love you too" Ashley hung up the phone. She smiled at Ryan relieved that it went so well. "Ryan she was glad to hear from me and guess what.. she can get me a typewriter" Ashley gleamed.

"I know I heard, I'm so happy for you, that is so cool. So we can go visit over the break, that would be great, maybe she can even get your typewriter by then. You are so pretty in this light I need a kiss, you are the most amazing girl I have ever had the pleasure of knowing." Ryan kissed her again and again. "Hey I have an idea, my dad is still at work he won't be home for another two hours, you want to take advantage of a private room with a real bed in it, my beautiful sexy lady?" Ryan winked and gave her another kiss, while wrapping his arms around her.

"Sounds good to me my handsome man, race you" Ash smiled and pushed him out of the way and raced towards the stairs.

"Oh no you don't" Ryan laughed and ran after her reaching up and grabbing her butt as they reached the top of the stairs laughing and getting to his room. They fell onto the bed into each other's arms starting to kiss, he gently helped her take off her shirt and then his. They made love with such freedom, it was so magical, afterwards they lay in each other's arms and dreamt of a time when they could do this all the time. Not stealing away and hiding in the shadows, down those long dead end roads at the lake. But the two of them in their own home their own house their own bedroom, no more hiding away no more secrets. They heard the grandfather clock downstairs strike five and they realized his father was due to arrive home in about 15 minutes. The two raced around and got dressed then bolted out the door.

Although only Ryan and his father lived there, his father wouldn't approve of Ryan having an underage girl, or any girl, there alone in the house. He was aware that Ryan was in an exclusive relationship with Ashley which, according to him, was all the more reason he should not be alone with her in the house. He was a very old fashion type of person, he had Ryan very late in life, he was now almost eighty and he still worked as a mechanic at one of the few full service garages in town. He could fix most anything you had and he could put preachers to shame over his knowledge of the Bible. He was a good man, a very well read man and a great father to Ryan, he taught him a great deal about life and mechanical things just a wide variety of things.

They made it to the car "Whew that was close" Ryan smiled as he leaned over and kissed Ashley. He put the car in reverse and just then his father pulled in beside him, "Oh shit" exclaimed Ryan.

His father got out of his car and looked at the two of them for a second then motioned to Ryan to come over to him. So Ryan reluctantly got out of his car and made his way over to where his father stood "What exactly were you doing here with a young lady, unsupervised?" his father demanded.

"Uh…Well she had to make a private phone call, that's all, honest" Ryan professed.

"To who?

"To her mother" Ryan answered.

"She lives down the street, why doesn't she just go to her house if it's so private? His father exclaimed.

"Well I guess she didn't want to go unannounced, even you know that that is rude" Ryan quickly came back.

"So the two of you made a phone call and that's all?" Ryan was sweating profusely "Yes that's all"

"I'm supposed to believe you wore your shirt inside out all day and no one said anything about it to you, hardly, you're a damn liar. Now take that girl home and see to it that something like this doesn't happen again or I'll be forced to take action, now go" he glared at Ryan

"Yes sir" Ryan answered obediently. Then scurried over to the car jumped in and raced off.

"Man your dad can be scary when he's angry his face was all red, but I didn't hear what he said" Ashley commented.

"Tell me about it, but he's never really hit me. Maybe a couple of times when I was young but only in situations when I could have really hurt myself. He was only trying to protect your honor, we're not supposed to be alone in the house."

"Well how would he know if we fooled around?" Ashley asked. "Because my shirt is inside out, can you believe it" Ryan shook his head.

"Pull over, you better fix it before we get to my house or my dad will flip out" Ashley exclaimed. So they pulled over and Ryan quickly fixed his shirt then they went on their way.

Once home Ashley filled Ruth in on how the call went and that she needed to call again tomorrow. Ashley also asked Ruth "Did it hurt your feelings that I called my mother?" she looked her in the eye.

"No no of course not, she is your mother, she will always be your mother and I can't take her place. I also don't want to take her place, maybe you could think of me as an extra mother figure, more of a friend. I never want to take her place and I want you to have a good relationship with her, OK" Ruth smiled at Ashley and nodded her head.

"Ruth you always seem to say the right thing, sometimes I wish you were my real mother believe it or not, I'm so glad you married my dad" Ashley looked her in the eye and smiled.

"You're a good kid and I love you, and I'm glad I married your dad too" Ruth clapped her hands.

The following day Ashley called her mother from home and they agreed on a price for the typewriter, her mother would order it and Ashley would pay her when she came to visit over Thanksgiving. She and Ryan were going to have dinner at Ashley's fathers then later go have desert at Ashley's grandparents' house with her mother.

Thanksgiving Day had arrived Ruth and Rodger arose at dawn to get the huge bird washed in order to get it cooking, However Rodger went back to bed, stating it's too damn early. Luckily Ashley heard the activity and actually came downstairs. "Morning" she yawned.

"Well good morning sunshine your up awful early" Ruth grinned glad for the company.

"Yeah I heard you and dad so I thought I would get up and see if you needed a hand"

"That would be great, because your Dad abandoned me, wimp," Ruth chuckled

Ashley breathed in deep, "You have any coffee?" she asked "Coffee? How long you been drinking coffee?" Ruth surprisingly asked.

"Oh a while here and there, I like it and I love the caffeine jolt" "Well you know where it is, go get yourself a cup then" Ruth answered.

After enjoying a cup of coffee with Ruth, Ashley was revved up and ready to go. First she and Ashley cut up celery, onion and apples for the stuffing, then they mixed up the stuffing, so then Ruth showed her how to stuff the bird and they got it in the oven. Then they made pies and put them in the oven. They put the ham in the oven and soon it was time to peel potatoes and fix the sweet potatoes then the green been casserole, cranberry sauce, rolls, and gravy, all the while basting the bird.

Hours later, grandpa and grandma Ames showed up, she was ready to help finish up in the kitchen all the while catching up with Ruth and Ashley. This type of talk in the kitchen with her grandmother and Ruth made Ashley feel almost grown up it was a very special type of feeling and Ash just ate it up. She so enjoyed this time with her family and her grandmother had a way of making her feel like she was the most important person in the room, she never wanted the day to end.

Finally, dressed in their best a small group had gathered Rodger and Ruth and Ruth's parents, Grandpa and Grandma Ames and Ryan and his Father, Henry, but he preferred to be called Mr. Fellman and all the children of course. The group gave thanks to the Lord for their bounty then they feasted on a perfectly cooked bird, and all the fixings, they drank and they visited, trading stories and memories, just enjoying the day and time spent with one another. All were happy and grateful just to be with each other, sharing and caring for each other. The day was a joyous success.

Several hours after dinner had ended Mr. Fellman decided to leave, at this point Ashley worked up the courage to ask her father to go out. She had decided to ask in front of Ryan's dad so her father wouldn't freak out. "Dad do you think I can go out with Ryan?" Ash nervously asked.

"Where are you going? I mean nothing's open it's Thanksgiving" Rodger asked.

"Well.. Uh.. I sort of wanted to go see my mother, if that's OK with you?" Ash wrinkled her brow ready for an onslaught of yelling and screaming.

"OK" He simply answered.

Ashley just looked at him stunned, along with Ruth and Ryan. Rodger looked back replying "What the doctor said she needs a relationship with both of us, I can't give her what she gives her, so I need to concentrate on what I can do. See I listened to that doc, you thought I didn't, well I did, so go have a good time I'll see you when you get home" Rodger playfully stuck out his tongue and nodded his head, then went back to his movie.

"Thanks dad you're the best" Ash smiled wide then dashed in and kissed him on the cheek and bounced out the door to the car. "I can't believe it, I mean was that my dad in there, can you believe it?" Ash was shaking her head, she thought wow my dad was so great he made my day, she felt so satisfied and happy.

Ryan got in and started the car "No I'm as shocked as you are, in fact, I'm getting out of here as fast as possible so he doesn't come running out here changing his mind" Ryan sighed heavily as they backed out of the driveway onto the roadway.

"You brought the money right?" Ryan asked

"Sure did, I hope she already bought the typewriter and I'm just paying her back for it" Ashley exclaimed. "Because to tell you the truth I don't really want to give her the money without getting it"

"So you still don't trust her? I can't say I blame you after she took all that money you saved for college?" Ryan exclaimed.

"Well I just want the typewriter, I have a report due soon and it would be so much easier if I had it now."

"Are you avoiding the question?" Ryan chuckled.

"Yes."

Soon after Ashley's arrival at her grandparents' house and all the fussing over her was done, everyone sat down and had some desert.

Ashley had forgotten how awesome her grandmother's homemade apple pie tasted, in fact she had another piece and asked if she could take yet another home. During desert they chatted about school, work and how things were going in general for everyone, on both sides, it was a good full conversation no one was left out. Then finally, Ellen stepped into the other room and came back with the typewriter.

"Here it is, I was lucky they let me take the floor model, and just ordered another to take its place. I told them you needed one immediately because you were taking a college course, while in high school, and you had a paper to do over the holiday." Ellen handed it over with a smile.

Ashley set it on the table and opened the case and inside was the newest model they made, her eyes lit up. "Thanks mom this means a lot, so how much do I owe you?" Ash looked her in the eye.

"Well I've been thinking and since you need this not only now but when you go off to college that this will be a gift to you from me." Ellen smiled warmly at her.

"Are you serious, you don't want any money at all ?"Ashley stood stunned.

"Yes I'm serious, it's a gift," Ellen nodded.

"Thank you, thank you so much. This means so much to me you have no idea. Thank you that's so nice of you, I so appreciate it, I'm serious I do," she was shaking her head in shock.

"Well I wanted to do this for you, because I know you're saving all you can for college, so this is a way I can help you do that, I'm so proud of you, you have come a long way from where you were even a year ago." Ellen confessed.

"Yeah I've been trying to take all of the classes I have to make up to go to college, and work and this college class, I'm very busy especially studying I need good grades, just to get in." Ashley sighed heavily.

Laura piped up "I think you're doing great sissy, I'm also proud of you. So now that you and mommy have made up when are you coming over for a visit because I really miss you and want you hang out with me." She raised her eyebrows and tilted her head.

Everyone had a little laugh and Ashley commented "Well we will have to make some plans maybe over Christmas break when I don't have so much homework deal?"

"Deal" that made Laura happy, she probably missed her sister more than anyone. They spent a lot of time together in the past, at night, up talking late into the night, giggling and being silly, sharing secrets and dreams, things sisters should do. They developed a bond that time, distance and circumstance just could not break, most likely it would last a lifetime.

Ryan and Ashley stayed a while longer and visited with everyone as they were leaving Ashley again thanked her mother for the typewriter. She was grateful for the gift and would certainly put it to good use, she had a paper at home that needed to be typed, which she had thought she would have to go to the library to get it finished.

The two were barely out of the driveway when Ryan made the comment "Wow who was that in there, I was in total shock when she just gave that to you. She must really miss the hell out of you to just give that to you, it totally goes against her nature."

"I know right, I almost hit the floor when she said I could have it and she actually said she was proud of me. You think she really misses me?" Ashley questioned.

"Well yes, of course she does, you're a good person and you're doing all of this extra stuff to go on to college, to better yourself. You need to be proud of yourself and all that you've accomplished." Ryan reached over and stroked the back of her head.

Ashley proudly carried the typewriter into the house and opened it up on the kitchen table. She then set it all up and messed around with it until she was familiar with how it operated. Ruth came in curious to see what was going on and was happy to hear it was a gift. Ashley then dove in typing her paper, she kept at it for a couple of hours before turning in for the night. As she lay down she thought things are going well, I can actually say I'm kind of happy for the first time in my life. I 'm not thinking about dying all the time but going off to college instead. All that praying must have helped, Thank God for small miracles.

Ashley went back to work and started to put in a lot of time, which helped with saving money but then she had to stay up into the wee hours to complete all the homework due. The pace was grueling and she was doing her utmost to keep up, but you can only go so long without a good night's sleep.

School had been in session for a few weeks when Ashley discovered if she was put on the absentee list she could skip class without any consequences. So she started to try and get on the list and was quite successful. Some days she spent a lot of time hanging out, well napping, in the bathroom, she was exhausted. Christmas break would be coming soon she thought all she had to do was hold on until then, and then she could get some rest.

One afternoon Mr. Shore, the drug counselor, came up to her and basically busted her, asking why she was on the absentee list so often when she was obviously there. Ashley tried to play dumb to no avail, so he demanded to know what was going on.

"Well I'm just so tired from working every night until 11pm and then doing homework, that I just want to rest up I don't feel like going to class, I just don't care anymore," Ash sighed.

"Well this is not a way to fix this, the head guy is going to figure this out sooner or later, then you're going to be in big trouble," He raised his eyebrows.

"So what am I supposed to do?"

"Stop working so many hours and go to class, I mean come on you don't need me to tell you, your no dummy. Besides if you don't go to class you won't get into college." He held out his hands.

"Yeah I guess I'm going to have to because there's no speed anywhere, no one has any," Ashley looked him in the eye.

"Yeah real funny kiddo, drugs aren't the answer they'll only prolong the inevitable which is you crashing. And we all know how dangerous that can be, right?" Mr. Shore looked her back in the eye.

"I just want it all to work out,"

"Then you need to manage it properly, your life needs to be prioritizing, you need to put things in an order and manage it, a piece here and there, you can't just go full out on all of it, you'll burn out."

"Yeah yeah I hear you," Ashley rubbed her face.

"Then do it,"

"Alright," she moaned.

Ashley called in sick that night to work and just went to bed and slept right through until morning. Returning to bed she slept until early afternoon, skipping school in the process. Ruth actually woke her around 2pm just to make sure she was OK, secretly she feared another suicide attempt, but, of course, would never admit it. "Hey Ash you've been asleep for well like forever are you OK, are you sick is everything OK?" Ruth cautiously asked rubbing her hands together.

"Oh no I'm not sick just exhausted, I've been so busy with all the extra hours at work, then school and the tons of homework. I couldn't focus, I was just so tired, I couldn't stay awake anymore everything was getting to me, I felt like I was sinking and couldn't get out. I really just needed to sleep you know just catch up on it, does that sound crazy, because sometimes I feel like I'm going crazy?" Ashley wrinkled her brow and scrunched her face.

"No.. no.. you're not crazy, just very over tired, you'll be fine trust me. I was just worried because you've been asleep for so long, and I guess I didn't really realize the extra amount of hours you've put in at work and all the stress you've been under, I just wanted to check on you to make sure you were OK." Ruth sighed relieved she wasn't sick or depressed.

"Oh I know what you were thinking, another suicide attempt right?

"Ash please don't….."

"Don't nothing, that's what you thought right?" Ashley sat upright.

"Please Ashley stop, it doesn't matter, you are…"

"I'm what I'm fine. You need to trust me, I told you if I was going to do that I would reach out, but you suspect me and it's not fair"

"Well what you did is hard to forget and…"

"And what even the doc said I'm a lot better and it's been a long time and you still went right to that, thanks" Ashley just shook her head. "Just leave me alone, please just go" Ashley pulled the covers over her head and laid back down.

Ruth left Ashley's room not sure if she was upset, frustrated or feeling guilty. She realized that her suspicion, although rooted in fact, couldn't be more wrong. She hated the fact that they were at odds and wanted to resolve the issue as soon as she could. But she decided to leave the matter alone and let it rest, hopefully time would heal their squabble.

That next Friday night after work Ashley talked to her boss about cutting her hours down to a few nights a week, he wasn't happy about it but agreed to it, because she was the best dish washer he had at the time.

Ryan picked her up as usual and they went up to the bluffs to smoke up and have a couple of beers. "So Ryan you know Christmas break is coming, in like two weeks, and we are staying home this year. Anyway I know my mom is going to want me to come and visit maybe even spend the night, so I thought maybe you could come by and hang out while I'm there." Ash raised her eyebrows up and down.

"Well that sounds good," As he lit the joint and then inhaled and held it, then coughed and coughed blowing out the smoke. He then handed the joint to Ashley she inhaled and held it in then exhaled "This is the best way to end a workday, well any day," she handed the joint to Ryan.

He took another hit off of the joint, they continued to smoke, talking as they went, until it was a tiny roach and put it out so they wouldn't burn their fingertips. They had also opened a couple of beers and were knocking back a few. It was late and they were the only ones at the bluffs, so they started to kiss and after a while things progressed soon they were undressing each other and then the question arose "Do you have a condom?" Ash asked panting heavy.

"No I used the last one the other day," as he kissed her ear.

"We have to stop then," she sorts of sat up.

"What if I pull out?" he is kissing her and his hands are caressing her hips.

Ashley is kissing him back and trying to think clearly "I'm not sure, that's still risky,"

"I swear I'll pull out," he continues to kiss her everywhere. "Promise," she pants

"Oh I totally promise," he's breathing heavy.

They continue and the time comes and he only halfway pulled out stating it felt too good and he couldn't help himself. Ashley got up and dressed and told him to take her home. Then "What if I get pregnant, then what?" she yells at him.

"You won't relax, besides I only partly came in you, look I'm sorry don't worry OK everything will be fine. If you get pregnant then we'll get a place of our own and be parents together, OK so just chill." Ryan put his arm around her and pulled her close.

"But I want to go to college, I want to get a good job" Ashley tilted her head.

"Well you may have to just put it off for a year or two, but don't worry eventually you can go, but we're getting ahead of ourselves because you're not pregnant," He shook his head smiling.

"Well even though you're being sweet I'm still mad at you,"

"OK, I'll tell you what, I will make sure I have condoms from now on, I won't ever run out again deal?" Ryan pleaded with a sheepish smile.

"You better make sure, cause this can't happen again,"

Ryan started the car and proceeded to take her home, as she cracked open another beer for the ride.

Once home Ashley immediately checked her calendar to see when she was due for her period one and a half weeks, shit she thought this is one of the worst times to have unprotected sex. She sunk in under the covers and just prayed to God please don't let me be pregnant, not now, it would totally ruin my life, she begged God to make sure she wasn't with child, offering and bartering, trying any method she could think of to appease Him in order to maintain her life as it was. After a while she thought about all she had done to get where she was and how a baby would mess all of that up. The thought of that reminded her of the desperation she felt and was now starting to feel again, then she realized maybe I'm not pregnant and all of this worry is for nothing. She lay there thinking about all the different outcomes, over and over and over again, her brain just wouldn't shut down. Finally she started to drift off at around 3 am only to dream her reality, there was just no escaping it.

CHAPTER 23

Rodger came bursting through the door. "Hey, I got us a tree. Come here and see." He dragged it in the house and Michael went nuts. "Oh cool! It's huge. Thanks daddy. Where are you going to put it?" He smiled. Jacob just kind of stood there. He had never remembered seeing a tree in the house before.

"Daddy, why you bring tree in da house?" Jacob asked bewildered. They all had a good laugh, "It's for Christmas," Ruth commented while patting the toddler on the back. "That's a great tree honey. I'll go get the stand. We can put it in the living room. Come on Jake. Come help mommy get the stand." She and Jake dashed off and retrieved the stand.

Ashley stood to the side preoccupied with her thoughts.

"What do you think Ash?" her dad asked.

"It's an awesome tree dad. I like it." She nodded her head.

They moved into the living room and set up the tree with just a little bit of yelling at each other to get it in the stand but otherwise not too bad. Michael jumped up and down demanding to start decorating the tree. Jake just imitated his brother. After a brief wait to allow the tree to settle, they started as a family to decorate it. Watching the boys do it was probably the best part of the whole endeavor. But it turned out to be a really good time and everyone enjoyed the decorating and each other. This was one of the few times where Ashley actually allowed herself to get lost in an activity. She tried not think about what had happened between her and Ryan. She was counting the days and they crawled by at an agonizingly slow pace. Ashley's thoughts were dominated by the thought of having unprotected sex and getting her period versus getting pregnant. Even though she desperately tried to focus on her schoolwork, those thoughts were just under the surface constantly popping up, invading her conscious mind, making her a nervous wreck as the days went by. She had always been quite regular with getting her period so the morning it was due, she woke up and said a quick prayer then rushed to the bathroom hoping to get the usual start to her cycle. She sits and urinates, then looks, no blood. Her mood plummets. She breathes in deep and then says to herself, put on a liner. It will come just later in the day. It just has to. She desperately wants to curl up into a ball and hide under her covers, but she knows she has to go to school or it could raise suspicion. She tries to comfort herself thinking maybe it's just late. Just relax. It's only an hour. It's way too early to even get upset about. People only worry about this if it's days or weeks late so chill. It will all be OK.

Once at school Ash went to hang in the bathroom. She ran into Karen and Emily. "Hey, where you been? Listen we are getting together to smoke around 3rd period. You have study hall then. You want to come?" Karen asked as she took a drag off her cigarette.

"Sounds like fun but I really can't today. I've got some important shit I have to do later. Sucks." Ashley held out her hands and frowned. She thought in case I am pregnant I don't want to mess the kid up.

"That sucks but maybe next time," Karen commented. "So how are things? You haven't been around lately."

"Yeah, well you know. I've been taking all these extra classes to get into college and that college English class keeps me really busy," Ashley answered.

"That's cool but you haven't even been to many parties, like at the Bluffs or anywhere,"

"Well, I have to work most every Friday and Saturday night and I don't get out until after midnight, sometimes one in the morning or later. Everyone is gone by the time I'm out of work, so it really sucks." Ashley shook her head.

"Guess you have to do what you have to do." Karen nodded. Suddenly the bell rang and everyone filed out of the bathroom. Karen put her arm around Ashley and said, "Don't forget your friends." She patted her back and smiled. "I won't," Ashley replied feeling a bit guilty for not hanging out with them. They had been there for her when things were hard for her. She thought for a minute and reconsidered their invitation for third period. How much could just a little bit of weed mess up a kid. But what if it really could. It would be messed up for life because of her and her selfish desires. This shit sucks. She kept going back and forth in her mind.

She managed to make it through the day without smoking anything. That evening she went out Christmas shopping with Ryan. They started talking about her being late for her period almost the minute they were alone in the car. "Ash, you're making a big deal out of nothing…"

"Nothing? Nothing. Are you serious? My, no, our future, is at stake here. All my dreams could come crashing down. Everything I'm working for here would be for nothing. This would change everything in our life: our relationship, my father, oh my God, my father would kill me, then you. Hello, do you realize the gravity of the situation here? Are you in dream land?" Ash's mouth was agape and she just stared at Ryan who was calmly driving them to the mall.

Ryan took in a deep breath. "Ash, you know I love you, but you're only a day late. You are freaking out way too early, so get a grip. I know, I know you're never late, but you've been under a lot of stress lately and that could be the reason, so you need to relax. You ever hear the saying "If you worry, why pray and if you pray, why worry?" Maybe you should take some of that advice because worrying isn't going to change the outcome, my love." Ryan reached over and gently stroked her cheek. After a few minutes of silence Ash started to calm down. Her breathing started to relax although her head was still pounding.

"You're right. It's only been a day. Guess I sounded a bit crazy. Shut up, don't answer that." She smiled at him.

"I'll tell you what. If it doesn't come by Saturday, that's 2 days from now, I'll buy a test kit, and then we will take it together, OK?" Ryan winked at her. "But I'm sure you'll get it by then."

"Deal."

"Good enough. Now can we stop talking about this?" Ryan gave her a pathetic look.

Ash just chuckled at him and they arrived at the mall to shop, shop, shop.

The two made it home around 10 pm and Ash was beat. She just went straight to bed, neglecting all of her studies.

Ash awoke to Ruth's singing a Christmas carol at the top of the stairs in place of the usual arise and shine my dear. She was usually very cheery in the morning unlike Ashley who dreaded getting up and facing the day. "Good morning Sunshine." Ruth came in and opened up the curtains "It's a lovely day. The sun is shining and it's Friday, the last day before Christmas break. Get up." She glided through the room as if on a wave, then out and down the stairs.

"OK I'm up. I'll be down in a few minutes." She took in a deep breath, sat up, and wiped her face with both hands and thought for a second. Oh, she hoped today she would get that damn thing. She raced to the bathroom only to have her hopes dashed. Shit, she thought after leaving the bathroom. She tried to remain calm remembering what Ryan had said. It's just stress. She went and got ready for school. Once downstairs she put on an act for Ruth so she wouldn't suspect anything and off to school she went.

Everyone was in high spirits at school, except for Ashley. She went into the bathroom to hang out from habit more than anything. Karen, Emily and Amy were in the back smoking cigarettes, along with everyone else she knew. "Hey," Amy spoke up "Ash come here." Ashley made her way over to the group while saying hello to the other girls she knew. "Hey, how's it going," Ashley asked.

"Things are good. Finally vacation." Amy cheered with a huge smile as she exhaled a huge cloud of smoke.

"I know, right! I've had enough of this place." Ashley smirked. Karen spoke up, "Hey we're going for a short ride during our lunch break. You want to go?" she asked Ashley.

"Sure, why not." Ashley answered thinking a little weed wouldn't hurt anyone. She was sick of the whole situation. Maybe all she needed was to relax a bit although she was nervous just thinking about doing it. "Hey, I've got to go. I'll catch up with you guys later. Thanks for the invite; I'll be there". Ashley left the bathroom to just get some air and clear her thoughts, when she ran into Mr. Shore. "Hey, kiddo, what's up?" He asked.

"Uh… well I'm just headed to class," Ashley answered flipping her books from hand to hand, fidgeting as she stood there.

"You upset? You don't look your naturally cool self." he observed bobbing his head from side to side.

"I…uh ..just ..uh ..have a lot on my mind that's all. I'm OK"

"Well, why don't we go chat about it?" He motioned towards his office.

"I'm.. uh.. I'm not really in the mood to tell you the truth," Ashley sighed deeply.

"Sounds like you're in deep, breathing like that."

"I don't want to talk about it, to you or anyone. I'm sorry, but I don't," Ashley curtly but softly answered so other students walking to class wouldn't hear.

"It's OK. You don't have to right now, but I'm here if and when you change your mind." He walked her to class so she didn't get into trouble for being late. He couldn't help but wonder what exactly was troubling her. She, however, did not trust him with the sensitive information she carried inside. He hoped she would let down her guard and trust him enough to allow him to help her with whatever it was.

Ashley took her seat and thought I've got to avoid him today. I certainly don't want him all up in my business. This vacation can't happen soon enough. As science class went on, she became lost in thought and before she knew it the bell rang. Mrs. Farmington had noticed Ashley's behavior. "Ashley, could you stay for a minute? What's going on?

You're not yourself at all?" Mrs. Farmington stated. "Oh… Um…I….Uh …just had a fight with my boyfriend last night and it being Christmas and all. Well, it just upset me a lot. You know what I mean," Ashley lied through her teeth, hoping Mrs. Farmington would believe her and let her go. Even though part of her hated lying to one of her favorite teachers, but what else could she do. She certainly couldn't tell her the truth. No one could know, just in case it's just a scare. And, oh how she hoped it was just a scare, a scare she would never forget.

"Well, the holidays can be stressful. A lot of couples can have words. Try not to take it to heart. Hopefully you can work things out before it goes too far. A little forgiveness goes a long way." Mrs. Farmington smiled. "Have a good holiday if I don't see you before school lets out." She winked at Ashley.

"Thank you, Mrs. Farmington, you too. Have a merry Christmas." Ashley waved as she left. Out in the hall she thought for a minute. She is such a nice teacher. I probably could have trusted her. But it only takes one slip of the tongue and the whole town would know or think they know and she couldn't risk that.

As the day wore on more and more people noticed how disturbed Ashley's demeanor was. Another one of her favorite teachers Mrs. Tallman, who taught art something she loved also expressed concern.

She, however, continued to stick to the story about fighting with Ryan. By the time lunch break rolled around, Ashley had had enough. She eagerly met up with Karen and the gang and they took a ride to smoke up. Karen was in the driver's seat while Emily rode shotgun and Ash and Amy sat in the back. "Light that baby up, Amy," roared Emily who was more than ready to party. She lit it and passed it to Ashley who savored it and after a few tokes a sense of relief took root within Ashley. They passed it around and around. All were happy to smoke and to share, life was good although Ashley remained quiet during the ride while the other three girls whooped and hollered the whole way. "Come on, Ash, it's almost Christmas break. Let loose for goodness sake." Emily cheered as she waved her hand out the window. Karen laughed while she sounded off at the top of her lungs, "Let's get crazy ladies" and she did a doughnut in the middle of the snowy road. The car came to a screeching halt still in the middle of the road. The four girls all looked at one another and burst into laughter, and there they sat for quite a while giggling as if they were small children. Finally, Karen took hold of the wheel and straightened them out onto the side of the road. A few minutes later she pulled out and started back towards school." Well, ladies, we need to head back. Free time is over," Karen sighed. "But on the bright side we only have three more hours and we'll be high so who cares," The girls continued to talk and goof around until they arrived back at school.

After returning to school Ashley's attitude had made a complete turn around. She was no longer worried or upset. She couldn't have cared less about anything. The rest of the day flew by and before she realized it, it was time to go home. She said her goodbyes and left for home.

That night Ryan came over to pick her up to go shopping again at the mall. And once again they had a conversation about her not getting her period. Ryan commented, "Listen we will get you a test tomorrow and take it together if you don't get your period tomorrow,"

"Can't we just get it tonight and then I'll have it, just in case. I think you're supposed to take it first thing in the morning. Let's just go read the directions on one to see, please," Ashley practically begged him.

"OK, we'll go read the directions. If you have to take it first thing in the morning, we'll get it tonight. Would that make you feel better?" Ryan asked.

"Yes, I would feel much better." Ashley breathed a sigh of relief. They stopped at a drug store in the city so as not to be recognized and the directions stated to be done first thing in the morning and she got two tests in one box, just in case she needed to retest herself. As they waited in line to pay for the test kit, the reality of the situation hit Ryan. "You know a baby sure would change our lives forever." He looked all wide eyed at Ashley.

"That's what I've been telling you these past couple of days. You're just realizing the enormity of the situation now?" She just looked at him. When they went up and paid, the older clerk just kind of gave them the once over and said, "Good luck, whatever you're hoping for." Ryan just grabbed the bag and trudged out the door with this disgusted look on his face.

They finished up their Christmas shopping and got something to eat. On the way home Ryan commented, "You know though a baby wouldn't be the end of the world. I saw some of the other shoppers with babies and those families looked cute. They looked happy." He looked over at Ashley. "We could do that, be a family. Yeah it would change everything, but we could manage. Just have to put plans on hold for a while. I love you so much and a baby would be part of you and I would love that. Yeah, your parents may be mad at first, but they would get over it, especially after they see the baby. We planned on getting married sometime in the future so the baby just came first. So what, it happens. We could do this. I know it's not how we planned it but we could adjust. Don't be so scared. I'm here for you and we are in this together." Ryan looked her in the eye and smiled. "I love you,"

"Well, we'll know soon enough tomorrow morning. I'll take the test and I'll call you if there's anything growing inside. But to tell you the truth, after you said that, either way would be OK with me." She smiled at him. "But part of me still really wants to go off to college. I don't think I'm mature enough to be a parent, you know in charge of a real live person. I mean that's a huge responsibility. You have to teach them everything they are supposed to know not to mention love them through all of their stages. Plus, I don't want to act like my parents. I think I need to take some college courses to teach me about child psychology so I know how to deal with them the right way," Ashley confessed.

"You know you're right. We need to think this through. We don't know shit about raising kids, but if you are pregnant we can read some books about it together. You know, get ourselves ready. At least that way we can get a running start. Hell our parents didn't do anything, so any thing we do would help," Ryan added while shaking his head up and down. "We could be a good team," he reassured her.

"All right but let's not get too far ahead of ourselves. We aren't even sure if I am. Any way, you are dropping me off in one minute so let's just be normal. It's late so I'm just going to go to bed. Why don't you come over tomorrow to help me wrap all these gifts and then I'll give you the results. Listen don't come over before 10am because they will think something's up if you come over too early. So make sure you are relaxed and remember just stay calm, whatever happens, I love you. I'll see you tomorrow." They had pulled in the driveway and continued talking. Then she kissed him goodbye and got out of the car grabbing all of the bags of gifts. She skipped inside leaving Ryan alone to go home.

Ashley quietly went upstairs to her room with all the bags. She quickly hid the pregnancy test kit. Having read the directions earlier with Ryan, she knew exactly what she had to do in the morning. After changing into her pajamas she lay down and prayed to God. "Please God let the test come out negative or the best way You want it to be for my life. Your will be done not mine, although I really don't want a baby out of wedlock and before I graduate from college. Amen. She thought at least I'm not thinking about killing myself as the answer to my problems so that's a plus. Although my father will kill me if I'm pregnant, so it doesn't really matter. But I will at least graduate high school before it's born so he really can't say much and I'll be over 18 years old before it's born so he can't say anything to that either, but he can throw me out. He would never do that; he loves me. These thoughts kept running through Ashley's brain over and over again.

She just couldn't get settled down. She kept looking at the clock as the hours kept rolling by. The last time she checked it was three am.

Finally she opened her eyes to a gray snowy morning. She sat up and rubbed her face, looked around, thought for a moment, and then realized today was the day. She searched way back in her junk drawer and grabbed one of the test kits and quietly went to the bathroom.

She secretly performed the test bringing it back to her room waiting the endless three minutes. Finally she looked and it showed negative. She was elated now to get rid of the evidence. She poured the sample in the toilet and wrapped up the remaining evidence in a brown bag to go out with garbage. She thought about it again and decided to send the kit out with Ryan to dispose of it elsewhere. She was so elated and relieved she could hardly contain herself. She went put the remaining test in a bag and placed it way in the back of her junk drawer in a way so she would know if it were disturbed in any way. She then proceeded to get dressed and went downstairs to enjoy her vacation.

With Christmas coming in just a few days Ruth had been busy getting the house decorated and the tree was decorated over a week ago, so the house was pretty much all done except for a few things here and there. Ashley offered to help and Ruth put her to work stringing lights up over the walkways throughout the house and then putting silver and red garland over the top of the lights. "We also need to start baking some cookies and pies. Would you like to help do that too?" Ruth asked with a glimmer in her eyes.

"Sure, sounds like fun," Ash answered.

"Wow, you sure seem different today. The last few days you have been down in the dumps, but now you seem much better. Any reason I should know about," Ruth inquired.

"Ah, I think I was just worn out, you know with school and homework and work. I guess I just needed a break from it all. To sleep in this morning was so nice. I feel more rested and relaxed, just better overall that's all." Ashley breathed a sigh of relief while nodding her head.

"One day and you feel that much better. That's great. Are you sure that's all it is?" She probed even deeper.

"Yeah, I'm sure. Don't worry about me. There's nothing to worry about. I'm fine." Ash smiled trying to reassure her.

Last night Ashley had told Ryan not to come over before ten in the morning so about quarter after ten he comes bursting through the door with a huge smile and a bunch of flowers for Ashley. "Hey, good looking, how's your morning going? What's new?" He smiled.

"Oh, it's great. Nothing's going on though, not really, just your ordinary getting ready for the holidays." She went over kissed and Ryan, then hugged him while she quietly whispered in his ear "Negative." Then she hugged him even tighter and said, "I love you so much."

"Now what exactly is going on between the two of you?" Ruth demanded to know.

"What are you talking about? Nothing. We are just in love," Ashley sputtered while nervously taking Ryan's hand in hers.

"OK, OK, I'll tell you the truth." Ryan looked Ruth in the face. Ashley became all wide eyed and shocked that he would say anything." We had words last night and I begged Ash for forgiveness and to please let it go and have a fresh start today. That's why I brought flowers and I think she realized she was partly to blame. I'm sorry to bring it up again but you were." Ryan looked into her eyes with a somber expression. "You do forgive me, right?" he pleaded tilting his head.

"I do forgive you and you're right I was a bit wrong but only a tiny bit." Ash hugged him.

"Oh, you two are full of shit. Next time just tell me it's none of my business. Unless of course it's something I need to know, like you're pregnant or something." Ruth just shook her head.

"Pregnant, hell no, where would you get an idea like that? That's insane," Ashley spewed it out.

"We are no where's near ready to be parents. Pregnant, that's crazy, no way." Ryan turned so only Ash could see his face. His eyes about bugged out onto the floor. She motioned him to calm down.

"Listen, Ruth, we're going to go upstairs and wrap the gifts we got for everyone, so I want to close the door but, of course, you can come in at any time." Ash sort of asked and sort of stated it.

"And you know I'm going to, so stay decent," she stated. "OK thanks." The two of them quickly retreated upstairs.

As soon as the door shut on Ashley's room "Oh my God, I thought I was going to have a heart attack," Ryan quietly confessed to Ashley as he sat on the edge of her bed.

"I know, right? I couldn't get us out of there quick enough." Ash just sat on the bed trying to catch her breath and settle her nerves. "Nothing gets by her. Do you think she knows or she just got lucky. Maybe she was just talking. She does that sometimes. She probably has no clue. She was just spouting off and carrying on like joking." Ashley just shook her head from side to side.

Ryan sat shaking his leg up and down 'Well, did you hide the test? I mean is there a way she could have found it?"

"It's here in my room. She hasn't even been up here today. That's not something I would leave out in the open. I put it in a bag. I was planning on giving it to you to dispose of after you left the house, just to be safe. I'm pretty sure she was just talking. If she knew anything, she would be up here talking to us until she was blue in the face. So let's just get a hold of ourselves. You know we need to get a grip and settle down. They know nothing." Ashley sighed deeply.

"You're right. If she knew something, she would be on our asses big time, so we need to get our shit together and just relax. Besides the test was negative so we're good. You're going to get it any day now." Ryan breathed a sigh of relief. "If we are freaking this much over a negative, could you imagine if it were positive? Thank God it was what it was. I don't even want to say it because I'm afraid they will overhear me even though I'm talking to you in a whisper," Ryan added.

Ashley got up and started getting out the gifts. "Come on, let's get wrapping. We have to start doing this." She tapped him on the knee.

"OK. What do you want me to do?" He stood up.

"Get the wrapping paper out of the closet. I'll get the scissors and tape." Ashley proceeded to gather everything and spread it out on the bed and they started to wrap up all the gifts.

They wrapped in silence for a while and as they started to relax they started to joke around and things went back to a normal state between the two of them. After a while Ruth popped in on them just as she had promised, bringing them each a soda. She surveyed the area taking note of how many gifts they had wrapped. "Well, you two got a lot of stuff. Are you done or is there more to wrap?" Ruth asked as she handed them their drinks.

"We're almost finished," Ashley answered as she opened her Pepsi. "Thanks for the sodas,"

"Oh, you're welcome." Ruth waved her hand.

"So what time will dad be home?" Ashley inquired.

"Well, he has to work a full day today in order to have Monday and, of course, Tuesday off. He'll be home around five tonight unless he has to work overtime, but I doubt he will have to today." Ruth raised her eyebrows and pursed her lips. "I wanted to ask you if you're done with your shopping?"

"Yeah, why?" Ashley answered.

"Well, I know it's short notice but I was wondering if you could watch your brothers tonight so your father and I could do some last minute shopping?"

"Can Ryan stay here too if he wants to?" Ash raised her eyebrows. "Yeah, I think that would be OK." Ruth shook her head up and down.

"Sure, I would be glad to do it for you." "Thanks. That means a lot to me."

"I'm glad you trust us to be alone. Well, not alone, but the only sort of adults at home to watch the boys. Don't worry, we'll take good care of them." Ashley smiled at Ruth.

"I'm sure you will." Ruth got up to leave, "Finish up, then come downstairs before your father comes home. I don't want his mental image to be of you two in her bedroom and us leaving you at home sort of alone, got it?" Ruth went downstairs.

"Got it," Ash answered quickly before Ruth left. So the two quickly finished up what little they had to do and went downstairs. By this time Ruth had just put Jake down for his afternoon nap so he was upstairs crying himself to sleep. Ryan also had to leave to do some errands, at least that's what he told Ashley. So Ash went back to helping Ruth with baking and whatever else needed to be done because everyone was coming to their house on Christmas day.

After dinner was done Ruth and Rodger left Ashley in charge of the boys, so they could finish up their shopping. Ryan had not yet returned from running his errands and Ashley wasn't sure what to think. So she focused on playing with the boys, something she hadn't done in quite a while. After being knee deep in Lego's and race cars for over an hour, Ashley put the boys in the tub to play before she washed them up. Meanwhile Ryan showed up. He strolled in the house and announced himself, "Hey baby I'm here." He laughed.

Ashley ran downstairs. "What are you doing? What if one of my parents were here? Are you crazy?" She was shocked. "The boys are in the tub. I've got to go tend to them. Just sit down. I'll be right back." She ran back upstairs. "Hey guys, let's get you washed up." She started to wash them up.

Michael asked, "Is Ryan here?" Then Jake asked, "Sissy, is Ryan here?" "Yes, guys, Ryan is here. Now let's get you two cleaned up," she insisted.

"Can we go see him when we're done?" Michael pleaded.

"We'll see. Depends on how good you are," Ashley answered trying to think of a way to get the boys in bed quickly because Ryan was drunk. If her father came home and saw him there drunk in front of them, he could get upset even though he has been drunk in front of them plenty of times. Shit, she thought, what to do?

Once dressed the two boys ran downstairs to see Ryan who was singing along to the radio while drinking yet another beer. "Hey, guys, how are you? Are you being good for your sister? They nodded their heads while saying yes. They wrestled around like usual for a good fifteen minutes or so then Ryan settled them down and suggested, "You should make Ash read you a bed time story. I don't know about you, but I'm tired." Ryan wiped his face and fake yawned. "Let's all go up and lay down to go to bed and have Ashley read to us,"

"I don't want to go to bed," wailed Michael as he rubbed his eyes.

"Me either, Ash, not now," bawled Jake.

"Listen, let's just go up and lay down and I'll just read you some stories. You don't have to go to sleep, just listen to the books and we'll just have some quiet reading time. That's all, OK? No one said you have to go to sleep. We're just reading stories and having quiet time." Ash herded them up the stairs and into bed. She started to read. By the end of the third book both boys were out cold and Ryan was also dozing off. Ash gently poked him and the two silently and swiftly made their way back downstairs. The two fell onto the sofa. "So where were you today? Obviously you had a few beers," Ash prodded him.

"Well, after I got done doing some shopping I ran into a few of the guys and we went for a few drinks at the bar. One turned into two and so on. I just lost track of time." He shrugged his shoulders. Then he put his arm around Ashley and pulled her close. They started kissing and he whispered, "I have a fresh supply of condoms." He smirked.

"It's almost ten. My parents could be home at any time now, are you crazy?" She gently pushed him away.

"Oh, come on Ash. They won't catch us. We have plenty of time. You're wasting time right now. Come on, please. You know you want to." He stroked her arm and then kissed her hand.

"I'm scared. Besides after our scare with the test, I'm surprised you're even asking to already."

"Well, it will make it come all the sooner. You know all that action down there." Ryan stroked her leg. "You don't even have to take off all your clothes, just the important ones. And you know how I like you naked. Oh, come on, I want you so bad. You could think of it as an early Christmas present and it would be an awesome present." He was breathing heavy. "I know, why don't you have a beer, but drink it quick because we don't have a lot of time." Ryan ran out to the car and snagged a couple of beers.

Ashley's mind was in turmoil. She realized she could get in a lot of trouble if her parents found out she was drinking especially when watching the boys. The pressure from Ryan was so strong, she wished her parents would just pull in the driveway immediately. Then she wouldn't have to deal with Ryan right now. She put in a quick prayer to God to have them pull in the driveway now. Ryan came back with the beer. Ashley got up and excused herself, "Ryan I need to use the bathroom. I'll be right back." She paced back and forth unsure of what to do, but after a few minutes she went back out.

"Here, have a beer. It will relax you." Ryan went to hand it to her. Ash refused it. "I can't Ryan. I'm in charge of the boys and I can't drink. Any other time and I would be down with it but not when I am watching the boys. I promised my parents I would be trustworthy and that's what I need to be. I'm sorry but I can't." She turned away.

Ryan sighed deeply. "Whatever." He slammed the one beer, then opened the second and started to pound that one down. "I'm out of here. You're acting like a prude." He grabbed his coat and left, without a decent goodbye.

Ashley looked at the clock. It was almost 10:30 at night. She locked the door and went up to bed. As she lay in bed, all she could think about was how mad he had gotten when she refused to go along with his plan to get a piece of ass. To hell with his drunk ass. How could he think that her drinking while watching the boys was a good idea, not to mention that she would have to answer to her father. And he would get into trouble with him for buying the alcohol for her. How could he not care about any of this? Then the thought occurred to her that he would never act that way if he were sober. But he shouldn't get a pass because he was drunk. He acted like a total ass and was trying to pressure her into doing something she didn't feel comfortable doing and that's just not OK. She thought about this a lot and decided if he didn't apologize, then to hell with him. Especially after the scare they just had and she still didn't get her friend so who knows if the test is even right. She would give it a week, then if she was still waiting she would redo it. Around 11pm she heard her parents come in. She pretended to be asleep when they checked on her and the boys. Then, sometime after they were home, she finally drifted off to sleep. Her mind slowly quieted down enough to allow sleep to creep in and take over.

CHAPTER 24

The following morning Ashley slept in late but Ruth didn't mind figuring the boys wore her out last night. She also knew that Ashley had a long day ahead of her, at the restaurant washing dishes, so she gladly let her sleep in. Around noon Ashley wandered downstairs. "I can't believe how late it is. You could have woken me up," Ashley went and got herself a cup of coffee.

"Well, you have been so busy lately and you're working all day today. You needed a good long sleep. So what time do you have to go in today?" Ruth asked.

Ash sat down sipping her coffee. "Uh, I have to be there at 1pm, so I only have enough time to shower and then I've got to get going." She sighed.

"And what time will you be done?

"They will most likely stop serving around nine tonight so I'll be done around 11pm." Ash sipped her coffee.

"Wow, it takes that long to clean up?" Ruth stood with her hand on her hip.

"Well, it depends on when the last person gets served and how long people hang out in the dining room. So if the last person comes in around Seven pm, then it's an early night but if the last one comes in around nine, then it's a later night." Ash shook her head while drinking her coffee.

"Yeah, I understand. Hopefully it will be an early night,"

"No, I would rather get the extra hours to tell you the truth. It's easy especially if it's only one or two couples." Ashley smiled while rubbing her eyes.

Ruth poured herself another cup and sat down next to her. "Well, I hope you have a good day." She sipped her coffee.

Ash slammed the last of her coffee and then headed upstairs to get a shower. First she paused to ask, "Oh, can I drive the truck or do you want to give me a ride, but then you have to pick me up because Ryan and I got into a huge fight last night and I doubt he's going to show up to bring me home." Ashley stood waiting for a reply.

"Wait a minute. What did you get in a fight about?" Ruth inquired. "I would rather not get into it right now," Ashley quickly remarked. "Well, I'm concerned if you don't even think he would pick you up. He always picks you up." Ruth was unsettled.

"He was just a jerk last night, that's all," she added.

"Well, that doesn't sound like an I won't pick you up offense." Ruth frowned.

"Trust me, he's not going to pick me up. He was a real big time jerk. If I was allowed stronger language, I would use it." Ashley stood, hands on hips.

"What did you fight about? Ruth demanded. "I will keep it between you and me but I need to know just to ensure your continued mental health because in the big picture it really hasn't been that long since you were, well.. in dire straights, OK." Ruth raised her eyebrows and looked her directly in the eye.

Ashley let out a huge sigh and plopped down in the chair. "Fine I'll tell you. He came over already drunk and we put the boys to bed. Then we went downstairs and we were kissing. He wanted me to have a drink with him and he went out and got two beers out of his car. When he came back inside, I told him I couldn't drink. I was watching the boys. Any other time it would be OK, but I just couldn't today. He got mad and left." Ashley sighed again and rested her head in her hand.

Ruth sat for a minute absorbing all that Ashley had said. "That doesn't sound very upsetting, just not drinking. There has to be more to the story that you're just not telling me." Ruth tilted her head and looked in her eyes.

"I don't really want to talk about it." Ash sat bouncing her knee.

"Did he pressure you to have sex with him?" Ruth asked.

Ashley's eyes bugged out of her head.

"He did, didn't he? That's why he got so upset and left. You see, honey, I've lived many more years than you, I know how boys act. Don't worry. He will get over it. They all do. If he truly loves you, he'll come back around." Ruth pursed her lips and shook her head up and down as if her mind was on overdrive, congratulating herself for figuring it out. "Remember this is just between us," She patted her arm and went back to her coffee. "You can take the truck to work. That will show him you don't need him and that, my dear, will upset him, trust me." Ruth continued to shake her head non-stop as if she were on a mission.

"Thanks," Ashley got up and went upstairs to shower. Ashley thought about how angry she was at Ryan and now Ruth was in their business and knows sex has come up in it. Right now she wanted to beat his head into the pavement. How could he act that way putting her in this situation? Oh, how she hated him right now. She thought I'm seventeen. I'll be eighteen this summer and be going off to college. How long do they expect me to be a virgin? Hell, I still haven't got my period I could be… No, I don't even want to think about it. I'm not. The test was negative. I'm going to get it any day now, I just need to relax. I'm driving myself insane with this. Like the doctor said don't over think the situation, calm down. It's only two days until Christmas and I'm not even enjoying the holidays. Damn you, Ryan, for putting me in this predicament. All right get a grip. Just get ready and get your ass to work. Don't waste all this time thinking about all this shit.

By the time Ashley arrived at work there was a pile of dirty dishes waiting for her, and she had to peel a 10 pound bag of potatoes before she could start in on washing the dishes. At this point though she was a pro at peeling potatoes and had that done in no time. She started in on the dishes and the chef's pans as soon as they came back. She caught up quickly. It wasn't a busy day by any standard. She had brought some school homework just in case it was slow, so in her down time she could study. As the night wore on a slow night became a dead night. It seemed no one was in the mood for fine dining. Ashley's boss told her to pack it up and meet him out front in the empty bar, so she did. He and a couple of the waitresses and Ashley sat and had a toast to the holiday and he gave them each a hundred dollar bill.

"Wow, are you serious? Thanks Thank you so much." Ashley sat stunned with a huge smile on her face. She couldn't believe he actually gave her so much money for a holiday bonus. She tucked it safely away in her front pocket and couldn't stop grinning.

"You work very hard for me and I appreciate it, so, Merry Christmas, enjoy it," Mr. Croy said with a smile and a nod. He poured himself another drink and took a sip.

"Well, thank you. I'm all done out back so I'm going to head out. Have a Merry Christmas." Ashley held up her hand to wave goodbye and the other employees were talking having another drink with their boss and they all said goodbye to her.

She pulled in the driveway about eleven that night and just sat there for a few minutes thinking how Ryan didn't show up at the restaurant. How could we be fighting at Christmas, a time for happiness and love.

This has got to be the worst Christmas ever she thought. A tear streamed down her face. She just sat there gripping the wheel lost in thought. How could this be happening? She remembered the gift she had bought for him and took special care wrapping it. And now we are not even speaking to each other. Some great holiday.

She made her way into the dark house, locking the door behind her hanging the key onto the rack next to the door. Silently she went up to her room and got into bed. Before going to sleep she prayed, "Please, God, give me strength and help resolve the problem between Ryan and me, Your will be done on earth as it is in heaven. I love You, Lord. Thank You for all Your blessings. Please protect my family and loved ones. Keep them happy and healthy. Amen." She was so tired emotionally and physically she drifted off to sleep rather quickly.

The warm morning sun was shining bright in through the window masking the bitter cold outside. Ashley awoke to the joyful sounds of her two younger brothers across the hall in their bedroom, singing "Jingle Bells." She quickly realized it was Christmas Eve day. Glancing at her clock, it read 9:30 am. She took in a deep breath and rubbed her face while exhaling. Then Ash thought for a minute. She couldn't help but wonder if Ryan was going to call or come over. Then she considered maybe she should just call him. I mean why should she be waiting on him to act first. Maybe he was waiting for her to calm down or call first. No sense wondering all day what he is doing when deep down you want to talk to him. She so wanted to make up and be on good terms. For God's sake it's Christmas. So she decided to get up and face the day and its difficulties head on. After a shower and no period yet she decided she would wait and not let it bother her until after Christmas. She went downstairs and had a cup of coffee.

Ruth met her with a smile and a cheery greeting. "Well, good morning, I didn't hear you come in last night. How was work?"

"Work was good although very slow, too slow. It just dragged by, but he gave us a Christmas bonus, a hundred bucks. Can you believe it?" Ash smiled while sipping her coffee.

"Wow, what are you going to spend it on?" Ruth inquired.

"I'm putting it in savings for college, of course. I can't afford to spend a cent of it," Ashley nodded her head.

"You're such a good kid. That's being so smart. I'm proud of you."

"Thanks, I needed that. So I've decided to call Ryan, I mean why sit around waiting for him to call me when I'm totally capable of calling him and settling this. It's Christmas. I mean he can't possibly be that angry with me and you have to promise not to let on that you know anything. Deal?" Ashley looked her directly in the eye.

"Oh, no, I won't say anything. That conversation was between you and me and that's that, I promise." Ruth raised her eyebrows up and remained looking at her stepdaughter in the eye.

"Thank you because if he knew he would never feel comfortable coming over again. That's how important it is."

"I understand. It will remain just between us."

"OK I'm going to call him," Ashley drank some more of her coffee and picked up the phone and dialed his number. After the third ring Ryan picked up. "Hi, Ryan, it's me," Ashley nervously stammered.

"I know. I'm surprised that you even called. I figured you had enough of me the other night," Ryan sheepishly offered.

"Well, you were kind of a jerk and I still can't believe you wanted me to drink when I was watching the boys." Ashley started to become more firm.

"Well, I was really drunk. I normally would never ask you to do that. I just wanted to party with you, and you were so hot I wanted you so bad. Then you said no and it pissed me off really bad. But now I realize it was wrong and your parents could have caught us," Ryan admitted.

"Well, Ryan, I had to be straight. What if something happened to one of the boys? I needed to be in control. There's a time and place for everything and when I'm babysitting my two baby brothers, that's not the time. I tried to tell you that. All you wanted was, well you know what you wanted."

Ryan took in a deep breath and let it out. "I know and I'm sorry. I should never have been so forceful with you. I'm sorry. Can we just go back to being normal? I promise I won't ever do that again," Ryan swore to her.

As soon as she heard his apology, she was ready to forgive him. "You promise, because I would really like that."

"I swear I'll never pressure you to drop your panties again." He chuckled.

"You are so bad Ryan Fellman. What am I going to do with you? Beat you maybe. So are you going to come over and pick me up," Ashley asked.

"What time do you want me to be there?" Ryan asked.

"As soon as you're ready," she stated.

"I'll be there in an hour." Ryan hung up the phone. Yes he thought, we are good again.

Ashley looked at Ruth. "Well, looks like things are back to normal. Ryan is coming over to pick me up. We are going to go do some last minute shopping." She jumped up and raced upstairs to get ready.

Ruth sat there thinking it must be nice to be young and in love, so easy to fight, forgive and carry on. She smiled to herself and then got up and started to bake some pies for the holidays. She was sort of hoping to have Ashley's help today but since their make-up, she now doubted that. Rodger's parents were coming in later in the day and she knew her mother in law would gladly help prepare anything they needed for tomorrow. Ruth thought how just two years ago Ashley would have been waiting all day for her grandmother to arrive, but now she was lost in love.

Ryan tapped on the door as he let himself in. "Hello," as he walked into the kitchen, and was met with the aroma of apple pies baking in the oven. Ruth rounded the corner just as he was passing the table. "Well, hello there Ryan. Haven't seen you lately. You here to pick up Ashley?" Ruth tilted her head to the side.

"Hi, uh…yeah Ash just called and we're going out," Ryan pointed out towards the driveway with no real direction in mind, just out.

Ruth nodded her head. "OK, she's upstairs. I guess you can go get her, but don't dawdle. You don't need to be spending a lot of time in the bedroom." She raised her eyebrows.

"Thanks." Ryan took off up the stairs as if he were being chased. Once in Ashley's room he came to an abrupt stop catching his breath, and asking Ashley," Does Ruth know why we were fighting?" He stood there waiting for her to ease his fears.

"Why would you think that?" Ashley remarked hoping to try to avoid answering him.

"She just doesn't seem like she's the same." Ryan vigorously scratched his head.

"Don't worry about her. Listen, we should do something fun." Ashley grabbed his arms, facing him. "Like go to the Bluffs and let loose. You know relax." She nodded.

Ryan still focused on Ruth. "Why would she say that unless she knew something?"

"Ryan, Ryan. Come on, forget about her. I'm right here. Let's go to the Bluffs and have some fun." She put her hands on his face, cupping it and gave him a kiss. Then she went to her drawer and pulled out a bag of weed, flaunting it in front of him and then quickly putting it in her pocket. "Let's go have some fun," and she slapped his butt.

After he saw the weed, he was all in. "OK, I'm in. Let's go." The two left the house bound for the Bluffs.

When they arrived at the Bluffs, the wind coming off the lake was frigid but the sun was bright. It was warm shining through the windshield. The two wasted no time packing a glass bowl with blue and red coloring in it. They took turns taking hits off of it.

After smoking a couple of bowls, they sat talking and listening to the radio. Before too long they had worked themselves into the backseat and out of their clothes enjoying each other and being in love. After both had received complete joy from the other, they laid naked in each other's arms and then the topic of Ash not getting her period came up, though they did in fact use protection this time.

"Well, maybe our little make-up session will make it come," Ryan squeezed her tight. "Don't worry so much about it. I'm telling you it's all nerves." He hugged her again.

"Come on, we better get dressed. You never know, someone might show up," Ashley commented. They put their clothes on and climbed in the front seat.

"All of this sneaking around sucks. We should be able to go to my house. After all, I pay half the rent. Besides, my dad's legs are so bad now he can't even climb the stairs to get up to my room." Ryan sighed.

"That would be nice but that's just not the case right now. We really need to get back. It's Christmas Eve and my grandparents will be getting in soon," Ashley strongly suggested. It being late afternoon the two agreed and headed off back to Ashley's house. First though, they stopped in town to pick up a few little trinkets to show they had been shopping.

When they arrived at Ashley's house, her grandparents were already there. She walked in and her grandmother was helping Ruth in the kitchen baking cookies and pies. The whole house smelled of heavenly aromas. "Well, there she is." Her grandmother turned and put down the spatula in order to give her a hug.

"Hi, grandma. How are you?" Ashley hugged her.

"Oh, I'm better now, and how are you Ryan?" She went and gave him a big hug.

"I'm doing fine thanks." He smiled.

"Well, it's nice to see everyone together for the holiday. Your grandfather is in the other room with your father doing who knows what. You know how they are," Grandma Ames commented. "Now, Ryan, is your father coming to dinner tomorrow?"

"Yes he is, around 1pm right?" Ryan replied Ruth jumped in, "Yes, that's right." "We'll be here," Ryan added.

"Ruth, can Ryan and I go up to my room and wrap these few last gifts? We'll keep the door open." Ashley boldly asked in front of her grandmother.

"Yeah, that's fine. The boys are up there so will you keep an eye on them for me?" Ruth asked as she kept on baking.

"Sure, I can do that for you," Ashley answered and then they went upstairs to her room to wrap the trinkets they had gotten in town. She also checked in on the boys. They were playing with their toys while watching a video. After they had finished up, Ryan mentioned he should return home since his father would be home alone and he didn't want him to be by himself tonight. So he gave Ashley a rather long good bye kiss and left, with the promise to see her tomorrow afternoon for dinner. She was sad to see him go but respected him for spending time with his father on the holiday, especially because he was the only family he had.

After Ryan left, Ashley wandered downstairs to the kitchen where her grandmother and Ruth were whipping up a Christmas eve buffet: a veggie platter, a meat and cheese with rolls platter, cheese and crackers platter, shrimp with cocktail sauce, chips and dips, and rye bread dip platter. Ash started picking right away. "Oh, this is great. I love Christmas and you coming down here." She was looking at her grandmother.

"Well, I love coming too. The holidays are a special time of year and should always be spent with the people you love." Grandma Ames hugged Ashley. "So how are you and Ryan getting along? Do you love each other?" She inquired as she tilted her head to the side.

"Uh, yeah, I think so." Ashley grinned. "And he's good to you?" she inquired. "Yes, grandma, he's very good to me."

"So, you'll be 18 this summer and going off to college in the fall. How does he feel about that?"

He's fine with it. I'll probably come home on the weekends," Ashley answered trying to reassure her of their commitment.

Her grandmother came in close and asked, "So have you given yourself to him or are you waiting until you're married?" She raised her eyebrows and jutted out her chin a bit expecting an honest answer. And since Ashley hadn't had her period and could at this point be pregnant, she wasn't exactly sure what to say.

"Grandma! Really I can't believe you asked me that!" Ashley hoped that would be enough and she would leave it alone.

"So that means?" She looked her in the eye.

Ashley was shocked. She didn't know how to get out of this. She looked to Ruth who seemed just as shocked as she was that this was the topic of conversation. On the one hand if she said no it would be the end of it, unless nine months later a bundle of joy came along. Then she would be labeled a liar. But if she said yes, then she would be a loose woman of poor moral character. She decided to lie through her teeth. "No way. We are waiting, so that's that. I don't want to talk about this kind of stuff anymore or I'm leaving." Ashley took in a deep breath and let it out.

Her grandmother eyed her up and down not really convinced of the truth of her answer but at the same time relieved it was the one she wanted. "Very good my dear. I knew you were a good girl. Now let's finish up here in the kitchen." She went back to baking.

Ashley asked Ruth, "Is it OK if I call my mother?" "Of course," she replied.

Ashley called her mother. "Hi, mom. What time will you be at grandma and grandpa's tomorrow? I was thinking I could come and see all of you in the late afternoon if that was OK with you?" Ash offered.

"Yeah, that would be OK, but not too late because I have to go in to work at three," Ellen answered.

"OK. We are having dinner here at one so I'll be there at two. I'm sorry I can't come earlier," Ashley sighed.

"It's all right. Why don't you come and spend New Years day with me? Then we can spend the whole day together," Ellen suggested.

"Yeah, that would be great," Ashley replied.

"In fact you have the whole week off so why not spend a couple of days at my house with Laura and me. Ryan is right up the street. We could have fun," Ellen offered.

"All right I would like that. We'll talk more about it tomorrow. Sounds good. I'll see you tomorrow. Love you. Bye," Ashley hung up the phone. She turned to Ruth. "She wants me to spend a couple of nights at her house with Laura and her. Think it's a good idea?" Ash looked at her.

Ruth stopped rolling out the dough. "Yes, I think it's a great idea. You need to spend time with her and especially Laura. When are you going?"

"Well, later in the week. I already told her I would spend New Year's day with her, so I guess later in the week. Just a couple of days though. See how it goes." Ash wrinkled her brow.

Grandma Ames pipped in, "I think that would be good. She just couldn't tame your father, and I think you, Ruth, have done a great job of taming Rodger. He is so much better now than ever before."

So the night went well with everyone eating, drinking, having a good night, chatting, sharing memories, making new memories, and leaving out cookies for Santa at bedtime.

Ashley lay in bed thinking about past Christmas Eves, when she was little, at church reciting little pieces of quotes they had to memorize. There she would be, up front, in front of everyone reciting her little quote she had spent weeks memorizing, hoping and praying she wouldn't forget any of it. Then at the end everyone including her parents would clap and cheer. She felt great as if she had accomplished some great feat. The thought of that made her smile, made her miss it. When she was little she used to love going to church on Sundays with her aunt who lived just up the road from her mother.

Oh, how life gets more difficult the older you get. Now she had to lie to her grandmother and she may find out if she doesn't get her period soon. What was she going to do if she was pregnant? She could always get an abortion or kill herself because if her father found out he would kill her for sure. She thought if I don't get it in two more days, I'll use the other test. Then I'll know for sure. Oh, please don't be pregnant. That would ruin my whole life. A tear streamed down her face. She pulled up the covers and snuggled down in to get cozy.

"Come on Ash, get up. It's Christmas. It's time to open all our presents. Get up." Michael was tugging on her covers. "Get up Ash, come on." He kept tugging.

Ash rolled over. The clock read seven am. "Come on. Give me another hour."

"No, get up. Mommy says you have to be up for us to open our presents, so get up, now." Michael was now taking her covers off of her.

"OK, OK. I'm getting up. I've got to go to the bathroom first. Go downstairs and I'll be right down OK? Why don't you ask Mommy to get me a cup of coffee?" Ashley shuffled to the bathroom, sat on the toilet and wham her period came full force. She almost shouted for joy. She was so happy. It was the best Christmas present she could have received. By the time she got downstairs, she was wide awake and as happy as if she had already opened her gifts.

Coffee in hand the family gathered around the tree and proceeded to open their gifts. By the time it was over, Ashley had acquired three new shirts, two pairs of pants, one pair of sneakers, a watch, some socks, underwear, new books, art things, and some perfume. She was totally satisfied and grateful for everything. She thanked her parents and grandparents.

Michael looked up from his pile of new toys and announced "Santa is awesome look at how many toys he got me," Then he went back to playing.

"Yeah I love Santa he got me all these toys," Jacob smiled.

As the boys played in the living room, the adults gathered in the kitchen at the table and enjoyed their coffee. Ruth and Grandma Ames started making a breakfast of bacon, eggs, and home fries.

After breakfast Ashley called her mother to wish her and Laura a Merry Christmas. Then she showered and put on some of her new clothes and played around with her art things. It was mainly drawing pencils and books to help draw better, but she loved it. Before she knew it, it was almost time for dinner so she went down to help in the kitchen. Once there Ruth had her mash the potatoes and get out the rolls to put in the oven. While she was busy, Ryan and his father, Mr. Fellman, showed up for dinner and made themselves comfortable while waiting. By 1 pm the food was on the table and everyone was seated enjoying the feast presented to them. Ashley's grandfather really hit it off with Ryan's father which made Ryan feel really good because his father was a bit of a recluse. Ashley and Ryan ate rather quickly because they had made plans to go see Ashley's mother's side of the family by 2 pm so it didn't give them a lot of time to waste. They made eye contact and silently agreed they were ready to leave so they excused themselves from the dinner and got up to leave.

"You're leaving?" Grandma Ames asked in front of everyone.

"Yes, I have to go see my mother before she has to go into work." Ash put on her coat.

"All right then, I suppose it's OK, if your father doesn't object?" She kept at it.

"Mom, it's OK. She needs to go now," Rodger broke his silence and gave his answer.

Ashley made eye contact with her dad and gave him a big smile and he returned a wink. This made her feel really good inside. She turned with Ryan and they scampered out of the house. Once outside Ash said to Ryan, "My dad was great wasn't he?"

"Yeah, he really stood up for you. That's great." Ryan opened his car door and climbed in.

Ash waited until they got into the car before she broke the good news 'Guess what. I finally got my period this morning," she sighed in huge relief, smiling ear to ear.

"See I knew it would come as soon as we did the dirty deed," he laughed. "But seriously, thank God because your dad would have killed me." He smiled while looking at her. "We're in the clear. Man that takes a lot off my mind."

"I thought you weren't worried," Ashley came back.

"Oh, I was worried but I knew I had to remain calm to help you stay calm. Just trying to be a good man." Ryan started the car and backed out of the driveway.

Ashley laughed. You are something else, but you are a good man." She leaned over and kissed him. The two had exchanged gifts earlier in the day. Ashley was wearing the diamond earrings Ryan gave her and Ashley got Ryan a new winter Carhart jacket which he was also wearing.

The two walked in at her other grandparent's house just before 2 pm and said all their hellos and Merry Christmas with hugs and kisses. Then they chatted for a while and had dessert and they opened some more gifts. Her mother had gotten her a beautiful cross on a chain. It was just exquisite. She knew it was very expensive and promised herself she would take good care of it. Ashley was so very glad that she came. She really had a good time visiting and spending time with her family. They made the arrangements for when Ashley was going to come over to her mother's house and spend a few days visiting. This really made Laura happy. "I'm so glad you're coming over, I really miss having you around."

"I really miss hanging out with you too. "Ashley pursed her lips and tilted her head slightly to the side.

"Well, it'll be nice to have you back even if only for a few days." Ellen smiled.

"Listen, it's getting to be that time. I have to leave in a few minutes to go to work. I love you and I'll see you in a couple of days." Ellen went over and hugged Ashley then gave Laura a hug and told her she would see her at home. She said goodbye to her parents and left for work. After Ellen left, Ashley's grandmother, Helen, caught her alone and told her that her mother was really trying to change and understand where Ashley was coming from, how she felt and what she was going through. She told her that her mother had actually spoken to a counselor of sorts. What that was supposed to mean, Ashley wasn't sure. But it did make her feel better about spending time at her mother's house and with her. Ashley thanked her grandmother for trusting her with that information and swore she would keep it to herself. As the day wore on it got to be late so Ryan and Ashley said their goodbyes to her grandparents and Laura and Ryan took Ashley back to her father's house.

Once in the car Ashley could not contain herself anymore. "Gram said my mother actually spoke to a counselor about our relationship. She is trying to change, see things from my perspective. She didn't say if she is going on a regular basis or anything. I swore to keep it a secret but I had to tell you, of course." She held out her hands like what was she supposed to do with this information. "What do you think?"

"Wow, your mom in therapy. I don't even know what to think. But if it's about your relationship, it can't be bad. I mean anything is a step up," Ryan kept his eyes on the road only occasionally glancing over. It had started to snow.

"Well, she said a counselor of sorts. What's that supposed to mean?"
"I don't know. Hell, that could be an old wise woman or anything.

Who knows?" Ryan chuckeled, keeping his hands and eyes on the wheel. "But she's trying,"

"Yeah, you're right. At least she is trying, maybe to make it better and not to just sweep things under the rug. I don't know. In six months I'll be off to college so it won't matter so much."

"It will matter. She is your mother whether you're here or there." Ryan coughed.

"Oh, I hate it when you're right. I just want this mess to go away." Ashley sighed.

They pulled in the driveway and Ryan spoke up, "I don't see my dad's car so I'm assuming he already left. I'm going to take off and spend some quality time with him. I'll call you tomorrow. Give me a kiss." The two kissed for a bit.

"You are such a good son." She smiled,

"Well, I'm fond of the old man and he's up there in age so I won't have him around forever. I want to spend some time with him especially since mom died, what five years now. I think days like today he misses her more. I know I do." Ryan winked at her.

"I'm sorry you miss your mom; you spending time with your dad is part of the reason I love you so much. Good night." She got out of the car and waved goodbye as he pulled off.

Inside the house everyone was snuggled down watching a holiday movie. the two boys were asleep laying like a blanket over Ruth who herself was nodding off. Her grandparents had already turned in for the night so Ash just quietly waved to Ruth and snuck upstairs to her room. She snuggled in under her covers and realized that she actually had a good day. She smiled to herself and drifted off to sleep.

CHAPTER 25

*A*fter being at her mother's house for a couple of days, Ashley felt more turmoil being around her. Ellen had gone out of her way to try and make things peaceful and pleasant while she was visiting. However, Ashley still felt anger towards her mother over her taking the money. Before she came over she thought she had overcome that issue, but the longer she stayed the more it bothered her. She knew if she brought it up to her mother that it would blow up into a huge argument, so she decided to just bury it deep inside. In some ways she wanted justice, but she also wanted her mother to love her, and if that was the cost, she would pay it. Even though at times she felt deep resentment towards her, she also felt responsible for the destruction of not only the car but also the disruption of their lives for the entire summer.

Laura and Ashley had been spending a lot of time just hanging out, gossiping and sharing all their secrets. Just being with her sister made Ashley realize how much she missed her. Ashley, however, did not tell Laura about her thoughts and feelings towards their mother. She felt it would be wrong to weigh Laura down with that information.

With only one more day left at her mother's, Ashley felt she could keep herself in check until she got home. And, that night she was going out with Ryan. Her mother had already given her permission. So she didn't have to spend a lot of time with her which was a relief to Ashley.

As much as she missed her mother she also resented her which caused her to feel a great amount of turmoil where she was concerned.

That afternoon Ellen came home in a chipper mood. She even cooked one of Ashley's favorite dinners, homemade macaroni and cheese, which made Ashley feel guilty about how she was feeling towards her mother. After dinner she thanked her for going out of her way for fixing it for her and then they hung out for a little while. When it came time for Ryan to pick her up, Ellen did not allow him to come into the house. Ashley felt she was still angry about him coming to the house and retrieving the rest of her money. However, Ashley didn't voice her feelings. She just quietly met him outside.

Once in his car, however, she vehemently voiced her opinions. "I can't believe her. She didn't want you to come into the house." Ashley shook her head in disgust.

"What's up with that? She doesn't trust me, yet she allows you to go out with me. I bet she is still pissed off that I came and got the rest of your money, but she just doesn't want to say so. Did she give you a reason?"

"No, and I didn't ask. To hell with it. Today is Friday and I go home tomorrow. In fact, why don't you pick me up around ten in the morning? That way I can sleep until like nine and then just go home, the sooner the better. I'll just tell her I have some unfinished homework that I need to do." Ashley sighed heavily. "She is still the same underneath it all and that bothers me, a lot."

"Listen, you need to relax and take it for what it is. For the most part you had a peaceful visit. She really tried hard to make it good for you. So what I'm not allowed in the house. It's not that big of a deal." Ryan pursed his lips.

"It's not only that. The longer I stay the more resentful I feel about her taking the money and then I feel guilty when she tries to be nice to me. I need to talk to my counselor about this whole thing. I'm so confused about it," she said, wringing her hands.

"Well, school starts up on Monday so hopefully you can get in to see him and talk about it then. For right now just try and enjoy your visit at least with Laura and try to cut your mom some slack. She is trying." Ryan looked her in the eye trying to help her feel better. "For now let's just stay out until curfew. Then you can go back and go to bed, and then I'll come and get you in the morning." He reached over and gave her a hug and kiss. Later the two met up with another couple, Rick and Mary. They hadn't hung out with them in ages. Rick was Ryan's friend and he had really just started going out with Mary about six months ago, and they seemed to get along great. They were always fun to hang out with. So, after a night of cruising around mixed with a bit of partying, Ashley made it back to her mother's by curfew and went straight to bed.

The following morning went just as planned. She got up around nine and explained to her mother she had some homework that needed to be done and by ten she was packed and, on her way, back home. Leaving Laura was the only thing that was really hard for Ashley, but she knew that she just couldn't stay any longer. Besides, she would see Laura at school and they could have lunch together. Holding in all these feelings was killing her and not being able to tell her sister the truth about how she felt about her mother, was also beyond difficult, but she knew she just couldn't. So she left without a word, with the truth buried deep inside where she hoped to keep it.

When she arrived back home Ruth was in the kitchen quietly enjoying a cup of coffee. "Well, hello. Didn't expect you so early. How's my girl?" She was met by a huge smile and a bigger hug.

"I'm good. Glad to be home, that's for sure," she said as they separated.

"And how are you Ryan?" Ruth warmly asked.

"I'm good, thanks." He nodded.

"Did you have a good visit at your mother's house?" Ruth inquired.

"Well, it was OK, but I had feelings of resentment come up left over from the hospital so that kind of sucked." Ashley looked at the floor.

"Well, you went through a lot, and a lot happened especially between the two of you. Plus, most teenage girls don't see eye to eye with their mothers, so hang in there." She half smiled with a tilt of her head.

"She tried to make the visit pleasant. She really did, but I don't think she has changed as much as my grandmother would like me to believe." Ashley sighed. "I'm going to go put my bag away, then I'll come back and have some coffee with you,"

"OK. Ryan can stay right here with me." Ruth winked at her stepdaughter as she left the room.

Once Ashley was out of ear shot Ruth asked Ryan "How did it go? Tell me the truth." She was all wide eyed.

Ryan, not sure of what exactly she knew about how much went on at the hospital, shockingly replied, "Actually it went pretty well. No harsh words or anything that I know of." He was praying for Ashley's quick return.

"So, why is she home so early in the morning?" Ruth came back with. "I think she may have some homework and she said she was homesick," Ryan offered.

Ashley returned to the kitchen overhearing the bit Ryan had confessed to Ruth. "Do I need a reason to want to come home early?" she questioned, a bit on the defensive.

"No honey. Not at all. I was just worried something went wrong and you were upset, that's all," Ruth replied.

"Well, the visit went just fine. Stop worrying I'm fine." Ashley sighed.

Monday morning came early especially after being able to sleep late all vacation. Getting settled back into classes again and turning in assignments done over the holiday was typical. Ashley had decided her New Year's resolution was going to be to stop getting high in school and pay more attention to her teachers, put more effort into her assignments and concentrate on getting good grades. She did this mainly because she needed to buckle down and get good grades in order to get into college. One of her first stops was the bathroom. She decided to tell her friends her plan and hoped they understood. "Hey, girly girls, how's it going?" Ashley smiled as she greeted the gang in the back stall of the bathroom.

The trio stood around smoking and talking. Karen was the first to speak up "Hey, Ash, what have you been up to? You look good."

"Well, actually a lot. I made a New Year's resolution this year and it was to quit partying in school, but I'll still come to the parties outside of school. I'm not turning into a goody goody, that's for sure. I hope you understand I need to do this to get into college." Ashley sighed deeply and raised her eyebrows.

"Oh, man, that's a bummer. Things won't be the same without you, but I can understand, I guess. I mean I know you've got to get into college and all. It's just going to suck without you around. But at least we'll get to party together outside of school at the parties so that's cool. "Karen shook her head as she took a drag off of her cigarette.

"Karen pretty well summed it up for me too," Emily added.

"Sorry guys, but I've got to get into college. I don't want to get some minimum wage job in this nowhere town and be stuck here forever with no future." Ash held out her hands.

Amy finally spoke up, 'I get it. I mean I plan on going to college, but I still have another year to go." She took a drag and exhaled.

After explaining her newfound, in school, sobriety to her friends, Ashley felt a renewed sense of strength and dedication to her studies. Having done that she looked up her counselor and sat down for a chat. He wanted to know what was going on with her before vacation. She again refused to tell him stating it was no longer an issue. It was taken care of. It's nothing to worry about so just leave it alone. Mr. Shore was kind of taken aback by her response and adamant attitude about not sharing whatever was going on with her. He, however, let it go without an issue knowing she still needed him as a confidant for other situations. She did share about how she felt after staying at her mother's over vacation and, how the feelings escalated as the days wore on. Her mother tried hard to make her feel welcome, but Ashley still harbored resentment towards her. She explained how she had prayed about it, feeling she had overcome these negative feelings. He listened intently and explained that she needed more time which would help and possibly more prayer if she so desired. But he also stated he was not allowed to encourage prayer, but if she wanted to that was up to her. Then he suggested maybe she should keep her visits to a shorter period of time, maybe fewer consecutive days. The two talked for a while about how she was doing in other areas of her life and things of that nature. When they finished, Ashley felt much better about her life and the direction it was going.

Ashley rededicated herself to her studies and to staying out of trouble. Days turned into weeks and weeks turned into months without her having any problems. After school she actually went home and studied which helped to improve her grades dramatically. She rarely went into the bathroom to hang out during her free time. When she did, she didn't partake in smoking weed and she rarely smoked cigarettes anymore. Things seemed to be falling into place for Ashley and her future.

However, one evening Ryan called quite upset. His father had yet again fallen ill. He needed Ryan to start changing bandages on an open wound on his foot. He feared his father would get an infection throughout his body, but his father refused to go to the doctor. He had had other wounds before and recovered, but this time Ryan said it was worse. He had waited until the wound was very bad before he had sought out Ryan's help.

"Oh, Ryan, I'm so sorry. Is he running a temperature?" Ashley asked very concerned.

"I'm not sure but that's a good idea to check it. Hold on. Let me do that. Don't hang up,"

A few minutes went by and Ryan returned. "Well it says 99.5. Is that high? I'm not even sure," Ryan confessed.

"Well, it's only a little high. Maybe you should give him some aspirin or something. I think you need to get him to go to the doctor. Tell him he has a temp and he needs to go," Ash suggested.

"I don't know if that's enough to get him to go, but I'll try. I'll talk to you later."

"OK. Good luck." Ashley hung up feeling helpless. His father was old school, but she still was very fond of him. She thought back to Thanksgiving and what a good time they all had. She just shook her head feeling sad.

Over the next week or so Ryan's father still refused to go to the doctor, so Ryan was faced with changing the bandages on his foot. There was little improvement and his father couldn't return to work, yet he remained optimistic about the future. So Ryan just changed the bandages and tried to remain positive, yet he confided his fears in Ashley.

"He is so elderly. What if he doesn't win the fight with this infection? Then what?" Ryan confessed.

"Well, let's hope he does. If he doesn't we will deal with that when and if it happens. Just spend time with him and enjoy his company right now. Try not to think negatively." Ashley tried to offer her best advice. "I mean you've got nothing to lose. He's your dad. Spend time with him. If he comes out of it, you spent some extra time with him. You will always value it."

"You're right. I need to spend more time with him and be positive.

Besides you're so busy with school. You won't even notice." He chuckled.

"Ha ha, very funny, but it is kind of the truth. I won't even be jealous. You're such a good guy taking care of your dad like you do. I love you."

Ash smiled.

"Thanks, I love you too. Listen I've got to go. Talk to you tomorrow."

"OK. Tomorrow then. Bye." Ashley hung up the phone feeling warm inside.

With about one month left in her senior year of high school, Ashley was feeling pretty good. This one afternoon she followed Karen and Amy into the bathroom to hang for just a few minutes even though she had a free hour. The trio got to talking and then they got to smoking a little weed. When they finished the joint they flushed the roach, after a couple minutes Ashley states "Man we have to get out of here it reeks". So they walk out into the hall right into the vice principal, Mr. Mills, who had been waiting for them. He smelled the weed too. He led all three girls into the office and they were caught dead on. He left them there and went back to search the bathroom to no avail. When he returned to the office, he started to question the trio about how he had heard them say they had to leave because of the smell. Suddenly Ashley became irate. She stood up and loudly stated, "I said that because it did smell and I knew we needed to get out of there because you would blame it on me because of my past. Here I'm trying to do the right thing and I'm still getting blamed for things that I didn't do. I knew we had to leave. I didn't want to get into trouble because of something someone else did and you not believe me. I'm really trying here."

Out of nowhere Mr. Mills stood up and said, "OK. OK." He dismissed Karen and Amy. Then he turned his attention to Ashley. "Look I'm sorry to have accused you of smoking pot in the bathroom. I know you've been working very hard here in school and taking the college course, plus you have a job. Please don't let this set you back in any way. You're doing so well and you've come so far. We are all proud of the progress you have made. So I apologize for accusing you of smoking in the bathroom. You were right to get out of there because of the smell." Then Mr. Mills escorted Ashley out of his office and she got a pass and went to class. Immediately following her class, she zipped over to the bathroom and explained to the girls what happened to her after they left. They all were stunned.

"Man, Ash, you have the best brain ever. I couldn't believe what I was hearing and they bought it. That's a classic." Karen smiled and shook her head from side to side.

"Ash, you should become an actress because I bought it hook line and sinker and I was there." Amy chuckled.

"I know it. I can't believe it myself. Listen don't tell people. I don't want it to get around and then get back to him," Ashley stated.

They both nodded and agreed that that wouldn't be too cool.

Things settled down and before she knew it finals were here. Ashley found herself studying around the clock. She also had to take a trigonometry regents exam usually for juniors. Ashley had struggled through the course with the help of a tutor at one point. After the exam, a grueling three hours, she felt confident she got the needed 75 on the test. If she didn't, she wouldn't be able to get into college this year. So she had a lot riding on the outcome of this test in particular. Once she finished all of her final exams, she was riding high at the thought of graduation. On the final day of school students were gathered in the auditorium as usual. This morning they were giving out awards. Ashley and her friends were very excited and she kept getting weird glances from a few teachers. Then after many awards were given out, Mr. Mills announced they were going to give out the James H. McGinn Award. This was the highest award in the school. They started out saying the student had overcome many adversities and had made up many classes to go on to college and had come a long way. He announced "Ashley Ames." She was in shock. She stood up and started to go down then stopped in the aisle. He had to wave at her so she would continue to come down to the front of the auditorium. She actually started to cry, being in total disbelief, she stood in front of her classmates. All of her stoner friends were standing up cheering at the tops of their lungs, feeling that one of the regular kids won instead of one of the "good" kids who usually won. Also cheering were many of her teachers who she was very fond of and went the distance with her, some knowing how hard it was for her in life. After this award was given, the seniors were led to the library to say goodbye and the underclassmen were left to move into the upper classes' seats.

Once in the library all the seniors lined up and said goodbye to all the teachers and talked of their future plans, after that they snagged Ashley to take her picture for the paper along with the teacher who won the McGinn award. Ashley, however, felt a bit sad because usually parents are there to see their child's accomplishment. They told her they didn't know which one to invite, so they opted not to invite either one. She understood, but it still hurt her feelings, although she didn't show it. She took it in stride. Back at the library her friends cheered her on and that felt good. She decided it had to be enough to fill her heart. Saying goodbye to some of her teachers was bittersweet, yes she was looking forward to her future but she was leaving behind a sense of security. Mrs. Burns suggested she look at it as a sense of adventure and remember to ask herself what's the worst that could happen when she was upset or uncertain, to be brave and follow her dreams. She took that advice and kept it close to her heart telling herself she would always remember it.

She arrived home on a happy note, finding Ruth at the kitchen table enjoying a cup of coffee. "Well, how's it feel to be all done with high school?"

"It feels good. On to bigger and better things. College here I come." Ashley smiled. She went up to her room and collapsed on her bed. Although it had been a good day, it was literally exhausting and she just wanted to relax for a little while before dinner. Soon she drifted off to sleep and before she knew it Ruth was calling her for dinner. She got up and went downstairs.

During dinner she told her parents about winning the award. Unfortunately her father didn't seem too impressed, but Ruth was really proud of her and voiced it several times trying to get Rodger to jump on board but to no avail. While Ashley and Ruth cleaned up the dinner dishes, Ruth kept on telling her how proud she was of her and that her father probably just had a bad day at work and not to let his dismal mood affect her and her accomplishments. She should be proud of herself. Finally Ashley told Ruth what bothered her was, the school didn't invite her parents because they didn't know which ones to invite. No one was there to see her get the award and get a picture in the paper with her. She said, "I actually felt alone, like really lonely, as if I had no parents that cared. And now dad doesn't even see how important this is to me, like it isn't important at all, no big deal, but it is to me. I came a long way and did a lot of hard work to get it. But to him it means nothing partly because he didn't see me get it and see what a big deal it is to get the McGinn award. Plus it will be the same reaction of my mother. Yes, she will be happy I got it, but she will never see what a big deal it is to win it because they weren't there to see it for themselves." She looked her in the eye with a tear in hers.

"Oh, honey, I'm so sorry I wasn't there to see you get the award. I bet it was fabulous. Everyone cheered for you and you were so happy. I'm so proud of you,"

"Yeah, they even stood up for me. I wish you could have seen it." She sighed then sniffled. Later she called Ryan and told him. He was so proud of her. He said he owed her a night out on the town and dinner at her choice of place. That seemed to cheer her up because he understood how important the award was. It was the highest you could win in the school.

As the summer wore on Ashley worked all the hours she could, trying to save as much money as possible. One night after coming home late, with everyone asleep, she went to put something away in her desk drawer. She noticed her things had been gone through. Her first thought was maybe one of her brothers got into it, but then she couldn't help but wonder if it were her parents. But then she thought, I'm going off to college. Why would they be going through my things now? That's just crazy. She just went to bed, not giving it any more thought.

The next day Ashley found Ruth downstairs as usual in the kitchen doing household chores. She asked if she could help and Ruth seemed to be quiet and distant. She gave off a weird vibe that made Ashley feel just out of place and unwelcome. So she retreated upstairs to her room, but not before calling Ryan from another area in the house and telling him what was happening and how her drawer had been gone through. He told her he would get there as soon as he could, later that afternoon. She was certain something was going to happen and was nervous being there alone.

Later that afternoon Ashley's father came home early from work and sat down in the kitchen beside Ruth waiting for Ashley, like prey. She was upstairs in her room when her father pulled in the driveway and she noticed he was home early. All she could think about was why. It seemed strange, but she could sense it was about her. She said a quick prayer to have Ryan show up as soon as possible. Ashley sat on the edge of her bed trembling. It had to be serious if he came home early. Using the upstairs phone Ashley called Ryan again and his boss told her he had already left about 15 minutes ago. She thanked him and quietly hung up. Armed with the knowledge that Ryan would be there within the half hour, a sense of strength and confidence arose. She stood up, looked in the mirror into her own eyes, told herself you can do this whatever it is, took a deep breath, straightened her shirt, and then marched down the stairs ready for battle. As she entered the kitchen, she put out the attitude of surprise that her father had come home early and left Ruth's behavior alone.

Rodger started out very calm, "Hey, Ash, why don't you sit down. I need to talk to you about something that has come up." He took in a deep breath and slowly let it out.

So Ashley slowly pulled a chair out making sure she had a quick exit, although she didn't feel threatened and her father did not smell of alcohol but she wasn't that close to him. "So what's up? I mean you came home early just to talk to me. I don't understand." She looked back and forth between them.

"Well, I got a phone call the other day and it was upsetting to say the least." He rubbed his beard and face.

"Who and what did they say? It was about me, right? I mean that's why you're here right?" Ash held out her hand.

"I don't even know how to ask. So…well…OK. They asked if you were pregnant." He kind of glared at her.

"What? Who called? That's ridiculous. I'm not pregnant. Who said that?" She demanded looking her father in the eye.

Suddenly Ryan knocked as he let himself in. "Hello. Is Ash around?" He rounded the corner to see them sitting at the table and, he could sense the tension. "Bad time?" He looked around, then into Ashley's eyes.

"Ryan, apparently someone called and asked my father if I were pregnant, which we both know I'm not, and he refuses to say who." Ashley, feeling much braver now, blurted it all out.

"Why would anyone think you're pregnant? That's crazy." Ryan added in shock.

"Thank you. Exactly my point. Dad, who called and put this crazy idea in your head?" she again demanded.

"That's not important. Did you ever think you were pregnant?" her father asked with his eyebrows furrowed.

Instantly Ashley thought about her drawer being gone through. Now she knew where the idea came from. How could they do such a thing, invade her privacy like that. She was instantly pissed off at them. "What do you mean, did I ever think I was pregnant? I'm going off to college in a month. What does it matter anyways? Who cares?" Ashley held out her hands in disbelief.

"Fine. You are all grown up trying to keep secrets from me. You are almost eighteen. You're not making it. You need to move out, immediately. That's, that. I'm done with this." He got up from the table and went outside. Ashley looked at Ruth who just stared into her cup of coffee and said nothing.

"Fine I'll go pack. Thanks Ruth," Ashley motioned for Ryan to come with her.

When they got upstairs, Ashley asked Ryan if it would be possible if she could spend the next month at his house before going to college. He actually paid most of the mortgage. Ryan then called his father and checked with him explaining the situation and also stating that then he would have some company during the daytime hours. With a bit of prodding, he agreed seeing it was only about a month and he was rather fond of Ashley. The two of them packed up her belongings and on the way out just before they left, her father actually told Ryan to take good care of her.

When he got in the car he told Ashley and said, "What an asshole." He shook his head, then backed out of the driveway. "I can't believe he threw you out a month before you go to college. He probably didn't want to have to move you up there so he threw you out. I'm sorry this happened to you; he's so weak." Ryan stroked her hair.

"Yeah I pretty much feel like shit. I graduated, I won that award, I have a job and I am going to college, but in his eyes it's not enough. And what is not making it supposed to mean? Plus he didn't throw me a graduation party like all my friends got, but I have you, so thanks." Ashley had tears in her eyes.

Once settled in at Ryan's house, things went well. She and Henry got along well during the day and he and Ryan especially enjoyed her cleaning and cooking even though it wasn't anything fancy. She did work several nights a week at the restaurant, but they insisted she keep her money for school. Her chores more than made up for the added expense.

Ashley needed to go up to college to do some paperwork but it was an hour away. She definitely didn't want to ask her father or Ruth. She didn't want anything from them, not that they would even be willing to do it. Plus she didn't want to ask her mother because she hadn't even told her they threw her out. It was too embarrassing. She was so ashamed of the situation she was in, almost as if she had failed. Not knowing what to do, racking her brain for days, she finally decided to call her former teachers. So one afternoon she called Mrs. Burns and her husband, Eli, and explained her situation and asked them if they would be willing to take her. They happily agreed to take her, which took a huge weight off of her. She felt so grateful to them.

They picked her up early on a Wednesday morning and Ashley thanked them profusely. The ride up went quickly. The school had sent some paperwork along with information about several places for students to reside. Mrs. Burns and Ashley carefully went through them and decided with her financial aid that she could afford this one establishment. (it was a dorm atmosphere) They also decided to call ahead and visit to reserve Ashley a room when school started.

When they arrived at the campus Ashley was so excited. "Wow, look at this place." There it stood three stories high with huge windows with wings flowing out on each side with brick towers splitting them up in the middle, there was a huge courtyard in front and a circular driveway, mainly for the city buses transporting students.

She looked at her teacher and said, "I can't believe it's actually happening. I'm so grateful to you both. Thank you so much." She smiled, happily.

"Oh, you are welcome. You have come so far. We are just glad to help," Mrs. Burns smiled back at her.

"Well, we need to find the financial aide office," Eli stated ready to get down to business.

After stopping and asking directions, they made their way to the financial aide office. Ashley got in line and waited along with many other students. Finally she got her paperwork, filled out what was needed and then was back in line again and more waiting. Some corrections were needed, so back in line to wait some more. Eli got upset about now and went up to the window. "Look we have been here over two hours and made numerous corrections. All we need to do is hand this in, but we have to wait again." Eli loudly stated.

The attendant waved Ashley to the front, checked over her paperwork and agreed she did everything she needed to do. They were finished here. As they walked away, Ash looked at Eli. "Thanks Eli. We could have been there another hour." She was amazed by him.

Mrs. Burns suggested they go to the cafeteria and get some lunch and they treated her to lunch which she was grateful for. They made plans to go into the city and locate where this place was she was going to live. Ashley was so excited she could hardly contain herself. They finished up lunch and walked around the school a little while so she kind of knew where she would be going. Then they left and made their way to Hill House, the place where she would be renting a room. Ashley met the property manager and she gave them a tour of the place. It was on the bus line and was a secured building. It was three stories high and had laundry facilities in the basement. Students also shared the kitchen area and they told her she would most likely have a roommate which was OK with Ashley. After discussing it with Mrs. Burns and Eli she signed a lease so she was guaranteed a room come September 1st.

They also told her they would be willing to wait until her financial aide came in to get their rent as long as she had the documents to show them that it was coming. This was a huge relief to Ashley. On the way home it was getting late so they stopped for a bite to eat at a popular restaurant and yet again treated Ashley. She offered to pay her own way, but they insisted with the comment, "save it for school. You're going to need every penny." Yet again she thanked them. They had no clue as to how grateful Ashley was. Without their help, she may not have been able to go to college. She was truly indebted to them. They actually saved her future. If she hadn't been able to go to college, she probably would have tried to kill herself again. These were the thoughts running through her head. Yet, she didn't share them with them. To her they were truly her heroes. They would always have a special place in her heart.

After arriving home, Ryan was waiting with mixed emotions: happy because he knew she wanted to go to school but sad because she would be leaving him behind. "I'm going to miss you so much. I'm used to seeing you most every day." Ryan kind of pouted.

'Yeah, I know, but we can see each other on the weekend. It's only an hour away." She tried to comfort him.

"Yeah, I know. Part of me thinks you're going to find some college guy and dump me."

"That will never happen. I love you. We will always be together." Ashley tilted her head.

"Promise?" he asked

"Of course, I promise. I love you." Ashley went over and hugged and kissed him. "Want me to show you, later tonight?"

"Oh, that's so sweet of you. Yeah, I need a little lovin'." Ryan started to smile. Then he raised his eyebrows up and down. The more he thought about it, the better he felt.

So the last couple of weeks crawled by for Ashley. She was counting the minutes. Poor Ryan felt as if it flew by. So as it happened, Sept. 1st ended up being on a Sunday so that Saturday Ash packed up all the stuff she would need for school and they loaded up Ryan's car. Sunday, mid-morning, the two left for Hill House. Ashley was so excited she could hardly contain herself. Upon arrival she got her room key and found out the elevator was broken so the two of them hefted all her stuff up three flights of stairs. Finally they got it all up in her room and they collapsed on the bed. Since she was the first one in the room, she claimed the lower bunk and one of the desks and cabinets to hang her clothes. She started to put things away, trying to get settled before school started in the morning. After getting everything put away and having dinner together, she and Ryan decided that he would head home so he would not have a two hour drive to get to work in the morning. He kind of wanted to stay but Ashley wanted him to go so she could get a good night's sleep for school in the morning. She kind of stayed to herself this first night as there were so many thoughts going through her head. Here she was, she could hardly believe it. She actually made it. Her father said she wouldn't make it, her mother wanted her to be a secretary, but, no, she was going to be a college student and eventually graduate. Just think a year ago she wanted nothing more than to die. She never thought about her future. She had no future, just death, but now, now she was headed in the opposite direction, to actually be somebody and contribute to society. She had been trapped in that terrible defeated mindset for most of her life. But she did it. She got out, any way she could, she got out. It took a lot of hard work but she got out. As she lay there in bed she thought, I've been through a lot, but I didn't just get any way out, I got the best way out, college. And, there's a lot more to go, my life has just begun.